Starlight

OLIVIA
WILDENSTEIN

Starlight

STARLIGHT
BOOK 3 OF THE *ANGELS OF ELYSIUM* SERIES

Copyright © 2021 by Olivia Wildenstein

All rights reserved. Printed in the United States of America. No part of this book may be used or reproduced in any manner whatsoever without written permission except in the case of brief quotations embodied in critical articles or reviews.

This book is a work of fiction. Names, characters, businesses, organizations, places, events and incidents either are the product of the author's imagination or are used fictitiously. Any resemblance to actual persons, living or dead, events, or locales is entirely coincidental.

For information contact:
OLIVIA WILDENSTEIN
http://oliviawildenstein.com

Cover design by *Olivia Wildenstein*
Naya & Adam art by *Salome Totladze*
Editing by *Becky Barney*
Proofreading by *Katelyn Anderson*

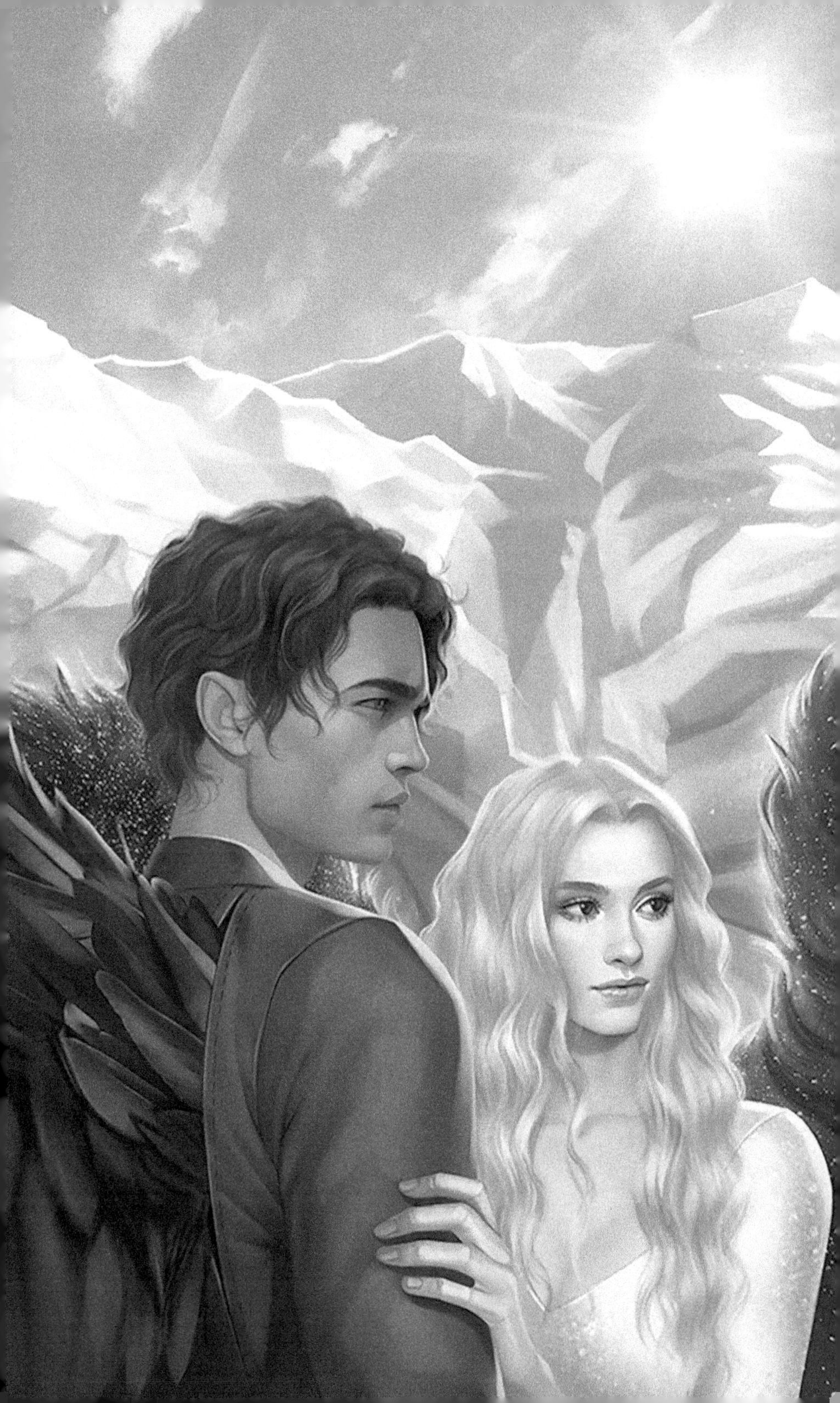

ANGEL HIERARCHY

Seraphim
Also known as archangels.
There are seven of them.
Highest ranking celestial being.
Verities (pure-blood angels).

Malakim
Soul collectors.
Verities.

Ishim
Rankers. They establish sinner scores.
Verities.

Erelim
Celestial sentinels.
Verities and hybrids.

Ophanim
Guild workers: professors and supervisors.
Mostly hybrids but open to verities.

Fletchings
Young angels who haven't yet completed their wings.
Verities and hybrids.

Nephilim
Fallen angels. Disgraced. Wingless. Mortal.

Shorhim
Guardian angels.
Verities and hybrids.

ANGELIC GLOSSARY

aheevaleh – my love
    ayim – celestial water
    haccoul – candy-colored Elysian wildcat
    kalkohav – starlight
    kaskaseem tobahat – rectum dandruff
    leh – my
    lehatsamehot – show yourselves
    levsheh – sweetheart
    motasheh – sweet doll
    naida – exquisite
    neshahadza - soulhalf
    ni aheeva ta – I love you
    shorhim – guardians
    vehnleh – my son

TO MY *Adam,*
ONE OF MY THREE *angels,*

DISCLAIMER

Starlight takes places 18 years after ***Feather***. I've taken the historical liberty to transform a presidential republic into a kingdom for story purposes. Please remember that this remains a work of fiction, and although not dystopian, it is paranormal.

Prologue

2 years earlier — Adam

ANGELIC FACT #1000
WING SIZE AND LUSTER AREN'T MEASURES
OF ONE'S WORTH.

"Not a fan of parties?"

I glanced at the angel who'd sidled up to me in a corner of the starlit atrium. Dark blond hair swept artfully up and to the side, trimmed beard, gray eyes, gold wings. Although he kept them tucked in, I didn't miss how they weren't just tipped but entirely metallic, as though he'd dunked them inside a vat of molten metal. I also didn't miss how full they were.

I returned my gaze to the swanning crowd. "Not a fan of *guild* parties. But I'm guessing you are, since you're attending one."

The ascended smiled. "I didn't come down from Elysium for the festivities."

"Then why'd you come? To flaunt your pure verity heritage?" My wing bones thrummed from the taunt, but astoundingly, no feather deserted me.

Two years growing and losing the downy black barbs on my back, and I still hadn't grasped the ishim's tolerance threshold.

The blond angel's smile grew wider. "Believe it or not, I made the trip to meet you, Adam."

He'd had my partial attention; now, he got my full one. I drained the glass of spiked pineapple juice Noah's current squeeze had smuggled into the London guild for the party and pressed away from the ivy-covered quartz to face my visitor.

I liked surprises as much as I liked strangers, which was to say, not in the plucking least. An Elysian citizen seeking me out made my feathers bristle.

I crossed my arms, glad that at sixteen, I was already as tall as this ascended. "Who are you, and what is it you want?"

"My name's Dov, and I want to recruit you."

"Like the bird?" I was still processing the second part of his answer.

"Without the -e." He held out his arm for a rainbow-winged sparrow. Usually skittish, the chanting guild mascot landed and pecked Dov's knuckle. Finding no food, it sprang off and resumed its concert.

"Recruit me for what, Dov with no -e?"

"For a clandestine project I'm spearheading."

My feathers still hadn't smoothed. I glanced toward Noah, but my friend was busy testing how far his tongue could go down his girl's throat to pay me and my Elysian visitor any mind.

Dov pushed away from the glowing quartz wall. "Our system has malakim, ishim, erelim, ophanim, but no shorhim. Did you never find that odd?"

Although I wanted to pretend he hadn't lost me with the Angelic lingo, curiosity got the better of me, and I caved. "Shorhim?"

"Guardians."

My pulse ticked faster.

"Humans talk about guardian angels all the time and yet guarding humans isn't one of our prerogatives." Dov stared around the vast room, pausing from time to time on one of the hundred or so teenage fletchings stockpiled around the seven fountains. "I believe humans would benefit from being guarded." He returned his attention to me. "My proposal, however, garnered no traction in Elysium, which is the reason for my trip down to the guilds. After studying thousands of profiles, I found you fit every criterion a guardian should possess."

I couldn't help the snort that escaped me. "Don't guardians need to be selfless?"

"And you're not?"

I used my holo-ranker to find my next hookup. And yeah, I eventually reformed the sinners I signed up for, but my primary intention was utterly selfish.

"I've studied you, Adam. You aid many of your peers in their missions, without it benefiting you in any way."

"Experience benefits everyone."

"What I meant was . . . you're aware and you care. Those are the qualities I'm after for my guardians." Dov squared his shoulders, making himself look bulkier in his toga-like gray uniform that was so at odds with my generation's denim-and-tee attire. "I'm an ishim, Adam. I know *everything* that happens to our fletchings. *Everything.*"

It sounded more like a threat than an encouragement, nevertheless I asked, "You said guardians. There are others?"

"You'd be the first."

"For how long?"

"Until we decide to bring in new pledges."

"You'd make their selection a *shared* decision?"

"I would. Unless you prefer I—"

"I'd like to have a say in it."

A satisfied smile curled the edges of Dov's mouth.

"Would I still need to go on human-reforming missions or will you just snap your fingers and make my feathers grow?"

He chortled. "I like you. I really like you."

That made one of us.

"Not even seraphim possess that sort of magic, so you'll still have to sign up for missions. You'll just draw them out longer. And once you're done, you'll stay signed on for a few more weeks. Months, would be even better."

"If you know *all* about me, then you know *all* about my fathers. Weeks might fly with them, but months . . . no dice, Ish."

"Then weeks, it'll be. Anyway, I expect you to be guarding humans in tandem with your missions. I'll bring you files on ill-intentioned sinners, and all you'll have to do is keep an eye on them to make sure they don't harm other beings."

My heart palpitated, my extremities tingled, and my stomach bottomed out. The last time I'd experienced such a rush was when my wing bones had finally drilled through the flesh along my spine two years ago. "Tell me more."

"I'll tell you everything, but only if you're in." He held out his hand.

I stared at it, stared at him, stared at his solid gold wings. "Any catch?"

"That this stays between you and me until I've built my case that shorhim have a place in our worlds."

I could work with that. "Last question. Would I be breaking any rules?"

"Has that ever stopped you?"

A slow smile spread along my mouth. "I suppose not."

Dov nodded to his hovering hand.

I shook it, marking my last day as a bat-winged fletching and the first as a black-winged savior.

ADAM

TODAY - 2038

ANGELIC FACT #34
ALL FLETCHINGS MUST EARN THEIR WINGS.

The elusive Elysian heiress was here, in London, standing opposite the human I was about to courteously dump.

Naya Moreau.

Angels didn't have last names and yet Seraph Asher's daughter had one. I snorted, which dragged both girls' attention my way.

"Moreau, huh?" The name rang familiar. I'd probably seen it on a holo-ranker. It wasn't a completely uncommon name. "Got that from your father or mother's side?" I taunted the blonde with the sparkly black wings.

Sure, it was a tad low. Even for me, but how in Abaddon had she gotten away with lying without losing a feather? Did they have a special scale in Elysium for the Seven's progeny? That would explain the density of her wings. I didn't doubt she went on missions —I'd heard *all* about them, and not only from my fathers but also from my fellow fletchings—but accumulating over nine-hundred feathers in five years was a feat no one before Naya had ever accomplished.

"My mother." Shaded by a fringe of lashes, her eyes glittered like her wings.

I'd gotten so sidetracked by examining the girl before me that my mind needed a couple seconds to play catch-up and remember what question she'd answered.

Right. Her last name.

I squinted at the ground, assuming I'd find a lone feather lying there. After all, her mother Celeste was an angel. The pavement didn't sparkle with black down. It hit me that she must've been referring to her biological mother.

"Why such interest in my family name, Adam?" Naya tipped her face up, which parted her curtain of blonde hair. The trickle of light streaming from the pub snagged on the fine slope of her nose, the bow-shape of her lips, and the graceful point of her chin. "Don't you have one?" She asked this pleasantly, even though there was nothing pleasant about her tone.

If anything, it sounded like a challenge, and although I wasn't one to shy away from challenges, I was done losing feathers for the day. At the rate I was earning them, I tried to stick to no more than one loss per week.

The air churned as Emmy stepped toward me and took my forearm. "Adam's last name is Tobiasson."

Naya studied my expression. "You don't say . . ."

Emmy hugged my arm tighter, giving Naya another once-over. "So, we were heading home."

"How fortunate for me." Naya smiled, her lips separating to reveal flawless white teeth.

Of course, her teeth were flawless. After all, the girl wasn't human. Yet her hair . . . It was full of volume, half-wavy, half-straight, as though she'd spent her afternoon rolling between the sheets.

My skin tightened at the image that thought sparked. I shrugged Emmy's hands off my arm, whisked away my wings, and set off at a brisk pace down the street. I'd been planning on leaving London in the morning, but I was bumping it up to tonight.

When I reached the white mews with the shiny black door and white Grecian columns, stuck between identical narrow white houses with black doors and white columns, my cheering crowd chime sounded. I fished my phone from the back pocket of my jeans, got comfortable against a pillar, and opened the message.

GALINA: *Have you seen the news, love? A serial killer is painting Chicago red. Meet me in the Windy City?*

A link to an article appeared on my screen. I clicked on it and skimmed the paragraphs. Well, pluck me.

GALINA: *Big D thinks you should stay in London to keep an eye on the Familia, but I think it'd be nice to get the gang back together. It's been too long.*

ME: *I suppose I could do round trips.*

A GIF of a dancer pumping her hands in the air lit up my screen.

GALINA: *Awesome. Everyone's on their way already. I got us this real perty house which we can use as our base.*

I didn't ask how she'd come by the house. Galina had a way with people, humans and angels alike, and that way gave her access to a multitude of perks.

GALINA: *Unless you prefer to sleep at Emmy's. Or at your next sinner's . . .*

ME: *I need to relocate or my fathers will get suspicious. Send me the address. I'll meet you there in a couple hours.*

After pocketing my phone, I tapped my foot impatiently. I could just hear Papa chiding me about how impatience stripped life of its sweetness. As a two-century old ascended, he had the luxury of patience. Once I was confined to the angelic world with nothing better to do and too much time to do it, I'd learn to sit on my ass and grin at dawdling people.

Emmy and Naya approached at a snail's pace, chattering on about angels-only-knew-what. Possibly the London weather—forever lousy—or perhaps Emmy was listing the amenities that came with the apartment—none.

"You're not a runaway, right?" Emmy asked as they finally reached number 9 Queen's Gate.

Naya hoisted her handbag farther up her wing-free shoulder, pushing her crazy hair out of the way, and sat her small suitcase on its wheels. "Why would you assume that?"

Bloody Abaddon, her voice . . . Raucous with a side of purr. If ascending didn't work out for the heiress, she could always land a job at an adult call center. The thought twisted my lips into a crooked grin. Daddy-dearest would just love that.

Emmy gestured to her. "Just crossing my Ts. I don't want to get in trouble with the authorities."

"I'm a tourist on a mission to discover your town and its people." She gestured to the colorful neighborhood with such excitement I almost fell for it, but every guild resident knew Naya was after one thing and one thing alone: reaching Elysium pronto. A feather-getter not a sightseer. "Maybe you could show me your favorite spots in the city? Unless you're busy with your internship."

Spending time with Emmy was probably part of Naya's reformation tactic. In spite of all the work I'd done on the girl in between my shorhim missions, the human still couldn't help herself from snatching things that weren't hers.

Emmy's blue eyes twinkled as she stepped onto the stoop of her family home. "I'm usually busy with Adam."

Your schedule's about to be wide open, darlin'.

I wanted to feel bad, but all I felt was relief. Where my best friend Noah got attached to everything that moved—be it animal, human, or angel—I got attached to nothing. Especially humans. What was the point? I was Elysium-bound, and although some of them would eventually find their way there, I wasn't waiting around for their souls to get collected by a malakim and carried through a channel.

As Emmy jiggled her key into the lock, she gazed over at where I stood with my arms firmly crossed. "You still have belongings in the apartment, Adam, or did you bring everything to mine?"

I willed the latch to click, so I could get in and out, but the ancient vermeil thing was more temperamental than Dov when we requested his help. Even though guarding had been his idea, the male didn't get his hands dirty.

"The lock can be finnicky," Emmy explained before adding proudly, "It's vintage."

Considering the direction of Naya's eyes—aimed at me—she didn't seem overly preoccupied by the faulty contraption.

The latch *finally* clacked. I shoved away from the column and pressed the door open, holding it for the ladies.

"Adam?" Emmy's ponytail flopped over her shoulder.

"What?" My harsh tone had her eyes springing wider. "Sorry. What?" I kept my tone downright placid this time around. I was many things, but not a dick to women. At least, not usually. Why Naya's presence was turning me into one was beyond me.

"I asked if you had any stuff left in the apartment Naya's subletting." Emmy played with the end of her brown ponytail. A nervous tic of hers.

I was about to tell her the apartment was vacant, had been forever, since I'd only used it as a pretext to get close to her, but changed my mind. "I better go check. Don't want Naya Moreau stumbling across anything that'll make her blush."

"No need to abuse my last name, Adam. Naya's just fine."

I smirked.

"I'll go get the key." Emmy scampered up the stairs to the first-floor landing.

When the hinges squeaked, I tilted my head to the side and observed the blonde fletching more thoroughly in the yellow light of the stairwell. I remembered hearing some of my guild-mates discussing her figure, after meeting her during an inter-guild dance I'd failed to attend. I'd thought they were exaggerating how shapely she was—after all, most female fletchings were sacks of bones—but Naya was all toned curves and sharp indents.

"Tell me, Naya, is it a coincidence that you picked Emmy Rogers?"

Eyes steady on mine, she replied with a single syllable: "No."

2

NAYA

I squared my shoulders as Adam's green eyes narrowed some more.

If Apa found out why I'd sought out his best friend's son, he'd kill me. Not literally, of course. As long as I had wing bones, I was unmurderable. Besides, my father wasn't the murderous type. He'd just tell me how disappointed he was in me and how he'd raised me to be above rule-breaking, then remind me how close I was to my thousand-feather goal.

Since my birth, I'd abided by *all* of my parents' rules, all of the worlds' rules, and earned feather after feather to prove my worth. It wasn't that I was done being a good girl, I was just ready to be a better one.

"You're not here for Emmy, are you?" Adam's breath slipped through the slender divide between our bodies.

"I did sign up to her, but you're right, I'm not here for Emmy. I'm here for you."

His pupils dilated, swallowing his colorful irises until only a slender emerald ring remained. "Ha. I knew it."

The fletching I'd cornered about Adam had warned me he wouldn't take well to my visit; he'd failed to mention the size of the boy's ego. "Conceited, much?"

Adam smiled, flashing me a single dimple and another wing-load of arrogance. "Let's cut the pleasantries."

"Not much of our interaction was pleasant," I interjected sweetly, which increased the camber of his lips and deepened his dimple.

"What is it you want from me, Naya Moreau?"

"In. I want *in*."

"*In*?" He seemed to grow stiller, taller. "You'll have to elaborate. *In* my old apartment? *In* my circle of acquaintances? *In* my bed?"

I couldn't help but roll my eyes. I mean . . . really? He thought I'd come all this way for a hook-up? Not to mention he had a girlfriend, who, from the creak of the first-floor landing and the jingle of metal, was on her way back down with the keys of the apartment I'd overpaid to live in for a month.

I took a step back from the tall male. "Noah directed me to Dov who directed me to you."

Dropping his best friend's name and the ascended in charge had the intended effect—Adam's smugness wilted. "You met Dov?"

"I did."

He dropped his voice to a rough whisper. "And he's on board with letting a seraphim's daughter join the fold?"

"I'm here, am I not?"

"Everything all right?" Emmy regarded me with slanted brows.

"Yes." I smiled. "I was just telling Adam that I ran into his best friend in Stockholm, and he says hello. Or rather, *hej*."

The vein at Adam's temple was throbbing hard.

"So you two know each other?" Emmy wrapped her arm around Adam's waist as though to remind me he was hers.

"No, but our fathers are best friends." I snagged a strand of hair that had gotten wedged between my silk bomber and handbag straps and set it free.

"Your dads are best friends, but you've never met?"

Adam's tendons flexed along his neck. "We have not had the pleasure."

Emmy blinked. In truth, I, too, found it odd that we'd never crossed paths. Especially since I knew Tobias and Gabriel well. Especially Tobias.

Two years ago, I'd asked Ama about Adam and why he never came along to family guild events. In usual Celeste-fashion, she'd smirked and replied, *Starlight, consider yourself lucky you've met any* boys. *If it was up to your father, he'd keep you stowed away until you were at least a century old.*

I'd sighed then and still sighed now, because my father was tremendously protective and did his best to drive potential suitors away from me. Since he was one of the Seven, his best was very effective. Boys looked at me, but none ever dared approach. My bestie Raven told me there was even a rumor flying around the guilds and Elysium that if anyone so much as laid a finger on me, they'd be assigned to Abaddon the second they ascended. How anyone believed this was beyond me, but my father could act mighty frightening at times.

I sidestepped the couple standing rigidly before me and walked over to the only door on this floor.

"The apartment's one level down." Emmy nodded to the staircase.

My forehead crimped. "I thought it had a garden and lots of natural light?" Just because I was planning on using the rental as an operational base didn't mean I wanted to live in a dank basement.

Adam made a sound that got under my skin. "You're better off going home, princess."

Home was not a possibility, since it was filled with hawk-eyed busybodies, and this new endeavor of mine would crash and burn before takeoff if anyone caught wind of it.

Emmy cocked an eyebrow. "Princess? You're royalty?"

I leveled a glare at Adam. "No."

Over the years, I'd heard Tobias's son described by many angels in many ways. The three most prevalent adjectives had been: conceited, tall, and gruff. Some people were generous enough to call him handsome. In my opinion, his features were all too large and dark. Except his eyes. Those were vibrant, but so calculating they may as well have been black like his wings.

"Follow me." Emmy trundled down the stairs ahead of me. There were two doors on this lower floor. She nodded to the one baring shiny fawn paint that was peeling in places, then inserted a huge key and twisted. The door opened swiftly but considering its thinness, it would've probably opened with an elbow jab.

She flicked on the lights, and a papier-maché ceiling lamp flared to life.

"Through here's the kitchenette." Emmy pointed out an ochre-tiled closet with a small white fridge, a toaster-oven, and a sink. "Bathroom's over on this side." She nodded to the door opposite the kitchen before striding into a square space with sliding glass doors, a laminated white dresser, a queen-size bed, and rolling racks outfitted with bare hangers. "Did you bring the down-payment in cash like I asked?"

I slid the envelope containing my monthly guild allowance from my jacket pocket and into her hand.

She peeked inside, counted the hundred-pound notes, then stuffed the envelope in the back pocket of her white jeans. "Fresh bedsheets are in the dresser. Towels, too. There's a utility room equipped with a washer and dryer down the hall. You'll have to buy your own detergent. Wi-Fi's free, though. The password's *emmyrogers111*, all in lowercase." She started back toward the door but stopped when she noticed Adam wasn't following. "Coming?"

"Just going to have a look around."

"I can wait."

His jaw twitched. "I'll be right up."

Emmy's expression stiffened. She stared at Adam, then at me, then back at him and flipped around, her ponytail swishing through the air. Since she hadn't closed the door, the creak of the stairs penetrated right inside the doll-sized space.

A minute later, a door thwacked closed. Adam walked over to the commode and methodically hooked his long fingers around the knobs, slid the drawers open, shut them, never once removing his gaze from my face.

Clearly, searching the apartment was an excuse for a chat, and he was going through the motions to avoid losing a feather. "What exactly did Noah and Dov tell you?"

"They explained what you do during all that extended time you spend on missions."

"You mean . . . seduce women, sample restaurants, patronize bars?"

"I'm sure you do all those things and more, but that's not what I was hinting at, Adam."

He smacked the drawer shut and stepped closer to me, the toes of his white sneakers knocking into my tan-heeled booties. "You. Know. Nothing."

I tipped my head, loath to be cowed by this growling male. "In

Sweden, I signed up to this woman who'd kidnapped a child. Guess who strolls into her house just after she'd promised to return the child to his rightful mother? The detective on the case *and* Noah." I took a breath, released it. "I cornered him after the arrest, and he said he was signed up to the guy, and what a funny coincidence that we were 'working' the same case, but then he lost a feather." I dropped my handbag onto the bed and parked the other one on the side of the commode.

I thought Adam muttered the word *weak*, but his lips were wedged so tight I'd probably imagined the sound.

"During our two-hour long trek back to the guilds, I dragged it all out of him." I dug my charger out of my handbag and hunted the baseboards for an outlet. When I found one, I crouched and plugged in my dying apparatus. When I stood back up, I pushed my hair off my face and returned Adam's unwavering stare. "I admire what you guys do, which is why I'm here. I want in. I want to be a shorhim too."

"No."

I blinked.

"I can't believe Dov even gave you the time of day. The daughter of a bloody seraphim!" Adam jammed a hand through his gelled mahogany locks. "Do you realize what would happen to our team if anyone in Elysium heard about it? They'd put an end to it, and possibly to us."

"I would never snitch."

"You have a *very* attentive father."

"Which is why I moved out of the guilds."

Adam let loose a frustrated growl. "That was error number one!"

I frowned. "How was that a mistake?"

"Have you ever lived outside a guild?"

"No."

He shook his head. "Then your father's probably already onto you. Which means he'll be onto me and Dov in no time." He strode to the wall, ripped my power cord from the outlet, and flung it in my bag. "Go home. I'll get your money back." He started for the door.

"And then you'll let me help?"

He wheeled around and stalked back toward me, backing me into the bed until my knees folded, and I was forced to sit. "Don't you plucking get it, Naya? Your help will only get the rest of us hurt."

"You're turning me down because of who I'm related to?"

"Ah . . . you're finally catching on."

His rejection and tone emptied my lungs. "Dov said I—"

"As the team leader, I get the right to veto his suggestions."

My lips thinned. "You know how many feathers I've—"

"Over nine hundred. *Everyone* knows. Your parents are oh-so-proud of their little girl."

"Nine hundred and forty-seven to be exact, so—"

"Bravo, Starlight." He slow-clapped.

"Don't call me that," I snapped.

"Don't worry. After tonight, I won't be calling you anything since our paths won't cross again. Not until Elysium, but that'll be in a few years for me. Before the end of this one for you. Maybe before the end of summer?"

"Do you just love the sound of your own voice? Is that why you won't let me finish a single sentence?"

My rebuke stunned him into silence. *Finally.*

"I didn't share my number of feathers with you for applause; I shared it to make you understand that my parents don't pry into my missions because I'm on track. They *trust* me."

"You'd be a liability."

"Dov doesn't think so."

"Well, I do." His gaze stuck to the window, that did, in fact, overlook a private garden. Although, could it be called that when it was no larger than the kitchen closet by the door? "You bloody already are." He reached the door this time. "Happy do-gooding, *Naya*."

The way he said my name, dragging it out as though the sound of it was unpleasant, made my invisible feathers bristle. "I was warned you were an ass, but you're worse than that."

The corners of his mouth drifted up as he backed away. "It was nice meeting you too."

In lieu of my middle finger, I flipped him my index, which was ishim-proof and just as evocative. My silent admonition merely increased his amusement.

After he was gone, I stewed in silent anger but then rose off the bed, grabbed my charger and shoved it back into the outlet. I didn't need Adam's approval or Dov's protection to guard unsuspecting humans.

All I needed was high-speed internet and holo-rankers, and I had access to both.

ADAM

ANGELIC FACT #6
ALTHOUGH WORDS ARE PREFERABLE, FISTS ARE ALLOWED.

When I reached Emmy's door, my blood was more pressurized than the water at a fountain show.

My plan for the evening had been to enjoy Emmy one final time and work on a compassionate break-up speech. Not worry whether my fellow fletchings' wing bones were in danger of seraphim flames, because if my team was discovered, everyone involved would suffer, including Dov.

The ranker was so cautious that I couldn't figure out why he'd taken the risk of sending one of the Seven's kids my way. Was it because Noah had blabbed, and Dov had felt cornered into confessing?

I ran my hands down my face, a growl lodged in my throat. Finally, I grabbed my phone and fired a message off Noah's way: *When were you planning on telling me about the company you kept in Stockholm?*

At the same time as I pressed send, a message from him appeared.

NOAH: *Galina just called. She says we're all moving to*

Chicago?

"Baby?" Emmy called out.

"What?" I gritted, few words irritating me more than *baby*. According to my fathers, I'd never liked being referred to as a child, not even when I *was* a child.

She emerged from the bathroom in only her underwear and a frown. As she strolled over, rolling her hips, I clicked my phone off and jammed it inside the back pocket of my jeans.

One mess at a time.

Emmy cupped the nape of my neck. "Hey . . . what's up with you? Did something happen downstairs?"

Huh? Oh, right . . . Naya. I glared at the floorboards, hoping the fletching would feel my annoyance through the old wood and painted plaster, then lifted my gaze back to Emmy, trying to banish the seraphim heiress from my mind, but her face bled right over my soon-to-be ex's. I shut my eyes and squeezed the bridge of my nose, pulse flaring at my temples.

Soft lips pressed against my hard ones, attempting to coax them open, but my mind kept sprinting to what my next move should be.

Should I go back downstairs, tell Naya I've had a change of heart, and give her something to do, so she believes she's in and keeps the organization a secret?

No. Her father would find out. He'd be all over us before I could formulate a lie ambiguous enough not to fleece me of my three hundred and sixty-three feathers.

Emmy made a sound, a choked cooing of sorts that dragged me out of my thoughts and cast me back into the human's apartment. What the Abaddon was I doing? I needed to break up and leave, then haul ass to Chicago to meet up with the others. Not only did we have a serial killer to stop, but I also had to warn them that Naya knew of our under-the-holo-ranker activities and that our chances of getting caught by the powers-that-be had just skyrocketed.

I skated my mouth off Emmy's and stepped back. "I can't do this anymore, Em. I'm sorry."

As far as breakup speeches went, I had to admit I'd delivered better.

Her jaw dropped and then dropped some more. "Are you dumping me?"

I frowned. My speech had been mediocre but concise, no?

"Something came up, and I have to go home." I looked around the living room, trying to remember if I'd brought anything other than clothes to Emmy's.

My eyes stuck to the log-shaped ceramic vase I'd crammed with yellow roses the day she'd returned the diamond studs she'd stolen from her stepmother. She'd never confessed to the theft and hadn't known that the bouquet was my way of congratulating her on her developed conscience.

That day had coincided with the growth of my feathers and the day I signed off from her. Exactly a month ago. I'd stuck around, because Dov had handed me a bothersome file on a family of supposed philanthropists with scores ranging from 47 to 100.

"When will you be back?" Emmy's voice sprang me out of my head.

"Here? Never." My fingers rolled into fists, stretching the scabbed skin over my knuckles.

"I don't understand—"

Was I speaking Viennese German again? I sometimes veered toward my father tongue. Or French, although I wasn't quite sure why I favored that one so much. I had a theory, that my biological mother was French, but Apa had briskly dismantled it.

Since Apa was still ashamed to have cheated on Papa, with a woman no less, I'd stopped digging.

The importance wasn't how you entered the world but what you did once inside. My fathers' mantra, and now mine.

If my guardian faction came with a baseline, that would be it.

"You know what? Screw my internship. I'm coming with you." Emmy whirled and headed to the bedroom separated from the living area by a thick beige curtain. "What should I pack?"

For a dumbfounded minute, I gawped at her and then I shuffled toward the bedroom. "Sorry but I'm not taking you with me, Em."

"Why? Because I'm not royalty like my new tenant?"

I snorted. Did she think Naya was an actual princess? "I couldn't take the King of England home if I wanted to."

The King had no wing bones, so I assumed he was entirely human. Unless, and this was quite unfortunate when it happened, his angel-blooded parent had failed to drop him off inside a guild before puberty, that magical age when our curved bones materialized.

"Why not?" she whined.

"Because my fathers are particular about who I befriend and bring home." There. Not a lie.

"And what? I'm not good enough?"

"You're a really sweet girl, and this—*us*—it's been fun, but I'm eighteen and not looking for anything long-term or serious. I'm sorry if I misled you." I spied my favorite forest-green jumper on the back of her desk chair, walked over, and plucked it up, then proceeded to dump all the other items of clothing I'd kept at her place in the lone duffel bag by the window.

After I zipped it up, I turned and *wham*! My cheek met an open palm.

I'd gotten slapped by one other person in my entire life—a frat boy I'd pulled off a girl at a house party and then beaten to a pulp.

Thanks to the self-defense law the Seven had implemented, which had apparently been Seraph Asher's idea, fletchings were no longer penalized when using force to defend themselves as long as said force didn't result in anyone's death.

Even though I found Naya's daddy obnoxious and unfriendly, especially toward me, angels-only-knew-why since he was buddy-buddy with Apa, I appreciated him for getting such a law passed.

Anyway, the day I'd gotten smacked, I'd enrolled in extra self-defense classes at the guild, and then, after Dov came to me with his guardian idea, I'd started profiling and nailing bunghole sinners like the frat boy who'd misunderstood the word *no*. All in all, that slap had done *me* and the human world a whole lot of good.

Cheek stinging, I shouldered my bag, wondering by how many points Emmy's sinner score card had just increased. Hurting angels was a major no-no. "Don't ever raise your hand on someone unless they're trying to harm you."

"You *are* harming me."

"No. I'm leaving you. And now, I'm doing it with no regrets. Or rather, one. That I stayed as long as I did."

Tears streamed down her face. "Get out of my house! Get out!"

"On my way." I paused by the front door of the mews and stared down the stairwell, giving the seraphim daughter one final thought before leaving.

Getting her involved would get her father involved, and we couldn't afford it.

4

NAYA

I awakened to loud banging. I checked the time on my phone and groaned—three o'clock in the morning. I pushed my hair off my face, my wavy strands out of control. Not that they were ever *in* control. Unlike most fletchings' hair, mine was always a mess, but styling it took time and made me resemble a woman I didn't yet feel like.

Maybe once I reached Elysium, sleek curls would be my thing. I'd have little else to do up there. Which was another reason I was putting the brakes on my ascension. I still planned on getting there within the next year or two, but unlike Apa hoped, I probably wouldn't reach it before the end of summer.

I padded over to the door and opened it before forgetting two major things: one, I wasn't in a guild, and two, I was only wearing underwear and a T-shirt, one of Ama's old ones. I'd inherited her full collection at fourteen, and although I loved them all, her Eagles tee was by far my favorite.

Emmy stumbled but caught herself on the door frame. "He fucking left me," she slurred. Her mascara was smudged, her brown hair loose and swinging around a denim jacket adorned with a dozen colorful pins. "Said he couldn't take me home. Said I wasn't good enough to meet his parents."

I frowned, trying to make sense of who this *he* could be. I was usually sharper, but it was the middle of the night. "Adam?"

"Who the hell else?"

I rubbed my temple. "I'm sorry."

"Are you?"

My fingers stilled. "Why wouldn't I be?"

"Let me see." She took a teetering step forward and knocked into the bathroom door.

I caught her forearm to save her from faceplanting against the beer-bottle green tiles.

"You waltz into London, and he leaves me. What did you tell him when you two"—she hiccupped—"chatted?"

I almost dropped her arm but ophanim had taught me to hold humans up. Although they'd meant metaphysically, I often applied it literally. "We didn't talk about you."

"Then why did he leave me?" she half-whined, half-sobbed.

"I don't know."

"You're not even pretty."

My grip stuttered. I was well-aware I was no beauty paradigm, but it nonetheless hurt to hear it said out loud. By a complete stranger, no less.

I didn't realize I'd magicked my wings into existence until my feathers brushed up against the backs of my thighs.

Emmy shrugged off my lax grip, then teetered past me, keeping one hand on the wall and squinting into the darkness of my bedroom. "Is he here?"

I crossed my arms. "No."

A door banged upstairs, and then a deeply-accented male voice called out, "Emmeline Rogers? Where the fuck are you? You can't blimey call me in the middle of the night and then hang up."

Emmy tottered back past me. "Downstairs! I'm downstairs"—she clapped her palm against her throat and released a strong-smelling burp—"with the new girl." She bumped into the wall so hard I worried she may have dislocated her shoulder, but then she turned, planted both her palms on it and repainted it with the contents of her stomach.

This was going to be a *long* night . . .

"Fuck." Footsteps resounded on the stairs and then a blond guy dressed in athletic wear appeared. He walked right up to Emmy and hooked her waist to keep her from toppling into her vomit. "How much did you drink?" Even though I didn't speak and was steeped in shadows, his gaze dropped to the beam of hallway light licking up one of my legs. Slowly, he trailed it up to my face. "I'm guessing you're the new tenant." Since it was obvious, I didn't answer. "You wouldn't happen to know what she ingested, would you?"

"Unfortunately not."

Emmy heaved again, more vomit splashing against the skinny baseboard.

I padded into the kitchenette. "I'll get her a glass of water."

"I think that'd be wise." He smiled, and although most of his teeth were crooked, I liked his smile, because it felt genuine.

I ran the tap a couple seconds until the water turned cool, then rooted around the wooden cupboard for a glass. I grabbed the first one I found and filled it, then carried it back out to the tiny vestibule and handed it to Emmy's friend.

He took it from me with a rapid thank you, then fit the plastic rim in her mouth and tipped it. The water sloshed down her chin and her neck, wetting her denim jacket and tank top.

"I don't want water, Gray."

"Tough luck, 'cause you're going to need a pint of it."

She shoved his wrist, and although his arm arced away, the second her fingers skidded off, he brought the glass back to her mouth. She reluctantly drank a sip, then coughed. Thankfully, no more vomit came up.

"I'll get her to bed and come back to help you." The guy she'd called by the color of his hoodie looked at me expectantly, I wasn't sure why. "Do you have a name, new girl?"

"Oh . . . it's Naya."

"Naya." Unlike Adam, he made the two syllables sound pretty.

"You don't need to come back."

His gaze flicked to Emmy, then back to me, dipping ever so slightly over my T-shirt before zipping back up to my face. "Five minutes." He extended the drained glass. "I'm Grayson, by the way."

After I took it from him, he heaved Emmy into his arms and was out my door and up the stairs before I could tell him not to worry. I heard her moan and mutter something, heard him reply softly. Whoever he was, it was a good thing she'd called him.

I sighed, wishing I possessed angel-fire. Would've made cleaning up the mess a breeze. Since I didn't, I went hunting for cleaning supplies and found a lone garbage bag and a half-used paper towel roll under the kitchen sink. I flapped the small plastic bag open, then wet the paper towel and rubbed the compacted bar of soap against it.

I mopped up the mess as well as I could and had gotten rid of the larger chunks of Emmy's dinner by the time Grayson trundled back down. I probably should've put on pants, but I was apparently not practical-minded at three in the morning. Not to mention Grayson had already seen my boy-short undies, and like Emmy had mentioned, I wasn't exactly a sight worth beholding.

He ripped off a few sheets of paper towel. "Got anything besides this soap bar?"

"Not presently. I was planning a trip to Tesco in the morning. Probably should've gone tonight." I tossed another soiled ball of paper into the garbage bag. "Is she okay?"

"She's sleeping it off." As he crouched beside the baseboards, he said, "Wouldn't happen to know why she dove headfirst into a bottle of gin?"

"Apparently, Adam broke up with her."

He stared steadily up at me, his expression so smooth it was impossible to read, but then he sighed. "She was very attached."

I wadded the last two sheets, soaked them, then rubbed them with soap. "And he wasn't?"

"Adam?" Grayson's head jerked back. "He was clearly with my sister for her money. Out at all hours and very vague about why he was in London and where he came from."

A gold-digger? Grayson's diagnostic may have amused me if I wasn't currently resentful of my fellow fletching, who'd looked upon me as though I was a plant louse.

I slid my teeth together as I leaned over to wipe up the last ochre streaks of Emmy's ginfest. "So, Emmy's your sister?"

"Stepsister. My mum married her dad."

Oh. "And you live here, too?"

"No. I live in Camden. You know, by Primrose Hill."

I had no clue where that was. "New in town, remember?"

"That's right." He straightened and tossed the grubby paper in the waste bag. He wasn't very tall but taller than my 5'6".

"You think it's safe for her to sleep alone tonight?" I asked, because ogling him in silence was getting a tad awkward. Not that he seemed perturbed, relaxed and smiley as he was.

"I was planning on spending the night."

"You're a good brother."

"I try." He rubbed a patch of shorn hair on the side of his head. "So, what brings you to London?"

I flicked my gaze to the wall, to the waterlogged paint, trying to decide how to explain my trip without lying. "I came for a job, but I didn't get it."

"A job? Here I assumed you were here for a summer session at uni. How old are you? If you don't mind me asking..."

"Eighteen." I glanced over at the rolling racks and the jeans I'd hung up, feeling underdressed for a prolonged chat.

"I should probably let you get some sleep. And check on snoring beauty up there." He rolled eyes that were a limpid shade of blue toward the ceiling, then swept his fingers through his bangs and backed up but paused on the threshold. "See you in the morning, Naya?"

I gave a sharp nod.

He dipped at the waist and grabbed the garbage bag, knotting it in midair. "I'll dispose of that."

As he walked toward the other door on the floor, which I was guessing led to the utility room, I leaned against the door frame. "Thank you."

Ambling back my way, he wiped his hands on his pants. "Anytime." He put a sneakered foot on the stair, then twisted around. "Great band by the way." At my frown, he pointed to my T-shirt. "The Eagles."

"Oh"—I stared down at myself—"yeah."

"Pity they broke up."

I toyed with the hem, trying to extend it past the edge of my boy shorts. "Three of them sort of... died." According to Ama, one of them was basking in the Elysian sun, giving sporadic concerts to flyersby, while the other two were atoning for their earthly sins in Abaddon.

"Sort of?"

I smiled sheepishly. "Okay... they died *died*."

His mouth quirked to the side. "Night, Naya. I was glad to meet you. In spite of the circumstances."

I rested my temple against the side of the door. "Good night, Grayson."

His jaw pinkened. He palmed it, flung me one last pleasant smile, then turned and climbed the stairs.

Why couldn't my meeting with Adam have gone half as smoothly?

5

NAYA

*T*here were times when I wished I could fly.

Right now was one of them.

Under the drumming summer rain, wings huddled around my sopping wet body, and arms curled around two soggy brown bags full of essentials, I hurried toward number 9 Queen's Gate. It took about three minutes of jiggling my key inside the lock to get the door open, and in the end, it wasn't even my key that did the job but Emmy's stepbrother.

The water beaded off my black feathers and plopped onto the ground behind me. It would take a well-trained eye to spot the odd rain-splatter, but I whisked my wings away nonetheless. Especially since Grayson was standing right there. Even though humans could neither see nor touch our wings, I wasn't keen on the staticky sensation of arms coasting through them.

"Let me get that for you." Grayson reached over to take one of the bags.

"Glad to see chivalry isn't dead."

"Like half the members of the Eagles?"

I laughed. "Yeah. Like that."

His blue eyes sparked in the watery sunlight that cut across his face.

"How's Emmy feeling?" I asked, as he closed the door behind me.

"Like those bandmates. The dead ones."

Death wasn't a huge thing for us angels, but for humans, it was, so I found morbid humor peculiar.

Arms pinned around the other bag, which weighed as much as my five-year-old sister Lyla, I preceded Grayson down the stairs, my house keys jangling from my fingers, echoing through the narrow space. "You'd think with full autonomous driving in large metropolises and light-speed internet, people would've done away with keys and locks."

"Keys can't be hacked."

I set down my bag in front of my door. "Oh, so you're one of those . . ."

He cocked an eyebrow. "One of those?"

"TCRs. Turn of the Century Revivalists." They were a worldwide group averse to technology and change. Some resisted in the name of whichever god they venerated; others by principle, because they didn't trust big corporations or had ethical concerns about how technology affected their race.

He snorted and smiled. "I'm most definitely not a TCR. I'm all for progress and technology. As for the keys"—he nodded toward the one I was digging into my lock—"I've been on Emmy's case about getting rid of them, but since her father cut her off, she's been trying to save up, even though she claims she's keeping them around because they're decorative."

"He cut her off?"

"Emmy was quite the party girl. She cleaned up her act a couple months ago." His teeth sank into his bottom lip as he followed me into the kitchenette and set the bag on the cramped counter. "I'm praying her stint last night was a one-off and not a relapse."

I briefly wondered if Adam had had a hand in that, but then cast him out of my mind, unwilling to let him stain my mood.

"I'm going to be sticking around for a few days to make sure." He strode out into the narrow hallway that still reeked of Emmy's nocturnal stopover. "You should probably air out the place."

"That was my next move." As I rifled through the grocery bags for the air freshener, sponge, and cleaning products, Grayson walked over to the patio door and slid it open.

I crouched and sprayed, then scoured the wall and floorboards, probably damaging both. What did I know? Worst came to worst, I'd buy paint. I may not have known much about human chores, but I was well-versed in art, thanks to Ama, who ran my home guild's art department.

I didn't have her talent, though, but I had her know-how. Lyla, on the other hand, had taken after our mother. Five-years-old, and she was already creating little masterpieces. My guild bedroom wall was full of them.

My nostrils tingled with the chemical smell of cleaning products, and my eyes watered. I rolled off the gloves and washed my hands repeatedly, and yet, I couldn't get rid of the smell.

Grayson leaned against the doorframe. "Lunch upstairs? I make a mean omelet."

My stomach growled.

His gaze dropped there, and he smiled. "I'm taking that as a yes."

If only all humans could be as pleasant as Grayson. Then again, if they were, fletchings would no longer have a purpose. I made a mental note to check his score the next time I visited a guild. More out of curiosity than because I believed he was concealing skeletons in his closet.

"Are you certain Emmy will be okay with me dropping by?"

"Absolutely."

Since I was supposed to be reforming her, and I could do with a warm meal, I thought *why not?* "Weren't you on your way out earlier?"

"I was actually on my way to get you cleaning supplies." He rubbed the back of his neck until the skin reddened. "You beat me to it."

"That's really thoughtful of you." Before shutting the apartment door, I looked toward the window. I had nothing to steal, but it was raining. "Should I shut the window?"

"Your patio"—even Grayson recognized it was a far cry from a garden—"is only accessible through the garden of the ground floor tenants, so you should be fine."

As I closed the door, not bothering to lock it, I asked, "Who lives upstairs?"

"A retired couple. Both crime novelists. She's really famous."

The mention of crime novelists lit up my synapses. How handy to have people fluent in criminology living upstairs. Sure, novelists meant fiction, but fiction was always steeped in reality.

"The lady on the third floor is a harpist with *a lot* of cats."

"How many are we talking?"

"More than a dozen. She has a pushchair for them and everything. Last spring, when she broke her hip, she tried to get Emmy to take her pride-and-joys out for some air. Em wasn't keen, so I ended up with the job."

This man was kindness personified. If he had even one point on his sinner card, I'd be surprised.

He glanced over at me as we started up the second flight of stairs. "I collected a startling amount of phone numbers during my cat walking."

I found myself laughing. "My best friend loves animals. She would totally have given you her phone number." Even though we were discouraged to date, especially humans, most of us still did it.

We may have been angels, but we were far from angelic.

"What about you? Would you have given me yours?"

I flicked my attention to his face, catching the barest hint of red streaking his cheekbones and nose. "To score a playdate with your cats?"

He ran a hand through his bangs, his blush deepening. "Or with me?"

My heart swooped as we reached Emmy's landing, and not from the physical exertion. "Honestly? No. I wouldn't have given you my number."

His blush dissipated, and the sparkle in his eyes blunted.

"But only because I don't give my phone number out to strangers, not even to handsome ones with a penchant for cat-strolls."

The sparkle was back. "Smart."

"Did you end up calling any of the girls?"

He pushed open Emmy's door and gestured for me to go in ahead of him. "I had a girlfriend back then, so no. But I've kept all the numbers."

Unlike the dim shoebox I was renting, Emmy's apartment was a bright rectangle with tall ceilings, crown moldings, an exposed brick wall painted white and inset with a modern kitchen, all glass laminate and stainless steel. On one end, two large windows overlooked a balcony, on the other hung a heavy cream velvet curtain, drawn from one wall to the other.

I twirled, taking in the recessed ceiling lights, the row of small glass chandeliers over the narrow but long kitchen island, the framed, flat-screen TV displaying legendary paintings, and the burgundy U-shaped couch. "This place is stunning."

"Emmy decorated it herself. She's studying interior design." He tossed his brown leather jacket on a wall peg shaped like deer antlers.

"She's got the talent for it."

"What are *you* studying?"

"This place." I turned back toward him. "And now, you."

He chuckled. "I meant in school." He was back to rubbing the side of his neck, my dark stare apparently making him nervous.

"I studied a little bit of everything, but sociology and martial arts were my favorite."

He looked me over, probably on the hunt for bulging muscles, of which I had none. At least, not bulging ones.

"I'm deceptively strong." I set my bag on the island and flexed my biceps.

Another grin brightened his eyes as he made his way to the stainless-steel fridge. "A good thing to be in this world. Especially as a woman."

Even though violence wasn't on the rise, it was also not decreasing. Which was why I planned on doing something about it while I still could. Who knew what the world would look like in a century? I could only hope it would be better, safer, but as long as humans were ruled by greed and envy, violence would endure.

"Ever take self-defense classes, Grayson?"

He set a carton of eggs and an armful of colorful vegetables down on the island. "No, but I lift a lot."

I assumed weights, and after a quick perusal of his biceps, I deduced my assumption was correct. "So boring."

"Not if you listen to what I listen to."

"What do you listen to?"

"True-crime podcasts. Some of the accounts are chilling."

Interest piqued, I perched on one of the bar stools. "I was thinking of getting into those. Do any of them report on local crimes?"

"A few. The *Big Ben Bang* is a great one." The knobs of his spine pressed into his T-shirt as he rooted around the fridge for more ingredients. "You can also check out the *High Tea Ladies*. They're a fun bunch."

As I looked both up on my phone and scrolled through the episodes, Grayson selected a chef's knife from a magnetic strip on the wall and began chopping all the vegetables into bite-sized pieces, the steady thwack the only sound in the apartment. He scraped his veggies into a large metal bowl, then tossed three garlic cloves onto the chopping board and smashed them with the flat side of the blade before breaking the eggs into another bowl and whisking the life out of them, which did really nice things to his arms.

I planted my elbows on the island and cradled my chin. "Where did you learn to cook?"

"Self-taught. Mum was a pediatric nurse in a cancer ward until she met Emmy's father. She worked ungodly hours, so it was either eat toast with Marmite at every single meal, or get creative. I went with option two." He lit a burner under a pan and swirled olive oil, then slid the garlic inside, followed by the rest of the veggies. Once everything was golden and smelled mouth-wateringly delicious, he showered the vegetables with cracked pepper and poured in the beaten eggs that sputtered and hissed as they settled around the colorful cubes in a pale web. "You wouldn't imagine how happy she was to come home to a hot meal."

My heart gave a little pitter-patter. "Do you have any flaws?"

The wooden spatula he'd been using to lift the edges of the omelet clattered against the pan. He caught it before it teetered off the countertop. "Doesn't everyone?"

"All his teeth are crooked, because he suffers from severe dentist-phobia." Emmy planted a hand on her hip. "Care to enlighten me why you're giving my new tenant a cooking show?"

Someone had gotten up on the wrong side of the bed. "Good morning, Emmy."

"More like, crap morning. Seriously, why is she sitting in my kitchen?"

"Be nice," Grayson mumbled.

"Why should I be nice to her? She's the reason he's gone."

Was I? Had Adam left London to escape me and my request to join his team?

Grayson's expression darkened. "Because Naya isn't to blame for your wanker ex leaving you."

"She arrives. They chat. And then two minutes later, he tells me we're not going to work out because he can't introduce me to his fucking family?" Her tapered gaze vaulted toward me. "Whom *she* apparently knows."

"I know Adam's fathers because one of them is best friends with mine. That's all."

"Fathers? He has multiple?"

Adam really hadn't been forthcoming about his heritage. "Just two."

"What about a mother?"

"He obviously had one but was raised by his fathers."

Emmy flung out an arm toward me. "See what I'm saying, Gray?"

"No. I don't."

"Adam and I were together for two bloody months, and I had no clue he was raised by gay dads."

"So?"

"So, we were together for *two* months. That's the sort of thing I should've known."

"He wasn't exactly an open book, Em."

"I *lived* with him."

"You told me he lived out of a bag."

Emmy's eyes flashed with something I couldn't put my finger on. Anger? Or was it frustration at the reminder of how casual their relationship had been?

"Besides, two months isn't all that long," Grayson added.

She rubbed her eyes, loosening dried mascara and smudging it before tapping on her phone. "In Grayson-land it isn't, but unlike you, I don't spend years with everyone I date."

The air churned with a low buzz and the bitter scent of charred beans.

As Emmy walked over to a hissing chrome machine sitting on the countertop, Grayson concentrated so hard on his pan that a groove formed between his eyebrows. "I don't spend *years* with all of them."

She held up her hand and bent a finger. "Val, two years. Susanna, one and a half." Another finger went down. "That Icelandic transfer, whatever her name was, you dated her three full terms. Oh, and the Polish girl I really didn't like, you stayed with her over *three* years."

"How old were you when you started dating? Ten?" I found myself asking.

Emmy glowered at me. "You're still here?"

I suddenly wished I'd signed on to Grayson instead of his hostile stepsister. *She's not a real mission; just a cover,* I reminded myself. I didn't actually *have* to spend any time with her.

"Stop being a bitch, Em."

"You're taking her side?"

"Right now, I am, because you're being ridiculous. Naya isn't to blame for your breakup." He suddenly side-eyed me. "Right?"

I raised my palms. "I swear I didn't know Adam until last night."

"See?" Grayson hissed.

"The only thing I *see* is that she's still sitting in my goddamn kitchen."

I got up.

"Don't go. Emmeline Rogers, apologize for not knowing your arse from your elbow."

She scowled at him, then at me, then back at him. "It's my house," she grumbled.

"And it's my omelet." Grayson swung his blue gaze toward me. "Naya, please stay."

I was already walking toward the front door. "Seriously, no worries. Whatever the pub was frying up earlier smelled really good."

Through clenched teeth, Emmy gritted out, "The food'll be better here, so just fucking stay."

That sounded as tempting as a channel ride to Abaddon.

"If you leave, Gray's going to withhold lunch from me, and I need lunch."

I doubted he would.

"I will." Had he been an angel, that would've cost him a feather, because a kid who cooked to make his mother smile was entirely too considerate to let his mood dictate his actions.

"I swear, it's fine."

"Please," he said again, which won him a raised eyebrow from Emmy instead of the previous daggers.

Not wanting to make a scene, I retraced my steps and sat, and the tension in his jaw and shoulders slackened.

He pulled his omelet off the stovetop and folded it onto a plate. "After her second cup, she gets friendlier."

"Oh, fuck off."

Grayson's mouth curved, revealing all his crooked teeth. Not that I'd judged him for it before, but now that I knew the reason he'd never had them fixed, I found it added to his overall charm. When he caught me staring at his mouth, he shut it and rubbed his lips.

"And to answer your previous question, Gray here started getting action at the ripe old age of twelve." She knocked her shoulder into his.

That was young. I hadn't even seen a boy at that age, other than in one of the ophanim-approved films we watched on guild movie nights. My wing bones thrummed, making me realize I'd inadvertently—thank Elysium or I would've lost a feather—forgotten another place I'd seen a boy.

On a holo-ranker.

Raven had snuck me into the Ranking Room after she'd gotten her wing bones, and side-by-side, we'd perused the system, alternately stifling giggles behind our fingers or blushing to the roots of our hair when we came across pictures of handsome male sinners.

Of course, Mira, had caught us and reamed poor Raven for having shown me content unsuitable for children. Mira still coddled me to this day, which surprised most, since the guild matron coddled no one.

I wasn't complaining. Where most fletchings barely saw their parents in the two decades they lived in the earthly dormitories, I not only saw both my parents on the regular, but I also had Mira, a grandmother of sorts.

Grayson pulled plates out of the cupboard, and I stood to help. "I got it, Naya."

So I sat back down.

"Gray's other flaw is that he's way too nice." Emmy shook out her napkin as she took her place at the head of the island, now set with flatware, glasses, and plates.

I ambled to the seat beside hers. "That's not a flaw."

"It is when it turns you into a pushover that every girl and her mother take advantage of."

My desire to lunch at the pub flared anew, but one glance at Grayson's pinched face and downcast eyes had me staying.

He tucked himself into the seat across from me and focused on his golden masterpiece, divvying it up with the wooden spatula. "It's a good thing I'm a pushover, or you'd have spent the end of your bender lying face-first in your vomit."

She scrunched up her nose, sufficiently chastised. "I didn't mean it like that, Gray. I just meant—"

"I know what you meant."

Emmy watched Grayson fill her plate. "On the upside, I'm going to be out of your hair for a full month soon. Imagine that."

He frowned, gliding a golden sliver onto my plate, before serving himself. "Where are you going?"

"Venezuela."

He set the serving platter down a little hard. "You're kidding?"

"Nope." She popped a piece of omelet into her mouth. "I was invited on a humanitarian mission a while back. I turned it down because of the internship. And Adam."

"Invited on a—Who gets invited on a humanitarian mission? Did you sign up for it? And what exactly will you be doing in Venezuela?"

"Feeding the hungry. Building houses for the poor."

"In *Venezuela*? The presidential republic turned kingdom?" Grayson had seized his fork but was hovering it over his omelet, too shocked to dig into his food.

"England's a kingdom too."

"Our country's not ruled by a murderous tyrant, Em," he growled. "Does your dad know?"

"Not yet, but imagine how proud he'll be to find out his pathetic daughter has been tapped by the illustrious Circle Foundation."

He set down his fork, and it clanked. "You're shitting me?"

"Nope."

He leaned back on his stool. "The Circle Foundation randomly emailed you to send you to Venezuela?"

She passed her phone over to her stepbrother. "Not randomly. I was recommended."

As he read, his brows drew closer. "By whom? This doesn't say."

"Why does it even matter who recommended me, Gray? You think I'm not good enough to go help out?"

"I never said that. I just think it's odd to be tapped for a humanitarian cause. People usually sign up for them."

Emmy sawed through her omelet. "Do *you* think it's odd, Naya?"

"A little. Especially if you didn't sign up for it. How did they get your email address?"

"Through my social media profile. Apparently, I fit the criteria for this mission."

"Which are?" I asked.

"Female, single, no kids, of uni age."

"Tell them no," Grayson said.

"I already said yes."

"Emmeline . . ." He growled. "I'm calling your dad." He started scrolling through her contact list.

She filched her phone away. "I *want* to go! I *need* to get out of London and do something useful."

"You do plenty of useful things around here."

"Like what?" she asked through gritted teeth.

"Like . . . I don't know"—he tossed one hand in the air—"your interior decorating internship."

"I'm not learning anything I don't already know."

"Em, Venezuela is corrupt and one of the most violent countries in South America. And the Circle Foundation . . . Well, you know my thoughts about them." Grayson jostled around a little cluster of glistening vegetables.

"I do, and I don't agree with them. I don't think their charities are fronts for nefarious things."

Grayson's eyes became as somber as the sky outside. "You're acting incredibly selfish."

"I think you've gotten your definition of selfless and selfish mixed up, Gray."

He worked his jaw from side to side. "When do you leave?"

"Monday."

"Mon—" Grayson spluttered. "Tomorrow?"

"No. Of next week."

The stepsiblings' tension clung to the air as vigorously as the frowns to their faces.

To defuse it, I asked, "So, Grayson, how did you come by your dentist-phobia?"

He sighed, the question slowly blowing away the shadows from his expression, and eventually, from Emmy's. As he told me the story of how a dentist had removed one of his adult teeth by mistake, my mind wandered to Emmy's untimely departure and what it meant for my mission.

The girl had been my cover. If I wanted to operate from London, I'd need a new one.

Grayson . . . I could sign up to him.

But then another thought slid over that one: I'd come here to become a guardian. If Emmy was being brought to a dangerous monarchy by a shady organization, shouldn't I be following her to keep her safe?

6

NAYA

"It's quaint," I told my mother as I sat cross-legged on my bed, towel-drying my hair, which was still damp from the scalding shower I'd taken after I'd gotten home from the guild.

I'd steeped under the hot spray, attempting to ease the disquiet my holo-ranker research had provoked within me, but like a teabag left too long to infuse, the hot water had only made my findings sink in deeper and my mood turn more bitter.

"Show me?" My mother's voice snapped me out of my storm-packed head.

Even though she insisted Apa was the worrier, she fretted more than he did. Probably because she wasn't allowed out of the guild to check up on me, unlike my father who could come and go as he pleased. And not because he was one of the Seven, but because he'd spent the requisite century away from the human world.

I recorded a video of the studio, making sure to frame the grayish-green dot Emmy had called a garden, then uploaded it to our chat.

"I think quaint may not be the best word to describe your new digs, Starlight."

"My new digs?" I snorted. "What century are you from, Ama?"

"Same one as you."

"You think Apa knows the word digs?"

My mother laughed. "I'll ask. Or better yet, you can ask him. He's planning to take you to dinner tonight, but, shh. It's a surprise."

I sat up so fast my head spun. "Is he planning on picking me up from Emmy's?"

"I think so. Did you have other plans?"

"No. No other plans."

"Act surprised, okay?" There was a little rustling noise on her end, then a grumbled, "Yes, yes, I'm coming, Mira. Gotta go, *levsheh*. Mira wants to discuss Arden's painting. She thinks it's very dark, too dark for a six-year-old, and denotes underlying trauma."

I tried to picture Eve's gap-toothed daughter splattering black paint over a canvas. Although Arden had a rather strong personality, like her mother and archangel grandmother, she was a surprisingly sympathetic child.

When she wanted to be.

That was probably just me being subjective, though. Arden was fiercely protective of my little sister, so I automatically liked her. I also liked her mother, who'd brought me presents from Elysium for each one of my birthdays—usually elaborate gowns that were tricky to wear outside guilds, what with them being so formal or sheer. Eve assured me they'd travel through the channel, since they were Elysian-made, and I'd have plenty of occasions to wear them *up there*. Angels adored dressing up, the glitzier the better.

Unlike Eve, Seraph Claire had never attended a single birthday of mine—why would she, though?—or of her granddaughter's—heartbreaking. But again, most angels weren't blessed with a tightknit family.

After I disconnected with Ama, I scoured the Circle Foundation's website, then looked up the family who ran it—the Dunmores —and pored over every article ever published about the doting, illustrious clan. Considering the amount of money they apparently gave back, their sinner scores should've been in the single digits, but the entire family—Susan, James, and their two grown sons—was, as Grayson suspected, corrupt to the bone.

The matriarch's score was 62 and her sin: Founder of the Circle Foundation.

The patriarch's score was 47. His sin: Purveyor of the Circle Foundation.

The eldest son, Henry, was rated 53, and his sin: Financier of the Circle Foundation.

But it was the youngest son, Robbie, who had the most alarming score: 100. His sin: Gatherer of the Circle Foundation.

So ambiguous...

Ama once told me that she'd ended up in the clutches of a human butcher whose sin had been labeled: *lawyer*. I'd asked Apa why the rankers couldn't just state the wrongdoings clearly. With a great sigh, he'd answered that it was put in place to protect us from the horrors committed by some, and then he'd kissed my forehead and left with my squirming baby sister bundled in his big arms.

I didn't understand how that protected us. If anything, it made us more vulnerable. Ignorance bred frustration, not bliss. Personally, I preferred knowing the devil's face than imagining it on everyone around me. And yeah, the devil wasn't real, but it got my point across best when I complained to my mother about the misleading terminology.

She shared my mindset and told me that once I ascended, she and I could embark on a mission to modify ishim legislature or, as she put it, *shake things up in the grand ole angel lair,* but only once I ascended.

I wondered how she'd react to hearing that Ish Dov was already attempting this. I'd promised him I wouldn't utter his name to either one of my parents, and I wouldn't, not even to ask if they knew him, but I couldn't imagine them not being enthusiastic about his plight. If anything, I bet they'd offer him the Elysian backing he needed, what with their ideals matching.

But again, I'd made him a promise, and I was a fletching of my word.

I refocused on my investigative work, trying to glean what made the Circle Foundation so terrible. What dark and terrible things did the twenty-seven-year-old Triple do behind the scenes? Hire hitmen? Launder money? Deal drugs? Run a prostitution ring?

As I listed the usual crimes that gave humans such a high score, my mind stuttered on the last one.

The Circle Foundation had recently reached out to young and unattached women. Could that be why?

No... that made little sense.

Girls usually stolen were the type no one reported missing or whose search dried up from lack of funds. Taking girls like Emmy made no sense. Especially taking them from a wealthy country and sending them into an underprivileged one.

Which led me to wonder: could this truly be a charitable organization? Even as a child, I believed that not all Triples were monsters. The same way I believed nephilim, the black sheep of our kind, the wingless angel-bloods, weren't intrinsically evil.

I took out the rainbow journal and sparkly pen Lyla had given me for my birthday, and jotted down the list of charities they'd financed. When I reached the one about the Venezuelan Aid program, I set down my pen and clicked it open and shut. A fancy website appeared with a link to an online application form which read CLOSED – *50/50*.

50 out of 50. Was that the number of girls they were taking? And if all the spots were filled, how could I get one?

Silly me.

I couldn't exactly enroll without an ID or a passport. I'd have to channel to whichever city or town they were flying to, and once I met up with Emmy, I'd tell her the truth: that I'd been worried and had followed her. Unless I guarded her from afar. Could I be that stealthy?

I went back to my information compilation, researching the people behind the foundation.

Susan and James lived in a manor on the outskirts of the city with their five cocker spaniels, their eldest son and his wife. The youngest son, the Triple, resided in an apartment in London with his flavor-of-the-day—all models from the looks of the girls on his arms.

As I scanned pictures of Robbie, I noticed he was often photographed in the same private club, a place called *Jardin Japonais*. The reason he was often there was revealed on the next page of results: he was part-owner of the place.

I chewed up the end of my pen as I weighed the pros and cons of heading there and interrogating him about the Venezuelan trip. How exactly would I go about it? I doubted a, "Hello, Mr. Dunmore, is this trip of yours legit, or are you planning on doing terrible things to these poor girls?" would go down smoothly. I'd probably get tossed out, or kidnapped and cross-examined.

But . . .

But I could question the staff. Maybe someone could enlighten me as to what was going on with this family. Humans were always so happy to gossip.

Or, I could just ask Ama. Tell her my sinner's going away with them. But that would get right back to my father, and he'd pull me off the mission immediately, not wanting me anywhere near criminals.

Apa!

I tossed my phone and journal aside, and dressed for my surprise dinner. After pulling on stonewashed jeans and a poppy-red sweater, I scrubbed my damp hair with a towel. Raven would've cringed because, according to my best friend, who ironically had the slickest, straightest hair in the history of keratin, wavy hair needed to air-dry with tons of serum and zero friction.

A shadow darkened my window, and I jumped, the towel sliding from my fingers and pooling at my feet. Palm flat on my heart, I watched as great turquoise wings retracted behind a chest so massive it took up the entire breadth of my patio.

I was about to open the glass door to let my father in when I spied my journal, lying open for all to see. I plucked the towel off the floor and tossed it on top of the lined paper, then let my larger-than-life father into my teeny-tiny home.

"Apa!"

He looked around the place, then looked again as though hoping he'd missed something—an extra bedroom perhaps. "Your mother mentioned the place you were staying was cozy." A frown bracketed his eyes and mouth. "As cozy as a jail cell, that's what it is."

I smirked. "I didn't know you were familiar with the size of jail cells."

My father's eyes finally settled on mine, and a small smile disrupted his scowl. "I may have spent a few nights in one when I was a fletching."

"What? Here I believed you eternally virtuous and law-abiding."

When a shadow blunted his expression, I wondered if he'd felt slighted by my words.

I tilted my head, and my half-dried curls rushed around my face. "Will you tell me about it during dinner?"

Apa released a deep exhale that blew away the darkness. "How do you know I'm taking you to dinner?"

"Ama may have let it slip."

His smile returned with a luminous vengeance. "Ah, your mother and keeping secrets..."

She was most terrible at it. Practically as bad as Raven. "So, where is it we're going?" I almost suggested *Jardin Japonais* to scope out the haunt but didn't think it'd be smart to be spotted with a man who was six-five and looked like he could bench-press Big Ben.

"Come. It's a surprise."

"Are we flying or walking?"

Apa cast a look over his shoulder at the dreary weather. "Definitely not walking. Why did you choose London again?"

"For a new experience." My pulse spiked, and my wings niggled as though about to expel a feather. "Ama says I should enjoy all the human world has to offer before I'm corralled inside Elysium."

"Let's not go overboard on human experiences, all right, *Kalkohav*? Once your wings are finished, you'll have infinite time to experience the world."

I sighed. "You mean, Elysium."

"Elysium, at first, but sooner than you realize, you'll be back here."

"A hundred years is not soon, Apa. Unless you're working on amending the law, so we can return to Earth sooner, and—"

"When you get your wings."

"Angels, you and Ama sound like broken records." I rolled my eyes. "What difference does it make whether I'm down here or up there?"

He swallowed. "Once I no longer have to worry about you, I can concentrate on our legislature."

"Once you no longer have to worry about me, you'll have to worry about Lyla."

He stared at me, but his gaze was unfocused, as though he were staring right through me. But then he blinked, and his eyes went clear again. "You're forgetting that I'll have a few years of respite between the time you ascend and she heads out into the world."

My stomach rumbled then, which made my father's expression soften. "Let's get you fed, Starlight. Any cravings?"

"I hear this country's famous for its puddings."

Apa laughed, a great big laugh that made the worlds a better place. "You and your sweet tooth."

"Hey... you made me this way."

His laughter petered out. "I did, didn't I?"

"Yeah. You did. Now, about those puddings . . ." I grabbed Ama's jacket, which had finally air-dried from my grocery store outing. "Know a place or should I look one up?"

Apa put his arm around me. "I know the perfect place."

7

ADAM

ANGELIC FACT #72
IF YOU DON'T CARE FOR ABADDON, CUT DOWN ON THE SINNING.

*D*renched in sweat, I pummeled the black leather punching bag with my fists and feet. I'd been at it since sunup. While all the members of my special ops team slept, exhausted by our late-night surveillance, I'd met up with Dov to discuss Naya in a vinyl-infested, twenty-four-hour diner. His answer that she was a good candidate and that I shouldn't have turned her away had sent me straight back to the gym, more wired and pissed than I'd been before our meeting.

"Something on your mind? Or rather *someone*?" Noah's voice came at me from the double-wide entrance of the home gym. "Maybe a certain black-winged fletching?" Noah had been fishing since I'd landed in the Chicago channel, and we'd shared a ride to the house.

I lobbed him a pointed glower that did nothing but flip up the corners of his lips. "Haven't thought of her once since I left London." I hissed as a feather dropped from my wings. Fine, the seraphim heiress had been on my mind, stuck there like a cheap decal. "Why did you have to go and tell her about what we were doing?"

"She cornered me, man. Stared me down with those really intense eyes of hers. Forkin' scared the soul out of me."

After shooting Noah the mother of all eye rolls, I assaulted the leather bag with my fists. "She's short, blonde, and blushes harder than a pubescent fletching at his wing bone ceremony. She may be a lot of things, but scary isn't one of them."

"That's because you fear nothing."

"What's there to fear when you're immortal?"

"We're not immortal *yet*, Adam."

"Technically, we are. For the next six years, at least."

Noah and I had gotten our wing bones at fourteen, exactly a month apart. By the time he'd sprouted his third pink feather, my first black one had appeared, the color shocking everyone but my fathers. Since Naya had gotten her wings the year before me, my fathers had known what to expect. After all, she and I were both born from extra-conjugal affairs.

"What time did you and Galina get home from the morgue last night?" Noah tucked in his gold-tipped, pastel wings, and yet tufts of his five-hundred-plus feathers stuck out around his shoulders, framing his deep brown face like that shower bonnet Galina had ferreted out of an upstairs bathroom and worn the first night we'd reunited.

She'd been trying to offset the nervous energy coming from all of us, and while the sight of her gorging on deep-dish pizza, wearing the atrocious thing, had been entertaining, it had done little to keep our minds off the serial killer.

"Late." The floorboards of the Prairie-style house creaked beneath the foam mats like my skeleton during my last visit to the chiropractor. "Are you and Levi done compiling the list of Chicago Triples for Dov?" My skin burned from where it had split, making me regret not having worn the sparring gloves my fathers, aggrieved by the constant sight of my pulped knuckles, had gifted me.

"We'll be done this afternoon. There are *a lot*."

I clapped the bag to steady it. "How many are we talking?"

"Over a thousand. Boone and I were going to head over to the guild after breakfast to finish up the list, then run it through Levi's new crosschecking program."

The youngest in our crew, a fifteen-year-old tech wiz, had managed to tap into the lead investigator's reports of the first three murders and was analyzing all the evidence in order to narrow down the unsub by age and physical attributes, something even our ascended mentor was unable to achieve with his nifty celestial tools. Apparently, the ranking system up in Elysium was as basic as ours.

"Did the unsub leave a calling-card yet?" Sociopaths usually craved recognition and 'signed' their murders.

"Besides the carved tear-shaped gashes and chopped . . . nether-regions?" Noah shuddered as though his junk was on the line. "Were you expecting he'd sign his name in blood on the crime scene?"

"Why do you say *he*?"

"I guess it could be a she, but the guys the unsub killed are massive." Noah cocked an eyebrow as I walked over to the water fountain for a drink. "You think we're dealing with a female serial killer?"

"Maybe. After all, dicks are being lobbed off."

Noah dry-heaved, then palmed his crotch, probably to remind himself it was still attached.

As the heavy leather punching bag swung, the chain rattling in the quiet gym, I crumpled my cup and tossed it into the trash. "You mentioned breakfast. I'll take eggs. Scrambled."

"Cook your own eggs."

"No one makes them better than you."

Noah sighed, unable to resist compliments about his skills in the kitchen. "Fine."

"Make a lot." I headed up the sweeping stairs that seemed carved out of a single piece of redwood. "I need sustenance before I go meet up with my sinner."

"What's her name?"

"Anthony."

Noah jerked, and the gold tips of his feathers swayed. "Anthony? You picked a *male* sinner?"

"Yeah. So?"

"So you've never picked a male sinner."

I shrugged. "About time I did."

"It wouldn't have to do with Naya?"

"Why would it?"

"What are you two prattling on about at nine-feathering-thirty-two in the morning?" Galina asked around a loud yawn. She stood just outside her bedroom door, wings and arms outstretched, artfully ripped tank top riding up her carved stomach.

The Russian nineteen-year-old recruit had better abs than Noah and Boone combined, probably because she worked out as religiously as the orthodox Jew that I'd reformed last year had frequented her local casino.

"Adam signed up to a guy," Noah said smugly, as though he'd somehow one-upped me by sharing the news.

"No deuce." Her wings curled in while her lips curled up. "Are you testing new waters?"

"Geez... I don't sleep with *all* my sinners."

"Beg to differ, Mr. Sinnerizer." Galina twisted the diamond stud in her nose.

"Well, I didn't feel like a distraction until we closed this case."

"You're missing out, love. The ladies in this town are delicious, especially the naughty ones." Galina cracked her neck from side-to-side.

"And fletchings call *me* the Sinnerizer," I muttered as I disappeared into my bedroom and kicked the door shut. My king-size bed was a rumpled mess. I flapped the comforter twice, fluffed up my pillows, then stuffed all my dirty clothes into the bag I'd traveled with from London.

There was a washer and dryer on premises, but nothing beat celestial hampers, and since Noah was heading to a guild, he could toss my clothes in, bag and all.

After a hot shower, during which I'd done my best to scrub Naya from my mind, I went down to the barn-style kitchen where everything was made of wood, except the kitchen appliances and glass light fixtures, and hefted my duffel. "Any chance you can stick my laundry in a guild hamper when you're there later?"

Noah looked up from the batter he was ladling on a griddle, then tipped his head toward the door that led to the garage. "Just leave it there."

After doing so, I took a seat in front of Galina and filled a plate with scrambled eggs. "How did you come by this place again?"

"Helped a woman shake the corrupt financial adviser I was signed up to. She felt indebted and loaned me her secondary home for as long as I needed it." Galina was sipping her beverage of choice

—green tea. How anyone could stomach something that reeked of dirty socks was beyond me.

I studied the shelving units topped with neat piles of cookbooks that were clearly only there for decoration, considering how pristine they all looked. "She won't stop by for a visit, will she?"

"No. She's touring Tahiti on her yacht."

"That sounds nice. I should've signed up to her." Noah deposited a plate stacked high with pancakes onto the table hewn from a giant trunk.

"You still could," I said.

Noah shook his head. "Stop trying to get rid of me."

I wished he'd take my out one of these days, but the guy was a giant stubborn ass. "It could get dangerous. I mean, we are dealing with a serial killer who has it out for tall men with buzzed hair. Wouldn't want anyone carving tears into those pretty cheekbones of yours or removing your family jewels."

"Tall, *human* men, who *used to* sport cropped hair back in college. Not to mention, all of them are in their thirties." He stirred something in a big pot. I was guessing refried beans from the smell. "Besides, I'm loving my new kitchen."

"And I'm loving you in your new kitchen. You're so very domestic, love." Galina blew on her tea, sending her foul herbal fumes my way. "We should get him an apron. Something frilly. Maybe a little lace. And obviously pink to match his wings."

Her quip won her a tossed strip of bacon.

She hissed. "So low, Noah. Attacking a vegan with animal product. I'm surprised you didn't lose one of your cute bubblegum feathers for the assault."

Noah fisted his fingers and flicked his wrist at Galina, a gesture meant to be obscene, a little like Naya's raised index finger.

No.

No thinking of Naya.

I shoveled down my eggs, then skewered a few pancakes and slathered them in maple syrup.

Galina propped one of her feet on the bench, bending her leg to balance her forearm on her knee. "Did you just sweeten your pancakes? I thought you hated sweet things."

I did. I disliked sweet food. Sweet people. Sweet smells. Everything I bet Naya loved. I squeezed my temples. For the ever-loving fuck, I was supposed to work her *out* of my system, not further in.

A hot jab made my shoulder blades flex.

Galina tracked my black feather's collapse. "What's with the rotten mood?"

"He's all worked up over Naya," Noah explained.

I mopped my sticky mouth on the corner of my napkin. "I'm not." Another feather loosened. I growled and got up, grabbed my plate, and dunked it in the sink. "I'm off to meet my sinner but I'll be back in time for dinner. Still planning on *bumping* into the lead investigator, Gee?"

She nodded. "Got his route memorized." She tapped her temple as she stood and rounded the table. "Let's see what Adam was up to when he earned this feather."

The girl had a passion for picking up stray feathers and replaying the memories lodged inside the shafts. As a kid, she apparently went around her guild picking up feathers to collect deeper intel on her guild-mates. Her passion for hoarding information made her a great profiler and a pain in my ass, because she'd learned way too much about me since Dov directed her to Bangkok eighteen months ago to join my *two*-person team. Even though I'd tried not to get Noah involved, he'd involved himself because . . . attachment issues.

The Dutch verity brothers, Levi and Boone, joined our little guardian gang last year. First, Levi, who'd become devoted to me after we'd found ourselves reforming two sinners from the same family back in Amsterdam, his first year out into the world. His sinner hadn't been very amenable until she and I had had a little chat about her weed consumption and how she financed it with money filched from her parents' wallets. Then she became putty.

Boone, I'd met a couple weeks later when he'd sought me out to express his gratitude for helping out his kid brother.

How did they end up becoming guardians? Turned out Levi was a sneaky little twerp who'd caught me debriefing with Dov over the phone about a motorcycle gang I'd been trying to nail. The kid got curious, did some digging, and ended up cracking my case. He'd then proceeded to blackmail me into letting him onto the team. He'd lost a feather for his threat but earned his spot. And then he'd blindsided me by bringing Boone into the fold.

I had *not* been happy.

Still wasn't.

Dov reminded me that growing the team was necessary, but not only was he an ascended, he was also a pure verity, and pure verities had more privileges than half-breed fletchings.

As I headed out into the bright Chicago day, the front door of the house flew open, and a flushed Levi, who seemed to have acquired an extra three inches overnight, thanks to an epic case of bedhead, rushed out, balancing a tablet on his open palms.

"Adam, wait!" He was breathing harder than when two brawny Russians had chased us down ten flights of stairs with loaded AKs back in Moscow. "You've got to—see this!" Although all that time he spent in front of screens was mighty useful, he seriously needed to up his cardio.

I retraced my steps toward him.

"I found a connection—between the—victims."

My gaze snapped off his puffing cheeks and onto the freckled, light-brown face of a teenage girl with piercing blue eyes. "Who am I looking at?"

"Felicity Gold. Committed suicide—twelve years ago—at fifteen."

Suicide . . .

Suicide meant her soul hadn't been harvested by the malakim.

Suicide meant true death—not only of the body but of the soul.

I didn't look away from those sparkling blue eyes so full of a life cut short. "What drove her to commit suicide?"

Levi grimaced. "She was raped."

"By the men being picked off?"

"Yes."

Although I was standing in bright sunshine, a chill barreled up my spine and spread throughout the rest of my body. So we weren't dealing with an amoral killer. We were dealing with one out for vengeance.

The three males' mutilated bodies flashed behind my lids. What had sparked pity now only sparked disgust. How could my people let humans get away with rape? How could they let innocents rot and criminals thrive? How could ishim leave the fates of souls at the mercy of scales calibrated during plucking Antiquity?

My wings niggled, reminding me not to criticize the system, but angels, I was furious. Maybe I should've let Naya onto our team after all. Maybe if a seraphim daughter got involved, I could convince Dov to let Asher in on our secret organization. Under the direction and protection of one of the Seven, we'd be able to put all our energy into guarding humans instead of our secret.

Anger churned low in my gut. "This changes everything."

I didn't care that these criminals would have accrued a higher score for their vile act, they'd led a girl to take her last breath, and in turn, her soul's last breath. Not to mention that the scores of the first three victims had been in the double digits, which meant their souls were getting another spin on the earthly carousel.

"How many men raped her?"

"The report filed posthumously by Felicity's parents says six."

"And they're named?"

"Two were. Four weren't. The three picked off weren't named."

So, our unsub knows every rapist's identity...

Boone, Noah, and Galina appeared behind Levi, their faces sporting varying degrees of grimness.

Boone ran a hand through his shoulder-length brown hair, still tangled from sleep. "I guess our investigation's a bust, and we'll all be going our separate ways?" His staunch disappointment was reflected in the others' expressions.

"No," I said.

Boone's brown eyes widened. "You want us to keep digging?"

I nodded. "But we're switching sides. Get me Felicity Gold's family tree. Any blood relative who would've been a kid back at the time of her suicide."

Noah tipped his head to the side. "A kid?"

"Because the killings are happening over a decade after the crime," Galina, forever on my wavelength, answered.

Noah's head straightened. "An adult could've waited a decade. Taken the time to plan."

"You're right," I said.

He blinked. "I... I am?"

"We shouldn't overlook older relatives, even though I still think it's more likely our unsub's young. We also need to look into who Felicity was friends with at the time of her death. And then run all the names through a holo-ranker and check for a spike in scores. That should give us the identity of our revenge killer."

"What do we do once we find out his or her identity?" The sun glinted off Galina's facial adornments.

"We'll go find our vigilante and help them finish the job."

Boone gasped. "Dov will never back this plan up."

Galina, who'd been flicking the little hoops speared through the shell of her ear, froze. "Boone's right. Premeditated murder would cost us our wings."

"No one's murdering anyone. We're simply going to cover our unsub's ass until they're done. And then one of us will sign up to them to help them atone for their *sin* so their soul doesn't end up like Felicity Gold's."

"Dov won't like—" Boone had the wherewithal to stop talking.

"Dov put me in charge of this team. If you're not happy with the way I run things, by all means, walk away."

They all stayed.

8

NAYA

I wasn't the quiet type, or at least, I didn't think I was until I spent time with my landlady slash sinner. I wasn't sure if it was excitement at her impending departure, or if she'd always been this way, but the girl could talk. *And* talk.

How had Adam endured *days* in Miss Chatterbox's company? The thought strummed my wing bones.

Just an observation, Ish. I looked up at the ceiling as though it offered a direct line of sight on the Elysian scales that weighed our angelic souls.

Miraculously, the ishim let it go, yet the uncomfortable tingle lingered, a reminder to be more compassionate. How much more compassionate could I be, though? I'd sat through hours of Emmy trying to figure out where she'd gone wrong with Adam, why he'd left, why she wasn't good enough to meet his fathers. And why hadn't he told her he'd had two fathers.

I wasn't quite sure why that last part stumped her so much. Then again, in our world, gender was of very little importance. It was all about soul connections. Had Ama been a man, Apa would've loved her just as passionately.

"You know how people say it takes half the time you were together to get over someone? Well, Adam and I were together for one month and twenty-nine days."

Oh, I know.

"And I'm already over the pompous prick." Emmy peeled away the wrapper on her third cupcake.

Grayson had whipped them up yesterday in a last attempt at dissuading her from joining the Circle Girls—the name the press had given the group heading to Venezuela—but his fudgy negotiation tool hadn't swayed his stubborn stepsister.

Mouth full, she added, "Don't even miss him. Not one bit." She sucked the frosting off her fingertips, then scarfed down the rest of her cupcake. "Oh, and I was researching Venezuela, and the men there"—she waggled her eyebrows—"they are *hot*, with a capital H. Especially the Prince. He sports this eye patch that just makes him hotter. Too bad the program's full, or I would've tried to get you on the list."

I balled up a polka-dot wrapper. "Maybe I could fly over and join on my own dime."

Her eyebrows shot up. "You'd have the means to do that?"

"Yeah."

"Then I take it that, on top of being a DILF, your dad's loaded?"

The polka-dot wrapper was no larger than an Elysian pearl between my clenched fingers. "A DILF?"

"You know, a Dad I'd Like to—"

"I know what it means, Emmy." I itched to sign off from her right then and there, because there were some boundaries that should *never* be crossed, and crushing on my father was one of them. "I would prefer never to hear you talk about my dad that way." How I wished Apa hadn't insisted on meeting Emmy after our dinner.

"I didn't see a wedding band."

"Well, he's been with my mother for years."

Emmy raised her palms. "Geez. Settle down, girl. It was just a question."

Her doorbell chimed then, piercing through the tension, and then a key rattled in the lock.

"That must be Gray. Either he's come to tell me he can't accompany me tonight, or he's come to tell me what a tit-head I am."

Emmy was right; it *was* Grayson. And considering his apparel—black dinner jacket worn over a button-down—I suspected he'd come to escort his stepsister to the private event Robbie Dunmore was organizing at *Jardin Japonais* for the Circle Girls and their families.

"Come to tell me off again?" Emmy removed the leather

scrunchie she'd wrapped around her top-knot and unfolded her legs from underneath her to stand.

"What do you think, Em?" There was an edge to his voice. A roughness. As though he expected this would be their last evening together.

Even though my contemplation to sign off from Emmy had lasted no more than a minute, his tone reminded me that I couldn't abandon the girl.

He smiled at me before studying the half-full platter of cupcakes and the little mound of wrappers littering the ashtray shaped like a child-sized, upturned top hat. "Em, the event tonight. You can bring your whole family, right?"

Emmy jerked to a stop in front of him. "If you told Dad—"

"I didn't. I was only asking to find out if you could bring a second date."

"Oh, yeah. Why? *Oh* . . ." She whirled toward me. "Have any plans tonight, Naya?"

The event was organized by the Circle Foundation, so even if Robbie Dunmore wasn't present, someone from the organization would be, and I could ask them all the questions.

I stood, dusting cupcake crumbs from my purple jeans. "I don't have any plans, but only if you're sure it's all right."

"Yep. All fine."

I pushed a long curl behind my ear. "It's being hosted at *Jardin Japonais*, right?"

She nodded as she gave my skinny jeans and pineapple top a lengthy once-over. "It's cocktail attire, so . . . *fancy*. Got a dress or do you need to borrow something?"

"I've got one."

I'd headed home to do laundry and pack fresh clothes yesterday, which had given me the opportunity to hang out with my little sister. After nine games of sardines with every fletching under the age of seven, I'd returned to London with a much larger suitcase, which had earned me an eyebrow raise from Mira. Nothing a kiss on the cheek didn't do away with, though.

Right before stepping past Grayson, I asked, "What time should I be ready?"

"In an hour."

Although my body headed down two flights of stairs, my heart rose inside my rib cage, and my fingertips prickled with adrenaline. Would I be able to negotiate a spot on the charitable mission? Would they even consider my candidature without an ID? But more importantly, did I want a spot on it, or would I be safer channeling over to Caracas and observing Emmy from afar?

I unlocked my door and rummaged through the exposed rack of clothing that sagged under vibrant fabrics. The color I lacked in my wings I made up for in my choice of attire. I ran my fingers over the row of dresses, settling on a neon pink frock and heels to match, then fought to flatten my frizzy hair, a fight I almost gave up on when my brush got stuck for the umpteenth time. The end result was semi-straight, at least around my face. I wasn't entirely sure what the back looked like, nor did I truly care. I made sure to slick my mouth with bright lipstick to distract from my temperamental blonde locks.

When I met up with Emmy an hour later, she smiled at my dress. "That is one *bright* outfit, chica."

I didn't ask if it was too much because I wouldn't go change even if it was.

"Cab's out front."

"And Grayson?"

"He had a phone call. Took it outside." Her smile slipped higher, misconstruing my curiosity for interest. I let her believe what she wanted. Whatever made her friendlier.

After fastening the buttons of her cropped leather jacket, she sashayed out to the idling black cab in her form-fitting dress. Grayson was already sitting inside, having taken cover from the rain.

He looked up from his glowing phone screen as I settled onto the banquette facing him, then powered it off and slid it inside his dinner jacket, his gaze skimming the fuchsia fabric peeking out from my teal bomber.

"I know, I know. It's *luridly* pink." I ran the short hem of my dress between my fingers. "Emmy didn't fail to point it out."

She snorted as she pressed the touchscreen to indicate we were strapped and ready to go.

Grayson's fingers climbed to his neck that poked out of his white button-down. "That's not—" He cleared his throat, but didn't finish his sentence. After a short beat, he asked, "I'm going to be drilling the organizers, Em."

"Are you informing me or asking me?"

"Informing you. And if any of their answers sound shifty—"

"You'll try to disenroll me."

His hand fell away from his neck, slapping his jean-clad thigh. "Fuck trying. I'll do it, even if I have to use physical force to carry you out."

Emmy's lips pinched. "I'm nineteen, Gray. Not even Dad can force me to do anything I don't want to anymore."

"Don't you care about your safety at all?"

Emmy rolled her blue eyes, which she'd dolled up with liquid liner.

I'd blackened mine once but had swiftly wiped my lids clean, because the makeup had intensified my irises' darkness, and who wanted to look like they sported sewer holes in the middle of their face?

"The Dunmores are billionaires, Gray. I guarantee you, we'll have our very own security details. They're not sparing any expenses for this trip. I mean, we're flying private for god's sake, *and* we're staying in the hotel owned by the Prince, in which he *himself* lives. Can you imagine how many guards will be around us at all times?" After a quiet beat, she added, "Hey . . . at least I'm not headed to Chicago."

Frowning, I turned away from the wet city. "What's in Chicago?"

"A serial killer. Don't you read the news?" Arguing with Grayson had regrettably turned Emmy back into her *pleasant* self.

"I've been busy reading up on . . . other stuff." *Most recently, the people you're about to travel with.*

Gray's eyes shifted off the drenched street and onto his stepsister. "The serial killer's targeting men in their thirties. Since you don't fit the profile, I'd much rather you head there than to fucking corrupt Venezuela."

"Gray, this is our last night together until next month. Can we please not spend it quarrelling?"

Jerking his gaze to the window, he muttered, "Fine." He didn't sound fine. I doubted he'd be fine until she landed back on British soil.

I wanted to reach over and pat his arm, tell him I'd make sure she got home safely, but he'd ask what I was going on about. It wasn't like I could impart my plans, so instead, I did what I seemed to do best when it came to my sinner and her stepbrother: I defused the tension. "You never did tell me what you do. Are you still studying or are you working?"

"I work in fintech."

Emmy yawned, which made Grayson flip her off, but I listened raptly. I had a very limited understanding of fintech—computer language, in general—because we weren't taught how to use them back in the guilds. That we were allowed smartphones was already a great concession on the part of the Seven. Apparently, fletchings hadn't had access to them for almost a decade after they'd become all the rage in the human world, because they were deemed too great a distraction from our missions.

When the ophanim realized students were buying them anyway, they'd looked more closely into the piece of technology and figured it wasn't overly nefarious; plus, it doubled as an excellent tracking device. This led to a guild-wide campaign to have them gifted to students on the day of their wing bone ceremony. I'd gotten mine then and had only upgraded models once, after a surprise visit to Raven's mission site that ended with my phone sinking to the bottom of the Mekong River.

Grayson was still in the middle of explaining cryptocurrency to me when we reached our destination.

9

NAYA

*L*ondon was loud on the outside, but the noise level inside *Jardin Japonais* took loud to a whole other level. Conversations rose from a knot of people gathered around a shiny black bar and bounced along the bronze bas-reliefs decorating the walls of the restaurant.

"Did Emmy call ahead to tell them I was coming?" I asked as waiters threaded themselves around tables as shiny and black as the bar, readjusting nameplates and cutlery positioning.

"I think so." Grayson's eyes trailed his stepsister, who'd veered straight toward the bar and was deep in conversation with the bartender. "If I comment on her alcohol intake, do you think she'll bite my head off?"

"Pretty sure she will."

He sighed. "I really wish she wasn't so adamant about doing this."

My instincts about Emmy's stepbrother had been correct. I'd thought he was kind, and his profile, which I'd looked up when I'd researched the Dunmores, had displayed a score of 2, which was almost unheard of for men of his age living in metropolises. His sin: *envy*. I assumed he'd envied something insignificant or the sin would've cost him way more than two points. Unless, he religiously balanced out his sinning with little acts of grace.

"You think Robbie Dunmore's here?" I scanned the room for the redheaded man.

Grayson cocked a brow. "Should be." He nodded toward a cluster of older women sporting dresses in varying shades of black, except one who'd dared a little brightness. "Right there. Chatting with concerned parents."

The woman in red laughed at whatever Robbie was saying. "They don't seem overly concerned."

"Wealth blinds people."

"It does, doesn't it?"

"Just as strongly as power."

We strolled toward Emmy, who was sipping clear liquid from a martini glass, making conversation with a girl whose skin was as luminous as the bronze wall decors.

Emmy gestured toward Grayson. "Natasha, can you please reassure my brother that we're not going to be returning to London in body bags?"

The girl—Natasha—gathered her mass of box braids and pushed them off her shoulder. "Body bags?" She smirked. "We have a medical team traveling with us. Some of the best surgeons and doctors in all of Britain, so if anything, we'll be coming home in better shape than we leave."

"You see, Gray? Nothing to worry . . ." Emmy's gaze vaulted over Natasha's head. She pressed away from the bar and squared her shoulders. "If it isn't the man who made all this possible?" She shot out her hand. "Lord Dunmore. A pleasure."

"Robbie. Lord Dunmore's my father. And the pleasure's all mine, Miss . . ."

A frisson tiptoed down my spine at the oily poshness of his timbre and mien.

"Emmeline Rogers."

His smile slipped higher, slick and smooth, a coral slash on his pale, freckled face. "Emmeline. What a lovely name." He picked up her hand and kissed her knuckles, then took Natasha's and repeated the same song and dance. "And you are?" He turned toward me, hand held aloft.

I stared at his blunt, clean nails, then at his blunt, clean face, and even though I wanted to touch him as much as I wanted to pet a mangy rat, I acted civil. "Naya Moreau."

A slight frown dented the space between his eyebrows as he lifted my hand to his lips. "I don't remember seeing that name on our list."

I was surprised he'd even glanced at the list. "That would be because I'm not on the list, Mr. Dunmore." I wiped my returned hand discreetly against my dress.

"Ah. That would explain it. American?"

"From New York."

"And you're here with . . . ?" His gaze drifted to Grayson, whose body went as stiff as a lamppost.

"They're my guests." Emmy took another sip from her martini glass. "My stepbrother and . . . his friend."

I cocked an eyebrow. *His* friend? I supposed that sounded better than introducing me as her tenant—who brought tenants to a private party? Besides, I did feel like Grayson's friend. Certainly more than I felt like Emmy's.

Robbie's amber-brown eyes seemed to glow red as he tipped his head in Emmy's direction.

The Triple was tall, as tall as Adam. The comparison took me by surprise. Out of all the tall people I knew, why in the worlds had my mind gone straight to my fellow black-wing? My father was impossibly tall. At the very least, three inches taller than Adam.

"Could I take a group shot?" A photographer wearing a plaid kilt over a white button-down lifted an old-timey camera outfitted with a telescopic lens.

"Why of course." Robbie turned to face him, then spread his arms out, and Natasha and Emmy stepped close, already grinning.

After the bright bulb flashed, Emmy waved at Grayson and me. "Come in the shot."

"I'm good, Em." Grayson's gruff tone and closed-off stance caught the attention of a woman in a dark pantsuit, standing a couple feet away.

From her strict attire, stricter hairdo, and tapered gaze, I assumed she was Robbie's bodyguard. A man of his stature must have a whole squadron of them. After staring Grayson up and down, she averted her gaze, probably deciding he wasn't a liability.

"Miss Moreau?" The sound of my name from the Triple's mouth made my gaze snap to his. "Would you like a picture?"

I didn't especially want one but thought better of turning him down. I stepped up to Emmy, who hooked her arm around my shoulders, and stared at the camera as it immortalized the moment.

Once that was done, Robbie thanked us for coming, then moved on to his next guests, the stern guard glued to his backside like his very own shadow.

"You could've at least said hi," Emmy hissed at Grayson, before turning to the bartender and pushing her martini glass toward him. "I'll take another one of these."

Over the ambient, loungey music, I thought I heard Grayson's knuckles click. I wrapped my hand over his balled one, trying to ease his billowing annoyance before it flared. For his sake and Emmy's, I didn't want their last interaction to be laced with antagonism.

"Want anything to drink, Naya?" she offered, once her glass was full and Natasha's flute was being topped with more bubbly.

"Just water. Thank you."

"And you, Gray?" Her gaze dropped to the hand I'd curled around Grayson's. When her smile broadened, I realized that she was, again, misconstruing my attempt to soothe as an attempt to seduce.

"Water, too." His grumble didn't peeve Emmy in the slightest.

As she put in our two orders, I murmured, "I know it pains you, Grayson, but let it go." I squeezed his fist one last time before removing my fingers.

"So, how long have you two been together?" Natasha was leaning against the bar, sipping her champagne.

I frowned. Looked around. When I realized she meant Grayson and me, I said, "Oh . . . we're not. We only just met."

Emmy tendered two glasses of water our way. "Never thought I'd be glad you arrived in London, Naya, but at least now, I'll leave for my trip with a lighter heart."

My pulse flattened at her insinuation, and Grayson . . . his face went all blotchy.

To lessen the awkwardness, I shot down my water, placed the empty glass on the bar, then hightailed it to the bathroom that was wedged between two bronze panels, at the end of an unlit corridor.

I jumped as a body shifted in the darkness beside the restroom door. It took my eyes a minute to realize it was Robbie's female guard. I supposed Robbie had also decided to visit the bathroom.

After I let myself into the ladies' room, I washed the Triple's touch off my hands, then finger-combed my hair, fixed my lipstick, and returned a text to my mother. Deciding I'd given Grayson enough time to cool off, I clutched my evening bag and was about to leave when the toilet stall door swung open and out strolled none other than Robbie.

Had I gone into the men's room?

I was about to apologize when the older woman in red, whom I'd spotted him with earlier, exited the same stall. As she readjusted the bodice of her dress, my gaze drifted to her left hand where a large, princess-cut diamond sparkled atop a wedding band. Even though I couldn't see her sinner score, cheating would've made her number go up at least two points, perhaps three. She paid me no mind. Merely murmured something into Robbie's ear, then licked her upper lip and let herself out of the powder room, hips swinging.

"Naya Moreau." The sound of my name made my attention snap to the mirror, to the reflected eyes of the youngest Dunmore. "What do you think of our program?"

I had more queries than thoughts about his program, but since I couldn't exactly question the nature of the trip, I replied diplomatically, "It's a wonderful initiative. I wish more people cared about helping others."

He turned off the sink and unrolled a towel from a basket. "Did you apply?"

"Unfortunately, I couldn't."

"Overprotective parents?"

My parents gave the word overprotective its very meaning. "Actually, it's my lack of passport that kept me from applying. I would've really loved to join your team."

Robbie raised a single strawberry-blond eyebrow as he continued wiping his hands. "You don't have a passport? How did you get to London? Did someone smuggle you into our country?"

Heat crept up my neck at my stupidity. Why hadn't I told him I was from around here? *Shoot. Shoot. Shoot.* "Yes," I ended up murmuring, and since my father had carried me through a channel, it wasn't a total lie.

Robbie finally discarded his hand towel into a wire basket under the sink, then propped his hip against the block of granite. "Tough family life?"

I picked silence since it spoke louder than words *and* it didn't cost feathers.

"If I procured you a passport, would you join?"

"Yes!" The more enthusiastic I sounded, the better, right? After a beat, I asked, "Was your question hypothetical?"

Even though there wasn't anything supernatural about Robbie, his eyes seemed to spark. "It wasn't."

"You could make it happen? I don't have a birth certificate, or—"

"You can make a lot of things happen when you know the right people and grease the right hands."

My heart tap-tapped my ribs.

"I'd need your fingerprints—to locate your birth certificate, if one exists—and your consent to run them through the system."

Without hesitation, I said, "Let's do it."

The grin he shot me was as bright as it was smug, because he considered me another fly caught in his web. Little did he know *he* was the fly, and he'd just flown straight into *my* web.

ADAM

ANGELIC FACT #131
TO SIN ISN'T JUST HUMAN, IT'S ANGELIC.

As I bulleted home atop my purring ride, I dwelled on ways to expedite my newest mission—reforming the forty-something baseball coach who lived for bribes. Although usually good at balancing my fletching missions with my shorhim ones, I had zero desire to invest myself in Anthony's plight.

The minute I stepped over the threshold of our borrowed home and caught the downward slashes of both Levi and Galina's eyebrows, my sinner flew out of my mind. "Who died?"

A glance at Noah's pinched mouth made my hackles rise. Something had happened.

Something bad.

Why the Abaddon had I hung out with my sinner today? I should've delayed my mission.

I wanted to kick myself for my lack of foresight. "The cops caught our unsub?"

"No. He or she is still on the loose." Galina sat up straighter on the bench, stretching her arms over her head, as though she'd been hunched over the kitchen table for hours.

I sank down on the bench beside her. "Then why do you all look like a malakim kicked a human soul?"

Galina exchanged a long look with Noah.

"They're worried you're going to be pissed by something I just found out." Levi trundled into the kitchen with his tablet.

My pulse, which had ramped up, held still. "What did you just find out?"

"You know that Circle Foundation's missionary trip you told me to keep an eye on? They just made the list of participants public."

"Okay. And?"

He turned his screen toward me. I skimmed the list until my gaze snagged on a familiar name. *Emmeline Rogers.*

Emmy had applied for a humanitarian mission? How had I not known this? And since when did she care about the rest of the world? She wasn't a fundamentally bad person, but she'd never given away a single penny she wasn't charged for, not to the homeless man sleeping in the Tube station near her house, not to waiters in restaurants. If anything, she'd filch stray cash as though her livelihood depended on it.

I finally looked up. "That's . . . unexpected."

"You weren't aware she'd applied?" Noah was draining pasta in the sink.

I shook my head.

Galina bent one of her knees and gathered it against her chest, blowing her rancid tea fumes in my direction. "Did your ex know you were looking into the Dunmores?"

"Of course not." I stretched out my neck, getting rid of the kinks my stressful day—*week*—had put there. "Why?"

"I had a theory she'd done it to get your attention." Galina shrugged. "Guess it's a coincidence."

No such thing as coincidences.

Had I inadvertently dropped the Dunmore name or mentioned their Venezuelan initiative? Maybe left a search page about the Circle Foundation open on my phone? Would Emmy really have gone through the trouble of getting involved with them to snag my attention?

It didn't make sense. What made even less sense was why she'd assume I'd come back to her if she got involved with them.

As I mulled all of this over, I caught Galina scrolling through a colorful feed full of pictures. One of them made me snatch the phone away from her and squeeze it so tightly, it was a miracle the glass didn't shatter.

I checked who the feed belonged to—Emmy—then checked the time stamp on the picture. It had been taken a half hour ago at that trendy dinner club owned by the youngest Dunmore. The caption read: *To new friends and new beginnings.*

I ground my jaw as I took in Naya's mouth skimming Grayson's ear, her hand wrapped around his. Whatever happened to her desire to save poor souls? Did she think Grayson's needed saving? I snorted at that. The guy's soul was cleaner than Noah's tighty-whities.

More importantly, though, she was all dolled up and smooching at an event thrown by a Triple.

"Can I get my phone back?" Galina held out her palm, just as Levi's tablet emitted a shrill chime.

He twisted it back toward him and dragged his finger across the screen as I relinquished the phone.

Galina studied the picture for a beat. "Who's the girl with your ex's brother?"

Levi spared me from answering. "The Circle Girl list was updated."

"What do you mean, updated?" I asked.

He shoved up the too-long sleeves of his lightning bolt tee. "A name was just added to the list."

"How? Didn't the application form close over two weeks ago?" Galina had blown-up the picture of Grayson and Naya and was studying it intently.

"It did. Not sure how she swung this." Levi ran a hand through the battlefield atop his head.

"Probably blew Robbie Dunmore," I mumbled.

The Triple loved getting people on their knees, whether it was to stick his cock into their mouths or his gun barrel. Men. Women. Old. Young. Didn't much matter to him. Humans, in his eyes, were there to be used, all of them disposable.

If only the new Circle Girl knew what she'd signed up for. Not that I was a hundred percent sure what he had planned for them. The only thing Dov and I were certain about was that the Triple was going to use the girls for personal gain.

Levi gaped at me. "You think?"

I shrugged a shoulder.

I was about to ask him for news on our case, when Noah rounded the island and peered down at the tablet. "*Naya's* the new sign-up?"

"What?" The word whooshed out of my mouth with such velocity it caught in the flyaways framing Galina's face.

She lowered her phone. "Naya, as in Seraph Asher's Naya?"

"Do you know any others?" I snapped.

"Geez." She rolled her eyes, raising her phone once again. "You're tense." She came upon a picture of me I didn't know existed. I wanted it gone but needed to prioritize my problems.

And the first one was Naya Moreau.

Noah returned to his pasta. "You think she joined in order to finish reforming her sinner or did Dov tell her about the Dunmores?"

Galina had returned to the picture of Grayson and Naya. "I really hope she didn't give Robbie a blowjob to get a spot on the team."

The image Galina dragged into my mind made me want to smash my fist into something, preferably Robbie's soul.

"Adam?" Noah's voice sounded amplified yet distant, like it was emanating from a loudspeaker atop a mountain. "You okay?"

I shot to my feet, adrenaline hurtling through my veins, tightening every single one of my muscles. "Naya isn't heading to Venezuela to keep track of Emmy; she's heading there because I turned her down."

Noah frowned. "I don't under—"

Before he could get the rest out, I was in the garage, revving up my bike, running through ways to knock sense into the fletching, without it costing me all my damn feathers.

One of the scenarios must've ticked off the ishim, because they bloody plucked me.

NAYA

*I*n the space of ten minutes, I'd gone from undocumented fletching to the proud owner of a birth certificate *and* a passport.

When Robbie had offered to fingerprint me, I'd assumed I wouldn't show up in the database, what with being of angelic descent, but lo and behold, my prints got a hit. They matched a certain Valentine Tremblay's, born in Paris on my birthday.

I read Valentine's mother's name—*Céline Tremblay*. Could she be my biological mother? Apa had never mentioned a Céline, but why would he? Although he loved me without fault, he wasn't proud of how I'd come into the world. An angel getting a married woman pregnant was majorly frowned upon.

Next to Céline's name was her husband's—*Lionel Tremblay*. I wondered why he'd allowed his name to be written on my birth certificate, if I was, in fact, his illegitimate child. Hadn't he known I wasn't his daughter when his wife gave me away to another man?

I was so focused on my budding ancestry that, as I reached for my water glass, I accidentally knocked it over, and the icy contents spilled across the table, right onto Grayson's lap.

He skated his chair back.

"Shoot. I'm so sorry."

"It's fine." Grayson smiled. "It's just water, Naya."

Emmy leaned over and slurred, "You could knock over a pitcher of soy sauce, and Gray would be absolutely *fine* about it."

Subtle. At least, she hadn't spoken too loudly.

After a server sponged away my mess, Grayson leaned forward and whispered, "Please bow out."

I startled, thinking he was talking to me, but I hadn't shared my recent enrollment, so I figured it was Emmy he was begging.

"And spend my summer moping about, wondering why I wasn't good enough for my ex? No thank you."

I studied her straight nose, bright blue eyes, and satiny hair. "You shouldn't measure your worth through other people's eyes."

She released a dull snort. "Has a guy ever dumped you, Naya?"

"No."

"Then you can't understand how that fucks with your self-esteem."

"I understand Adam hurt you."

"Says the person who's never been dumped."

"I've never been dumped because I've never dated anyone." Frustration that she thought so little of my sympathy *and* of herself made me admit that way too passionately. It also made my invisible wings bristle.

She blinked. "You're kidding?"

My cheeks heated as I gripped my newly-filled glass. "No."

"Why?"

"Because . . . I just never did." I drained the glass, then set it down brusquer than necessary.

Natasha, who'd switched around her name card to sit at our table, leaned over Emmy to look my way. "You've snogged someone, though, yeah?"

I shook my head, wings tingling as though the ishim were reminding me not to lie, but my mouth had never been on anyone else's.

"Are you serious?" Emmy's lids were pulled so high, she made me think of Lyla, whose eyes took up a third of her face. "You've never kissed *anyone*?"

She made it sound like I'd missed out on a quintessential stage in my development. Most fletchings didn't date until they made it to Elysium. I had to remind myself that Emmy was seeing this through human eyes where two decades constituted a huge chunk of life instead of the dew-drop it was to angels.

"I have my whole life to kiss and fall in love."

Natasha stared at me, communicating her shock with rounded eyes. "But aren't you curious?"

Thankfully, the server arrived with our appetizers, putting an end to that conversation. Emmy ordered another cocktail, which made tension writhe in Grayson's jaw as he chewed his chive crumpet topped with lemony cream, raw salmon, and a dollop of glistening caviar.

"Still don't want anything more fun than water, Naya?" Emmy had spent the better part of the last hour alternatively fussing with her glossy brown locks and trying to entice me to consume alcohol.

"No."

"You don't drink, do you?"

I speared the seafood concoction on the tines of my fork. "I prefer to keep a clear head."

"So it's not for dietary or religious reasons?" Emmy fixed her hair for the trillionth time, then puckered her lips and took *another* selfie, making sure her décolleté was front and center now that Robbie Dunmore was no longer in attendance. Before he'd left, apparently needing to head out to his parents' manor to ready it for our arrival—we were spending the weekend there to be prepped for the trip—most of her selfies were wide shots that had encompassed the notorious billionaire.

I shook my head. "A life choice." Also, drinking cost feathers. Or rather, the abuse of alcohol. One glass apparently didn't hurt.

Emmy finally stashed her phone back into her little designer bag, and it clinked against something that looked a lot like the mother-of-pearl napkin ring which had been wrapped around the crisp linen on her lap. Since people rarely brought their own napkin rings to dinner parties, and the model was a replica of the one I'd placed beside my plate, I assumed she'd filched it.

Emmy, Emmy, Emmy.

I almost clucked my tongue but decided to keep quiet and wait for her to fish it out and articulate a lame excuse. Although she caught me staring, she zipped up her bag and tucked it behind her back.

Our appetizers were cleared, and her drink served. The ice

clinked as she tipped it to her lips. Maybe because she was flustered that I'd caught her red-handed, she turned toward Natasha, which left me to speak with Grayson, my table-end companion.

I opened my mouth to make conversation when Natasha purred, "Um, yum. Dessert just arrived."

Already? Whatever had happened to the main course? Not that I was complaining.

Emmy hissed, and my gaze snapped off Natasha's place setting, following her line of sight instead. No wonder Emmy looked like she'd bitten down on a lemon wedge. Her ex was arrowing straight for our table, eyes a radioactive shade of green, mahogany hair sticking out haphazardly around his head, and skin plated with sweat. Instead of shrinking, Emmy sat up and squared her shoulders.

Adam's eyes locked on mine as he pounded past curious diners. I briefly wondered how he'd gotten into the private soirée. *Dov.* He must've called Dov.

The real question, though, was, why had he come? To rekindle his relationship with Emmy? To convince her to drop out of the program? Was he even aware she'd been tapped to be part of the Dunmore mission?

As he loomed nearer, I noticed the muscles in his arms bunching as though he were gearing up for a fight.

Grayson shot out of his chair.

"I'm not here for your sister," Adam gritted out. "I'm here for Naya."

Emmy, who up till then, had sat as still as an ice carving, thawed to life and whisked her attention toward me. I didn't meet her accusatory glower. Instead, I leaned back in my chair and crossed my arms.

"She and I need to have another little chat."

I'd heard of serrated gazes, but I'd never experienced one until Adam's eyes cut to mine.

Under his breath, he added, "Since our first one didn't quite do the trick."

Grayson glanced over at me, forehead pleated in confusion.

"Naya." Adam jerked his chin toward the exit. "Now."

I didn't get up. "I'm not a dog, Adam. And I heard you loud and clear the first time around."

"Guess she's not interested in what you have to say." Grayson took a step forward, trying to force Adam to back up.

"Fuck off, Gray." His molars clenched as the ishim extracted a feather from his invisible wings. To think he'd lost the black down for his word choice, when he should've lost it for his rotten tone.

"If Naya wanted to talk to you, arseface," Grayson hissed, "she'd have gotten up already. Now shove off before I tell Dunmore's bodyguards to toss you out on the curb where you belong."

Except Dunmore's guards had all departed with their boss . . .

"It's not a game, Naya." Adam vibrated with barely contained rage.

So, he knew I'd joined the Circle Girls and had dropped by to talk me out of it? Although his manner was brash and ill thought-out, I appreciated that he'd cared enough to make the trip.

Unless . . .

Unless it had nothing to do with concern and everything to do with this being his case, and him acting territorial.

My arms tightened in front of my chest.

When he realized I wouldn't stand, he shook his head, flipped around, and stormed off. His visit was so surreal that if I hadn't caught heads swiveling between the restaurant entrance and the end of our table, I would've wondered if it had actually happened.

"What was that about?" Natasha asked.

Arms finally loosening, I chose my words carefully. I didn't want to lose my first feather because of him. "He tried to talk me out of hanging with Emmy."

"He what?" Her cheeks puffed with shock. Or was it indignation?

"I don't know him well—admittedly *at all*—but I don't think he wants us to become friends."

"Why? Because I'm not good enough to be your friend?" Emmy spat out.

"What I meant was, maybe he's worried you'll tell me stories about him he doesn't want getting back to his fathers."

Her pupils seemed to dilate as she weighed the pros and cons of trusting me. Finally, she released a little huff. "He *should* be worried. I have many stories." She swiped her gin off the table, dumping the liquid down her throat, then smacked her lips. "Oh, where to begin?"

Natasha asked for the dirtiest one. I didn't want to hear about it, so I turned to Grayson who was watching me silently, intently.

"You honestly only met him the night you got to London?" he asked.

With a sigh, I nodded. "I honestly did." I let my forearms collapse onto the black glass tabletop, before reaching out to snatch one of the fried rice puffs from the ceramic bowl a waiter had left on our table.

I chewed, unfortunately too riled up to enjoy the taste of it. I ate another, which went down like wet plaster. However hard I tried to focus on the delicious food and the mission I was about to embark on, I kept replaying Adam's tempestuous outburst.

And replaying it...

All the way back to the mews.

Still thinking about the fletching, I parted ways with a moody Grayson and a drunken Emmy—his efforts to curtail his sister's drinking had died a quick death after the Adam-fiasco.

As he helped her up one flight of stairs, I headed down to my hidey-hole and unlocked the door. Before I could reach for the light switch, the cheap lamp on my nightstand flared, and my heart, which had thumped erratically all night, all but derailed.

ADAM

ANGELIC FACT #12
ELYSIUM IS NOT A PLACE ON EARTH.

The keys slipped out of Naya's hand, and her cheeks hollowed with a gasp.

I rocked on the hind legs of the iron chair I'd dragged in from her underground terrace. "Had a good time at *Jardin Japonais?*" I popped the *p* in that last word.

I'd waited almost two hours for her to get home. If I'd been pissed beforehand, it paled in comparison to how riled up I presently felt.

She crouched to retrieve her keys, then stuffed them inside her jacket pocket. "How—How did you get in?"

"First rule of living in the human world, learn to lock your doors."

Her fingers clenched around her keys, knuckles turning as white as the walls surrounding us. "My door *was* locked."

"*Doors*. Plural." I nodded to the patio door behind me as I banged the chair's front legs into the vinyl flooring meant to look like real wood and stood. "Pack your bags. You're going home."

"I'm not going anywhere." Her blonde mane vibrated. Her entire body vibrated, beatmatching her mood, and mine. "How did you even find out?"

"The Circle Girls list is public, that's how. Now, pack up. We're leaving."

"I'm not leaving."

I worked my jaw from side to side.

I was about to ask a tad more nicely when she added, "Grayson's right. You are *such* an overbearing arse."

I smirked. I'd take that as a compliment, considering how yawn-inducing Emmy's stepbrother was, a runner-up to Ophan Franz, my home guild's etiquette professor. I'd never slept quite as soundly as during his classes.

Back to the point, though . . . "Do you have any idea how vile Robbie Dunmore is, Naya?"

"I've done my research. I know he's a Triple and I know the family's foundation is a cover for lots of bad stuff."

Although her sky-high heels lent her several inches, she still had to tip her head back to look me in the eye. Papa Gabriel may not have been my biological father, yet I'd somehow inherited his height.

"Bad stuff?" I snorted. "That's putting it mildly. The man has more blood on his hands than the Red Cross Foundation has in their banks. He's as corrupt as they come."

"Good thing I got a spot on this mission then."

Whoever said the girl was pliant and sweet obviously hadn't spent much time in her company.

I tugged at the roots of my hair. "Are you always this stubborn?"

"Are you always this ornery?"

My fingers froze mid-tug. "Do you have any idea what he's planning to do with his little delegation?"

She pursed her lips. "I've entertained some thoughts on the matter, yes."

"And yet, you're still going?"

"These girls are defenseless. They're going to need a guardian angel, which is where I come in."

"They're going to need more than one," I groused.

"Are you offering to join *my* mission?"

"*Your* mission?" I stepped into her space, looming so close I noticed her irises weren't black like I'd assumed. "I came to London to look into this family. Why do you think I signed up to a sinner as easy as Emmeline Rogers, huh? Why do you think I stuck around so long?" The girl had been a great alibi and a pleasant method to blow off steam while I investigated the Dunmores. "Imagine my surprise when I saw your name pop up on the list." My rough exhales fluttered a strand of her hair. I was momentarily distracted by how smooth it was, so unlike the first time we'd met. "Look, I'll say this one last time, but unless you want to see girls trafficked or murdered or angels only know what the bunghole's got planned, you need to bow out."

Her lips were still welded shut, but her throat moved, dipping with swallow after swallow; I'd finally shaken her. Was it the trafficked or murdered part? Was she finally afraid for her own safety? Naya may have been immortal, but there were some forms of torture even we couldn't escape from.

She pivoted on those sky-high heels of hers and drew open her drawer. "How's the weather in Venezuela at this time of year?"

My gaze stuck to her calves, long and lean, toned muscle covered by milky flesh, but then her words smacked me upside the head. "Venezuela?"

Her fingers stilled on the lip of her drawer, and then she shoved it shut and perched her hand on her hip, crushing the neon pink fabric. "You didn't actually think I was packing to escape London, did you?"

This girl was going to give my brain whiplash. I shut my eyes, trying to calm down before I thought or did something that would cost me another handful of feathers. How many had I lost since I'd met Naya? Undoubtedly all the ones I'd earned for Emmy.

"Let me explain something to you, so you understand how bloody reckless you're being right now, *Starlight*."

Her fingers wrinkled her skirt some more.

"My team and I, we work under the guidance of an ishim and alongside cops, feds, and detectives." The detective bit was tru*ish*. As for the feds and the police . . . we'd stumbled into the former twice while working the same case and the latter were perpetually trying to book us for trespassing or tampering with evidence. I didn't clarify since that would greatly depreciate my point. "Our goal is to dismantle crime organizations, not just skip alongside crime lords until they locate their conscience."

A chuckle sputtered from her mouth. She stifled it with the back of her hand, but her eyes remained aglitter. "You thought I was planning on reforming Robbie Dunmore?" Another chuckle, the sound raucous yet satin-smooth.

I sidled against the wall, beating down the goosebumps rising on my arms. Since when did I get chills at the sound of someone's laughter, especially when that laughter was at my expense? "Walk me through your grand guardian plan."

"I would," she said sweetly, "but you and I aren't a team. You turned me down, remember? And since we're not friends either, I don't see why I owe you any insight into how I'll be protecting these girls."

I snorted. "You don't even have a plan, do you?"

Her wings sprouted from her back and curled ever so slightly around her shoulders. "I do, actually."

I checked the air around her legs for a fallen feather, then the floor around her treacherous stilettos. When no black fluff sparkled, I towed my gaze back up the length of her body to her face. "Since you're so determined in seeing this mission through, and I'm determined in annihilating Robbie Dunmore once and for all, indulge me."

Her mouth stayed motionless for a minute . . . two. Just as I was losing patience, her lips parted. "We're going to the Dunmores' manor to prep for the mission before we leave for Venezuela." She added air quotes around the word *prep*. "I was planning on collecting evidence that it's not a humanitarian endeavor and bringing my findings to the police, so they could intervene before the girls leave British soil."

I couldn't stifle the snort that bolted out of me.

She glowered. "What?"

"Good luck finding a cop willing to go against that family. You'd have better luck grafting wing bones to human flesh." As I scrutinized the girl, the old adage Papa had hammered into my brain about honey and bees and vinegar seeped over my current approach. "I applaud your initiative, though."

She huffed. "How did *that* not cost you a feather?"

"Because it isn't a lie. But I'm serious about you being out of your depth. Besides, my team and I are monitoring the whole thing. No need to put yourself at risk." I pushed off the wall and opened the top drawer to help her pack when my fingertips bumped into a trove of lace and satin. My blood warmed. I'd pegged Naya for a neutral-cotton type of angel, not—

"So what exactly is *your* plan?"

I froze at the rough breathiness of her voice, my fingertips hovering over things I had no right seeing, much less touching. I balled them up and locked them at my side, then pivoted toward her and cleared my throat.

"Getting one of Robbie's enemies involved once he's in Venezuela." With my eyes, I traced the curve of Naya's cheek to the point of her chin. "In this country, he's untouchable."

"Involved how?"

"Murdered."

Naya's breath caught.

"One less vile soul floating around the worlds."

"Okay."

"Okay, what?"

"Okay, I'll help get Robbie in his enemy's path."

I powered down every part of my brain that had perked up at the sight of Naya's underthings, leaving only the common-sense section on, since clearly, she'd flicked hers off. "Absolutely not."

"I'll be on the ground. Plus, Robbie knows me and believes I'm some vapid girl with family issues. He'll never see it coming."

"No."

"What's the worse the Triple could do to me?"

"He could sequester you! Torture you!"

"So? I'm immortal. I'm also extremely well-trained in martial arts."

"I'm still not using you to trap Robbie."

"I can handle it."

I suppressed a growl. "It'll stain your soul."

She rolled her eyes. Actually rolled them. "I'm not asking to be part of your team, only part of *this* mission."

I stared at the angel before me, took inventory of her body, looked for the strength she claimed to have. She was far from frail, and angel-blood did flow through her veins, but she still struck me as vulnerable. "Your father will murder me."

A smile flipped up the corners of her mouth. A plucking smile. Maybe Dov had been right about her. Maybe she did have it in her to prowl the noxious, black pockets of this Earth. Why else would she grin at the idea of partaking in a mission that was bound to get ugly?

Unless that smile had been produced by the idea of my impending death, because I had no doubt that if anything happened to her, Asher would see to my soul's extermination.

"You're crazier than I thought," I muttered, gaze pinned to the steady flutter of her pulse.

"Braver."

I returned my eyes to her obsidian ones and arched a brow.

"It takes courage to head into battle."

"Sure. When you have no choice. When you do have a choice, it's pure madness."

Smile brightening, she said, "Then I must be just as mad as you."

NAYA

A knock on the door had my heart spinning in time with my body.

Robbie Dunmore wouldn't knock, I reminded myself. Robbie Dunmore wouldn't visit, period, and there really was no reason for him to send someone my way. Unless he'd been told about the altercation I'd had with Adam and was reconsidering bringing someone with complicated ties aboard his mission.

I stared at the door. "Who is it?"

"Grayson."

My heartbeats spaced out. "Coming."

I nodded to the bathroom door. Adam either didn't understand my silent request or didn't care for it. Either way, he didn't budge from where he was rooted, arms now crossed in front of his torso.

"One second, Grayson," I called out, nodding toward a corner of the room.

With a gruff sigh, Adam finally stepped out of sight. As I padded toward the door, I realized I hadn't yet removed my jacket, which would surely strike Grayson as odd. After all, I'd left him and Emmy a good twenty minutes earlier. I magicked away my wings, then simultaneously kicked off my heels and shrugged out of my jacket.

Taking in a deep breath that did little to settle my nerves, I drew the door open and leaned against it. "Hey. What's up?"

Grayson perused my face, his features crimping into a look of muted amusement. "Were you exercising?"

I raised a palm to my neck, felt the flush of my skin and the thump of my pulse. "Taking off this dress requires demonic body contortions." I bent my arm over my head to prove my point.

His amusement increased, then transformed into another look altogether, one that spread ice through my veins. Grayson was sweet, but his timing was awful.

"I could help with that." His blue eyes skimmed the demure neckline of my bustier top.

I was about to let Grayson down gently when a deep, nonchalant voice said, "She's all set. Thanks though, Gray."

My lips snapped together, and I whirled. The nerve of Adam! I was going to throttle him once my visitor left.

"Didn't mean to interrupt." Grayson's voice had lost several degrees of warmth.

After volleying over another eloquent glare Adam's way, I turned back toward Emmy's stepbrother. "It's not what you think."

"I'm not really sure what to think anymore."

My hold on the door was so strained that my nails clawed the wood. "Adam dropped by to gripe about having been dismissed earlier. He's got a very sensitive ego."

A snort sounded from behind me.

Grayson stared at Adam before shifting his gaze to mine. "Just don't let Emmy find him in here. For all her insistence of being fine, she's not over the wanker." He backed up toward the stairs. "I'm going to meet up with a mate." A long beat ensued.

Was he asking me whether I wanted to come? Was he hoping I'd suggest going with him?

Even if Adam hadn't been there, I would've turned Grayson down. I was leaving tomorrow, perhaps forever. Once I returned Emmy and the rest of the Circle Girls safely to London, I'd travel someplace else.

"Anyway"—he palmed the buzzed hair along his temples—"see you around."

"Have a fun rest of the night."

Once he'd climbed the stairs and left the building, I smacked my door shut and whirled on Adam. "Was it really too much to ask that you stay hidden and quiet?" My sharp tone didn't even make him flinch.

"Instead of shooting daggers my way, you should be thanking me for getting the deadweight out."

"Grayson's *not* deadweight."

"You think he offered to assist you with your zipper out of gallantry?"

I glowered so hard my hairline felt taut. "You're missing the point."

"Yeah. And what point is that?"

Our combined frustration suffused the small room.

"That I can handle myself just fine, Adam."

His jaw ticked. "Pardon me for assuming you were serious about succeeding in nailing criminals. If I'd known you were more interested in nailing men, I'd have—"

"Oh, for angels' sakes, stop talking." I clutched my forehead and squeezed. "Seriously. Just stop."

Surprisingly, he did, but his jaw spasmed as though he were biting back words.

"I can't believe we're about to collaborate on a mission when a minute in your presence gives me a headache."

"You're not exactly a ray of sunshine yourself, Starlight."

I, Naya Moreau, the fletching with the most placid disposition in the history of guilds, growled.

And how did Adam react to my articulated annoyance? The green-eyed fletching smirked.

"I'm off to the manor tomorrow," I said tightly. "Since you've been studying the Dunmores, any words of wisdom you'd like to impart before I go?"

"Many." He fished his phone from his track pants pocket and began typing.

When he still hadn't said anything after a full minute, I cleared my throat. "I'm listening."

"Oh, we're not talking here." He stamped the screen one last time, then slid the cell phone into his pocket. "Our cab will be here in ten."

I frowned. "Where are we going?"

"To get you outfitted with a tracking device."

"In the middle of the night?"

"Where we're going, it's the afternoon." Adam pushed off the wall and walked toward me.

"Don't they make tracking devices in England?"

"Not the sort that'd fly beneath the Dunmores' radar."

I regretted having kicked off my heels, because I had to crane my neck to look Adam in the eye. "This isn't some devious ploy to get me out of the city, is it?"

"Nope."

I checked the air around his legs for a renegade feather.

"Glad we've got the trust down pat."

"You expect me to trust you?"

"I have zero expectations, only irrepressible hope."

"Well, keep hoping."

He gave my dress a slow once-over. "May want to change into a more appropriate traveling outfit."

"What's wrong with this dress?"

"You claimed to have ninja skills. I want a demonstration."

"I don't owe you a demonstration."

His lips pinched. "And I don't owe you any help, yet I'm giving it to you, so the least you can do is reassure me that you're not some damsel-in-distress I'll end up needing to save along with the humans."

Our eyes locked in a stare-off that lasted ten full breaths.

I averted my gaze first, then purposely bumped him as I walked to my dresser. I'd change, and not for his sake. I was changing, so I didn't flash him while I flattened his ego.

A damsel.

However childish it was to pout, I pursed my lips.

"Will you require assistance with that tricky zipper of yours, heiress?"

As I carted a pair of stretchy jeans and a T-shirt into my bathroom to change, I flipped him my index finger. "Naya. Not heiress. Not Starlight."

Adam had the audacity to chuckle.

"Maybe that's the reason Apa never introduced us," I quipped through the closed door. "Because you're insufferable."

I almost dislocated my shoulder tugging down my zipper—I needed to find a better system for this dress. Maybe Raven, who suffered from *restless finger syndrome*, could crochet some pretty beads together and hook them to my zipper when she was allowed out of Elysium.

She'd been gone six months, yet it felt like six years had trickled by since our last hug in front of the channel. I could still hear her soft voice in my ear, promising me she'd be on her best behavior—she didn't have a bad bone in her body, so her best was also her *only* behavior—to earn a channel key in time for my eighteenth birthday.

Unfortunately, behaving was one of two factors required to travel back down to Earth. The webbing between our feathers took months to dry and solidify, a process that only occurred in Elysium, thus our initial, lengthy stay.

My birthday came and went, and Raven had still not returned. I wondered what'd she think of my new guarding endeavor. Would she encourage my initiative or tell me I wasn't keeping my promise to meet her in Elysium before the year was out?

"Jumping on the wanker-train, are you?" Adam's voice carried Raven away.

"Can't jump on something you're already riding." Wrangling my hair into a ponytail, I returned to the bedroom for shoes, settling on sparkly silver sneakers that matched the angel wings embroidered on my jacket. I poked my arms through the sleeves and zipped it up. "Is my outfit satisfactory?"

He glanced at it, his gaze sticking to my sparkly shoes. "Cab's here." And then he was striding toward my door and drawing it open.

I took that as a yes. I checked the battery life on my phone, then thought better of taking it with me. If Apa caught me traveling midmission, he'd get curious, so I slid the slim apparatus onto the kitchenette counter before palming my keys.

As I stepped out, Adam nodded to the countertop. "Your phone."

"It's traceable. Don't want my father finding out where I'm going."

"I can turn off the GPS."

"Because that won't worry him . . ."

He released my front door, which he'd been holding open, even though no mechanical arm threatened to shut it. "Good thinking."

"You seem surprised I'm capable of such a thing."

"No expectations, remember?"

"How could I forget?" I sighed as I locked the flimsy piece of wood and climbed the stairs ahead of him, glad Emmy was knocked out. I didn't want to risk her finding me going anywhere with her ex. I needed her trust, not her anger.

Once in the cab, I asked, "So where is it we're channeling to?"

"Chicago."

"What's in Chicago?"

"My team."

Anticipation made my pulse skip. I was about to meet the team I'd come all the way to London to join.

Funny how it hadn't worked out like I'd assumed, and yet, I was still getting what I wanted.

NAYA

A half-hour after we left Queen's Gate, our cab pulled up alongside the narrow celestial dwelling wedged in between two equally skinny houses on Notting Hill, and I stepped out into the wet city.

"I'll pick you up on the other side." Adam's voice barely registered through the downpour.

"On the other side of what?"

"Of the channel. I'm going through the male guild, so we're not seen together."

"Oh." I was about to say *good thinking* when I decided his ego didn't need a boost.

He nodded to the cornflower-blue mews. "Get inside."

Even though I didn't *love* taking orders, I also didn't love getting soaked to the bone, so I sprinted to the guild and drew open the door, feeling Adam's eyes on me until I stepped past the threshold.

Whisking away the rain from my hair and cheeks, I peeked into the front office for an ophanim but found none. Maybe they were at dinner or putting the younger fletchings to sleep.

I strode so briskly through the atrium that the yellow English roses bled together like watercolor splashes on snow-white vellum. "Ophan?" I called out, my footsteps squeaking on the fire-lit quartz. As I turned into the dormitory hallway, I found myself nose-to-wing with Ophan Kate, the matron of Guild 37. "Sorry, Ophan. Didn't mean to run into your wings."

She lifted one eyebrow at the sight of me. "Have you reconsidered your sleeping arrangements, Naya?"

"No. I'm just in transit. Could you actually give me a ride?"

She sighed but nodded to the channel. "To New York, I suppose?"

"Actually, to Chicago."

That made her tilt her head. "Are you already done with your mission here?"

"Not yet. I'm just going to meet a"—I'd been about to use the word *friend* but swapped it out for the more accurate—"an *acquaintance* for the evening."

"I suppose you're so ahead of the game, you're allowed a break now and then."

I hadn't been aware my feather-count was so popular a topic. Unsure how to respond, I pasted on a smile which I wore straight through to Chicago.

As soon as the sparkling smoke dissipated, I darted away from my carrier, firing a rapid *thank you.*

Although I'd never traveled to the Midwest, the Chicago guild was fashioned like every other fletching dwelling—fire-veined white quartz and skylights that gave onto the always clear Elysian sky. The only variants were the flora and floor plan.

After two wrong turns, I found my way to the red-ivy choked atrium where seven quartz angel fountains glimmered under a patch of cerulean sky. I speed-walked past them, then pushed open the front door and emerged onto a piece of sundrenched sidewalk. After a week of nonstop rain, I couldn't help but close my eyes and tilt my head back.

Even though I wasn't excited to move to Caracas, dangerous as the mission and kingdom were, I *was* excited to live in a place where the air wasn't forever moist.

At an approaching motor, I squinted. An SUV slipped by, jampacked with kids. And then three smaller cars. Two cabs. One bus. I was starting to wish I'd asked Adam for the address of where we were going when a motorcycle swerved my way, and atop it, my newest associate.

Adam twisted the grips, and the bike, matte black like his feathers, rumbled. "Planning on getting on sometime today, Miss Moreau?"

"I've never been on a motorcycle."

"Never?"

I shook my head.

"Nothing to fret about."

I rolled my eyes. "I'm not scared."

"Right. You're the reckless seraphim's daughter, not the coddled one with the voice that rivals Elysian sparrows."

"Excuse me?" *What an odd thing to say* . . . Was it a compliment or an underhanded slight?

He revved the bike again, knuckles whitening around the grips and eyes straying to the steady ebb of traffic. "Your mother's words. Obviously not my own."

"Obviously."

Without looking my way, he jerked his head to the seat. "Get on already."

"Any chance I can drive it?"

His gaze snapped back to mine. "You've never been on a motorcycle but want to drive one?"

"How hard can it be? *You* can do it."

His dimple pressed into his cheek. "Tell you what . . . abandon your guardian angel dream, and I'll let you take this baby out for a spin."

"Nice try." I swung my leg behind Adam.

"Hold on."

I grabbed on to the back of the bike.

"To me, Naya. Hold on to me."

Oh. He shot forward, and I strangled his midriff, the hard muscles beneath his black T-shirt bunching and flexing as he tilted the bike to take sharp turns. Once my body adjusted to the movement and speed, my death grip slackened.

"Is the bike yours?" I asked at a red light.

"Rental. Can't exactly bring them through channels."

Although my arms were nowhere near his heart, his pulse resonated through my skin.

"Do you have a license to drive these things?"

The light turned green, and he rocketed through the intersection. "I do."

"A legal one?"

"Depends on your definition of legal."

I snorted. Had I really expected a fletching, who ran a league of guardians, to be rule-abiding? How naïve of me.

Once out of the heart of the city, Adam throttled the motor. Since I preferred not becoming roadkill, I pinned my body to his and watched Chicago unfurl, neat rows of brick-and-stone buildings on one side, an expansive blue lake on the other.

Beautiful.

I decided I'd look for a mission here after Venezuela. Which, of course, sent my mind tumbling right back to Robbie Dunmore and his "humanitarian" mission. I was still thinking of him when Adam pulled into the driveway of a rectangular house outfitted with large bay windows, ruddy bricks, and a flat roof.

A motorized garage door lifted, and Adam rolled in, parking beside a vintage cherry-red sportscar and a whole lot of clutter. I hopped off the bike, taking in the assortment of boxes brimming with saw-toothed tools, machines with missing parts, rope, rubber, screws, and electrical wires.

"Did you rent this house off the serial killer that's making all the news?" I scanned a shelf bowing under the weight of industrial-sized cleaning products.

"Boone has a passion for collecting and repurposing broken crap."

"We call him the tinkerer." Noah appeared in a doorway, pink wings tight against his back, eyes tight on Adam. "Fancy seeing you here, Naya." He was still looking at Adam, one eyebrow arced high. "What brings you to our part of the world?"

"I came to collect data and a tracking device."

"A tracking device?" His eyes went so wide his brown irises bobbed in pools of white. "You let her onto the team?"

"I'm just freelancing." I kept my tone sweet, even though I was still salty about being snubbed because of who my father was.

The ball in Noah's throat bounced up an inch, then down one. "Freelancing on the serial killer case?"

My attention swung between the two male fletchings. *"That's* the case you're working here?"

"Uh..." Sweat dotted Noah's brow.

Adam's jawline sharpened, probably because he was grinding

down the enamel. "Naya's dead set on joining the Circle Girls expedition, so we're going to help her." He turned and walked past Noah, and although he had his back to me, I sensed him mouthing something to his perspiring friend.

I speared my hands into my jean pockets. "He's not too happy about my decision to help out."

"Funny. I couldn't tell when he rushed out of here earlier as though his ass was on fire."

"You mean house?"

"Nope. I mean ass."

I smiled; Noah smiled.

What power there was in a simple curve of lips. I didn't presume it marked the beginning of a beautiful friendship but hoped it meant the poor guy would stop breaking out in hives in my company.

"What smells so . . ." I lifted my nose and inhaled a lungful of sugared air, "delish?"

"I just pulled a lava cake with vanilla-bean ice cream from the oven." He swiped a hand over the buzzed hair along his temple. "Well, the cake. The ice cream wasn't in the oven."

I laughed. "Any chance I could sample it? I *love* chocolate cake."

Grin broadening, he gestured to the doorway. "After you."

I stepped past him and into a bright and wooden space four times the size of my basement shoebox. "Are you baking to blow off steam, or is there a lull in chasing your serial killer?"

"Noah mans the home front." Adam was leaning against a kitchen counter, also made of wood.

"What he means by that, is that when the team gets together, I somehow land the housekeeping gig."

"Aren't you being a little dramatic, love? We all pitch in." A girl with raven-black hair cut into a sharp bob, reminiscent of Mira's, swung into the kitchen. Her resemblance to my guild professor stopped there though. This girl's jaw was soft, her cheeks full, her skin freckled, and she sported more piercings than my mother had rings. Little loops adorned the ridge of her ears, a diamond glittered in her nose, and a gold stud was speared through her tongue. "You must be Naya. I've simply been *dying* to meet you." She extended her hand, cheekbones pushed high from her grin.

"Down, Gee," Adam muttered.

Galina rolled her eyes, smile intact. "I'm just showing our newest member a proper welcome, since I imagine you haven't, sullen as you naturally are."

"She isn't—" Adam started at the same time I said, "I'm not—"

"Part of the team," both he and I said in tandem.

Noah whistled as he ladled barely cooked dough onto a ceramic plate and topped it with a dollop of ice-cream, but it did little to disrupt the growing silence.

"Hey, Boone, have you heard the wonderful news?" Galina called out over her shoulder. "You're on bathroom duty for the rest of the week!"

A groan came from somewhere inside the house, then the stairs creaked, and a male fletching with a short ponytail trundled in.

"Boone and I struck a *non-monetary* bet about whether Adam would be bringing you back here." Galina rubbed her palms. "Loser scrubs everyone's toilets."

"Naya won't be staying, though," Adam said.

Boone perked up but then bit down on his lip, flattening the hopeful curve. "Didn't mean to look excited about you leaving so soon, Naya. Toilets are just the worse."

I offered him a tentative smile. "I'm with you on that one."

Adam snorted. "Because you've had to scrub *oh so* many toilets in your life."

"I have actually. During a mission." I'd once picked a pregnant sinner who'd suffered from acute morning sickness. While reforming her, I'd helped around the house, and one of the chores I'd pitched in on was scraping dried vomit off the toilet bowl. I didn't bother relating any of that to Adam because I didn't care to justify myself to him.

Probably to break up the tension, Galina said, "Good thing our bet didn't specify a number of hours."

Boone let out another groan as he plopped down at the wooden dining table.

"So, what's your role in the group, Boone?" I asked. "Besides scrubbing toilets?"

Galina chuckled.

"I make things."

Right. Noah had called him the tinkerer. "So you're the one supplying me with a GPS?"

"I am?" He cast a glance toward Adam. "Um . . . why?"

Adam raised a water bottle to his lips but didn't drink. "Naya refused to drop out of the Circle Girl mission. I offered to lend her some tech support so we can swoop in and save her ass when Dunmore realizes she isn't who she claims to be."

My fingers clamped down on the plate Noah had given me. Had I possessed superhuman strength like my father, the ceramic would've shattered. *Don't engage. Do not engage.*

I engaged. "*Save my ass?* I know you think I'm some weak fletching, but I won't require any saving. If that's the only reason you've offered me a tracking device, then I guess I came for nothing." My fingers shook so hard the cake bobbed.

Noah stepped in front of me and pressed a spoon into my hand, effectively blocking out Adam. "Nobody thinks you're weak. A weak person wouldn't sign up for field duty. Now try my cake and tell me it isn't the best damn cake in the history of chocolate cake."

Although my appetite was shot, I carried my dessert over to the table and took a seat on the bench across from Boone, whose brown hair was as ruffled as the edges of the table.

"When do you fly out to Venezuela?"

I tucked my spoon into the mound of melting ice-cream and swirled it around, trying to ease my tetchiness before I took it out on any of the others. "On Monday. Tomorrow, we're headed to the Dunmores' manor on the outskirts of London, so they can prep us for the humanitarian mission."

Galina plopped down beside me, pulling one of her knees into her chest. "That sounds shady A.F."

"The tracking device, Boone. Get it." Adam pushed away from the kitchen counter.

Boone shot up to his feet. Geez. How did they stand to work with the disagreeable black-wing?

"Will you be outfitting the rest of the girls with a tracking device?"

"No." Adam parked himself by the head of the table, toying with the cap of his bottle.

"Why not?"

"Because we don't have fifty-one tracking devices laying around."

Boone paused between the doorjamb of the garage door. "Naya, are your ears pierced?"

Frowning, I touched my lobes. "Yes."

"Cool." After that strange query, he vanished into the garage.

As I scooped up a bite of cake, a shallow hiss sounded from my right. "You brought her *here*?"

Well, hello to you, too, kid.

"Aren't you happy you didn't take me up on my bet, Levi?" Galina propped one elbow on the table and laid her cheek in her open palm, gazing at the newcomer, a boy with a mane of disheveled brown hair. "Your brother's now on bathroom duty."

So Boone was this boy's brother . . . Several years older, I imagined. "Is that all of you, or are there more?"

"That's the whole team. Me and four boys." Galina sighed. "Why aren't you joining us again?"

"Because Adam's scared of my father."

He made a choking noise. "I'm not bloody scared of your father. I just don't want him getting involved, and all of Elysium knows how obsessed he is with his precious daughter."

I glowered at him. "Protective. Not obsessed."

"Same plucking thing, heiress."

Even though there was no backrest, I leaned back. "You do realize that calling me heiress is a misnomer since I can't inherit my father's title, right?"

Adam's brows gathered low over his emerald eyes, turning them the shade of the forest at dusk.

"I say we put Naya's candidacy up for a vote." Galina's eyes twinkled like her many earrings.

"No." Adam squeezed his bottle, and the thin casing crinkled. "There'll be no voting. It's my team, and Naya doesn't qualify."

Galina flicked her hand. "It's also Dov's team, and he okayed it, didn't he?"

"Did he really have a choice?" Adam glared at Noah, who grimaced as he secured the top of a bag of flour with a clip.

"She's more qualified than I am, yet you let *me* onto the team." Was Noah saying this to divert the attention away from his oversharing?

Adam's cheeks hollowed with an annoyed breath. "You bring plenty to the table."

Although he didn't add, *Naya won't*, his opinion about my added value—or rather, lack of—came across loud and clear. In his eyes, the only thing I'd bring was my father.

Galina jumped to my defense. "You can be so obtuse, Adam."

I raised my hand to stop their bickering. "I don't want you guys to fight. Especially since I don't even want a spot on the team." A sharp jab to my shoulder blade made my spoon slip from my fingers and clatter loudly against my plate.

Shock shot down my spine, which had snapped very straight. My wings spilled into existence, vibrating from the resonating ache. I breathed until the electrical current of pain stopped radiating through the right side of my body.

Without glancing at the floor, I knew.

A feather had just unhooked itself from my body.

I thought of Raven, of how she was so convinced they were unnaturally stuck.

And then I thought of my father, of how disappointed he'd be if he looked up my score. Would Ama also be mad? She'd lost so many feathers during her fletching life, I doubted disappointment would be her go-to feeling. If anything, she'd be curious about the cause, which would cost me another feather, seeing as I couldn't speak of Adam and his guardian team.

Moistening my lips with the tip of my tongue, I pulled my wings in tight and finally glanced at the dark feather casting tinsels across the hardwood floor.

Now that the pain had abated, the loss felt momentous. A milestone I wanted to not quite celebrate but commemorate because I finally felt normal.

I picked up my spoon. "I've never lost a feather before. I wasn't even sure I could." I carved out a bite of chocolate cake topped with melted ice-cream and brought it past my lips.

Perhaps I should've cared that losing it had revealed my lie and subsequent desperation for a place on the team, but—as Ama would say—I couldn't seem to give a feather about it, much too consumed by other emotions.

And now, cake. And I'd thought I'd lost my appetite . . . "This is amazing, Noah."

The pink-winged verity was gaping at me along with the others.

"What?" I scrubbed my thumb along my lips, hoping I wasn't sporting smudged chocolate.

Adam's gaze trailed my finger. "What do you mean, you weren't sure you could lose a feather?"

Oh. I dropped my hand back to the table and shrugged. "My best friend is convinced their peculiar color makes them adhere unnaturally to my bones, since everyone else sheds feathers, and up till today, I hadn't."

Galina pressed her head off her palm. "Wait . . . this is the first one you've lost?"

I nodded.

She twisted the stud in her nose as she side-eyed my feather. "Will you be picking it up?"

I wrapped my mouth around another bite of cake. Did I want to relive my past? Fearing it would taint my present state of tranquility, I shook my head.

She hinged at the waist to reach for it. "May I?"

"No," Adam barked.

Galina froze. "Naya's feather, Naya's decision."

A vein along Adam's temple throbbed almost spastically. Clearly, he didn't want Galina to pick up my feather, but why? Was he worried it may make her feel closer to me and thus strengthen her crusade to get me on the team? Touching someone else's feather was an intimate experience, not sexually but psychically, because you got to inhabit someone's soul.

It struck me how I could use the loss to my advantage. "Actually, I think *you* should pick it up, Adam. It'll speed up our whole trusting each other issue, which will be beneficial to working together."

He startled. Yeah . . . he hadn't been expecting me to offer him a front-row seat into my psyche.

Once he recovered from his surprise, his brow lowered, and he took a step back. "I don't pick up people's feathers, Naya. Besides, your past won't influence my trust. Only your skill. So if you're done with the tea party—"

"I'm done." Annoyance made my pitch dip a full octave. "Let's get this over with." I slung my legs over the side of the bench to stand, careful to avoid my feather, even though I couldn't absorb it through the soles of my shoes, then grabbed my plate and toted it to the sink. I wiped it down so energetically, foam splattered all four sides of the sink basin. Once I'd slotted the dark ceramic into the drying rack, I turned. "Do we fight here?"

"In the gym." Adam ticked his head toward the double-wide entrance Levi and Boone had come bounding through earlier.

"I want to watch that." Galina stood, rubbing her palms together.

"Don't you have somewhere to be, Galina?" Adam asked. "Someone's childhood bestie to meet?" They didn't sound like questions. They sounded like elegant dismissals.

Galina glanced at the large clock hooked over the doorway and sighed. "Damn. I really wanted to see Adam get his ass handed to him. Noah, tape it for me?"

"No video. No spectators." Adam's tone was low but sharp.

Was he afraid the others would lose respect for him if he took a few blows or did he not want an audience because he was planning on fighting dirty?

ADAM

ANGELIC FACT #256
ANGELS OFTENTIMES BEHAVE UNANGELICALLY.

Galina lingered in the garage doorway. "Is this goodbye or will you still be here later?"

Naya smiled kindly at Galina, adding fuel to the little flame the female shorhim harbored for the seraphim's daughter. "Guess that depends on Boone."

"He works quickly, so she'll be gone." I sent a pointed glower Galina's way, because Naya wasn't fair game. She was too much of a wild card.

"In that case, it was really nice to meet you, Galina, and I sincerely hope we'll see each other again. Either here or in Venezuela."

"Me too. Good luck, love." With complete disregard for my subtle warning, she shot Naya a wink before leaving, the river of colorful pompoms hooked to the zipper of her leather backpack bumping around noiselessly.

"I could hack the list and erase her name." Levi was looking up at me from the bench.

My gaze flicked between his tablet screen and the sink where Noah had sidled in close to Naya to whisper something in her ear.

"So? Want me to scrub it?"

"I'd need to talk to her stepbrother first. Organize an intervention . . ."

"Naya has a stepbrother?" the kid asked.

I tore my gaze away from Noah and Naya, who were still chatting quietly. "I was talking about Emmy."

"Oh." Levi rammed a hand through his unruly hair. "I can remove her, too. But I meant—"

"I got who you meant. Let me see how she fights." I smacked my empty water bottle down on the table and raised my voice. "You two done wasting my time over there?"

Noah side-eyed me, then spoke loud enough for me to hear. "His go-to persona is donkeyhole when he's worried."

Before she assumed I was worried about her, I said, "The only thing I'm worried about right now is someone destroying what I've spent the last two years building. Dismantling criminal organizations, whatever their size or reach, requires training, preparation, and commitment. It does *not* require indulging in cake and flirtations. That goes for you too, Noah."

My friend squashed my authority with a drawn-out eye-roll.

"Naya. The gym. Now."

She narrowed her dark gaze as she shuffled forward. "You *are* aware that the use of the word 'please' won't diminish your fostered wankerness?"

My fostered wankerness. I snorted, then proceeded to flatten my amusement as she walked ahead of me into the gym. I also proceeded not to let my eyes stray below the silver wings embroidered on her jacket.

What was it with angels needing to advertise what they were? Wasn't it enough to know?

Naya stopped walking so suddenly that I bumped right into those silver wings.

I froze.

I wasn't even sure why. They weren't real wings, just flattened copies made with thread.

Naya glanced over her shoulder. I probably should've apologized, even though, technically, *she'd* caused the pile-up, but I was still trying to process my reason for turning into a statue.

Pushing my fingers through my hair, I sidestepped her and bulleted toward the mats.

"Should I take off my shoes?" she asked as she shrugged out of her jacket and tossed it on the weight rack.

"I don't know, Naya. If you'll be asking Robbie Dunmore whether you should remove your shoes, then by all means, kick off your sparkly footwear."

"You're such a . . . a . . ."

A feather drifted from her invisible wings. I must've graduated from wanker to something way more awful.

After sucking in a shallow breath, Naya gaped at the sparkly black down for a full minute before shutting her eyes and squeezing them so tightly that a bead of perspiration rolled down her cheek. Or was it a tear?

Had I offended her *that* profoundly? "Are you crying?"

"I'm fine," she gritted out, clearly *not* fine. Or maybe she was, since she didn't lose a feather after declaring it.

She stalked toward me and slammed two open palms into my chest, making me stumble backward.

Someone was out for blood.

When her knee started to rise toward a part of me I did *not* want socked, I blocked the hit, then spun her around and held her in a chokehold, careful not to crush her larynx. For all my talk of not going easy on her, I wasn't planning on injuring the girl.

Her vein pumped hard beneath my forearm as she twisted her head and nicked my ear with her teeth, not hard enough to draw blood but hard enough to startle me. The second my arm slackened, she dipped her chin, slid her head right through the lax noose of flesh, and dropped into a crouch.

Before I'd fully recovered, she rocked onto her palms, kicked out her leg, and swept both of mine from under me. I went down hard.

She unfurled from her crouch, pupils pulsing with satisfaction. "Reassured?"

Air stuck somewhere between my solar plexus and spine, I wheezed, "No."

She stared out those big, unfathomably dark eyes of hers. "I just knocked you down. What more do you need? That I knock you *out*?"

"Even if you knocked me out, I wouldn't be reassured."

"Why not?"

I pulled the same move she had, minus the ear-nibbling. Her knees buckled, and her back clapped against the mat.

Before she could roll up, I straddled her hips and pinned her wrists down. "Because you're getting into bed with Robbie Dunmore, Naya, not a lone, knife-happy tweaker."

As she squirmed, her T-shirt strained across her breasts and rode up, revealing a slice of firm skin. This girl was such a conundrum—hard and soft, wild and calm. Before she could notice the chain reaction her wriggling had on my body, I lurched to my feet and extended my arm to help her up. She contemplated my proffered hand so long that I began to lower it, but then she slapped her hand into mine, accepting the lift.

I was about to tug my fingers free when she crushed my phalanxes between hers, flipped my wrist, and reached between my legs to seize my balls.

I froze, unsure whether to move or to stay *very* still.

Her fingers tightened, getting my dick's full attention. My brain's too, for that matter.

She moved her lips to my ear, her sweet breath warming my still-wet earlobe, and whispered in that phone-sex operator voice of hers, "If I got into bed with Robbie Dunmore, Adam, you can bet I'd rip this part of his anatomy right off."

Her threat and grip should've been the source of my entire focus, and yet my blood zinged with barely contained horror at the image she'd just conjured behind my lids—her seducing Robbie Dunmore.

My gaze narrowed on the pulsating pinpricks of her pupils, on the determined set of her jaw, which somehow had retained its softness amid her rage. "Not much point in ripping off a dead man's genitals. Now, unless you plan on finishing me off . . ." She could interpret that the way she wanted. "Let. Go."

Her fingers sprang open around both my groin and shackled hand.

"You want to fight dirty, Naya? Fine. Let's fight dirty."

16

NAYA

Not much point in ripping off a dead man's genitals.
What did that even mean?

Before I could ask, Adam clasped my wrists and pinned them against my tailbone, then pressed his front flush to mine, forcing my feet to shuffle backward. He held on so hard and moved so fast, I was certain he was about to slam me into the floor-to-ceiling mirror.

I braced myself for impact. Although my back did meet the wall, the collision was far from brutal. I supposed Adam didn't want to pay for any repair work and replacing a mirror would be pricey.

I cranked my neck as far back as it could go. "Are we done *now*?"

"I'm trying to help you, Naya, not piss you off. Why the Abaddon are you so angry anyway?"

"Because you treat me like a weakling and keep reminding me what a nuisance I am."

"I'm just trying to uncover your strengths and weaknesses." His voice caressed the perspiration glazing my hairline. "See if you're suited for this job."

"Except the choice is mine, not yours." I tried to shove him off but had zero leverage. "I'm done proving myself to you." Ticked off, I growled, "Feathering release me, Adam."

"Make me. Make me let you go."

I rolled onto my toes and smacked my forehead into his jaw.

Even though I didn't break any of his bones, my attack broke his hold on my wrists. I'd never fought with such aggression, not against the martial arts ophanim or the human black-belts I'd sought out to master more techniques.

Adam rubbed his reddened skin, eyes flashing. With surprise. Possibly contempt. Definitely not admiration. When he still didn't back up, I sidestepped him.

He whipped his forearm out and snared my waist, twirling me back until my front collided with the mirror, then stepped into my body, immobilizing me like a fly. "You've only just started proving yourself."

"I came to Chicago because you promised to help me; I didn't travel here to be evaluated and browbeaten." My ragged breaths fogged the silvered glass beneath my cheek. "Up till now, you've taught me nothing besides the fact that I'm not some freakish new breed of fletching with superglued feathers."

I rocked my head, my cheek skidding uselessly up and down the mirror. His grip didn't waver, but his body grew eerily still. "How is it that you'd never lost a feather?"

"I actively try not to think badly of anyone, even sinners, and I've skirted the truth but never lied. Can you please let go already?"

This time, he did. He even took a step back as I spun, seething.

His lips stayed pinned shut for a long while before he muttered, "Hope you're ready to part with more, because you'll be lying and doing all sorts of unsanctioned things as a guardian."

"Like I've told you, I'm ahead of the game, so I don't consider that a problem."

"As much as you don't seem to care about your wings, I bet your daddy will care. What will you do when he asks why you're shedding? What will you tell him?"

"I'll tell him I'm trying to save humans. And before you assume otherwise, I won't toss you and your team under the bus."

One of Adam's eyes squeezed as though he didn't believe me.

"Why do you assume he'd be so against it anyway? Ama believes guardians should exist, and my father agrees. I've heard them discussing it."

"If he thinks guardians should exist, then why hasn't he brought it up with the Seven?"

"Because he's still getting other laws ratified." My breathing had finally regulated itself. "He believes that if you bring too much change at once, it'll backfire."

Although Adam's gaze didn't relax, the line of his shoulders did. "If your father's so pro-guardian, why are you doing it behind his back?"

I tightened my ponytail. "Because he believes the *ascended* should be guardians."

The creak of floorboards followed by the low patter of footfalls had my attention turning toward the doorway.

Boone peered in, head tilted to the side. "I'm done. Are you?"

"Yes." I trod over the black foam mats, giving my fallen feather a wide berth. The sight of it no longer pained me, but it was still unsettling to see a part of myself just lying there, in waste.

"Your feather, Naya."

I paused and hooked a look over my shoulder. "What about my feather?"

"Aren't you going to collect it?"

I tapped my temple. "I remember each and every sinner I've helped."

Sometimes, I even remembered sinners I hadn't helped.

Sinners who only existed inside my mind.

I'd asked Mira if my strange and vivid dreams could be premonitory. She'd scoffed and told me there was no such thing as prescience. Sort of ironic coming from a supernatural being, but hey, who was I to question someone who'd been around since the European Renaissance?

I flicked my finger toward it. "Pick it up. It might reassure you that I'm not completely worthless."

NAYA

"So, how'd you get yourself tangled in the Dunmore web?" Boone asked, as I took a seat on the bench in the kitchen, the one under which resided my other fallen feather.

Noah was gone, but Levi was still there, clicking away on his tablet, sky-blue headphones poking out of his bushy hair, leaking a head-thumping bass.

"I signed up to Adam's girlfriend, who received an email invitation to partake in the Circle Girls mission. When she got the news, her stepbrother freaked out and told me how shady a family they were."

Boone frowned, his scraggly, blackened fingertips stilling on the side latches of a plastic container. "And *that* made you want to get closer to them?"

"I want to be a guardian, Boone. This case is bigger than I imagined, but as they say, go big or go home."

A smile ghosted over his mouth. "Doubt that applies to guardian missions." He reached into the box and lifted something swaddled in oilcloth, which he untucked with great care, as though tugging apart a sheet of unbaked puff pastry. Against the ochre cloth gleamed a pair of pearl studs as large as frog eyes. Had Boone unwrapped the wrong packet?

"So you're a jeweler in your downtime?"

"These," he said, with a flourish of his hand, "are my latest invention: ornamental tracking devices."

I blinked at him, then at the earrings. "You're kidding?" I pinched one between my thumb and forefinger and brought it up to my face, marveling at how inconspicuous it was. "Amazing."

Levi lifted his eyes off his screen to scrutinize his brother's handiwork. His lack of surprise told me he'd either known what to expect or was used to his brother's creativity.

"The calcium carbonate casing—" When my head tipped to the side, Boone clarified, "That's what pearls are made of. Anyway, it'll render the embedded trackers invisible to the most high-tech detectors."

"Wow." I set the miniature gadget down next to its twin. Instead of settling beside it, it rolled away.

At my puckered brow, Boone explained, "The magnetic force repelling them allows them to autonomously recharge."

Boone removed his smartphone from the back pocket of his shorts and pressed here and there on the screen until a grid appeared. A single, red dot blinked intermittently. I assumed the dot was our location.

"They're fire resistant and waterproof."

I really hoped I wouldn't find myself in a situation that tested the fire part. "And I can't inadvertently turn them off or anything?"

"No." Boone's honeyed-brown eyes set on my earlobes. "Ready to try them on?"

I removed the slender diamond hoops that forever hugged my ears. Ama had given them to me after Raven had taken me to get my lobes pierced at the birth of my hundredth feather. My bestie had followed up my tiny transformation, which had felt like a full makeover, with a celebratory ice-cream sundae that we'd slurped to its last creamy droplet on a Miami boardwalk.

After stowing the hoops in my jeans pocket, I speared in the pearls. They felt heavy and foreign on my lobes. "Will you be able to track me during the flight from London to Caracas?"

I still couldn't believe I was about to fly in an airplane. Was it strange how excited I was about adding that to my ever-expanding list of human experiences?

Boone nodded to his brother, still busy typing away, fingers as limber as a concert pianist's. "Levi'll be tracking the flight in real-time. If anything happens up there, he can take control of the plane and land it."

My heart picked up speed at the idea of anything happening midflight. "That's"—I gulped—"reassuring."

"Nothing'll happen." Boone tipped me a reassuring smile that didn't quite do the trick. "Levi accessed the passenger log. Both Susan and Robbie are listed."

In other words, he wouldn't explode the plane to create chaos. "What do you think he plans to do with the girls?"

Boone glanced toward the doorway. I turned but found no one standing there. "Adam thinks he may be trying to orchestrate a hostage situation to launder money. Get the girls kidnapped and then swoop in and save them by paying hefty ransoms in cash. Clever way to move cash."

A chill scampered over my skin. Even if the girls didn't get physically injured, being kidnapped would leave them with a wing-load of psychological issues, because he'd have to make it look and feel real.

I toyed with my new earrings. "If that's his plan, I hope he'll keep us together."

Boone propped himself on the edge of the table, hooking his ankles. "He won't be orchestrating fifty different kidnappings, that's for sure. Imagine how messy that'd get."

"Good point."

"What's a good point?" Adam's wet hair soaked the collar of his white tee.

"Boone was telling me about your hostage-money laundering theory. He pointed out we'd all probably get kidnapped by the same organization and kept in the same place." I released my high-tech earring. "Any other theories?"

Adam exchanged a long look with Boone. "You don't want to hear about my other theories."

"Actually, I do."

Adam pressed his mouth together, before relaxing his lips around words that chilled my blood. "Prostitution. Assassination. Imprisonment. Forced pregnancies."

Some of his theories would explain why Dunmore's criteria had been single women over eighteen years of age. "How would being used as wombs benefit him?"

"I'm just listing possibilities, Naya. In truth, we have no plucking idea what he's planning."

Boone shrugged. "For all we know, you guys are really going to be building houses for the poor."

"Maybe." I doubted it, though. "Adam, we haven't yet discussed this, but do you have a contact on the ground? Someone in the Venezuelan police force I can call if I need backup down there?"

Boone's thick eyebrows shot up. "A contact in the Venezuelan police?"

"Adam told me you worked with human law enforcers."

"We do?"

"If anything goes sideways"—Adam fired off a look Boone's way that made me wonder if he'd embellished the truth, because Boone certainly didn't seem aware of any relationship with the police—"*I'll* be pulling you out. There isn't a single member of the Venezuelan police that isn't corrupt."

"What about the CIA?" I was now almost certain Adam and his team didn't work with human law enforcers, and I wanted him to confess his deception.

"What need would you have for mortal, fragile humans with firearms when you've got *me*, Naya?" Adam possessed an unprecedented manner of skirting the truth.

"What about Dov? Would he intervene?"

"No. He trusts me to do it."

I supposed an ishim intervening on behalf of fletchings would raise Elysian eyebrows. After all, ishim rarely traveled down to guilds and even more rarely out of them.

"You got her outfitted yet, Boone?"

The tinkerer nodded to the pearls. "She's all wired up."

Adam swiped a damp lock from his forehead. "What happens if they bring her underground or someplace surrounded by jammers?"

"They'll work up to twenty-five hundred feet underground. As for jammers, they're broadcasting on a frequency jammers won't hinder."

"And you're sure they're undetectable?"

"Hundred percent."

Adam strummed his sweatpants-clad thighs with his fingertips. "It's a real shame we can't graft them beneath her skin."

Geez. How useless did he think I was? "I'm not going to

misplace them." I stuck my elbow on the table and pillowed my cheek on my fist. "And if they confiscate the pearls, I'll find a way to get in touch with you. Who's got the easiest phone number to remember?"

"If they confiscate them, you won't have time to get in touch with us, 'cause they'll know you're working against them, and—"

"The pearls come from Elysium." Boone clasped the edge of the table. "They're uncrackable."

Adam's eyes veered toward his friend. "Did Dov give them to you?"

Boone shook his head. "I clipped them off one of my mother's necklaces. She won't notice." He shoved away from the table and beelined for the fridge, then grabbed a bottle of juice and downed half of it in one go. "Hey, Levi! Tell Adam how many Ama owns."

Levi plucked one headphone off his ear. "Our father gets her a new strand each anniversary, and they're celebrating their one-hundredth and sixth. She won't notice."

Adam crossed his arms in front of his chest, his attention returning to me. "Last time I'll ask, Naya, but are you sure you want to infiltrate the Circle Girls?"

"I'm sure."

Levi looked up from his screen. "One click, and she can be gone."

She? He couldn't mean me, could he?

Adam's gaze flicked to Levi, then to me. "She said she was sure, so don't mess with the list."

He *had* meant me. "Hey, Levi, you may take your orders from Adam, but this is *my* mission. *My* decision."

Boone tossed the empty bottle in the recycling bin where it clinked against other discarded glass items. "Levi. Come on, bro, be civil."

Levi squared his shoulders, making them appear narrower beneath the flaccid cotton. "She's not part of the team."

"And you won't be either if you disrespect her or anyone else, be they a guardian or not." Adam's tone brooked no argument. "I'm serious, Levi. Apologize, or you're out."

I blinked at Adam, surprised he'd sacrifice a teammate for an outsider. Surely, he was putting on a show to gain my confidence.

A grumbled, "Sorry," finally airlifted from Levi's drawn lips.

"Look at her when you say it," Adam growled, "and bloody mean it."

Levi's eyes flashed an angry blue as they finally met mine over his tablet's frame. "Sorry, Naya." He still didn't sound sorry.

I nodded to acknowledge I'd heard him. "Can one of you call me a cab, so I can get back to the guild?"

Adam nodded to the garage. "I'll drive you over. Head out to the bike. I'll be right there."

After thanking Boone for my earlobe gear, I stood and headed for the garage, but then remembered I'd discarded my bomber on the weight rack. "Forgot something in the gym."

The second I passed the threshold, my gaze struck the foam mats. At first glance, I didn't spot my sparkling feather, and my heart's tempo notched up. If Adam had picked it up, that'd mean he was interested in—

Something glimmered. And it wasn't settling dust motes.

My feather came into sharp focus.

So much for assuming the guy cared about getting to know me.

18

ADAM

ANGELIC FACT #28
WINGS AREN'T ALWAYS USED TO FLY AWAY.

After dropping Naya off at the guild, I went to visit my fathers in Vienna. Only Apa, forever the night owl, was awake. I sat with him in the cafeteria while he tried to feed me *sachertorte*, his go-to remedy for any and all ailments, be they of the heart, spirit, or body.

Ever since I'd told my fathers I'd ended things with Emmy, they assumed my heightened level of stress and ill temper were byproducts of the breakup, and although I was most definitely torn up over a girl, that girl wasn't Emmy.

I toyed with telling my father the truth. Confessing would keep Naya from getting into bed with Robbie Dunmore, but ultimately, it would doom me and Dov, and I was entirely too selfish to shed light on our forbidden undertakings.

I twisted my fork by its tines. "Not to worry. My flighty heart will heal in no time, Apa."

My quip earned me a smile and a small headshake.

Before he could help me dissect what went wrong in my relationship—Apa loved nothing more than matters of the heart—I talked about my current deadbeat sinner. My use of the word made his smile wither and sparked a quietly articulated plea to treat humans with compassion.

"Some humans don't deserve compassion, Apa."

"Everyone deserves compassion."

"Even Triples, Apa?"

He went quiet for a full minute. "Depends on their sins. But yes, Adam, even they deserve compassion."

"What about nephilim?"

His throat bobbed as he lifted his gaze to the mural adorning the ceiling, which had been painted by a man who'd given up his wings because Elysium wouldn't listen to his plea to raise children in the land of angels until their wing bone ceremony.

Leveling his gaze back on me, Apa murmured, "The absence of wings does not mean the absence of a heart."

My father was compassionate to a fault. Both my fathers were, but Apa was the type of man who forgave before the offender had even started formulating an apology.

We chatted about Noah and his mission, then about two recent ascensions from our guild. When I got up to leave, Apa touched upon my upsurge in lost feathers.

I'd come prepared. "If Seraph Asher overturns the curse words rule, I'll be that much"—I held my hands aloft, palms facing each other but far apart—"closer to immortality."

"Adamleh," Apa sighed. "The human languages are rich with vocabulary and your mind fertile with imagination."

In other words: *get creative*.

As he escorted me back through the channel, he added, "Next time you see Celeste, ask her for some tips. She curses so colorfully."

My pulse twanged at the mention of Naya's mother, because another one of Celeste's talents was diluting the opacity of our minds the same way she diluted her paints. That woman could see right through you if you weren't careful. I hoped Naya had learned to shield her mind, or the lot of us would be in trouble.

Although I hadn't gotten much off my chest, I felt surprisingly lighter after leaving Apa, but that lightness shriveled up the moment I stepped out of the Chicago guild, and both the Felicity Gold case and Naya's upcoming mission pressed down on my shoulders.

I gunned my bike through the sunset-gilded streets, my mood

darkening like the sky. By the time I reached our borrowed house, not a flicker of light remained within me.

Naya had spent all of an hour with my team, yet somehow, I could picture her standing by Boone's pile of rubble, bantering with Noah, shooting Galina those polished smiles that made her delicate chin pointier and curling those sparkly black wings around her feminine curves. Somehow, I could *smell* her. I lifted the collar of my shirt and took a whiff. I was still sniffing my T-shirt when I plodded into the kitchen.

The chatter and laughter died at my arrival, and eyebrows hefted. I released the cotton and beelined toward the place setting they'd set out for me, the loud playlist Boone had cued echoing against my pounding skull.

I wasn't prone to headaches, but the Circle Girls expedition had been harrowing before Naya. Now it was—

It was—

I searched for a word to encompass how bloody alarming it had become. I'd had half a mind to sequester her here against her will, but that would've brought her father out of the quartz-work, and as much as I didn't care if he surprised Naya mid-mission, I didn't want him to show up at our headquarters.

I scooped a large portion of Noah's vegetarian lasagna onto my plate. "How was the meeting with Felicity's friend?"

"Enlightening." Galina scraped up the congealed cream sauce and sucked it off her fork. "I found out Felicity was a Big."

I waited for Galina to add a word. When she didn't, I asked, "A big what?"

"Big's short for Big Sister. It's a school-based mentoring program where older kids help out younger kids. Anyway, she was helping out this little kid with learning difficulties." Galina set her phone down next to my plate, then zoomed in on a picture of a brown-skinned teenager with a buzz-cut and a tank top that read *Justice for Felicity*. The girl stood in front of a drab chain-link fence, hugging a framed picture of Felicity.

I scrolled to the caption: *Calliope Underwood, age 15, 8 years after her Big Sister took her life.* The picture had been taken four years back, just after one of the guys who'd raped Felicity had gotten paroled.

"That guy's still alive," Levi said. "But check this out."

He slid his tablet toward me. A picture of six guys standing in front of a fraternity college house with their arms around each other lit up his screen. I checked the mugshot of the blond jock named in Galina's article, and sure enough, found him in Levi's picture.

A tingle shot through my gut. Even though fifteen-year-old Calliope was slight, there was already something fierce about her. She'd be nineteen now. Possibly in college. "Do we have an address for Calliope Underwood?"

"She lives at home with her grandfather, a retired gym coach. And guess where he taught?" Galina pivoted on the bench and sat cross-legged. Excitement made her legs flap. "At the same college these six attended."

The tingling intensified until my stomach was as hard as the fist clenched around my fork. I slung a look around the table. "He's our guy."

"Or . . ." Galina drew out the word. "She's our girl."

"Or they're working as a team." Noah lifted a beer bottle to his lips, took a pull, then set it down. "Is that a parting gift from my favorite black-winged fletching?"

"Huh?"

"The bruise you've got right"—Galina pressed her fingertip against my jaw, awakening the dull ache I'd attributed to my clenched jaw—"here."

I jerked my head out of reach. "You just had to shove your finger into my face?" I muttered.

"Too tempting." Galina smirked. "By the way, have you changed your mind about the feather?"

"What feather?"

"The one under your ass." She flicked her gaze to the shadows beneath the bench.

Right. The feather. The first one the straightlaced fletching had ever lost. The first of two. "Vacuum it."

Galina hopped off the bench and crouched. Before I could ask why the vacuum was stowed beneath the kitchen table, her eyes glazed over. I shoved away from the table and grabbed her wrist, but by the time I pulled it back, the feather had disintegrated into sparkling dust.

"Oh, bloody Abaddon, Galina, I said vacuum it."

Several seconds later, she blinked out of her trance. "You failed to mention with what." She stood up, her spine clicking as her vertebrae rolled into alignment. "Our undercover agent's a very sweet creature. Want to know what—"

"No."

Shared memories created bonds, and I was bonded to enough fletchings as it was. Besides, I didn't want another reminder of the girl's sweetness, because sweetness would only get her hurt, and my mind was already conjuring up all the ways Robbie Dunmore was going to crack Naya's soul like a walnut and let her untainted light seep out.

Anger flaring at the lack of control I had over the situation, I vaulted off the bench and pulled open the freezer door, then grabbed the bottle of Grey Goose and walked it back to the table. I filled my empty water glass with vodka.

"Dude," Boone said. "That's going to hurt your wings."

"Do I look like I give a pluck?" I grumbled into my glass of syrupy liquid.

Noah regarded me with concern.

"Don't you dare give me your two cents."

He released a deep sigh as he got up and grabbed his plate, then stacked it atop Galina and Levi's empty ones. "It better make you more pleasant."

As my drink spread fire across my chest, slowly but steadily dousing my crackling nerves, I attacked my lasagna. The others began chatting about the Felicity case again. After we made plans to meet with Calliope and her grandfather at daybreak, I tuned both them and the music out and retreated into my head.

One case almost down. A grueling one to go.

I ran through all the scenarios of what could happen to the Circle Girls. Each one sparked a fresh wave of rage. Two servings of lasagna and a refill of vodka later, my blood was simmering and my wings were down a feather. I stood up so abruptly that the bench skidded backward, almost knocking Galina onto her ass.

"Where are you going?" To steady herself, she clasped the table and braced her bare feet on the ground.

"For a ride."

The vodka hadn't made me more pleasant. Maybe another blast of fresh air would. Hopeful thinking, that's what it was.

The only thing that'd quiet my nerves would be Naya phoning me up to announce she was pulling out.

As I sat on my bike, I dragged my phone from my sweatpants pocket and pulled up her contact information that Levi had sent me when I'd waited for her to return from *Jardin Japonais* a couple hours ago.

Felt like days.

Weeks.

I clicked on her phone number, which led me to a blank messaging thread. I stared at the digital keypad until the letters began to blur.

I typed out: *Don't do it. You're going to get hurt.*

I erased it, then typed. *I'll put the earrings on Emmy, and we can monitor the situation remotely.*

I erased that too, because what the actual pluck?

I was ready to let my ex dance with the devil but not Naya? I should've been knocking down Emmy's door and bartering with *her* not to go. She was the human one, the mortal one. I bet it would've taken hardly any convincing to sway Emmy. A second-chance at dating me may even have done the trick.

My eardrums chafed at the memory of her voice and my skin itched at the memory of her touch. I was a wanker through-and-through.

In the end, I typed: *This is my cell phone. Memorize the number.*

I put my phone away, clutched the handlebars to power on the bike, and rocketed down the quiet, suburban neighborhood toward the moonlit lake.

NAYA

Getting awoken by a phone call was never pleasant. Getting awoken by a phone call from your mother to ask when you'd be arriving to your little sister's birthday brunch was downright calamitous.

I blinked and blinked at the time display at the top of my phone—1:30 p.m. I *never* slept in late. Then again, I rarely stayed up till dawn, mulling over a mission.

ME: *Be there in thirty!*

I ordered a cab, then tossed my phone aside and leaped out of bed. After stabbing my legs through last night's jeans, I traded the T-shirt I'd slept in for a pale pink one that drooped off one shoulder, pulled on Ama's bomber jacket, and hopped to where I'd lined up my shoes, sticking my feet in the first pair I saw. Probably should've gone with the second pair, because I almost twisted my ankle going up the stairs in my candied stilettos. And then again when I dove through drab gray drizzle into my awaiting taxi.

How could I have forgotten Lyla's birthday? I was the absolute worst sister ever. I didn't even have a present for her and couldn't afford to stop by any shop on my way to the guild, late as I was already.

At least the adrenaline rush of waking up to Ama's phone call had supplanted the nervous anticipation of my upcoming trip to the Dunmores. I couldn't believe I'd be staying in a house full of high-ranking sinners and flying with a Triple into a country where violence was a way of life.

Any sane person would balk instead of feel excited. Perhaps even run the other way.

I fingered my nifty studs. Were the others tracking me? Were they wondering why I was moving deeper into the heart of the city instead of away from it?

What would they think if I registered in New York? That I'd come to my senses and bowed out?

As the cab splashed down the capital's streets, I noticed I had a new text message.

UNKNOWN NUMBER: *This is my cell phone. Memorize the number.*

I frowned. Who would send such a—

Even though our phones didn't project holograms, the dry tone conjured up Adam's face. I was about to fire back a message about civility before deciding on: *I was hoping you'd send it to me. Consider it memorized, Grayson.*

I added a smiley-face emoji, then figuratively patted myself on the back for the wonderful comeback that was sure to nick Adam's ego, since he was clearly not a fan of Grayson.

Before clicking out of the chat, I memorized the string of numbers until it turned into a jingle, then drew the sequence in the condensation on my window as fat droplets splattered the cab. By the time I arrived in front of the cornflower-blue house on Notting Hill, I knew Adam's number as well as I'd known Raven's.

Wild hope that she might be at Lyla's birthday blustered through me. I tried to tamp it down to avoid being disappointed, but it grew and grew, took up so much space that I all but floated from the cab, across the drab expanse of sidewalk, and into the forever-temperate guild.

I was so focused inwardly that I ran smack dab into Ophan Kate, knocking the poor matron into a fountain. The sodden ophanim pulled herself out of the shallow basin, the angel-fire in her veins already transforming the water into steam. "Fletching Naya, must you always be in such a rush?"

Her question gave me pause. *Was* I always in a rush?

Up till a week ago, I'd been in a rush to earn my feathers. Now, I was in a rush to get home and back in time to begin my new job.

A group of fletchings around Lyla's age, who'd caught my grand entrance, giggled in a corner while I apologized profusely to Kate, before asking her for a ride through the channel.

A grumble followed by a sigh later, she gestured to the quartz hallways. As I walked past the group of younger tittering fletchings, I winked at them. One of the girls tried to wink back, but she couldn't dissociate her lids, so they both ended up closing and opening. I smiled, because it reminded me of Lyla, who had also yet to master the art of winking.

In a matter of minutes, I'd traded the yellow English rose shrubs of the London atrium for the honeysuckle vines of home. "Thank you, Ophan!" I exclaimed as I lunged out.

Her low *tsk*ing made me aware that I'd, again, been about to set off at a very fast trot. I forced my limbs to draw out each stride.

"Whatever are you doing, Naya? Impersonating a robot?"

I jerked my attention off the quartz floor and onto Mira's pursed mouth. "Ha. No." My cheeks pulled up with a grin. "Ophan Kate pointed out how I always seem in a hurry, so I was making a conscious attempt at slowing down."

Mira smiled, and there was something wistful about it. "How observant she is. As a child, you were always rushing through our halls."

Because I'd been perpetually worried I'd miss something important if I dawdled.

"Most fletchings learned to walk at the normal age of one, but you, my dear Naya, learned to walk at twelve . . . or was it thirteen?"

I went as still as the atrium statue and gawped at her in astonishment. "Did you just make a joke, Mira?"

"It was merely an observation, dear child." But the corners of her mouth said otherwise. "Lyla has been bouncing around all morning waiting for you. You'd think a tranquil father would breed tranquil girls."

"Are you calling my daughters high-spirited heathens, Mira?"

"Apa!" There I went again, cantering, but his arms were open, and I loved hugs too much to slow.

To this day, I believed hugs were magical and the world would be a better place if everyone hugged more often. I had a vision of Adam getting scooped into an embrace. I bet he despised hugs or expedited them when he found himself caught in one.

Mira smiled up at my very tall and very imposing father. "I was just pointing how much more alike your daughters are to their mother than to you, Asher."

My father's turquoise eyes sparkled with pride and love for our mishmash of a family. "Are you calling Celeste a high-spirited individual?"

Mira's smile increased, creating concentric ripples around her mouth. "That's one way of describing her."

Shrill squeals followed by peals of delight echoed over the slabs of white quartz.

"Tobias must've given Lyla her gift." In my ear, Apa whispered, "It's a baby *haccoul*."

My question should've been: how in the worlds had Tobias managed to carry an Elysian wild cat through the channel. Instead, I asked, "Tobias is here?"

Had he heard I'd met Adam? And if Tobias had heard, had he shared the information with my father?

"When has Tobias ever missed one of your birthdays?"

True. "It's only his son who's missed out on all of them." I was testing the waters. "Why is that, Apa?"

My father stiffened. "You know how I feel about you mixing with boys."

"But it's Tobias's son. Don't you want us to be friends?"

My father flinched. Visibly flinched. I was guessing he wasn't a fan of Adam, which led me to wonder why, since he was a huge fan of Tobias and Gabriel. "What I want, is for you to concentrate on your ascension. As soon as you've made it up there, you can build as many friendships as you so please."

It struck me that perhaps Apa knew about Adam's extracurricular activities and was worried he'd rub off on me. Of course, that didn't explain why we'd never been introduced, but it did explain why my father was so reticent we meet now.

Apa slung an arm around my shoulder as we walked toward the cafeteria. "Are you done with Emmy yet?"

"Not yet. I'm probably going to need another week. Or two."

"Sometimes, the easiest missions turn out to be the hardest ones."

I gripped his arm and looked up into his pensive face. "And the hardest ones turn out to be the easiest?"

He released a cumbersome sigh. "No. The hard ones usually remain hard."

"How very pessimistic old age has made you, Apa."

He grunted, applying a kiss to the crown of my head that grazed the underside of his jaw thanks to my four-inch heels.

No wonder Adam was terrified of my father. Although my fellow fletching was tall, my father was a beast.

With Mira at our heels, we reached the cafeteria. What a sight it was. Lyla, Arden, and several other little girls were running amok, toppling piles of jeweled fruit and miniature glazed cakes as they chased after a lime-green furball that could fit in Apa's palm. My sister's furry birthday gift was causing quite the chaos. The ophanim in attendance were desperately trying to corral the wild kitten while Tobias, Eve, and my mother watched on, in hysterics.

"Oh, Great Elysium . . ." Mira gasped. Had she been human and Catholic, she would've crossed herself. Because she was angelic, she snapped her wings out and screeched, "Tobias!"

More laughter puffed out of the women bracketing him.

When Ama spotted me, her laughter turned into a wink and an extended hand. "Starlight, come meet the newest member of Guild 24."

I abandoned my father for my mother and laid my head on her shoulder. "I'm worried Lyla's pet's residency will be cut short."

Ama's deep dimples excavated her freckled cheeks.

"You are loving this aren't you, Ama?"

"We are *all* loving this." Eve flipped the long black hair she'd inherited from her mother and passed down to her daughter. "Aren't we, Celeste?"

Ama's amber gaze tracked Mira and Tobias's passionate exchange. "Oh, so very much." She gently knocked the side of her head with mine. "So, what's new in your life? Met any handsome Brits?"

Unlike Apa, Ama never failed to encourage me to acquire experience in the dating department so that when I met *the one*, I'd have lived a little.

"I once dated this British lord—"

Ama's voice cut through Eve's. "If it's the one your best friend introduced you to, then it's not a suitable story to tell Naya."

"Why? It was all very PG."

Ama shot Eve a look that stapled her reddened mouth shut.

"What?" I asked.

"Not that PG after all." Eve's voice had gone up a full octave. "I should go check on Arden."

I frowned as she took off for the drinks table instead. "What was that about?"

"Nothing." Ama's smile was so tight it definitely hinted at something. "So, you were telling me about handsome Brits?"

"*Hmm* . . ." I thought of Grayson, with his charming heart and topsy-turvy teeth. I wouldn't have called him handsome, though. Handsome was a word better suited for men with blunt jaws, wanton mouths, and shrewd eyes.

Men like Adam.

I searched Tobias's face for similarities. Besides the color of their hair, brightness of their irises, and cut of their jaws, father and son were vastly different. Adam's complexion was deeper, a shade of olive so dark he looked like he sunbathed in his downtime, which I may have assumed before bumping into Noah.

Adam was also broader and bigger than Tobias, as though someone had taken the father and zoomed in on every one of his features. He must've taken after his mother, whoever she was. Like mine, no one ever spoke of her.

"Handsome men are much too inimical, Ama."

"You're telling me," she breathed, gazing adoringly at my father.

Where Lyla would've mumbled a *gross*—partly to be tickled and partly because, at five, physical love was still a revolting concept—I let out a small sigh. What my parents shared was beautiful.

A shrill gasp had all of our attentions turning toward Mira and the *haccoul* presently nesting atop her head.

Shoulders shaking with silent laughter, Apa reached up and seized the green kitten by the scruff. "Why don't you go get him a strawberry, Lylaleh? *Haccouls* are very fond of fruit."

My sister pushed aside her long brown hair and skipped toward the quartz buffet. She plucked a handful of strawberries and returned toward the baby *haccoul* burrowed against our father's brown suede tunic.

The tiny cat raised its head and sniffed, but upon seeing the small crowd, smooshed it back against Apa.

Tobias clapped his hands. "Girls, form a line behind Lyla."

Arden squeezed in behind my sister, who'd kneeled and flattened the back of her hand against the floor, a plump strawberry resting in her palm. Apa crouched, so that the quivering feline was at eye level with my sister. The animal sniffed again, growing braver this time. Keeping one hand on its back, Apa set it down beside Lyla's hand. The creature snagged the strawberry and tore through it as though it were live prey. Lyla reached out and petted its small head.

The animal froze, pink juice dripping from its muzzle. "Hello, Nitznootz."

"*Nitznootz?*" I asked Ama.

"It means Twinkle in Angelic," she whispered back. "Lyla and Tobias came up with it together."

"Cute."

"I still can't believe he managed to trap a *haccoul*. Mimi must be so jealous."

Mimi was Ama's surrogate mother, the original Moreau, a soul I had yet to meet but whom I already loved. I couldn't explain it, but every time I thought of her—like now—I'd smell cookies.

I often found myself associating scents with feelings. Sugar with love. Wind with freedom. Rain with sorrow. Even the lone fig tree in the corner of the cafeteria provoked feelings within me —heartache.

However hard I attempted to recall the origin of that one, I had trouble putting my finger down on what it was about the mineral sweetness that made my heart smart. There had been a stretch of weeks during which Apa had been stuck working in Elysium when I was Lyla's age. Perhaps I'd waited too often for him to return beneath that tree?

Lyla's tinkling laughter sprinkled the air, garnering my attention but also the kitten's, who was rubbing up against her bent legs, emitting a purr as melodious as a sparrow song.

The thought of our celestial birds made me think of Adam and what he'd said about my voice. How very odd a comment it had been. I'd decided to take it as a compliment since their chanting was lovely.

"Raven couldn't come?" I lifted my gaze to the painted ceiling of the cafeteria—one of Ama's many projects.

"Not yet." Ama kept her gaze steady on the jittery line of little girls, which was more of a curve, since each one strove for a better look at Lyla and her new pet. "But she sends her love."

Considering the secrets I was keeping, it was probably best she hadn't come.

My mother pushed aside a lock of my hair, which the London humidity had turned frizzy. "Who gave you those pretty pearls?"

Shoot. I should've unscrewed them and tucked them into my bag. "A boy."

"They look like Elysian pearls." Her eyebrows slanted. "Does this boy have wings?"

My cheeks blazed. "Maybe."

"What's this winged boy's name?"

"Ama, it wasn't a romantic gift or anything." I twisted my head so my blonde locks obscured my ears.

"Your complexion tells another story."

"But my wings tell the same one." I gestured to the quartz floor. "See. No feather."

"Can I at least know his name?"

I almost suggested a trade: one name for another. In the bedlam that had been my evening and the frenzy that had been my morning, I hadn't looked up Céline Tremblay. Even if Ama had never met my birthmother, Apa must've spoken about her—those two told each other *everything*.

In the end, I decided against sharing Boone's name. "Nope."

My mother's dimples flattened along with the curve of her mouth.

I hated the disappointment I was causing her. Absolutely hated it. "I swear that if I ever contemplate dating anyone, you'll be the first person to know. I also swear that I have zero interest in dating the boy who gave me the earrings." I stuck my hand in my jeans pocket, my fingertips grazing the diamond hoops I'd stashed there yesterday. I dug them out. "Can you keep these safe for me?"

Ama pocketed them without glancing away from my face. "This boy obviously has a vested interest in dating you. Why else would he give you jewelry?" Her gaze returned to Tobias, who stood beside my crouching father, putting order in the squiggly line of wide-eyed girls. "You're certain I don't know him?"

"You've never spoken to me about him. Then again, the only boy you ever speak about is Adam." I nibbled on my lip, then released it.

"I've been meaning to ask . . ." I shouldn't have brought more attention to the team, but I was genuinely curious. Especially now that Adam and I had met. Sure, the male was a touch bullish and a lot reckless, but he was passably-mannered. I didn't think he and I would ever become the best of friends but assumed we also wouldn't turn into the worst of enemies. "Apa's always so vague about this, but why is it you never introduced us?"

Her narrow throat dipped. "Why would we introduce you?"

"Because Tobias and Apa are as close as blood brothers, which makes Adam sort of like my cousin."

"Except, he's not your cousin." Her tone was as sharp as our quills. "Sorry. I didn't mean to snap at you. Your father and I are just extremely anxious for you to join us in Elysium, and boys are—"

"Distractions?"

"Yes. And I would know. I was a little . . . wild in my fletching days."

"And yet you still made it to Elysium."

"But I almost didn't, Starlight. I almost didn't." Her amber gaze went unfocused. She blinked back to the atrium. Back to me. "I don't want you to ever have to experience that level of anguish."

"I would never let a boy come between me and my wings, Ama. Never."

My mother's body, which wasn't supple to begin with, seemed to grow steelier, as though her muscles had morphed to bone and her skin to stone. Her reaction, her devouring anxiety that I'd, somehow, fail to cement my wings to my shoulder blades, strengthened my theory on the scarcity of parent visits in the guilds—by staying away, they spared themselves an immeasurable amount of stress.

"Naya!" my sister squealed, putting an end to our strange conversation and frightening her new friend right back into Apa's lap. She grimaced and leaned over, murmuring, "Sorry, Nitznootz." The cat peeked out and accepted the pat between its pointed ears. "I'll be right back." And then she sprang up and pranced toward me.

My arms were already stretched wide when she reached me. I hooked them around her small body and lifted her, singing my own version of the birthday song after which I apologized for coming empty-handed to her big day. "Although I'm sort of glad I didn't bring anything, because how is anyone supposed to top a *haccoul*?"

"He's *super* cute, isn't he?" She tossed the same adoring gaze Ama reserved for Apa toward her new pet.

"Super *mega* cute." Cheek to cheek, we looked on as the other fletchings all took their turn stroking the guild's new mascot. "I like the name. Suits him."

Lyla shot me a toothy smile, then directed me toward the gathering. We sat beside each other on the warm quartz. Nitznootz poked out from between Apa's legs to sniff my hand, before jumping into the circle of my sister's crossed legs.

"Domesticating a *haccoul* is unheard of." Mira was saying, eyeing the animal with great suspicion.

"But you have to admit, he's precious." Eve had one hand on her daughter's shoulder.

Although Eve resembled Claire in many ways, Arden resembled her mother in every way. It was as though Eve had cloned herself. If I hadn't met Arden's erelim father, I may have wondered whether cloning was a thing up in Elysium.

Mira thrust her hand toward the little guy. "He's a wild creature."

As though Nitznootz decided to thumb his triangular nose at her, he rolled himself into a tight ball of green fur and stopped moving.

Lyla lifted her brightly-hued, worried eyes to my deep brown ones. "Is he—Is he asleep?"

Between her dark hair, aquamarine irises, dimples, and smattering of freckles, my little sister would be one heck of a heartbreaker someday.

"Obvs," Arden droned. "Celestial creatures can't die, Lyla. Well"—she shrugged the bony shoulder Eve was clasping—"besides us."

That robbed the adults' faces of most of their joviality. Even Mira's expression went from crimped to crumpled.

The reminder of nephilim had me biting my lip. It wasn't that I ever *forgot* about this celestial loophole—I was well aware that the absence of wing bones meant death, and forever-death at that, since nephilim souls weren't harvested—but I tried not to contemplate this too often as it made dread billow within me.

I magicked my wings into existence and wrapped them around me to ease the dread Arden's words had conjured.

Safe.

I was safe.

But so many weren't.

Cocooned in twilit darkness, I was more than ever determined to use my angel-given gift to pay that protection forward to deserving humans.

ADAM

ANGELIC FACT #322
A FLETCHING WITH A PLAN CAN OUTSMART A HUMAN WITH NO PLAN.

At 7 a.m., after a pitstop at the guild to look up the Underwoods' individual scores, we parked four blocks away from our serial killer's house, a modest two-story brick unit. Like we'd planned the night before, Noah and Boone rounded the property to block off the back door while Galina and I strolled right up to the front one, past a low fence outfitted with locks, even though there were none on the actual fence door.

All the locks were hooked into the loops of wire. Since it was only in front of the Underwoods' property, I imagined it was their doing. Probably something symbolic. I briefly wondered if they had anything to do with Felicity Gold or if they were a memento of Granddad Gregory's days as a beloved college coach.

I poked a rigid finger into the doorbell repeatedly.

When it didn't ring, Galina used the rusted knocker. "You should've gone behind with Boone and left Noah out here with me." At my frown, she added in Russian, "You look like you're out for blood, which won't help convince Grandpa we're on his side." I grunted, which made Galina's eyebrows quirk. "What's eating you, anyway?"

Worry for a certain fletching who'd insisted on prancing into the devil's lair with zero preparation and zero qualms.

Stress that two enormous cases were going down at the same time.

The team needed me here in Chicago, and Naya, even if she refused to admit it, needed me in London. Those trackers speared through her earlobes were flimsy safety nets, and nets could be clipped. And then what?

"I don't like having two cases happening at once," I finally said.

The front door opened a crack, straining a flimsy chain.

"Good morning, Mr. Underwood." Galina's voice was as chipper as the bumblebee-yellow top she'd donned to match her nail polish.

"Mornin'?" Clearly, he was unsure if it was going to be any good.

"I'm Galina and this is Adam, my . . . partner."

The whites around the man's deep brown irises broadened.

"We're not undercover cops," I added in a low voice.

Gregory's lashes lowered a fraction, confirming that was where his mind had gone at the mention of the word *partner*.

"Or romantically-involved," Galina piped in, although I doubted he'd jumped to that conclusion. "We're just here to see Calliope, sir."

"She isn't home." He started shoving his door closed.

I whipped my palm up to keep it from settling in the frame. "Can you tell us where she is? It's important." The door chain tensed so hard, I estimated it was on the brink of unhooking itself.

"She's a grown woman. I don't keep track of her."

"Probably should. I mean, her extracurricular activities are getting quite a lot of airtime these days." I waved hello to an old lady peeping through a windowpane hung with frilly lace sheers on the opposite side of South Parnell. She froze mid-pat of her curler-pinned hair, blinked, then sprang sideways, surprisingly lithely for her age. "We're happy to continue discussing Calliope out here, but we imagine you'd rather keep your neighbors out of it."

A scuffle sounded on the other side of the house, complete with muted grunts and a heavy thump. My gaze met Galina's. She nodded and sprinted around the brick wall.

Underwood's Adam's apple jumped a full inch. "Where's the girl going?"

"To check out the disturbance at the back of the house. Probably a raccoon digging through your trash." I tilted my head. "Unless it's Calliope. Does she usually come in and out through the back door?"

It grew quiet except for the old man's heavy inhales, some distant wheezing, and the word *bitch* being grunted on repeat.

The former sports coach gave me a thorough once-over.

"I'm unarmed. You can pat me down if you'd like, although I prefer you don't. I'm not a big fan of being felt up by strangers."

His brown eyes snapped back to mine, then sideways, to Boone who was walking up to us, rubbing the back of his head.

"She used a track trophy. Darn pointy," he mumbled. "Galina wants to know if she should take her to the car?"

"Really all depends on if Mr. Underwood's feeling hospitable."

The old man's nostrils flared. "Let go of the door," he grumbled. "I'll let you in."

"That's more like it." I eased my fingers away, and the door slapped shut.

Seconds ticked by before the door opened again. Boone's sigh told me he was of the same mind as I was—the man was gunning up. Unless Boone was sighing because of his injury.

The chain finally rattled, and the hinges squeaked. "Get in."

The room we stepped into was homey and clean, the two-seater couch plumped and decorated with needlepoint throw pillows of birds. Pictures in mismatched frames battled for space with sports trophies and figurines of ladybugs. Four years of reforming humans had gotten rid of most of my preconceived notions, yet I couldn't help but wonder where Calliope stashed her arsenal of saw blades, pliers, and rope. Under the couch? It certainly wouldn't all fit under the seat of her yellow scooter . . .

"Now don't you move a muscle." Underwood backpedaled into a compact, green-tiled kitchen, eyes trained on us, hand on the small of his back.

I didn't ask him to put the gun away since it was helping him feel safe.

Smoke wafted from the stove top. Underwood swore as he pulled a pan full of charred bacon strips off the fire before unlocking the back door—guess Calliope had gone out a window—and in tumbled the nineteen-year-old, wrists bound behind her back.

Galina stepped in behind her, kicking the door shut. "Noah's standing guard outside."

Underwood raised his gun and aimed it at Galina. "Untie my granddaughter."

Galina picked lint off her T-shirt. "Not until you put that weapon away, Mr. Underwood. Like my colleague said, we're here to help."

"Pops, don't." A vein stood out in Calliope's neck.

I settled against the linoleum table in the corner and crossed my ankles and arms. "Let him keep the weapon, Gee." I sniffed the air. "Is that coffee I smell? Wouldn't mind a cup. I'll take it black."

Calliope's hazelish eyes narrowed. "Who the hell are you people?" Since the picture taken of her at fifteen, the girl had grown sideways and up, not body-builder bulky, but firm and muscular, a clear match for the men she was stabbing to walls with strategically-placed knives.

"Consider us your guardian angels." As always, my wings itched upon uttering the phrase, but since guardian angels didn't exist in our world, I was never stripped of a feather.

Calliope snorted, a corner of her mouth tucking up. "I don't need no guardian angels."

"Perhaps not yet, but you will soon. The Feds are going to come knocking on your granddaddy's door any day now."

Her mouth realigned.

I nodded to Boone. "The cruise ticket?"

"Cruise ticket?" Gregory murmured, gun still raised but no longer leveled at my skull.

"Your defensive attitude confirms that you're aware of your granddaughter's revenge scheme, so we've decided to send you on a relaxing, all-inclusive Caribbean cruise, Mr. Underwood," I announced as Boone handed him the printout of his travel itinerary. "The cabins on the ship are on the small side, but I hear they're cozier than prison cells."

The old man's breathing shortened whereas Calliope's seemed to have stopped entirely. "Says Jimmy Oakley on these. My name's not Jimmy Oakley." He tried to stuff the papers back into Boone's hand.

Boone pushed them away. "It is now. My brother's working on your passport as we speak."

Underwood's stubby lashes fluttered in confusion.

"Knowing makes you an accessory to murder and will get you jail time," Galina explained. "Not to mention you were the guys' basketball coach, which also makes you a suspect."

The air vibrated with heartbeats. Theirs. Ours.

Underwood turned to his granddaughter. "I won't leave. Not without her."

"Pops. I can't leave yet. I'm not done."

"Well then, I'll wait, and we'll leave together like we planned."

They stared and stared at each other. Into each other.

Finally, she turned her gaze on me. "There's no such thing as guardian angels, so who the hell are you people really?"

"Concerned citizens." I pushed away from the table and held my palm aloft. "Key?"

Galina dropped it into my palm, and I unlocked the cuffs.

The second they were off, Calliope spun and backed up toward her grandfather, rubbing her wrists. "And you're concerned about us, why?"

"My team and I, we're all for getting rid of lowlives, but the police . . . they have a diverging view on justice and have just caught a whiff of your trail. We want you to get away with your revenge killings. You're good, but the Feds are better, and that detective on your case, he's close to making the same connection we did between the men being murdered and the girl they"—my molars clenched in revulsion—"raped."

Galina joggled her head. "The detective's still convinced the executioner is male, which works in your favor, Calliope, but not in yours, Mr. Underwood."

"He'll be catching on before you can take down the last three standing. Who, by the way, have realized they're being targeted." I cast a longing look at the coffee machine. "One of them hit the road this morning with his whole family."

Calliope's pupils pulsed.

"We're tracking him. You're welcome."

Calliope didn't say a word, but her jaw ticked.

"She's tracking him, too." Galina twisted the diamond in her nose. "Right, Calliope?"

She glanced at Galina but didn't bother answering.

"Anyhoo"—I stuffed the cuffs inside my sweatpants pocket—"Noah'll give your grandaddy a ride to the airport while you fill us in on your plan of action, so we can help you get away with murder. Murders."

Calliope swallowed. "What's the catch?"

"It's not really a catch," Galina said. "It's more of a promise we want from you."

"Just spit it out."

So I did. "We'd like you to agree to let us rehab your murderous soul once you're done."

"Huh?"

"Once you've avenged Felicity, you'll let one of us—you get to pick who"—Galina waved between us—"help you start over with a clean slate. New name. New papers. Legit job. No more bloodshed."

Although Gregory Underwood still held the gun, the barrel was facing down, and his grip was so lax I was surprised the firearm hadn't plummeted right out of his hand.

"What's in it for you?" A ray of sunlight caught in Calliope's lashes and lit up the green flecks like bits of confetti.

"We get nicer halos." I avoided mentioning wings, since speaking of those with humans was usually, depending on context, a costly faux-pas.

Calliope's full lips pressed into a firm line as she rolled over all we'd said. "How much will the cruise and new papers cost us?"

"It's part of the soul-rehab package we're offering," I said.

"It sounds too good to be true."

Not much to do about how it sounded.

"Your offer is generous, and we both appreciate it, but I'm not leaving without my Calliope."

"Pops, if you're a suspect—"

"No." He shook his head. "I'll wait until you're done, and then we'll leave together."

"Pops—"

"No." His tone was so final that I realized we better get that cruise refunded stat.

"You still both need to pack." Galina tucked her black hair behind her pierced ears. "This house will be crawling with cops soon."

"Boone, call Levi and tell him to find Jimmy and Annie a safe-house," I barked.

"Annie?" Calliope asked.

"It's your new name. Better get used to it."

"You called me Annie Oakley?" The murderess sounded peeved.

I smiled. "Thought it was fitting, even though she was famous for her sharpshooting, and if all goes according to plan, you won't become famous for your sharp*stabbing*."

Calliope shook her head. "Y'all are weird."

Says the serial killer...

"Can't believe we're trusting you with our lives," she added under her breath.

I could hardly believe it either. I'd imagined it would take more negotiation. Perhaps even a stray bullet or two.

In a way, though, it confirmed what we already knew about Calliope and her grandfather: they weren't bad people, just good people doing a bad thing. Well, bad according to ishim and human law.

My crowd-cheer chime went off. Levi's name flashing over the screen had me hitting the accept button. "You already got the safehouse?"

"No." Lightning-fast tapping rang out from the other end of the phone as Levi's fingers danced on his keyboard. "I just heard police chatter about a hostage situation in Englewood."

"Thanks for the head's up." After ending the call, I strode over to the window and peered through it. Sure enough, the little old lady had her face smooshed to the glass. "Your nosy-ass neighbor just phoned the cops on us."

I didn't want to take the Underwoods back to HQ, and hotels were out of the question.

"Britt means well." Calliope's grandfather sidled up next to me and waved at the woman whose wrinkled brow furrowed deeper. "You all get out of here. Take Calliope. I'll handle the cops."

"That's a bad idea, Mr. Underwood," Galina said. "They're going to use this opportunity to question you."

Calliope glanced at Galina out of the corner of her eye. "Hate to admit it, but I agree with Yellow."

"Galina, but you can call me Yellow, Annie."

Calliope grumbled something about how Annie was a lame-ass name.

I clapped my palms to get everyone's attention. "You have five minutes. Take only the things you aren't willing to part with. Everything else stays."

Calliope snapped into action, tugging on Gregory's tattooed arm.

"Oh, and, Calliope?" I called out. "Don't leave any murder . . . *tools* lying around."

"I don't bring my work home."

Her grandfather's skin dotted with perspiration at my counsel. To think we'd pegged *him* for the murderer. The man had probably never even squashed a fly.

"Galina, Boone, help them. You have five minutes." I opened the back door, found Noah standing vigil next to a battered couch. "Cops are on their way," I told him in our father tongue. "Get the car running."

Adrenaline counteracted the fatigue which had crept over me when my motorcycle had finally run out of battery at dawn and I'd passed out on the couch for two hours before Noah woke me.

I was about to put my phone away when I saw I'd gotten a new message from Naya.

NAYA: *I was hoping you'd send it to me. Consider it memorized, Grayson.* :)

My blood went ice-cold. Did she really think it was Grayson? I jammed my fingers through my hair, mussed on one side by my twilit motorcycle ride and flattened on the other by my comatose spell on the couch.

As the floorboards creaked overhead, I typed: *It's Adam, not Grayson.*

My thumb hovered over the send button, but I shut down the conversation without responding. I didn't want to play into her joke. 'Cause that's what it was, right? Naya didn't actually assume Grayson had sent her his phone number?

A blaring police siren had me almost dropping my phone. I shoved it back into my leather jacket and peered out the kitchen window that overlooked the street. Britt was still at the window, working the curlers out of her mousy hair.

We needed to scram.

I pushed up onto my toes and rapped two knuckles on the ceiling. "Let's go, people!"

Galina trundled down first, Calliope hot on her heels, a backpack slung across one shoulder and a stuffed duffel swinging from the other. "Pops!"

He came down a couple beats later, his strides ricketier, his breathing labored, the front of his undershirt plastered to his puffing chest with sweat. Boone shadowed him, a small rolling suitcase swaying from his fingers.

Galina and Calliope sidestepped me, then Grandpa and Boone. We were halfway across the neighbor's yard when the old man started patting his chest as though his heart was about to blow.

"Sharon's wedding ring. I forgot my Sharon's wedding ring."

"Pops—"

"The chain broke, and I was going to have it fixed, but—"

"Shh." Calliope rested her hand on the side of his neck. "Where did you put it?"

"In my nightstand."

The sirens blared louder. They were definitely heading toward this neighborhood.

Calliope dropped the duffel. "I'll be right back."

"No." I bent at the waist, grabbed the duffel, and tossed it at Galina. "You all head to the car. I'll go grab it and meet you there. If I don't show in five, start driving."

I took off at a brisk jog, past the fence separating the properties, past the disemboweled couch Underwood had relegated to his lawn, then climbed up the porch steps, flew through the kitchen and up the staircase. Took me all of five seconds to figure out whose room was whose—Calliope's was powder green, with fake flowers outlining everything, from her bedframe to her vanity mirror to her windows. Surprisingly winsome for someone who chopped off dicks.

Blue and red light splashed across Calliope's plastic garden as a cruiser slid to a stop in front of the neighbor's place.

Move. I needed to move.

As the lady with the poodle hair cracked open her door to greet the two uniforms, I backed out of Calliope's room and sprinted down the short hall. The last thing I needed was to be carted off to a police station. Since I wasn't in the system, it'd raise a whole bunting banner of red flags and make quite a lot of feathers bristle over in the guilds, especially my fathers'.

I dug around the nightstand, jostling a pocket-sized Bible whose gilt edges sparkled like Dov's wings. Between his concealing dust and flying, the ishim would've made an awfully handy sidekick right about now.

Just as my fingers closed around a gold chain, the brass knocker thudded. I snatched the necklace and stuffed it inside my jacket pocket, then started for the door when I heard hinges creak downstairs. They must've found the back door.

Couldn't Britt have offered them a muffin or something?

I tiptoed over to the open window overlooking the broken couch. After ascertaining the yard was empty, I gripped the ledge and swung my legs over. The landing wasn't pleasant, in spite of my wings snapping open, angels only knew why since they were useless until fully-feathered.

"Suspect jumped out the window!" I heard a cop yell.

Pluck. Me.

"Put your arms where we can see them," the uniform hollered through the living room window as her partner rushed back toward the door that I'd dumbly left open.

The flash of a gun barrel had me pouncing out of my squat and tearing through the neighbor's yard. I was about to book a left in the direction the others had taken when footfalls crunched behind me.

I turned right, weaving through cluttered yards and hopping over desiccated shrubs, pricking my palms more than once on jagged fences. Just as I jumped over a stubby hedge, a whip-like snap echoed, followed by the mother of all stings in my calf. Dizzy with pain, I stumbled, barely catching myself on a plastic playground set.

The cop yelled again, but his voice was out of focus, the same way my vision was. Gritting my teeth, I pushed away from the swing set and stumbled through another yard, round another brick house, sheer willpower propelling me forward.

Calliope would be fine—after all, she had my team—but what would happen to Naya if I was put away?

Although the bullet had greatly diminished my velocity, adrenaline kept my mind clear, clear enough to realize that I needed to give up outrunning and start outsmarting.

NAYA

My father insisted on escorting me back to London. I prayed he wouldn't insist on seeing me all the way back to my flat, because my bag sat packed and bulging beside my front door. A glance at it would lead to a cross-examination, one that would inevitably harm my wings, and in turn, my mission.

When he strolled alongside me through the atrium, I nibbled the inside of my cheek, evaluating escape plans.

I decided on a hug goodbye. Sweet and final. "Thank you for walking me home."

Apa's big hand landed on the back of my head and smoothed my hair. "You haven't changed your mind about staying here instead of at your sinner's by any chance?"

I pressed away from him, raising a rueful smile. "No."

He sighed. "You're going to make my hair go prematurely gray."

I laughed and patted his arm. "You can be so dramatic."

He grunted.

"*Ni aheeva ta*, Apa." I'd been told *I love you* in Angelic enough times over the years to store away the melodious sound.

"I love you too, Starlight."

As I pulled up the app to book myself a ride, my father clasped his hands behind his back and stared up at the statue of the quartz angel spouting water from her spine in the shape of wings.

"You better go check that Mira hasn't shipped Lyla's gift back to Elysium." I hoped I didn't sound too frantic to be rid of him.

My father snorted but then grew serious. "Your mother would never allow that to happen, but you're right. I better head back." He started to pivot but paused. "Naya?"

"Yeah?" I shifted from one stiletto to the other.

"What Arden said. It seemed to rattle you."

I stopped shifting, surprised by the train of his thoughts. "Rattle me? Have you counted my feathers lately?"

"Every day, Starlight," he murmured. "Every day."

Since he hadn't mentioned my two fallen ones, I assumed he'd skipped a day. Or that his mind wasn't on math.

My phone vibrated, alerting me that my cab was arriving. "I'll be caged in no time, Apa." I blew him a kiss before fleeing out the guild door.

The London air was damp and carried the chill of a day lacking sunlight. I dashed toward the already open door of the cab and settled in the back seat. As my ride pulled away from the curb, I perused my messages and found a retort that made a smile rise over my lips.

UNKNOWN NUMBER: *It's Adam, not Grayson.*

Adam may have inherited his father's supple hair and bright eyes, but the sense of humor gene had passed him right by.

ME: *I imagined as much. Especially since I already have Grayson's number.*

ME: *I'm heading out to the manor in 30.*

When he didn't write back, I looked up the manor's address, input it, then closed my eyes and thought of my upcoming undercover op. Emmy would be surprised. Happy-surprised or weirded-out-surprised? I didn't want her to view me as a stalker, even though all good vigilantes were.

Sooner than anticipated, the cab slid in front of 9 Queen's Gate. I stepped out, one of my feet hitting a puddle, splashing dirty rainwater onto the hem of my jeans. *Ugh.* Wrinkling my nose, I traipsed quickly toward the front door. My key rattled a full minute in the lock before it found the cradle and clicked.

I clopped down to the basement, my ankles itching from the damp denim. I contemplated changing, but that would waste precious minutes, so I grabbed my bag and rolled it out and up. I'd packed it so full of clothes that it thumped against each stair.

"Moving out?"

I whipped my face up. Out of all the people I hadn't wanted to run into . . . "Hey, Grayson."

He stared down at me from the landing, eyes a shadowy shade of blue. When my suitcase began to tip me backward, I clamped my hand around the ramp.

Sighing, Grayson trundled down and lifted the bag from my clammy fingers as though it weighed as little as my wings. "So? What's with the luggage?"

I bit at the inside of my cheek, trying to decide how to answer his question. Finally, I chose the truth. "Last night, Mr. Dunmore offered me a spot on the expedition. I accepted."

Grayson's stare grew more intense. "Emmy failed to inform me of that."

I blew a breath out the side of my mouth that lifted a terrifyingly frizzy curl. Humidity had an unrivaled way of adding volume to my hair. "Because she doesn't know."

The laces on one of his sneakers were loose. I thought of pointing it out. I didn't want him to trip. When I looked back up and found his eyes still on mine, heavy with disappointment, I forgot about his laces.

"Why?" His question was barely louder than his exhale.

"Because I like to help people." I didn't clarify it was the Circle Girls I was planning to help and not the Venezuelans. I didn't want to alarm him anymore than he already was.

"The cab outside. It's yours?"

I nodded.

"Emmy forgot her passport. I was going to bring it out to her." That explained why he was in the building when his stepsister wasn't.

"I'll give it to her."

He reached into the back pocket of his jeans but didn't immediately extricate it. After giving his head a small shake, he reluctantly extended the passport my way. I clasped it, but he didn't let go.

"Will you come back after?" My suitcase still dangled from his hand.

"I don't know. I go where my heart takes me."

"Where your heart, or where *Adam* takes you?"

"I assure you, Adam doesn't dictate where I go." Yes, I'd come here for him, but I was leaving for me.

His freshly-shaven throat dipped. "Then for what it's worth, I hope your heart takes you back here."

"Perhaps, it will." I smiled at him.

In companionable silence, we climbed the rest of the stairs. Grayson insisted on wheeling my bag into the cab. After he'd set it at my feet, he held the door open as though contemplating getting in.

"You have a beautiful soul, Grayson."

He winced.

"What? It's true."

"That's what girls tell a guy they're sticking inside the friendzone."

I reached out and grazed his knuckles. "To me, nothing's more important than a person's soul. Everything else fades. Only the soul remains."

A flash of dark eyes rimmed by darker lashes appeared over Grayson's face. A statue of an angel with stumps for wing bones. A scent, mineral and sweet. My heart started and stopped, started and stopped.

I snatched my hand away from Grayson's and rubbed at my chest. It wasn't the first time I'd envisioned this scene, but it was the first time it scrolled through my mind while I was wide-awake.

His eyebrows bent. "Are you okay?"

I swallowed and blinked, forcing the smell and sight away, then nodded. Since his eyebrows hadn't leveled out, I said, "Yes." But was I?

That scent . . .

I hadn't lost a feather, so I must've been relatively okay, yet something felt amiss. Someone. I scooted back into the seat, keeping my palm against my murmuring heart.

As a child, I had these episodes where I'd wake in cold sweats. Mira or my father would walk me around the guild for hours before I accepted returning to bed. If I'd been human, I would've assumed I'd had a past life and a malakim had done a sloppy job of purifying my soul, but angelic souls weren't reincarnated. Which reinforced my belief in premonitions.

I slipped Emmy's passport, which I'd been bending out of shape, into my jacket pocket, then lowered my hand from my chest and laid it flat against my drumming thigh. Grayson's face came back into perfect focus, complexion as milky-white as the soggy air and the columns lining Queen's Gate, eyes as blue as the shirt on his back.

He looked nothing like the man from my visions. Smelled nothing like him. Grayson was as sweet as the man I dreamed about wasn't.

"I'm going to be so late." I cleared the gravel from my throat. "Until we meet again, Grayson." Because we would. On Earth before I ascended or in Elysium after he died.

"Safe travels, Naya." He stepped back, and the door snicked shut between us.

"Here goes"—I substituted the word nothing for—*"everything,"* not because I was overly confident in my guarding capability, but because I was going to give this mission my all.

As the cab crawled away from the city center, a bakery with a French name made me think of my birth certificate. I retrieved my phone from the pocket where I'd stashed Emmy's passport and typed out Céline Tremblay's name.

It was an unfortunately popular name. I added Paris to my search, which decreased the number of hits to four candidates, then narrowed my search by age bracket. I was left with four profiles—a naturopath, a financial consultant, a jewelry designer, and a dentist. All had pictures attached to their profile.

I studied each one, my skin prickling from my hiked-up pulse. After a close examination of their faces, I found I had the same pointy chin as the naturopath, the same deep brown eyes as the dentist, the same fair complexion as the consultant, and the same wavy mane as the jewelry designer. How was it that I could resemble four women who looked nothing alike? Was it because I wanted so badly to find myself in one of them?

A notification startled me out of my intense scrutiny—it was the picture Apa had taken earlier of Nitznootz wrapped in Lyla's arms, my sister wrapped in my arms, and me wrapped in Ama's. I smiled at the colorful accordion we made.

Sighing, I glanced back at the jewelry designer's face, then closed the page. Closed all four pages. Not because I was worried my parents would examine my search history but because I already had a family.

A loving and extraordinary one whom I didn't want to hurt by finding the human my father had impregnated almost two decades ago and refused to speak of. There had to be a reason behind his silence, one I hoped he'd tell me of his own free will someday.

22

NAYA

The Dunmore Manor should have been dubbed a palace what with its stone turrets spiraling into the misty sunset, its manicured land spilling down to a mirror-flat lake, and a sprawling terrace that could easily fit our entire fletching population.

A white-gloved parking attendant dressed in a uniform that seemed stolen right off a nineteenth-century lord's back insisted on handling my bag and helping me out of the taxi. I plodded up the curved stone steps, expecting a river of maids and butlers to stream out, but I was neither an extra in a period piece, nor was I a celebrity.

As I stepped over the threshold, past a sculpted wooden door inset with copper grommets, the nickname Adam had used tiptoed into my mind. I was no heiress. Merely a fletching born to an elected official. If Apa ever stepped down, I'd inherit nothing.

"Naya Moreau?" The woman who'd shadowed Robbie at last night's event appeared on the landing with another black-garbed guard.

"That's me."

"For security purposes, I'll need to pat you down and have your bags searched."

I nodded, gave my handbag to her partner, then raised my arms.

She ran a wand up and down every one of my limbs. When she reached my face, I held my breath. The wand passed over one pearl, then over the other. No beeping ensued.

"Supper's about to begin. Let me show you to your room."

I trailed her long strides. "You are required to wear a cocktail outfit. If you didn't bring one, one will be lent to you."

"I'm all set. Thank you, though." I briefly wondered if borrowed dresses came from Mrs. Dunmore's closet or if there was an attic stuffed with garments intended for guests.

I tipped my head back as we passed through a gargantuan hall girdled by a glass mezzanine. The coffered walnut ceiling that loomed two stories high was breathtaking, each square filled with art that would've made Ama weep.

Laughter and chatter stole my attention off the painted ceiling and carried it toward a set of open doors, to a room brimming with people.

"Once you've freshened up and have dressed appropriately"—my escort turned her nose up at my ripped jeans—"proceed to the drawing room." She gestured in the direction of the noise before striding beneath an archway that led to wide stone stairs covered in a midnight-blue runner. "You'll be sharing your bedroom with two other girls. I believe you know them both—a Miss Emmeline Rogers and a Miss Natasha Cumming?"

"Do they know they're sharing a room with me?"

"They've been made aware of their roommate's identity, yes."

I wondered how Emmy had reacted to the news.

At breakneck speed, we strode down the mezzanine I'd spied from below, dotted with a row of identical doors. It reminded me of the guild dorm hallway, if it were made of dark wood instead of quartz and lit by acorn-shaped sconces instead of veins of angel-fire.

My room ended up being at the very end of the wide corridor. The guard indicated each amenity with a flourish of her hand—the white-tiled jack-and-jill bathroom, the walnut sleigh dresser, the raw silk curtains made of the same teal fabric as the bedspreads. The room was devoid of the pomp of the reception area, yet still luxurious.

My suitcase must've been brought up another route for it already rested at the foot of one of the beds, right beside a terry bathrobe monogrammed with a loopy D. "You may keep and pack the robe for your upcoming trip. A present from the lord and lady for your service to the Venezuelan people."

"Thank you."

"Thank them."

Okay then . . . Not that I was looking to become besties with Robbie's guards, but a little warmth would've been welcomed. "I will."

"Now, for the rules during your stay. There will be no wandering through the halls, no entering private quarters, no screaming, squabbling, loitering, or running. Sealed doors are sealed for a reason. Remember that you are a guest, and nothing more."

My brow furrowed a little harder at each one of her bullet points, but that last one elicited a snort.

"Something funny, Miss Moreau?"

I forced the smile off my lips. "I'm well aware that this isn't an episode of the *Bachelor*."

"That makes one of you." At my sobering, she added, "Most of the participants have no regard for the Venezuelan children they'll be aiding, only for the unattached man organizing the trip. Now get ready. You're already extraordinarily late." She spun around and let herself out, shutting the door.

Friendly. But what had I been expecting? She worked for a family of monsters, and although that didn't automatically make her one, her loyalties laid with them.

After a lightning-quick shower, I unzipped my suitcase, selected a sky-blue dress, then attempted to pass a brush through my hair before giving up and patting serum haphazardly over my tousled curls.

Raven would've cringed at the uneven effect. Mira would've clucked her tongue at my impatience. Ama would've stroked my wild mane and reminded me that it was a thing of beauty, but my mother was completely biased and loved me and my hair unconditionally.

As I tried one last time to tame my locks, the bedroom door clicked and a familiar voice drifted toward me. "Naya, you little sneakster, you didn't tell me you'd be joining the Circle Girls!" Emmy sidled against the doorframe, big blue irises sparkling between thick swipes of black eyeliner. "Grayson told me he gave you my passport."

"He did." I dug it out and handed it over, observing her outfit—another black dress that fit her like a Band-Aid, coupled with strappy high heels.

"We're about to sit down for dinner." Her floral fragrance battled with the fumes of gin drifting off her words. "I scored us seats at the Prince's table. He's delish in spite of his missing eye. Looks like a pirate." She checked her makeup in the bathroom mirror, while I returned to the bedroom to put on my dress.

"How come he's here?"

"He wanted to meet and greet the women about to change his country's landscape."

"That's giving us a lot of credit."

"We're about to touch a lot of lives, so we deserve *some* credit. Are you ready?" She popped back out of the bathroom, just as I zipped the back of my dress. "Whoa. Where did you get that? If you tell me from the Dunmore closet, I'm going to ask to visit the place."

I lifted the strapless neckline embroidered with Elysian pearls, then smoothed my palms over the cinched waist and silk skirt that swirled around my legs like water. "A family friend."

"Must be a really wealthy friend. What brand is it?"

"Um. No brand. She had it made for me."

The arch of Emmy's brows heightened. "I wish I had family friends like yours. Anyway, let's go before one of the Circle Bitches steals our spots."

"Circle . . .?" I let my voice drag on the other word she'd pronounced. I wasn't sure if it would cost me a feather and didn't care to find out.

"There are these five girls. They're horrible. Conceited as fuck." She wrinkled her pert nose.

Before leaving, I checked my phone. Sure enough, Adam had replied to my little quip.

BLACK HOLE: *Why do you have Gray's number?*

I smiled at the creative nickname I'd found him during my cab ride.

ME: *Because he and I are friends.*

ME: *Why do you care?*

Since no answer came, I assumed he was offline. As Emmy removed a tube of lipstick from her tiny bag, I quickly typed out two more messages.

ME: *By the way, the Prince of Venezuela is at the manor.*

ME: *Just thought you'd want to know.*

And then I stashed my phone inside my roomy bag and followed Emmy out. When we hit the carpeted hallway, she hooked her arm through mine and filled the quiet with a running commentary on each participant. By the time we reached the drawing room, I knew who was who and who was doing who—apparently Robbie's older brother, Henry, had a wandering eye and unabashedly cheated on his socialite wife, who preferred the company of women anyway.

What a family . . . I tried to recall Henry's score—in the fifties, if I wasn't mistaken—like his father. It was the mother who was a high scorer, but not as high as Robbie.

Emmy guided me through the drawing room that was empty of guests but full of staff removing cocktail glasses and fluffing up throw pillows, returning the grand room to its catalogue-ready shape. Even though I hadn't come to admire the Dunmores' possessions, I couldn't help gazing around the room and admiring the detailed carvings in the wood paneling, the pastel mural covering the ceiling, and the rich upholstery.

All paid with blood money, Naya. The reminder dimmed the abounding splendor.

When we reached the terrace, a black-tailed waiter escorted us to one of the central tables. Although there were far more women than men at the event, there were still quite a few men. Most around Robbie's age.

"They saved us seats," Emmy murmured excitedly, at the same time as I asked, "Who are all the men?"

"Most are business associates. Some are Eton friends of Robbie's. That's how Robbie and Prince Pablo met actually."

Even though I couldn't guess sinner scores at a glance, I imagined most people here ranged in the high double-digits, and that assumption made my tight bodice feel as though it were cinching far more than my waist.

All five men seated at the table rose when we arrived. I established who the Prince was, thanks to the eye patch. His uncovered eye ran over me in a way that made my skin crawl and my wings spring out of hiding.

I forced a smile onto my lips and introduced myself, my voice striking my throat to the rhythm of my unsteady heart. I needed to calm down or these sharks in tailored suits and sparkling cufflinks would scent my distress.

"Your Highness"—Emmy batted her lashes—"thank you for saving seats for me and my friend."

Pablo nodded to Emmy, before stepping lithely around the table and lifting my hand to his lips. "The pleasure is all mine. Will you do me the honor of dining at my side, Señorita Moreau?"

I was so concentrated on the fact that Pablo wore leather gloves that I almost squeaked when Emmy breathed inside my ear. "Shit. There goes my chance at becoming queen."

I would've offered her my seat in a heartbeat but decided that if anyone could shed light on Robbie's mission, it'd be the monarch's own flesh and blood. Besides, encouraging Emmy's affection for the son of a corrupt leader, surely corrupt himself, defied the purpose of protecting her.

Emmy gave me a little shove but not before whispering, "On the upside, I'll be going straight to heaven if you two tie the knot."

There'd be no tying of any knots. What there'd be plenty of—hopefully—was unravelling of knots. The quicker I could understand what we were up against, the quicker I could put a stop to it.

23

ADAM

ANGELIC FACT #415
SOME ANGELS ARE FAR GREATER THAN THE SUM
OF THEIR FEATHERS. SOME... ARE NOT.

"Good afternoon. I'm back with breaking news on the apprehension of Englewood High's beloved and retired gym coach, Mr. Gregory Underwood. Where the police force wasn't able to lift prints from the female offender"—a 3D generated picture of Galina materialized on the screen followed by one of me—"they were able to collect DNA from the male suspect."

"Why is it that they make me look like a twelve-year-old with chipmunk cheeks but make you look like an Adonis?" Galina tossed popcorn at me.

I picked up the kernels that landed on my lap and ate them.

Noah side-eyed her. "That's what you're choosing to focus on? Not on the fact that the two of you are on the news. On the forking news!"

All afternoon, I'd been expecting a call from my fathers. Papa Gabriel would chew my wings off and demand answers, while my other father, as always, would play good, sympathetic cop.

Thankfully, in spite of blood loss and lack of sleep, I'd prepped a solid defense. As I'd waited out the uniform in the bed of a pickup truck, sweating and bleeding beneath gray moving blankets that smelled like musty wood and wet dog, I'd decided to drop my current sinner and sign up to Calliope's grandfather, which would give me an angelic reason to have been on the premises.

So that's what I'd done.

After Galina had come back for me in the cherry-red sportscar, I'd told her to drive to a guild. Next thing I knew, I was slapped in the face by a roll of gauze and a bottle of water.

"Patch yourself up before you give the ophanim a heart attack," Galina had grumbled, staring at the tan upholstery I'd painted red in spite of having stuck the moving blanket, soaked in my DNA, under my ass.

Grunting like a pig, I'd worked the bullet out of the wound. It probably would've popped out on its own, but that could've taken a couple days, and I didn't have days to limp around with a bullet lodged in my calf. After mummifying my bum leg, I'd cleaned the blood off my hands with half the water bottle's contents, then guzzled the other half to replenish the sweat I'd lost hiding from the cop.

"Whoa," Galina whispered, as I scanned the transcript from Naya's earrings.

Yeah. The transcript.

Before I'd driven her home yesterday, Boone had informed me the pearls were also equipped with mics. He'd asked whether to turn them on or leave them off. I hadn't hesitated, because more than an infringement on Naya's privacy, I saw them as an extra way to keep the girl safe from the Dunmores.

I hovered over two particular segments of the transcript: a conversation she'd had with Celeste, where they were discussing me and our lack of kinship, and a piece of the chat she'd had with Grayson.

That one made my eyesight taper so hard it livened up the throbbing in my forehead.

I go where my heart takes me.
Where your heart, or where Adam takes you?
I assure you, Adam doesn't dictate where I go.
Then for what it's worth, I hope your heart takes you back here.
Perhaps, it will.

I was aware she liked the guy, but to the point of making sappy promises to return? I scrolled through the rest of their talk, while the software Levi had installed on my phone transcribed her latest conversation, then flipped back to our text thread and reread her answer to the messages I either hadn't meant to send or shouldn't have.

The painkillers Noah had jammed down my throat were toying with my good sense to stay out of the girl's personal life.

NAYA: *Why do you care?*

"This is bad, Adam," Noah murmured.

Agreed. The girl had way more important things to focus on than flirting with Emmy's stepbrother. And yeah, I was the pot calling the kettle black, but she wasn't merely guarding humans from a bad person; she was guarding humans from the devil himself.

Noah elbowed me, jerking my gaze off my phone, but not my mind off the girl on the other end of it.

"What?" I growled, everything pissing me off today.

We'd stowed the Underwoods away from the cops and I hadn't gotten booked. I should've been rejoicing over so many wins, but it felt like a countdown had begun, like someone had just lit a wick and our luck was on the melt.

"What do you mean what? They have your freaking DNA." Noah's feathers were bristling as they always did when his mood spiked.

I let my head loll back against the couch cushion just as my phone chimed again. "So? I'm not in the human database."

Galina raised the volume on the TV.

"This is where the case gets really strange, Maddox," the newscaster was telling her fellow reporter. "The suspect's DNA matches the DNA of a stillborn child from a French hospital. A boy of Middle Eastern descent born to an Aicha Bennani and an unknown father. Police are working with French authorities and the mother of the presumed deceased infant to exhume the body."

I frowned. *What the—*

"So that's how they remove hybrids from their mortal parent." Galina wrinkled her nose. "By pretending we're stillborns..."

Noah grabbed a fistful of popcorn from Galina's bowl. "I don't think that's what they do for all hybrids."

"Do you know a single one who's met their birth parent? Because I've never met mine, nor have I ever been given the man's name."

"Aicha Bennani," I whispered, as my past locked into my present. I stood, and in spite of the flaming pain eating my calf, I limped the length of the room.

"Dude, you were shot. Sit down," Noah said.

I needed to move, even if it was just across the living room floor.

Galina's earrings glinted from the reflection of the TV, where the picture of a woman wearing scrubs filled the screen. Her skin was a deeper olive shade than mine and her hair a darker brown, but her eyes were identical—Granny Smith-green.

I thought of calling Apa to tell him I'd found out his dirty little secret, but then thought better of it, because he'd ask how, and if he hadn't heard about my stint on the news, then I certainly didn't want to be the one to inform him of it.

I stashed the information under my sleeve for later use. If my fathers reamed me for negligence, I'd pull out the Aicha-card to divert the interrogation.

"Can you imagine your mother's shock if she decides to exhume you?" Galina mused. "Poor woman."

"She can't exhume him," Noah whispered.

"She can and probably will." Galina shoveled in another palmful of popcorn. "If I were her, I'd do it."

"That's because you're morbidly curious." Noah tossed a look at Galina before turning to me. "We need to tell Tobias, so he can take care of it."

"And how exactly should we preface the news? *Adam was running from a cop, and the dude shot him and recovered his DNA.* He'll ask why the guy shot me, and then what?" My blood was burning up in my veins. "It's not like I can lie to him."

"He's going to find out sooner or later, Adam." Noah's voice was as quiet as static. "You're making headlines. There's a very accurate police sketch of you out there."

"Then let him find out. After all, *he* buried my existence once. Let him deal with burying it again. Besides, it'll give him something to focus on. The last thing I need is for him or Papa to start looking more closely at me. At any of us, for that matter."

I finally glanced at my phone, which had chirped not two minutes ago.

NAYA: *By the way, the Prince of Venezuela is at the manor.*

NAYA: *Just thought you'd want to know.*

I stared so long at my screen that Galina shoved the popcorn bowl onto Noah's lap and walked over to me.

"Perez's son is at the manor? That's not good," she muttered.

I stretched my jaw from side-to-side, which was wound as tightly as the rest of my body. "Levi, run a full background check on Perez Junior."

"Am I looking for anything specific?" Levi asked from where he'd sunk into the armchair, tablet on his thighs.

"I want to know what businesses he runs, who he beds, and what organizations he's aiding. Find out every damn thing on the guy."

Galina straightened. "How can I help?"

"You head over to the safehouse and take the next shift. Tell Boone to stop by the guild and look up the Prince's score before coming home." She bit down on her lip as though peeved I wasn't putting her on Naya's case. "Check with Calliope when she's planning her next move. The sooner the better."

Because the sooner we were done with her case, the sooner we could give the Dunmore situation our full focus.

Galina sighed. "Fine. Send Naya my love."

Yeah . . . like that would ever happen.

After Galina left, I looked over the information Levi had unearthed on Pablo Perez Jr., and that lit wick burned hotter, melting what little advantage and luck we'd gathered. Pablo was one of Robbie's Eton friends, a man just as influential as his father and surely just as awful.

My gut told me he was a Triple before Boone confirmed it, but hearing it out loud made my flesh smart harder than my perforated calf.

Naya was about to share air with two Triples, while I hobbled around this room, an ocean away. I thought about sending Boone or Noah, but what could they do, besides extract her against her will? It wasn't as though they could take her place. Not even Galina could.

Hopefully by tomorrow, my leg would be healed enough, and I could travel to London. Maybe pose as a waiter to gain entry into the manor. I'd stay in the shadows so Emmy wouldn't recognize me. Maybe I wouldn't even let Naya see me.

As long as I had eyes and ears on her . . .

"Have you read the recent transcript?" Levi flipped his tablet screen toward me so I could read what the devices speared through Naya's ears had collected.

Son of a cherub.

My stomach bottomed out at all I read, and a violent urge to punch the man sucked away every last ounce of my pain and fatigue. I grabbed my jacket and soared into the garage, Noah hot on my wing tips.

While I ripped the charging cord out of the bike, he took root before the front fender, arms crossed, pink feathers extended like a gate. "What do you think you're doing?"

"What's best for the mission, that's what I'm doing. I'm going in."

"That isn't what's best for the mission."

I tossed my hands in the air. "Naya is surrounded by Triples."

"And I'm certain she's aware of it."

"She's plucking flirting with him!"

Noah tipped his head to the side. "You're acting like a raging lunatic because Naya's using her feminine wiles on a Triple?"

"Her fem—What century are you from, No?"

"It means flirting."

"I know what it means. Now get out of my way before I get a faceful of your pretty feathers."

Noah raised his chin. "Not until you calm down."

"I'm fucking calm," I hissed, the unmodified curse word costing me a feather. Or was it the lie?

"Clearly."

After a minute of breathing like a dragon, I growled, "You know what happens to people who play with fire? They get burned. Even angels."

Noah magicked away his wings. "Scoot forward." When I frowned, he added, "You know what happens to shorhim who go into missions half-cocked? They get caught. If you're going to England, I'm going with you. Someone has to keep your reckless ass in check."

"Noah . . ."

Before I could plead with him to stay here, he threw a leg over the back of the bike. "Shall we make a plan? I really like plans."

I side-eyed him, contemplating revving the bike and dashing forward brutally in order to toss him off.

"Don't." As usual, he read right into my thoughts. We'd spent way too much time together. "Your calf is blacker than mine and your mood is darker than your wings, so don't you even think about getting rid of me."

"Fine, but I call the shots. If I tell you to hang back, you hang back." I twisted the handles, and the bike rocketed forward.

"I'll hang *at your* back." Over the rush of wind, he added, "Now, tell me the plan!"

I didn't have one. All I had was a gut feeling to pull Naya out of that festering pit of monsters before they did more than graze her skin with their blood-soaked hands.

NAYA

The Prince was one handsy man. This was the twelfth time his palm connected with some part of my body, and appetizers had only just been cleared.

"Have you ever been to my country, Señorita Moreau?"

I met his one-eyed gaze, goading my lips into a smile and tucking my arm out of his reach—again. "I haven't had the honor yet. Will you tell me about it?"

"For starters, the weather's nicer than here."

"That's not such a feat." I peered at the sky that seemed to sag against the transparent tent that had been erected over the terrace. Something shimmered above my head, something spread wide. Wings. My heart held still, expecting those wings to be attached to a large body, and it was. But thankfully not my father's.

The angel overhead was none other than the one Noah had put me in contact with and whom I'd had one pleasant interaction to date. Had Adam informed Dov we were working together? Had the ishim come to check up on me?

Pablo's leather-cloaked fingers brushed over my wrist, jolting my attention off Dov. "What interesting thing did you see up there?"

"I was watching for rain." My original intent. "So, you and Robbie went to school together?" I peered up. Dov was gone.

"We did. Since the age of seven."

I glanced over in the direction of the tawny-haired Triple, who was regaling his table with a story that had everyone doubled over with laughter. "Now, I understand why he picked Venezuela."

"My country is in dire need of help. I don't know how much you've heard about it, but my father, the King . . . he's let poverty fester. When jobs are scarce, taxes exorbitant, and social aid used for whores and parties, there is much unrest. Since I have no political pull myself, I'm employing my personal connections to bring about change. I'm hoping this expedition will create a big splash, the first of many."

I studied his lightly stubbled jaw, his cropped blond hair, and ice-blue iris, wondering if I'd misjudged him by association. "That's a munificent incentive, Your Highness."

"Please call me Pablo." As he readjusted his black eye patch, I couldn't help but wonder if something had also happened to his hands since he kept them covered.

"May I ask how you lost your eye?"

"How very direct you are."

"Curious. And yes, I suppose, direct."

"I'm a great fan of both qualities." Pablo reangled his chair, and his knee jostled mine. "*Lo siento.*" His palm settled on my thigh as though saying sorry wasn't enough, and he wanted to manually soothe my bumped knee.

I shifted my legs to the side to dislodge his hand. "No harm done," I answered in unaccented Spanish, before realizing I probably should've stuck to English.

Brow furrowed, Pablo leaned back in his chair. "So you speak my language?"

"I learned it in school."

"You have no accent."

"I'm good with languages."

"What other hidden talents do you possess?"

"I've been told I'm a great listener."

"I'd much rather hear you talk than watch you listen. You have a most wondrous voice."

Like the warble of sparrows, I thought, before shaking loose Adam's comparison. I much preferred the term Pablo had just used: *wondrous.*

I'd never considered flirting to obtain what I needed, but didn't special agents charm confessions out of criminals? If I could learn this man's secrets with a few well-timed smiles, I'd be ahead of the game. And if Pablo got the wrong idea, I'd explain I wasn't open to anything until marriage, a surefire way to make a man back off.

And if, for some reason, he didn't, I'd accompany my well-timed smile with a well-placed kick. "I'm flattered."

"Simply the truth, Señorita Moreau."

I studied his expression again, trying to glimpse the soul beneath the cage of flesh. If only portable holo-rankers existed. Or a soul-rating app. *Huh.* Not to blow my own horn but what an ingenious idea that would be. One I'd need to discuss with my father.

I redirected the conversation, because talking about myself would get me nowhere. "Was it an accident? Your eye?"

"No. My father removed it to punish me for having spearheaded a protest the summer after I returned from university. He swore to remove the other if I didn't bury my political ambitions."

My mouth parted around a soundless gasp. "That's awful."

What if I'd signed up to the *one* mission Robbie wasn't using to launder his soul? What if this delegation Robbie and Pablo were co-organizing was genuinely altruistic?

Pablo's score would enlighten me. If only I'd brought my phone. I could've messaged Adam, and had him drive over to a guild to check. Organized as he was, he probably already had the information.

I was about to excuse myself when Emmy tapped her raised wine glass with her bread knife to offer a toast.

"To new friends," she said, lips curved with a shiny smile.

Calling these people *friends* was a definite stretch, but I raised my wine glass to support the sentiment.

"Naya and I met only last week, yet it feels like we've known each other for *years*."

Oh. She was talking about me? That was . . . sweet.

"Here's to you, friend." She winked at me.

"Here, here." Everyone cheered.

In the heat of the moment, I dipped my lips into the wine but came to my senses quickly and set down my glass, licking away the droplets, which were as unexpectedly sweet as Emmy's toast. Although I eyed my glass, curious for a full sip, alcohol interfered with our senses, and I needed them as sharp as Emmy's polished nails tonight. Perhaps I'd allow myself a drink once I completed my first guardian mission.

I mouthed a thank you to Emmy. For all her thorniness and opinions, the girl had a kind soul, one that deserved to be carried away from these people, no matter if this wasn't a maleficent mission. Perhaps I'd hide her passport when I went upstairs to text Adam.

I scooted backward, but again, missed my cue to get up when waiters descended upon our table with the main courses. Politeness compelled me to stay. As I cut into my white fish, the man to my left, Luis, Pablo's cousin, instigated a conversation. Where Pablo had been flirtatious from the get-go, Luis was pleasantly not. He kept his hands to himself and, from time to time, darted glances over my shoulder.

At his sixth furtive glimpse, I turned in my seat and found Pablo's pale eye leveled on his cousin, even though he was actively partaking in the table conversation about British food started by one of the Circle Girls, whose dream was to become a world-famous chef.

"Perhaps I'll organize a cooking class with the best chef in Caracas for all of you?" Pablo proposed.

The girl—Lexi—clapped excitedly, which had the bodyguards lining the wall of the tent shifting. Here I'd assumed they were Robbie's, but, unsurprisingly, really, they worked for the man at my side. A monarch's son necessitated quite the entourage.

"With all due respect, Your Highness"—unlike when I'd called him by his title, Pablo didn't correct Ruth, a girl I'd spoken with briefly at the meet-and-greet yesterday—"I thought we were there to help, not *be* helped."

"Consider it a recompense for services rendered," Pablo replied smoothly, giving the dark-haired girl a cursory glance before returning his eye to me.

"Our recompense will be seeing your people's lives improve." Ruth was the eldest of seven, determined at eighteen to devote her life to succoring the needy.

"No one's forcing you to cut loose and have fun, Ruthie," Lexi said.

"Ruth, not Ruthie."

Lexi rolled her eyes. Although Ruth kept her chin raised high and her spine straight, she grew silent, gaze poised on the floral centerpiece—white and blue stargazer lilies packed in the shape of Perez's Venezuelan flag.

As the conversation accumulated vigor, and our main courses were collected, I folded my napkin and scooted back my chair. "Excuse me. I'll be right back."

Pablo rose and pulled out my chair some more, then hinged at the waist to murmur into my ear, "*Eres cómo el sol, Señorita Moreau.*"

My entire life I'd been compared to starlight, so being compared to the sun was quite jarring. "It's probably my hair that gives this impression." I stabbed my fingers through it self-consciously, trying to flatten it in the process. "Blonde and voluminous as it is."

"It's not your hair; it's your aura." He leaned forward and coiled one of my strands around the smooth leather ensconcing his finger. "But your hair *is* incredibly pale. Naturally so?"

A waiter pushed in between us with a pitcher, breaking Pablo's grasp on my hair. I couldn't have been more grateful for the man's brusque sense of duty, even though he splashed more water onto my lap than into my glass. When I gasped at the chilliness, Pablo gripped the waiter's biceps and spun him away from me, but not before I got a glimpse of his face.

While Pablo voiced his irritation with a string of expletives, my heart beat double-time. Dov had shown up and now Noah? Was there a development I wasn't aware of? Why else would they *both* be here?

"It's only a little water, Pablo," I murmured, scanning the room.

"My apologies, Miss." Noah, who'd finally managed to turn back my way, flicked his eyes sideways, and I followed their movement, finding a familiar set burning an emerald path straight for me.

Dov. Noah. And Adam.

Either something was terribly wrong or they were all terribly distrusting.

I couldn't decide which reason pained me less.

NAYA

*A*dam stood in the service entrance being used by the army of waiters, dressed like one of them, but not resembling any mortal I'd ever seen with his simmering eyes and black wings. He jerked his head toward the manor, then receded through the door and out of sight.

I glanced at Noah, unsure where it was Adam wanted to meet. I knew nothing of the floorplan of the mansion.

"May I show you to the powder room?" my fellow fletching suggested, thankfully reading my expression.

"I'll take her." Emmy jumped up and out of her seat.

Shoot. I looked at Noah for a quick fix to that problem.

A nerve twitched in his jaw. Interceding would raise eyebrows, so he trudged back the way he'd come, probably to warn Adam I wouldn't be arriving alone.

Emmy speared her arm through mine, hips swishing as she led me back through the drawing room. "Pablo cannot take his eyes—eye—off of you." She glanced over her shoulder. "He's looking right now." Her face glowed with the same exhilaration that had animated my sister's expression when Nitznootz had curled into a ball on her lap. "If you become queen, Naya, do *not* forget me."

Common sense made me say, "I'd have to marry a king for that."

"You're in luck then. Pablo's next-in-line."

"If you take into account how long humans live nowadays, his children will have more of a chance of inheriting the throne than he does." I stabbed my lip with my teeth for my slip-up. *Humans? Really, Naya.* Emmy didn't seem to notice, too far gone in her reverie of me becoming queen.

"Robbie mentioned his friend would sit on the throne in no time. Maybe the King's terminally ill," she added in a conspiratorial whisper. "Or maybe they have a plan, and we're part of it."

One of my skinny heels caught in a seam of the oiled parquet. Although Emmy's footfalls weren't all that steady, she surprisingly managed to keep me from face-planting into the behemoth stone hearth.

"What do you mean?" Had she figured out what I still hadn't? Or had she heard something?

"Well, by bringing a delegation of do-gooders, Pablo's showing his people how resourceful and generous he can be."

My anticipation drooped like the damp fabric of my dress. "But to unseat him, he'd have to . . ." My eyes grew wide, and my mind, crystal-clear.

"Powder's room through there. It's to *die* for." She dragged me past a door and into an octagonal room festooned entirely in gold mosaic.

The room was beautiful enough to give my thought process pause, but not for long.

If Robbie was helping Pablo plan a coup, what was *our* purpose? To distract or to participate in the crusade? Maybe some of the Circle Girls had military training or were daughters of influential men?

I was about to ask Emmy when she blurted out, "BTW, if you need condoms, I brought a shitload. Although, making a baby with a future king could ensure you one hell of a future. Can you imagine? Living in a palace? I bet the loos are made of solid gold."

If she was right, then I'd hope he'd melt them to give back to his country. Otherwise, he'd be no better than his selfish father. "I'm way too young to have a baby."

A shiver ran through me at the idea of bringing a child I'd have to abscond with to raise in a guild. The same way Apa had taken me from Céline. Even if she'd been on board with giving me up, she must've felt my loss.

Or maybe not.

No thinking of her, Naya. You have way more important things to dwell on.

As Emmy reapplied her lipstick in front of a gilt-framed mirror, I grabbed a hand towel and blotted the wet spot on my dress, wondering how to get rid of my chatty friend so I could speak with Adam. Where was he anyway? Hiding behind one of the four closed doors in this powder room?

Asking Emmy about the men who bookended her at dinner, I discreetly went to open the first stall door. No Adam. Then the second. Also empty. The third and fourth were empty as well.

"What are you doing?" One of Emmy's eyebrows hooked way up. "Checking what the toilets are made of?"

I smiled to avoid lying, then deflected the attention off myself. "Grayson was really worried. You should give him a call."

She huffed a sigh. "Definitely not. He's too much of a Debbie Downer. Don't get me wrong, he's awesome and caring and everything, but his predisposition for pessimism really takes its toll on me."

The powder room door opened, and a dark head popped in—Noah. "Miss, I wanted to apologize again."

Emmy waved her hand. "*Pshh.* I'm sure she's forgiven you already. She forgives *everyone.*"

Noah pushed the door wider. "I was told to show you to the laundry room, so one of the maids could help dry your dress."

Emmy gave Noah a long once-over as she sidled in close to me. "I'll go with you," she whispered. "To keep you safe."

My heart rapped against my rib cage, partly because of her compassion and partly because of her clinginess. "Thank you, Emmy, but it's unnecessary. Promise."

"Are you sure?" She eyed Noah's broad frame again. "He's—"

"Fired, if he doesn't fix his mistake," Noah finished for her.

I grazed the back of her hand. "Before I was allowed to leave home, my father made me learn self-defense."

"If you're certain . . ."

"I'm certain." And with those words, I trailed Noah down a dimly-lit corridor dotted in a series of watercolors depicting horses and hunting. "Did something happen?"

"Not here." His full lips barely moved around the words.

I tossed a glance over my shoulder to make sure no one was in hearing range. Emmy stepped out of the powder room then, and I fell back a step, not wanting to pique her curiosity.

When we turned a corner, I expelled a breath. Perhaps because the entire waitstaff was busy with the festive dinner, we didn't bump into anyone as we traveled down a narrow staircase, deeper into the belly of the manor. Instead of wainscoting, the basement was outfitted with sturdy jute, drab gray tiles, and ceilings low enough that if I extended my arm, my fingertips would skim the white plaster and bright, recessed bulbs.

"Why are you three here?" The powdery scent of detergent was so thick I tasted lilac and talc.

"Three?"

"I saw Dov earlier. He was hovering over the terrace."

Noah nodded, a thoughtful expression overtaking his face. "He likes to check in on us from time to time. Especially during our first missions. As for why we're here, Adam was worried."

"About *me*?"

"About the company you keep." Noah stopped in front of a door and rapped his knuckles four times with a second between each beat. "Did that sleazeball really call you his sunshine?"

"No. He told me I was *like* the sun."

"Does that line even work on women?"

"It beats being called Worm."

"Worm? You've been called a worm?" Noah guffawed softly. "Let me guess. By the guy waiting in there?" He tipped his head toward the door, which had just opened.

"I never called her Worm." Adam's lips slammed shut and his nostrils flared.

I frowned at his strange reaction. That was, until I caught a lone black feather sailing beside his pant leg. I'd been wondering where the thought had even come from. Now, I knew. He must've muttered the moniker at some point during our brief time together, and my mind had stored it. Maybe during the motorcycle ride.

"You sure about that, Adam?" Noah's smirk strengthened as he pointed to the collapsing down.

"Can we drop the pointless chitchat?" Adam hissed.

"I wouldn't call it pointless." Noah's brown eyes shimmered like his wing tips. "It's rather illuminating."

"Bloody get in here before Robbie or Pablo's security teams gun you two idiots down."

Noah's hilarity only increased. "After you, sunshine."

I elbowed him in the ribs as I stepped into the moonlit room—an extra-large linen closet. Sheets were stacked neatly beside fluffy towels, and packaged toiletries lined row upon row of shelves.

"You know what cell phones are for, right?" Adam snapped.

Without turning to face the tetchy fletching, I said, "Why, of course. For taking selfies and sharing memes."

ADAM

ANGELIC FACT #97
YOU DON'T SCREW A TRIPLE,
YOU SCREW THEM OVER.

*N*aya's taunt chafed my already raw nerves. It had taken Noah and me one hour to reach the Dunmore manor, and then another twenty minutes and a feather each to incapacitate two waiters to borrow their starchy penguin uniforms.

The seams of the one stretched over my body would probably blow, but since I had no plan on handing it back, what with my DNA soaking the pant leg, it didn't matter. The *only* thing that mattered was that this guardian-wannabe started taking her job seriously and stop cozying up to Triples.

"This isn't a game, Naya. It's a matter of life and death for most of the humans on that terrace."

She spun around, hands on her hips. "I'm well aware it's not a game. And just so you know, right before Noah poured his whole pitcher of water on my lap"—she gestured to the wet spot on a blue strapless dress better fit for an Elysian ball than for a dinner hosted by a Triple and attended by another—"I was on my way to my bedroom to text you to find out Pablo's score."

I couldn't help the snort that wedged its way up my tight throat. "You two are on a first-name basis now?"

Noah, who'd elected residence against the stacked towels, said, "They're on a *nickname*-basis."

I glowered at him, then at Naya. "Your new buddy, Pablo, is a Triple. You were seducing a plucking Triple."

One of her hands skidded off her hips. The other's pressure must've turned lax because she was no longer strangling the fabric. "I wasn't seducing him." Her nose crinkled. "But I was thinking about it. I was trying to understand the use of the Circle Girls. Dov still has no clue?"

"No." I yanked on the shirt collar strangling me, popping the top three buttons. "As for your seduction scheme, the first rule of guardianship is: *don't screw the bad guys.*"

A nerve feathered her jaw. She'd just admitted she was thinking about making a move on Junior, so I didn't see why my advice ticked her off.

"Just screw them over?" Her voice rumbled across the dimly-lit space.

"Exactly."

"Since I imagine you didn't race through a channel just to inform me of Pablo's score, what else is happening that I should know about?"

I looked at Noah, who was whistling some song while admiring the thread-count on a folded duvet cover. "We're pulling you out."

"Why?" She let go of her dress.

"Because you don't need to be a victim to play the hero."

"I'm immortal, Adam. As long as I have wing bones, I can't die."

"Leave with us, and you get a spot on the team." *There.*

Dream come true.

Plan executed.

"They have my ID. Robbie will hunt me down, which will make me a liability to the team."

You're already a liability. I kept my thoughts to myself, smart enough to know reiterating the reminder would rub her the wrong way. "Except you know nothing, so he'd have no reason to hunt you down."

"I do know something actually."

Noah stopped whistling, confirming he'd been eavesdropping the entire time.

"Pablo's planning a coup."

I released a breath that had gotten lodged in my lungs. "We already figured he was."

She frowned, as though miffed we hadn't looped her in, then wetted her lips with the tip of her tongue. "Well, I believe he's going to use the Circle Girls to accomplish it."

I tore my gaze from her glistening mouth. "Junior told you this?"

Her palm settled over her stomach as though her dress was zipped up too tight. Considering how it seamlessly displayed her figure and pushed up her breasts, it most definitely was. "Yes. He admitted he wanted to conquer his people and that bringing us would show them just how resourceful he could be." Her cheek dimpled as though she were biting the inside of it. "Why is he a Triple? What are his sins?"

"Making people disappear," I deadpanned.

Her fingers stilled. "That's what's written on his sinner scorecard?"

"No, but since I didn't lose a feather, I'm guessing I'm right."

"You think he's planning on making fifty-one girls vanish?"

"Would it be such a stretch?" Noah asked, fully invested in the conversation.

"How does that help him with his coup?" Naya's eyes glazed over in thought, but a sweep of her dark lashes later, and the glassiness was gone. "One of your theories was a hostage negotiation. You think he'll use us to get the UK involved in his plight and pin our disappearances on his father?"

I hadn't made *that* connection.

Noah pulled his phone out of his jacket pocket. After a look at the screen, he said, "Ten minutes since Emmy returned to the table."

In other words, someone was bound to come looking for Naya at any moment.

She palmed the damp blue spot. "You guys have to get out of here."

I nodded to the narrow horizontal window Noah had already propped open. "After you."

"Adam, I'm not coming."

I stepped close, so close she had to crane her neck to keep her eyes on mine. "Well, I'm not leaving without you."

"There are fifty girls upstairs. If they're going to kidnap us, then I want to make sure I'm among them so you can track and save them."

"We'll put the bloody earrings on another girl."

"Adam," she gasp-whispered.

"We'll keep guarding them." We were so near, I could smell the warmth of her skin, could hear the tumult of her breaths, could sense the unrest of her heart. "This is what you wanted, Naya." I took another step closer, bumping her body to herd her toward the window.

She stood her ground. "I can't leave them, but . . ." Her chest lifted, grazing mine.

Through the silk of her dress and the starch of my shirt, I caught the flutter of her pulse, rapid and strong, a mirror of mine. "But what?"

"But take Emmy away from here. She's really sweet and doesn't deserve whatever's coming."

My knees locked, which sent a spasm through my convalescing calf. "She signed up for this."

"She didn't sign up to be a pawn in the Machiavellian scheme of two Triples. None of these girls did." She splayed her palm against my chest and pushed, but I didn't ease off her. "Except me. *I* signed up for this."

I didn't want to take Emmy; I wanted to take Naya.

Away from Junior.

I didn't want him to call her his sun.

She wasn't *his* anything.

I wished I could've gone back in time, to the night Naya and I had met, and offer her a spot on the team. If I'd played my cards better, she wouldn't have inserted herself into this hapless expedition.

"I need to get back upstairs." Her tone was as soft as down but as sharp as a quill.

"Feather," I murmured, the word rolling off my tongue.

Instead of pushing, her fingers curled into my shirt. "Excuse me?"

It felt so right, I could only wonder how I hadn't thought about it earlier. "You're not in line to inherit a title, so heiress is erroneous. You're not spineless, so a worm doesn't do you justice—and for the life of me, I don't remember calling you that, much less thinking of you and invertebrates in the same context." Her eyes had honed in on mine, dark and luminous as the ocean at night. "Even though your hair is light and *bouncy*"—I had the strangest urge to touch it but kept my fingers balled loosely at my sides—"it's utterly offset by your eyes, and thus comparing you to a sun is nonsensical." Also, Junior had thought about it first, and I wasn't the type to recycle. "Starlight suits you because of your sparkly wings, but it's what your parents call you." I kept my eyes steady on hers, and I could've sworn her pupils had tightened, even though her face was cast in too much shadow from my own looming one. "The most fitting nickname to encompass all that you are, Naya, is Feather."

Her breathing seemed to grow ragged, but then Noah was muttering something about my untimely lunacy and us having to leave immediately.

The pressure of her palm disappeared from my shirt, leaving behind the phantom shape of her five slender fingers. It was as though she'd branded me with that hand the same way I'd branded her with that name.

She stepped back. "Promise to save Emmy?"

Annoyance swirled inside of me. "Fine, we'll get her out, but if Junior so much as makes a move on you, we're extracting you, too."

She opened her mouth, probably to protest, but in the end, she said, "Okay."

I stalked toward Noah, who stood with his hands outstretched, as though to give me a leg up if mine decided to give out. Well, in my head, I stalked.

I must've limped, because Naya asked, "Are you injured?"

Gritting my teeth, I set my palms on the window sill and hoisted myself out through the narrow opening, glad for my daily regimen of pull-ups.

"Is he all right?" she asked again.

"He got shot in the leg earlier. I made him take a bunch of pills for the pain. Probably too many."

That'd explain the psychotic break I'd just had. Once my mind cleared, I'd hopefully forget I'd given an inane monologue about nicknames to a fletching who probably already considered me a few feathers short of a full wing.

I didn't catch the tail-end of their conversation, because, as I lumbered to my feet, a cramp seized my leg, followed by a bolt of white-hot pain that sent me sprawling face-first into the Dunmore's manicured hedges.

NAYA

*R*obbie Dunmore organized a picnic lunch the next day, followed by a horseback trek through the woods. Albeit frivolous, the activities helped the girls bond, and they'd need these attachments soon.

Hooves clacking on the mulch had me turning in my saddle. Pablo sat astride a chestnut gelding, whose coat glistened with sweat, two of his ten bodyguards a few paces behind.

"Señorita Moreau, why do I get the distinct impression that you are avoiding me today?"

Because I am avoiding you . . .

But also, I was worried.

About Adam, who'd passed out after crawling out the window last night.

About Emmy, who was still among us.

Noah had messaged me an hour after tossing Adam over his shoulder and carrying him away from the manor to assure me that his grumpy leader was all right and that they were going to get Emmy today, but the sun was already dipping over the horizon, and she was still right there, trotting on a white horse like a seasoned equestrian, chattering with some of the other girls.

"I have a lot on my mind."

"So, it is not I?"

I decided to deflect his question with a truth. "A friend of mine was shot last night in some freak accident. It's a flesh wound, but he's in a lot of pain."

"Ahh." Pablo's eyes scraped over my face before leveling on the horizon. "This friend... you care a lot about him?"

As our horses clip-clopped through the drizzle-chilled woods, I said, "Enough that his poor welfare pains me."

"Any way I can help?"

"No. He just needs time. But I appreciate you asking."

Not too much time thanks to what we were, but the deeper the wound, the longer it took to heal.

"You missed out last night," Pablo said, after a beat. "The DJ Robbie booked for the end of the evening is the best in London. *Everyone* was dancing." He leaned toward me and whispered conspiratorially, "Including that staid girl, Ruthie."

"Ruth's not dull. She's just extremely focused."

If his cause truly had been charitable, I'd have pointed out what a great asset she'd make but decided not to spark a baseless debate since we weren't actually going to be aiding his people. At least, that was the conclusion I'd drawn, upon finding out his score. Hasty perhaps, but in my wing bone marrow, I sensed the only people this mission would benefit were Pablo and Robbie.

Keeping my voice free of contempt, I asked, "Did you dance?"

"You weren't there." His score materialized over his debonair posture, over his clean-shaven face and gelled blond hair, the three numbers clear as holograms. Perhaps not all Triples were terrible human beings, but Pablo's friendship with Robbie caused me to doubt every word that came out of his mouth and every look that came out of his eye.

"Will there be another big party tonight?"

"No. Just an early supper, so you can all rest before the big trip tomorrow. It's a long flight."

"Will you be flying with us?"

"My security team prefers I travel separately. For *your* safety."

It took me a moment to grasp what he was implying—that a father capable of removing his son's eye was also capable of shooting down a plane carrying that son home. Humans couldn't accrue scores higher than one hundred, so it was impossible to tell who was truly worse between father and son.

"Will we be meeting your father?"

Pablo stared ahead of him, at the thinning copse of trees and the pond shimmering like a mirage through them. "My father doesn't much care about social delegations, so you may be spared a meeting." His attention returned to me. "But if you were to be invited to his palace, I'll enlist extra security personnel."

How I wished I could ask him what he intended to do with us.

"I didn't mention this yesterday, but your earrings are lovely."

My heart stumbled in time with my horse. I tugged on the reins and leaned back, managing to stay in the saddle.

"Are they real?"

Once the creature had recovered his equilibrium, and I, mine, I said, "They are."

"A gift from a lover?"

I bit my lip. "No. Just a friend."

"The same friend who got shot?"

Was Pablo onto me?

A high-pitched gasp followed by a, "What? When?" rose from the group riding in front of us.

It took me no time to realize the voice belonged to Emmy. She had a very discernible pitch. Plus, her phone was pinned to her ear.

I coaxed my horse into a trot to catch up with her. "What happened?" I asked, when I'd managed to push my way into the throng.

"Gray. He just collapsed." She was clutching her phone, but it was no longer sandwiched underneath her helmet. "They brought him to the hospital."

A chill sank into my veins. Was this part of Adam and Noah's plan? "Did they say from what?"

"A seizure." Emmy had turned as white as her horse. "Oh, God, do you think he has cancer? Or meningitis? Oh, God."

As she pressed her knuckles against her mouth, I touched her arm. "It could be nothing, Emmy. Heatstroke—"

"Heatstroke in London?" She raised her gaze to the canopy of trees blotting out the thready afternoon light. "I have to go home," she murmured.

I couldn't tell if her moroseness was borne from concern for her stepbrother or annoyance at having to forfeit this trip.

Tears didn't well up, but she was distraught the rest of the way to the stables. I galloped beside her, then helped her repack the few clothes and toiletries she'd unpacked from her giant suitcase. Nestled between two folded T-shirts, I found a gold tissue box.

"Emmy?" I pulled it out. "Is this yours?" How had Adam earned points for this sinner when her kleptomania was still rampant?

She stared at it through glassy eyes. I wasn't even sure if she saw what it was I was holding. "Robbie's mother gave it to me when she saw me admiring it."

I stared long and hard at her, then sighed as she wrestled it from my fingers and placed it back inside her suitcase. I prayed for her soul's sake that it had been gifted to her.

Before we left the bedroom, I stepped into the bathroom for a little privacy and sent Adam a message, asking him if Grayson was all right. When I returned, Emmy was zipping up her suitcase, cheeks flushed as though the zipper had gotten stuck and was giving her trouble.

I stuffed my cell phone into the back pocket of my jeans and walked over to help her, but she sprang to her feet and pulled out the handle. "I'm ready."

She dragged her luggage to the door and handed it over to the white-gloved attendant, lingering in the hallway, aware of her departure. As he carried it down the stairwell reserved for the staff, Robbie's female guard escorted Emmy and me down the sweeping stairs reserved for family and guests.

"You know what would make Gray feel much better?" She blew her nose with one of the many tissues I'd kept on hand. The tears hadn't come until we'd descended the stone steps of the manor, but now a torrent streamed from her bright blue eyes.

"A detailed essay on cryptocurrency?" I suggested, as we waited by the entrance of the manor for her cab to roll through the ostentatious gates.

Her lips quirked upward before trembling back around a sob. "If you came back with me. I know he's not next in line for a throne, but he's smart, and he's a fantastic boyfriend. Loyal and attentive and—" She flung the back of her hand against her mouth. "I can't lose him."

I pulled her into a hug. "You're not going to lose him."

"I'm sorry I called you a bitch, Naya. You're not. You're actually really nice and stupid pretty."

Snorting, I rubbed her back. "Stupid pretty?"

"Like nauseatingly so. You don't have a single blemish, and you just sort of shine. I swear, it's like you're otherworldly."

My hand froze on her back.

"I hated you so much the night you showed up, because the second Adam saw you, he stopped looking at me."

I rubbed her back. "I swear he's not attracted to me, Emmy."

She picked her face off the wet spot on my T-shirt. "How could he not be? Every man you cross paths with is. Gray. Pablo. Even that waiter last night. I mean, he came back to *check* on you. Who does that?"

"Someone considerate." And who needed to get me alone . . .

Car tires crunched over gravel.

Emmy fastened her reddened eyes to mine. "Come with me."

Adam would just love that.

I raised my gaze to the manor, where too many innocents were caught between two Triples.

As I towed my gaze back to Emmy, I caught three figures standing beside one of the reception-floor windows—Robbie, Pablo, and that cousin of his. Unfortunately, I couldn't read lips, so I wasn't sure what was being discussed, but emotions seemed to be running high, considering Pablo's rapid-hand movements.

Suddenly, his arms fell back along his sides. His cousin's chin bobbing toward the window had the Prince pivoting. Our eyes crossed for a fraction of a second. Not wanting him to get suspicious of me, I didn't tear my gaze off his instantly. Instead, I smiled and waved.

Emmy sighed. "Do you want my condoms?"

That snapped my attention off the Triple, who'd yet to return my smile.

The female guard let out a soft snort as she blustered by us to check the automated vehicle with that wand of hers. *Great* . . .

"Thanks, but no thanks." Not only would Adam use it as an excuse to extract me from this mission, but, for all my talk of flirting, I'd also never sleep with a murderous human.

My wing bones thrummed . . . and thrummed. In the end, no feather loosened, but the sensation lingered, as well as a solid dose of confusion. Did the ishim think I was lying?

"When you get back, give me a call, and we can go out to lunch."

Emmy blotted her eyes, kissed my cheek, then entered the cab, inside which the attendant had already placed her luggage.

"Give Grayson a hug from me," I called out before her door shut.

When the taillights faded, I fished my phone from my jeans pocket. An unread message from Black Hole was awaiting me: *He's fine.*

ME: *Emmy just left. Thank you.*

The sun set behind the gates, spreading burnished light across the trimmed lawn.

ME: *And you? Are you okay?*

Dots danced on my screen, as though Adam were composing a long-winded message.

BLACK HOLE: *I'm fine, Feather.*

Feather. The nickname made goosebumps dot my skin and a chill sweep up my spine. It had had the same effect last night. I'd wanted to tell him not to call me that, but since I couldn't explain why it affected me so, and I'd been desperately trying to get him and Noah far from the manor, I hadn't brought it up.

So I brought it up now . . .

ME: *I'd rather you don't call me that.*

BLACK HOLE: *And I'd rather you'd left with Emmy.*

ME: *Adam . . .*

BLACK HOLE: *Delete this conversation.*

I stared at the message above his curt order until a new line appeared on my phone.

BLACK HOLE: *Is it done?*

I sighed and pressed delete, then sent him a checkmark to let him know it was done. I wondered what they'd do now. Sequester Emmy against her will? Keep Grayson locked away until the flight to Venezuela departed?

I turned to climb the stairs, startling when I bumped into a hard body.

"Shame her stepbrother fell ill." Robbie's hazel eyes were trained on the road that led out of his family's domain. "Would you happen to know which hospital he was transported to? I'd like to send him a convalescence gift."

"I'm not sure, but I can find out."

"I'd greatly appreciate it." He held out his arm. "May I escort you back inside? Supper's about to be served."

Even though I didn't want to touch Robbie, I made myself thread my arm through his and paste an obliging smile on my lips.

"Did you enjoy the horseback ride today?"

"Very much."

"I'm pleased to hear it." His gaze slid up the side of my face, lingering on my ear. "What beautiful pearls you have."

My heart took off as though I was mountaineering instead of ascending a few steps.

"Pablo's convinced you have an immensely rich lover. He's terribly jealous."

I fingered the pearl he was staring at, wishing I'd worn my hair loose instead of in a ponytail. "No lover. Just generous friends." Why couldn't Boone have borrowed smaller pearls from his mother? Their size was going to get me in trouble. "If you like them so much, I could get you a matching pair when we return from Venezuela."

Robbie laughed. "I'll pass. Although . . . my mother does love pearls, and her birthday is next month." He looked in the direction of the window that framed his friends, both of whom were watching us. "I may take you up on that offer once we return."

So, we'd be returning . . . That was reassuring.

"Well, when *I* return. Not sure Pablo will let you leave."

My throat spasmed, causing me to croak, "Why wouldn't he?"

"I don't know what you've done to the poor bloke, but he thinks you're some sort of divinity come to life. He's as superstitious as he is religious that one."

Like my throat, my skin felt too tight. I wanted to shrug Robbie's arm away. I wanted to scramble back down those stairs and take off after Emmy's taxi. All I did, though, was put one booted foot in front of the other. "I can assure you, I'm no divinity."

"An angel, then?" The lopsided curve of Robbie's mouth told me he was teasing me, yet his joshing only increased the feeling of my skin compressing my organs.

I smiled. "You don't strike me as the sort of man who believes in angels."

He smiled, teeth as freckled as his face, stained by poor life choices, just like his soul. "Wouldn't you agree that if God and angels existed, Miss Moreau, the fate of humans would be greatly improved?"

"It's not a question of existing; it's a question of doing. *The right thing*, I'll add. If the sun existed but didn't emit heat and light, then it'd be as useful as a shiny bauble."

Robbie's lips stretched wider and then he laughed. "How droll you are, my dear."

Except I wasn't being droll; I was being honest. "Would you live your life differently if you had proof of a higher power, Lord Dunmore?"

"Certainly." Grin chiseled like a Halloween pumpkin carving, he added, "If saviors and saints existed, then I'd be out of a job."

I stopped walking. Did he really believe he was saving humans and behaving like a saint?

"Have I baffled you? You appear baffled."

"She's merely shocked by your modesty, Robbie. Forever comparing yourself to a saint and a god." Pablo held out his arm, his jeer shadowed by a hint of annoyance. "Señorita Moreau, may I walk you the rest of the way to the terrace?"

I didn't want to be *walked* anywhere, but I traded one Triple for another, praying Adam wouldn't equate being escorted to being hit on. Or better yet, that he had no memory of the stipulation he'd made under the influence of painkillers.

NAYA

A fine mist touched my face and slipped inside my mouth, chemical and pungent.

Had my roommate Natasha just doused me in her perfume? Couldn't she have gone to the bathroom to get ready?

When my nostrils and throat began to tingle, I wrenched my lids open. The room was dark with only a splash of moonlight across my roommate's bed. A soft snore whirred from her lips. I guessed I'd dreamt the smell and sensation. I tried to turn onto my side, but it felt like the mattress had transformed into a giant, melted marshmallow.

The air even smelled of the fluffy candy Raven would bring me back from the human world during those first two years she could leave the guild and I couldn't.

A soft *pshhh* droned overhead. What in the worlds were they spraying through the vents? Air freshener? I blinked as another fine layer of mist sank from the ceiling, glittering like sunlit dust motes.

I reached up to shield my face, but my hand stayed pinned to the mattress, my arm heavy as an anvil. I shut my mouth and lids, and kept my breathing to a bare minimum. When the chill of the gas stopped tickling my exposed skin, I dared to open my eyes.

The inside of my mouth tasted like chalk, and my muscles felt numb. Not air freshener then. A muscle relaxant?

"Natasha." The syllables of her name came out garbled, as though my teeth were glued to wads upon wads of extra-sticky gum.

She didn't stir.

I tried calling out to her again, but my tongue lay as limp as my limbs.

Doors clacked outside. Footsteps thudded.

So the entire household hasn't been affected . . . I couldn't decide if that was reassuring or not.

My heart rate leaped when the doorknob turned. Instinct made me close my lids and rely on my hearing to parse out what was happening. I distinguished two distinct patterns of footfalls.

Sheets rustled and then cool air licked across my legs and arms, pebbling my skin. Someone had just pulled the bedcovers off my body. Ama's story of the organ farm she'd been detained in made my pulse lash at my eardrums with such violence that it momentarily drowned out all other sounds.

Even though my limbs were weighed down by the drugs, I could feel the pressure of a palm sliding up the inside of my thigh. "*Tan sutil.*" *So delicate.* The voice sounded almost robotic, spaced as it was between rushes of air, yet the timbre was unmistakable: Pablo's.

I wanted to grip his wrist and twist it until it cracked. How dare he fondle me while I lay unconscious! What sort of man did such a thing?

His hand crawled higher, over the fabric of my sleep shorts, over the planes of my stomach, settling atop the globe of my left breast. "*Tan perfecta.*" *So perfect.*

"I'll start with the other one." Another man's voice resounded through the bedroom, its quality also punctuated by whooshing air.

They must've been wearing gas masks to protect their airways from the noxious gas.

Pablo pinched my nipple so hard it took everything in me not to react, even though the current extent of my reaction would've been a glower. "How stable is the detonator?"

Detonator?

"It can only go off once the SIMs are activated." It was Robbie's nasally voice this time that resonated through the bedroom. "As long as you don't call the telecom company, the detonators stay dormant."

Detonators? They were about to put explosives inside of us? Were they doing this to all the girls or a select few?

"*Bueno*, because I may want to keep this one."

"You can always remove the device, but considering how fast you tire of women, my friend, I'll wager she'll go boom just like the others." In spite of the gas mask, Robbie's voice lilted.

My soul coiled in a corner of my chest, taking refuge beside my pounding heart. There had been no *good* fates, but there had been preferable ones. Being used as bombs was the worst of the worst, so horrific it hadn't even crossed our minds.

A clap sounded as I imagined Robbie slapping his friend's back. "Unless you want to inject her, give Luis some space."

Pablo stroked my stomach, tracing the edge of my waistband.

A part of me hoped Levi had eyes and ears on the room, that Adam was watching this, that he'd storm the manor and punish the Triple for his indecency and cruelty. Another part hoped no one was witnessing this degrading moment.

"You can play with her later," Robbie said. "We could even bring her on your jet."

"With a lump of Semtex in her body? Pass."

"Only you can activate the SIMs, Pablo."

The mattress shifted, the dip filling out. "I'll have her in Caracas."

He'd have my nails gouge all the soft parts of his body, that's what he'd have.

Pablo must've stepped toward the door, because his voice had lost much of its volume. "What have you decided to do about her friend?"

My revenge reel came to an abrupt stop. Which friend were they talking about? Emmy?

"I have someone following her and looking into her brother's collapse," Robbie said in a low voice. "She seemed genuinely disappointed to leave, so I don't think she heard anything . . . *problematic*." A beat. "But if she did, I'll take care of it."

Fear like I'd never experienced before swirled beneath my skin, growing to a crescendo as something penetrated my navel. There was no pain, only a meddlesome pressure and presence.

"Done," Luis said, as I fought hard to conceal my state of consciousness. I was almost glad about the anaesthetizing gas agent, or I may have strangled the lot of them right there and then. "Squirt some clotting gel on the puncture wound."

Something wet and warm dripped along my numbed skin. A hard swipe later, and the dripping was replaced by a prickling burn. The sheet was tossed back over my body.

"Are all the girls ready?" a female voice asked from the hallway. I hadn't interacted much with Robbie's mother, yet I recognized her voice immediately.

"All ready, Mum."

"What time do we fly out?"

"I'm going to leave with Pablo. I've arranged that you depart at noon. Message me when you've boarded the jet with the girls."

"Of course, darling." The wet sound of lips smacking cheeks faded as the door hinges creaked and the wood settled carefully into its frame.

So, Robbie wasn't flying with us . . . I supposed being airborne with fifty IEDs wasn't ideal. Then again, he *was* sending his mother.

It took another hour of staring catatonically at the moonlight swaying across the ceiling for my skin to awaken and my muscles to twitch. I peeled away the bedsheet glued to my navel, which had popped back open to evict the foreign substance a few minutes after the butchers had departed.

A glance toward Natasha's pristine white sheets told me the clotting agent had worked flawlessly on her. I kneaded my skin trying to feel the lump and coax it out, but they'd wedged it in so deep, it would probably take days to emerge. Gritting my teeth, I prodded the hole left behind by the needle. Could I fish it out?

The thought alone threatened to upend my stomach and made my head spin. I stayed still until the floor rocked back into place, then rolled onto my side slowly and retrieved my phone from where I'd put it to charge on the nightstand. It took my fingers a full minute to detach the power cord and more precious minutes to retrieve Adam's contact.

I contemplated typing a message, but my fingers shook too hard. After hitting dial, I wedged the phone between the pillow and my cheek.

"Please pick up," I murmured. "Please—"

The phone clicked. "Did you just have a dirty dream about me, Feather?"

I swallowed as the scent of copper and sour almonds thickened.

My heart ached, my navel ached, and a sob blubbered through my lips before I could stifle it with my pillow.

"Naya? What is it?" Adam's voice had lost its mischievous edge. "What happened? Did someone hurt you?"

Vocal cords vibrating as hard as the rest of my body, I croaked, "Th-they made their . . . m-move."

"What do you mean? What move?"

"They p-put . . ." I hissed as my stomach contracted, expulsing so much blood that a hot puddle formed beneath me.

"What did they put? Where?" Things rustled and thumped on his end, then keypad tones shrilled as though he were typing on his phone. A sudden hiss leaped through the phone. "Those motherpluckers."

I could barely breathe as what felt like lit kerosene chewed through my abdomen. Had my blood somehow activated the Semtex? Was I exploding?

"Feather!" *That name again* . . . It hurt but not in the same way my body was hurting. It jolted me from one chasm of overwhelming sensation into another, a darker one that seemed to exist on the rim of my consciousness.

"They put Sem—" I winced as my insides wrung themselves out.

"I know."

I briefly wondered how, but a debilitating wave of agony washed away the room and then Adam's voice.

ADAM

ANGELIC FACT #1
FLETCHINGS ARE ALL BORN IMMORTAL, BUT NOT ALL REMAIN SO.

"Naya! Heiress!" My voice went hoarse calling out her name. Every name I had for her. "Feather!"

Noah loomed over where I sat on the couch, eyes large and spooked by my yelling. He'd already ended his call to Levi and was checking his phone for a link to the Dunmores' security footage, which our tech genius had managed to hack.

"Feather, answer for fuck's sake. Please . . ." My shoulder blades tensed. "Feather? Come on. Come back to me." I shot to my feet and paced around the round bedroom Levi had found us after Noah's distress call last night.

I'd been in and out of consciousness, yet flopped like a dead fish over Noah's shoulder, I remembered him telling Levi I was unfit to travel through a guild and to find us something in the area stat. Levi had come through with an old-timey inn converted into a boutique bed-and-breakfast.

In the time it took for Noah to carry me there, Levi had booked us the "suite," which was no more than a bedroom wedged inside an ancient grain-mill with whitewashed walls, puny windows, and a peaked roof. The cherry-on-top: it cost a bloody fortune.

My rail about wasting funds came to a quick end when Noah yanked off my shoes, telling me to shut up—Dov would cover the expense—and sleep it off. I hadn't thought I would, but I passed out and stayed that way until morning, at which point I woke up just as wired and pissed as I'd been after leaving the manor without Naya.

If I hadn't been spaced out by my pill-popping, I would've built a better case. Investigated every person she was shacking up with and provided her with their scores. Even though she wasn't the backboneless doe I'd first assumed, the number of sickos surrounding her would've surely made her see reason and flee.

Instead, she'd returned to the party, had slept beneath a roof the Dunmores may as well have painted crimson for all the blood they'd spilled, lunched and ridden horses with the sleazy Venezuelan Prince who'd tried to wheedle information about the origin of her pearls, and now . . . now . . .

"Naya, bab—" I stopped myself short. Had I really been about to utter the word *baby*? Who was I?

Upon waking, I'd forgone the painkillers Noah had unrolled in his fist, but I must've still been high on something, because I didn't call girls *baby*, and I certainly didn't dream of shredding humans from limb to limb for hurting an immortal.

I reasoned that if it had been Noah or anyone else from my team, I'd have been just as riled up and out for blood. But that's where it didn't make sense. Noah and the others, they were my family, my brothers and sister. Naya . . . I barely knew her.

"Naya?"

The line went dead, and dread, like I'd never felt before, sheeted over me. Wave upon wave that frosted my flesh and everything beneath it. Noah wrestled the phone out of my hands and looked over the pearls' transcript, his eyes growing as wide as when I'd come up with the plan to "give" Grayson a seizure.

Had it only been this morning? It felt like days since we'd taxied over to Gray's flat in London. Days since the short, muscled blond scrutinized us as though we were Triples out to get him. But he quickly saw reason when we explained we were working undercover to nail Dunmore. Since Gray also hated the prissy lord and wanted Emmy to come home, he'd gone along with our scheme.

Even though I'd volunteered to give Grayson a black eye and a bloody nose—we needed to make it look real after all—Noah had shoved me aside and sacrificed one of his glittery pink feathers. He'd forfeited another to call 999 after Grayson had fake-collapsed in his building's staircase and proceeded to shake for two full minutes to make sure that if any neighbors came across him, they'd corroborate his condition.

After he was transported to the hospital, we'd paid him one final visit to inform him Emmy was on her way.

"*Naya, is she one of you?*"

We were already at the door of his hospital room when he asked this.

I knew he didn't mean *an angel*; I knew he meant to ask if she was part of our team. "Yes."

"*So you're leaving her there?*"

His question had sounded like an accusation.

Like *I'd* put her in Dunmore's path.

Like I hadn't tried to get her out.

"*She won't leave.*"

"*And you're okay with that?*"

Of course I wasn't okay with it!

Noah had propelled me toward the exit before I could snatch Gray's food tray and fling it against a wall to show him just how *not okay* I was with Naya's decision.

Diplomatic as always, my friend said, "*We're working on getting her out.*"

But we hadn't worked hard enough on it. And when she'd asked if I was fine, instead of playing up the truth, that I wasn't, I'd chosen my usual MO of not showing weakness. Not only didn't I want her pity, but I also wanted her focused on the mission, since she was so adamant about seeing it through.

If I'd told her the truth, would she have run to me like Emmy had run to Gray?

What was I going on about? We didn't have that sort of relationship. The seraphim's daughter and I didn't have any sort of relationship.

I'd been on the phone with Galina, who was guarding the cellar in which Calliope was ending one more bunghole's life, when Naya's call had come through, and I'd downloaded her earrings' transcript.

Although some words were missing, probably spoken too low to have registered properly, the important ones were there: *Semtex. Injection. SIM cards. Boom.*

"Get us a car!" I yelled at Noah, shoving my feet into my sneakers. I had to do it twice before I got the right shoe on the right foot.

Because we were out in the plucking boondocks, and it was an unangelic hour, it took thirty minutes for a cab to roll in. I'd just inputted the manor's address when the red dot of Naya's GPS coordinates started moving across my screen, at first slowly and then faster.

"You think she got away?" Noah asked.

My gut throbbed as though I'd gotten sucker-punched. "No." I pressed pause on our route. Without glancing at the transcript, I typed in a new address, redirecting the cab down the public road that laced around the Dunmore's property. "They're headed to the marsh."

Noah's eyelashes rose because he knew what laid on the farthest edge of the Dunmores' land: a cesspool Robbie and his family had transformed into a mass grave.

I'd pinpointed it on a map to the detective who'd looked into the disappearance of a high society debutante when I'd first landed in London. The last place the woman had been seen was at the Dunmore estate. I was certain the man would request a warrant and comb through the grounds, but he'd merely scratched his rubbery jowls and informed me, eyes darting every which way, that the woman had run away to the States with her lover. Case-closed.

Except, I'd checked her profile on a holo-ranker. The eighteen year old's current residence was Elysium. It was only after checking the detective's score that I understood the Dunmores had hushed him with a copious amount of money since his current sin was—*takes bribes*.

While Noah tinkered with the screen to make sure our cab idled, I jolted out into the tangle of tree trunks, skidding on brambles and fallen pinecones. I was so jacked up on adrenaline I barely registered Noah hissing out my name until he gripped a fistful of my T-shirt and jerked me to a stop.

"For fork's sake, Adam, slow down!" Noah panted. "Levi's not done deactivating the cameras."

I could see the noxious black pond gleam between the dense

forest like a predatory eye. Had they already tossed her in? I patted my sweatpants down for my phone, but my pockets were empty. All the blood pooled at the back of my throat drained away. "My phone. I forgot my—"

"I have it." Noah lit it up at the same time as Henry Dunmore's green Jeep coughed down the hill.

Just before his headlights splashed the bushy beech trees behind which we stood, Noah caught my biceps and shoved me down. An *oomph* fell from my lips as my shin smacked the forest floor, sending shards of pain across my injured leg.

"A warning would've been nice," I grumbled, swiping my wrist across my mouth to dislodge the dirt just as light licked the gilded tips of Noah's feathers. "Your plucking wings, No," I grumbled.

"What about my wings?"

"They're out."

"So? You think anyone in that family has angel-blood?"

"Good point." Only Naya would see them, if she was even conscious.

The second the car veered and plunged us back into darkness, I started to get up, but Noah caught my wrist.

"We wait," he murmured.

"We've waited enough."

"Well, we're waiting some more. We'll retrieve her as soon as they're gone and Levi's shut off the security feed." He cinched my wrist tighter, sensing I didn't have it in me to wait. "She's immortal, Adam. We'll fish her out and heal her. She'll be fine."

I glared at his hand, then at his face. Anyone else would've grown antsy under my scrutiny, but not Noah. Never Noah. There wasn't a thing I could do to the guy to intimidate him.

"Fine. Fine I'll *wait*!" I shook his hand off as we got to our feet. "I can't believe they put bloody Semtex inside of her. *Semtex!*"

"Keep your voice down."

"What if they decide to detonate her?" I hissed.

"They won't detonate her. It'd cause too much noise," Noah said calmly.

Not under water. There, it'd cause only ripples.

We may have been immortal, but what happened if our bodies blew up? Did we break into a trillion pieces that magically superglued back together? It wasn't the sort of thing ophanim taught in the guilds, because getting used as dirty bombs didn't factor into normal fletching missions. I retrieved my phone from Noah's hand and pounded out a message to Dov.

Angels, how I wanted to smack something. *Someone*. Henry. His mother. Junior. Robbie. I rolled my restless fingers into fists that I kept locked against my strumming thighs.

"I know you don't believe in soulmates, but your fathers clearly are."

"Soulmates? What the pluck, Noah? Did you just sniff some shrooms?"

"I heard that when souls find their mates, they can't live without each other. Maybe Naya's yours?"

Had my lips not been stretched tautly over my teeth, I may have laughed. What was he going to come out with next? That cupids were flitting around, stabbing humans in the ass with enchanted arrows?

"I've been around you for eighteen years, and this is the first time I've seen you act this unhinged."

I glared at Noah before going back to tracking Naya's GPS toward the silty marsh. "I'm not unhinged." What I was, was finally acting like a responsible adult.

The skin over my knuckles strained so hard it snapped open one of my scabs. Noah gripped my shoulder and gave it a squeeze. I shrugged his hand off, not in the mood to be coddled or whatever it was the pink-feathered mother hen was attempting.

"Breathe, Adam. You're turning blue in the face."

Even though it felt like a 747 was parked on my chest, I sucked in a breath and held onto it, not sure I had it in me to take another until Naya was out of the Dunmores' hold and safely in ours.

30

NAYA

My head smacked against a wall.

"She called someone. We're trying to figure out who, but they wiped her phone."

It took my puffy eyes a moment to peel open and realize I was inside the boot of a 4-by-4. Another bump in the road made me roll forward so brutally that my forehead banged into the trunk door.

"We're driving her out to the marsh . . . Yes, she was the only one who hadn't cauterized. Your father, brother, and I checked up on all the others personally."

"Put Rob on speakerphone, Mum."

There was a slight clank followed by a slew of curse words pronounced so elegantly one would've thought Lady Dunmore was reciting poetry instead of insulting her son for his hasty driving.

The Triple's affected voice trickled into the car. "—the bedding?"

"What was that?" Susan squawked after going off on her son again about his driving. "We missed the beginning of your question, Rob."

"Have you remade the bed? We can't afford for the others to see the blood."

"It's already been done." Lady Dunmore *tsk*ed. "Not my first rodeo, son."

What had this woman done before? Goosebumps rose across my

tender skin, stapling each inch with the painful awareness that these monsters weren't done torturing me.

"What do we tell the other girls when they wake, Rob?" Henry asked.

"That Emmeline Rogers was a wreck, and compassionate Naya went to offer her friend emotional support."

The car hit another bump. Even though I braced myself, it didn't lessen the agony that spread through my rib cage when it jostled my body. I bit back the whimper and swallowed down my tears. I'd pull through this.

Somehow.

"How do you want us to get rid of her?" Henry booked such a sharp turn that the crown of my head pressed painfully against the side paneling.

"Store her in the usual place." Robbie's voice was barely above a murmur.

What was their usual place? The marsh they'd mentioned earlier?

I hoped the pearls in my lobes were transmitting my location. I hoped the others— The memory of having called Adam slammed into me as violently as my body against the trunk door. What had I managed to tell him?

A gunshot rent the air.

I held my breath, expecting pain to explode somewhere in my body, but if I had been shot, I couldn't feel a thing over the pain radiating from my middle.

"Robert?" Susan's voice writhed with nerves. "Robert!"

"I'm here, Mum. I'm here."

"What was that?" she all but screeched.

Robbie's voice dropped to a whisper. "Pablo just offed Luis for botching the job on his favorite Circle Girl."

Not that I had any love for Luis, but holy Abaddon . . . Pablo had shot his own cousin?

Would a malakim come for the dead man or had maiming an angel made him a Triple?

Perhaps, he'd already been a Triple . . .

"I'll call you when I land. Make sure to weigh her down." And then the phone clicked off.

For as long as I could remember, I'd been warned that humans were capable of cruelty, but how it paled in comparison to experiencing it firsthand. How could they discuss drowning someone with such detachment?

The car came to an abrupt stop, which sent my body spiraling over the trunk mat that smelled of wet dog and fresh blood.

"Lay the cement bricks beside the shore, Henry. I'll fetch the girl."

Their doors clacked. I made sure to keep my lids sealed as the car door rose automatically. Even though I couldn't see Susan Dunmore, I could smell the thick rose perfume springing off her botoxed skin, I could feel her cool hands wind around my bare ankles and tug.

"A shame your body rejected the coagulator. You would've made a great asset for my family." A finger stroked down my cheek, halting the tremors rushing through my body. When that same finger curled around my earlobe, everything in me seized. "Pretty."

My eyes sprang open, and I shook my head.

Her fingers recoiled, but then a sneer rearranged her features. "Darling, you won't be needing those where you're going."

I blinked at her, murmuring, "Mine... don't."

She slapped me, the sting of her palm startling me long enough for her to pry one earring off my lobe. After she pocketed it, she grabbed my hair and used it as a leash to access the other side of my face.

I tried shaking my head again, but that merely led to Susan tightening her grip until my strands felt like they'd pop clean off my scalp.

"Hold still, or I rip it off."

I growled at her threat. "Monster."

"Oh, darling, I've been called far, *far* worse." The post back thankfully sprang open, preserving that tiny bit of my skin.

After she put the pearl away in her robe pocket, she yanked again on my hair, this time, to pull me out of the car. I roared with indignation and pain when my tailbone hit the ground.

Panting, I croaked, "Don't do this, Susan. For your soul's sake, don't do this."

She peered down at me, her unnaturally plump lips kinked in amusement. "My soul's sake? *You* signed up to help. I had nothing to do with your candidature or your selection, so do not blame me for where you've ended up. This is entirely on you, Miss Moreau."

She dragged me by the hair toward where Henry stood ready

with rope and cinder blocks. I writhed and kicked, catching the eldest son on the underside of his chin, which sent him teetering backward. When he fell onto his backside, his mother muttered something about raising feeble sons and needing to do everything herself.

Steeling my spine, I kicked my leg out, the momentum spinning me onto my front and destabilizing the matriarch who lost hold of my hair. Even though stars spangled my vision, I heaved my knees under me, then attempted to stand, but the effort robbed me of breath and strength, and the ground came at me before the Dunmores.

NAYA

*I*cy water shocked my lips apart. I gagged around a mouthful of silt, my lungs contracting, attempting to filter the air from the water, but I had no gills. Only wings. I called upon them, forcing them to open, forcing them to flap even though the sheer energy this required made my shoulders ache and my lungs scream.

My body didn't miraculously rise, the same way my lungs didn't miraculously fill with air.

Again, I flapped, but all that did was disturb the sandy bottom and blacken the already murky water. I tugged at my wrists, trying to loosen the coils of waxed rope biting into my skin, but with every tug, the knots grew snugger, and I, weaker.

My lips quivered around the fraying threads of oxygen as agony raged through my whole being. Agony and shame. My father had raised me to be strong and resourceful, a warrior with wings, not a drowned insect pinned to the bottom of a marsh.

How easily I'd been subdued.

How swiftly I'd lost control.

Adam had been right. For all my confidence, I hadn't been prepared for this mission.

In a few seconds, I'd pass out, and then what? Would my body sway in this liquid grave until someone towed me out? Would I lose consciousness and then regain it every now and then, just to realize I was still a prisoner of the Dunmores' swamp?

I suddenly wished they'd detonate the explosive inside me, because an explosion would snap the rope off my ankles and wrists, or at the very least, create a tidal wave that would wash me up on shore.

That was probably wishful thinking.

Sick wishful thinking.

Dov would come looking for me.

Or my father. He'd move Elysium and Earth to find me.

My wing bones strained to propel me upward, but like storm clouds rushing over the moon, darkness enveloped me and gobbled me whole.

32

ADAM

ANGELIC FACT #464
FEATHERS MAY KEEP US AFLOAT IN AIR BUT NOT IN WATER

The second Levi gave us the green light, I was off and running. The ground sucked at the soles of my shoes and jostled my bruised calf, but I plowed on, splashing into the marsh before diving under. It took me mere seconds to locate her wings bobbing like an open chute that had failed to carry her to safety.

I scraped my hands across her body until I felt her wrists and the rope wound around them, then tracked it to the knot that anchored her to the sandy bottom. I worked it until my fingernails tore and bled, until it loosened and slithered like an eel. I broke the surface and inhaled a lungful of air before diving back under toward her ankles.

My head banged against something hard that made me startle and sip water. It took my blurry eyes a heartbeat to realize it was Noah. Noah who was sawing through the rope with what looked like a pocket knife.

I ripped back to the surface and sucked in a lungful of fetid air before diving back under. Since the marsh was shallow, I weaved my arms around Naya's back, beneath her sagging wings, and pressed the soles of my sneakers into the bottom to lever her body upward while Noah finished untying her ankles.

Her torso was ice, her lips blue, her skin marbled like the Elysian quartz when it lit up at night. "Naya," I croaked so close to her mouth that if she failed to hear her name, she'd feel it. "Feather, you need to breathe."

When her mouth didn't part, I snaked one of my arms off her waist, keeping her upright with the other, and cradled her chin between my fingertips, raising her face toward my own. With my thumb, I broke open the seam of her lips, and water dribbled out.

"Breathe," I ordered her, less softly this time.

She was still listless and rigid as a corpse.

I gathered her close. "Angelsdammit, breathe!"

A slight tremor stole through her torso, stealing through mine in turn, and dirty water spurted from the corners of her mouth and ribboned down her chin.

The cinder block keeping her fastened to the watery tomb finally released her body, and she drifted up. Noah splashed to the surface, drawing in air and whisking his palms across his eyes and mouth.

"There was a bone down there." He shuddered, palming the grime off him. "A forking bone." Another shudder. "Remind me why the seraphim don't just incinerate Triples' souls?"

In that moment, I couldn't concentrate on the whys and hows of our system, because a spasm rattled Naya's body, and then she was gasping and retching, her lungs expelling the swamp.

Although I released her chin, I held her to me until every last drop of water drained from her body, until her breathing turned from ragged to even, until her heartbeats went from harsh to soft, and her body from stiff to pliant.

Noah stared at me over her shuddering wings. "Want help carrying her out?"

I shook my head, bent at the knees, and scooped her up. When I stepped onto the shore and the moonlight hit her waist, I gnashed my teeth and swore to plucking end the Dunmore line.

If I lost a feather for my unangelic thought, I didn't feel it. I felt nothing but pure hatred for the blackness oozing out of Naya's abdomen, the pallor of her skin, and the puffiness of her lids.

"Adam?" She batted her waterlogged lashes, as though surprised to see me.

"What? You thought I wouldn't come?" I snapped, nerves as sore and shredded as my nails.

"I—" A swallow deepened the hollow at the base of her throat. "No."

My sweltering anger grew hotter at her lack of faith, and I tore my gaze off hers as we waded through the forest.

Noah trotted to catch up, his feet squishing in his sneakers. "Adam, hand her over. You're limping."

"I got her," I growled at him, then at her, "Magick away your wings. They're dragging." My tone was as punitive as my pulse.

The darkness stopped glittering around her limp form. The soft down, that had peeled away from my wet forearms, left behind a streak of goosebumps.

Minutes or maybe an hour later, we reached the cab, still idling on the deserted backroad. Noah pulled open the door. I hunched over her as I plowed into the puny vehicle and dropped in the middle of the bench seat, cradling her body to mine. She wriggled to break free but then winced and stopped struggling as Noah slid onto the upholstered bench in front of us and input the mill's address.

"Where did they put the Semtex?" I all but barked, examining her exposed abdomen, the soiled rag of a shirt that stuck to her skin like wet paper.

"Inside my stomach."

I felt her dark gaze seeking mine, but I didn't give her my eyes, the buildup of anger and guilt too great. One look, and both would spill into her.

"They injected it through—my belly button."

My gaze narrowed there. "Did it come out yet?"

"I don't know. Maybe when I was underwater."

I set her legs down carefully, then prodded the mottled flesh around her stomach with the tips of my index and middle fingers. When she hissed, I snatched my hand back.

"Is it still there?" she rasped.

"I don't know. I didn't want to press too hard."

She squeezed her lids tight. "I want it out."

So did I.

So. Did. I.

Noah wiped his cell phone against the fabric bench, then clicked it awake. "Boone thinks the Semtex will dissolve but that the detonator should come out."

"Should?" she croaked.

"*Will*," I said.

"He's hoping it's still inside her, so he can study it."

And I was hoping it was buried six feet under the marsh.

"How long did it take the bullet"—she pulled in a rickety breath—"to come out of your leg?"

"A few hours." But I'd helped it along.

"Good. Then maybe it's still there."

"*Good?*" Without meaning to, I looked into her eyes. "How would that be good?"

"Because they put one in all of us." Her lids slid shut, and her forehead grooved. I wanted to take her pain and pulp it. "Maybe if he studies it, he'll be able to dismantle the others."

I stared at her bone-white face, shocked by how calm and clear-minded she was when I was primed to tear out jugulars.

Her colorless lips parted. "Adam, see if you can feel it."

My hand, which had landed on her hipbone when she'd winced, refused to lift. "No."

"Fine." She swallowed.

I turned my attention to the window, to the stretch of road still drizzled in moonlight, but a hiss of pain made my head jerk back toward Naya. The crazy girl was feeling up her abdomen! I shackled her wrist.

"It's there," she murmured.

"You felt it?" The excitement lacing Noah's tone made me skewer him with a glower. "Don't tell me you would've preferred a swim in the skeleton-infested marsh?"

"The only thing I would prefer is for Naya not to bleed out all over my lap." After a beat, I added, "The cab company would send us a hefty fine."

I couldn't care less about a fine, so I wasn't sure why I was making a plucking fuss about it.

Noah rolled his eyes, and Naya . . . she smiled. And that smile, it loosened something inside my gut.

She was alive.

She was safe.

And she was with me.

My phone erupted with my crowd-cheer. I readjusted Naya to yank it out of my pocket, glad I hadn't lost it in the swamp.

DOV: *Our bodies can't explode, but she'll bleed profusely.*

I tossed my phone at Noah. "Ask him to meet us at the inn." And then I concentrated on Naya's porcelain features and veined lids.

I wanted to wake her, to keep her conscious, but Dov's words spiraled through my mind: *Our bodies can't explode.*

As selfish as I was, as much as I wanted to keep her conscious, I knew it would be kinder to let her sleep through the healing process. Time would go by faster for her, even if it'd crawl by for me.

"You're going to be okay, Feather," I murmured. "You're going to be okay."

ADAM

ANGELIC FACT #538
NOT EVERYTHING ROLLS OFF OUR FEATHERS.

Naya remained unconscious as I carried her inside the mill and laid her limp body on the towel Noah draped over one side of the king-size bed. He'd suggested bathing her, but I wasn't undressing a girl without her consent or waking one who slept this soundly.

"You don't think they embedded a tracking device inside the detonator?" Noah asked, as I drew another towel and then the comforter over her glistening pallor. I hated how waxen her skin had become, how it made her resemble an atrium statue.

I cracked my knuckles. "Let them come."

"Adam . . ." Noah warned. "There'll be no man-slaughtering, or woman-slaughtering, tonight. Or any other night. I don't want you to lose all your hard-earned feathers."

"I bet slaughtering Triples doesn't cost a thing. Especially those who harm angels." I grabbed my phone to ask our trusty ishim.

"I'd prefer you don't find this out first-hand." Noah poked the fire he was coaxing to life in the round chimney, because, of course, every angelsdamn thing in this mill was circular. "Well, I'm going to go wash off the marsh." He put the poker back in place and stretched his arms over his head. "Unless you want to go first?"

"I'll wait."

I sat beside Naya, elbows on my thighs, clasped hands supporting my forehead that throbbed with its own pulse as it computed the use of the Circle Girls. What a dungshow this was going to be, if we didn't find a way to extract or block fifty explosive devices in time.

How much time did we even have? Would Pablo set them off tomorrow? The day after? A week from now? Would he make them go off all at once and wipe out the entire Venezuelan court or would he detonate the girls here and there in his city to create a diversion?

I kneaded my thumping temples with my thumbs. This felt too big for a bunch of fletching guardians, but even if I begged Dov to call upon the Seven, he wouldn't, because it'd compromise his project.

I expelled a deep breath and scraped my hands down my face, then phoned Galina, hoping she'd have good news. I was desperate for a spark of sunshine in this endless night. "Is she done?"

"Yep. One more disgusting human in a body bag. Hopefully, he'll be doing a lot of soul-searching down in Abaddon."

I grunted. A year for every sinner point. That hardly felt like enough for what he'd done to Felicity Gold. "The malakim didn't see you?"

"Nope. Got Calliope out of there before one of ours came down to collect the man's soul. So, why'd you hang up on me like that?"

I looked over at Naya and picked a lock of hair off her cheek. Wet, her curls were a burnished gold, like the midafternoon sun instead of the one at daybreak. "Boone and Levi didn't fill you in?"

"I just dropped our favorite murderer at the safe house, so I didn't get a chance to call. So . . . what happened?"

I told Galina everything, and besides gasping an unangelic word that made her breath whoosh sharply through the receiver, she didn't interrupt me.

"But she's okay?"

"She will be. Eventually." *I hoped.* Pluck, would she be okay?

After I was caught up on Calliope's timeline for the last two rapists—the ones named in the papers and currently under police protection—Galina and I hung up, and I stood, the effort almost knocking me back onto my ass. In the adrenaline rush of getting to Naya, my leg injury had become white noise, but the torturous burn was back with a vengeance.

Naya stirred and let out a soft whimper that shut down my pity-party. I reached out to touch her cheek to remind her that she was safe when she murmured a two-syllable name.

A name that was not mine.

Although I had no reason to be jealous, when she repeated it around a soft moan, I balled my fingers into fists and pried myself off the bed and away from this girl who was getting under my skin, even though, apparently, another man had gotten under hers.

I reasoned that fear for her life and guilt for her pain was making her far more important to me than she was.

34

NAYA

Although my mouth felt like it had been wadded up with steel-wool and my body, like it had been scrubbed with it, my head was clear. That clarity quickly faded, though, when I attempted to lift my hands out from underneath the comforter to scrub the sleep from my eyes.

As my fingers collapsed limply back alongside my torso, I blinked at my surroundings. Above me, stretched a thatched peaked roof, and around me, a ring of whitewashed stone walls. Fire crackled in a modern glass hearth, combatting the ambient grayness. The sky outside shone milky through the four-paned windows set so high that I'd need a chair to see out. Where was I? The windows screamed dungeon, but the rest of the space, the soft sheets in which I lay cocooned and the pristine walls, hinted at luxury.

Even though my neck creaked, I managed to pivot my head. When I found Noah curled on the bed beside me, intermittently snoring and garbling things in his sleep, I couldn't keep emotion from flooding me.

I hadn't dreamt being succored.

Adam's team had come through for me. They'd managed to find me in spite of Susan Dunmore stealing my earrings. Tears welled and spilled, sluicing down my cheek like the swamp water that had clogged my airways. My heartache took a different direction, and the taste in my mouth became so sour I wanted to chug a bottle of mouthwash.

The rest of the evening trickled back through me with such clarity, it felt like I was reliving it, each terrible instant. Pablo's unwelcomed touch. The syringe too wide and long and sharp slicing through my navel. The bitter scent of blood laced with plastic explosive. The salty taste of silt and terror.

Even though my arm trembled savagely, I gripped the comforter and eased it down the length of my body, then caught the edge of the towel stained crimson with blood and rolled it down. My tank top had dried, but the fabric was crusty and rumpled. And the smell . . .

Angels the smell of me was eye-watering. How had Noah endured it? How had he managed to fall asleep next to it?

Between the fire burning out and the lifted cover, the air turned so pungent that my stomach convulsed. The spasm made a whimper spill over the soft pop of charred logs and blood ooze from my navel.

Breath wedged inside my throat, I skipped a finger over my blackened stomach, hoping the color was due to the mineral deposit of the swamp, but no dirt adhered to the tip. My torso was gangrening. At least, that explained the stench. I studied my wrists, patterned red and purple from the cord the Dunmore duo had wrapped around them, and three feelings raced through me—revulsion, dismay, and relief.

Revulsion for what they'd done.

Dismay that they'd done it without a second thought.

Relief that it had been done to me instead of to a fragile human.

Stealing a deep breath, I gripped the side of the nightstand and gently towed my legs off the bed. When my feet hit the floor, it felt like stepping onto a mat of tiny needles instead of a plush beige rug stained with dirty shoeprints. I studied the wave-like pattern as I waited for the prickling to abate in my soles and skull.

When all was calm, I towed my torso up to sit and listed forward. *Oh, angels, no.*

No, no, no.

I tightened my hold on the nightstand, as my vision fragmented into tiny pixels. I tried to recline backward, so I'd fall against the mattress, but failed to even straighten my torso, which had curled in on itself.

My vision became as fine as dust and purloined the color from the room. I swayed forward and fell. Although the landing was abrupt, nothing crunched in my face. The rug must've been plusher than it had felt beneath my toes.

"Not that black isn't your color"—a voice, which seemed to rise from beneath the rug, quipped—"but perhaps try not to match the entirety of your skin to your eyes and wings."

I smiled in spite of how close to the truth Adam's statement was and how feathering much all the bruises mottling my skin hurt. "Were you sleeping under the bed?"

"Only monsters sleep there." As he propped me on the rug with my back against the side of the mattress, he asked, "Are you calling me a monster, Feather?"

As my skin awakened, it tingled like a colony of ants was marching over it. "Not now that I've met real ones." He smelled like thunder and rain-slicked grass, so clean and fresh that I filled my lungs with him. "Thank you for rescuing me last night. And again right now."

Angels, how I hated being so weak . . .

A lock of hair swung in front of my right eye. My hand shook as I reached up to tuck it behind my ear, but the strands were so gnarled and hard, they sprang right out.

"Just doing my job, heiress."

I wondered why he downplayed his compassion. "Since when is getting me out of trouble *your* job?"

"Would you rather I'd phoned your daddy?"

"No." I bit my lip. "Definitely not." A realization made my mouth pop open. "My clothes. My phone." Neck creaking, I glanced around what I could see of the circular space, hoping I'd find my sapphire suitcase blunting the cream décor, but found only men's clothes, food wrappers, and a plaid cover dangling off the couch.

"I got you a new phone, which Levi rebooted remotely. He disabled and wiped the other one."

The discussion the Dunmores had about the uselessness of my phone while they'd driven me to my resting place in the woods finally made sense.

"Love the moniker you gave me, but I do wonder . . . did you nickname me BLACK HOLE because I suck you in or did you mean to add a three-letter word before the *hole* part?"

I managed a smile even though my insides were weeping. "You'll never know."

"Want to bet?" The male sounded positively chirpy, which was odd considering the dark circles beneath his eyes.

"Angels don't bet."

"They also don't attempt to thwart terrorist attacks." His comment sobered me up. "Anyway, I got you an outfit to change into. Well, more of a T-shirt-sleep-shirt thingie." He nodded to a paper grocery bag he must've dropped when he'd slid onto his knees to catch me, because it was resting on its side, contents poking out. "I ordered you some clothes, but they haven't arrived yet."

"You ordered me clothes?" I couldn't help the smile that bent my lips.

He shrugged, jaw tinged pink. "Galina did. I told her to keep everything functional."

"Thank you." Head still spinning, I reached over and uprooted the T-shirt from the bag. A white logo was printed on the amethyst cotton: *Save water. Drink beer.* "A real poster child for fletchings everywhere."

"Got it at the pub. It was either that, or an apron from the minimart."

"I love it."

His gaze skimmed the rug, probably on the hunt for a feather. He wouldn't find one, because it wasn't a lie. I was grateful for this shirt, like I was grateful that he and Noah had come back for me.

"Ama will be so jealous. She loves T-shirts with sayings." Almost as much as she loved her—

Oh, no. Her angel-wing bomber! Even though material goods were replaceable, if I'd lost that jacket . . .

Adam's eyes dropped to my black-and-blue midriff, misinterpreting my sudden contrition. "Do you—Are you in pain?"

Since I was in pain, physically and otherwise, I nodded, not wanting to elaborate that a jacket was at the root of my grief. He surely thought me shallow enough.

"Can you help me get to the bathroom?" My low voice scraped across my chattering teeth.

He stared at my extended palm as though I'd just asked him to be my square-dancing partner. I lowered my hand to the rug. Maybe I could manage by myself. Before I could even try, he slid one arm behind my back and the other underneath my knees, and airlifted me.

Even though I was racked with chills, my cheeks heated. "You don't have to carry me, Adam."

One of his eyebrows quirked. "How else were you planning on getting to the bathroom?"

My ego would've preferred crawling to it. "What about your leg?"

"My leg's feeling much better." And yet, he limped around the bed.

I glanced over at Noah, dead to the world, in spite of all the noise we'd made.

"Heaviest sleeper you'll ever meet. When we were kids, I used to borrow instruments from the music room to wake him. The trumpet worked best."

"Ouch."

Adam flashed me a dark smile that showed he'd enjoyed torturing his poor friend a little too much. "Don't worry. He got me back."

"Glad to hear it."

"I'm sure you are."

"What did he do?"

His gaze traced the huddled mass under the comforter that was Noah, before the dozing fletching vanished from our line of sight and a bathroom made of tinted pine, teal paint, and brushed black stone appeared. "He wrote a love note in my name to this friend of ours. Creeped the guy out so much, he felt like he needed to give me this longwinded explanation, in the middle of the cafeteria no less, about why it wouldn't work out between us and that he preferred girls anyway." Adam smirked as though he was somehow fond of the memory. "He still gives me a wide berth every time our paths cross." He set me down on the lip of the built-in bathtub, knocking back the row of packaged salts and soap bottles so I could lean against the cool wall. "Shower or bath?"

"Shower." I wanted to strip away the layers of grime on my body, not steep in them.

He stepped toward the glass-walled shower and spun the valve until steam coiled off the spray, then returned to get me. One palm flat against the wall, I reached out the other to Adam. With his help,

I heaved myself upright. When the lines between the floorboards turned squiggly, I shut my eyes.

Adam wound his arm around my waist, his grip all at once feather-light and firm. "I'm going to sit you down inside. Do *not* attempt to stand."

I didn't think I could.

When fabric rustled, I cracked my lids open in time to see Adam shoving down his sweatpants. His underwear stayed in place. Yes, I checked.

"What are you doing?"

"Trying to salvage some clothes, so I don't have to spend the day in a bathrobe."

Before I could wonder what in the worlds he meant, he stepped right inside the shower with me, then crouched to ease my body down.

"Your T-shirt—" *And briefs...*

"Needed a wash anyway. Saves me a trip to the guild."

Because I'd bled all over him. I scrunched up my nose in apology.

He pointed to my soiled clothes. "Want to keep those on?"

I didn't, but I also didn't feel like getting naked in front of a virtual stranger, so I nodded. Adam rose, fisted the bottles of soap on the metal shelf, then dumped them beside me on the floor. Before he dropped into a squat, I noticed that the color of his calf, the one that had been shot, was a kaleidoscope of purple, orange, and yellow beneath the dusting of dark hair.

I grabbed the shampoo bottle and attempted to open it, but between the water making it slippery and my hands shaking, I failed at the easy task. He filched it from my hands and unscrewed the cap, then poured the contents into my tendered palms. I raised them to my head with the intention to wash my hair, but the best I accomplished was useless patting.

Adam, who'd removed his T-shirt and was scrubbing it energetically with soap, tossed it beside the hodgepodge of soap bottles. He eased my hands off my head and worked the shampoo into my hair. Just like his grip, his fingers were gentle and firm against my scalp, and although I tried to stifle it, a moan escaped. I couldn't decide if I was more embarrassed by the breathy sound or by the situation in its entirety. At least, it was taking my mind off the pain.

"I usually don't shower with girls until the sixth date."

I smiled at his attempt to put me at ease. "And yet here you are, breaking your rules for the loathed seraphim's daughter."

His eyebrows pulled in close as he concentrated on his task, which along with the sound of falling water and the herbal scent of the soap, sloughed my prickling nerves. "I seem to be breaking a lot of my rules around you."

"That terrified of my father, huh?" I meant it as teasing, but his grim expression told me I'd hit a nerve.

My stomach roiled then. Even though the sight was sickening, I lowered my eyes to the blood oozing from my navel and searched the stream for a lump.

The chip had to be small, since they'd used a wide needle, but I'd notice it, right? "Do you have any idea how big the mechanism will be?"

"From the images he's retrieved, Boone assumes it'll be little larger than a green pea."

"What images?"

"Just hallway stills. He managed to zoom in on one."

"Did he get images from inside our bedrooms?" Modesty and shame made me hope not.

"No. They don't have any cameras in there."

Which explained how I'd gotten away with calling Adam . . .

A sigh must've escaped me, because Adam's fingers paused in the mass of suds and blonde hair.

After a beat, his fingers began to move again. "I don't know if we have enough shampoo for all that hair."

"As long as you have conditioner."

He cracked another bottle open and massaged it into my lengths. When his fingers sailed neatly through, he sat back on his haunches, thick lashes shading his eyes, water roping down the knobs of his bare shoulders like oil. "Want help with the rest of your body?"

"I should be able to manage." Hopefully.

I held out my palms for soap, then proceeded to slick it down my arms, across my collarbone, and over my bent legs. After appealing to him for more soap, I peeled the ribbed material off my abdomen and inched my hands beneath, careful not to graze the raw, navy skin.

Pablo's face flashed before my eyes, spiking my temper. I made sure to soap my breasts thoroughly to remove the phantom touch of his fingers.

How feathering dare he...

In my frustration, I towed my hands down too brutally and winced as they connected with the giant bruise. I popped them away but not before they skimmed against something small and hard.

I prodded the area around my navel again. "The mechanism—it's right there."

Adam's eyes flipped off a bottle label he'd been studying intensely.

I took his fingers and pressed them against the lump, which seemed to come alive and vibrate. Sucking in a sticky breath, I tossed away his fingers. "Did you feel that? You think we just set it off?"

Adam shoved wet hair out of his eyes. "*We* can't trigger it."

"You think *they* did then?"

A slender groove appeared between his eyebrows.

"Adam, get out of the shower. Get away. In case—"

"You're not blowing up."

"How do you know that?"

"Because you're an angel, and our kind doesn't go *kaboom*."

I so wanted to believe him, but he didn't know. He *couldn't* know. My father might know, but I couldn't very well phone him up and ask. If the dirty bomb they'd put inside of me didn't kill me, he would.

"Plus, Dov confirmed you'll be bleeding it out."

Thank Elysium.

Adam's fingers returned to that inch of skin above my navel. My stomach jerked so hard at his touch that blood spurted out of my gaping belly button. Although we were ensconced in a cloud of steam, cold sweat ran off the nape of my neck.

"You think you can maneuver it out?" Bile carved a path up my throat, but I swallowed it down.

"I think your body's doing that for you."

The throbbing in my stomach became so insistent that I saw stars. "Angels, I'm going to be sick."

His hands caught either side of my face. "Look at me. Focus on me." The emerald gleam of his irises spread across his straight nose and strong forehead, over his carved cheekbones and sharp jaw. Even the steam and black stone took on a green hue. "Feather, keep your eyes open and on me. Don't pass out."

I grunted. "I don't like that name."

"I know." His thumbs brushed along my cheeks.

He knew but didn't care. And yet . . . yet he must've cared a little, otherwise, he wouldn't have dove into a marsh in the middle of the night to rescue me. Otherwise, he wouldn't be squatting in a shower, cleaning up the mess other men had made of my body.

As I focused on his pupils and the steadiness of his palms, my breathing eased and the brilliant shade of his irises stopped tinting everything around them.

"Still want me to get it out or should we leave your body to do it on its own time?" He lowered his hands from my face.

My neck felt suddenly too weak to hold up my head, so I leaned it back against the wall. "I want it to stop hurting. I want it out."

His dimple appeared, and since he wasn't smiling, I assumed it had deepened, because he was prepping himself for the gory job ahead.

Feebly, I said, "I can try doing it myself."

He glowered, but I didn't think it was in anger. "Lean into me. I don't want you to flop sideways and knock yourself out."

His rough order made my lids close and my neck dip until my forehead rested in the scoop of his corded neck. "I wouldn't mind getting knocked out a little."

He grunted as he slid one arm around my hunched spine. His chest rose and fell five times before his fingers finally found their way to my stomach. At first, he barely pressed down, but then he ran two knuckles down the flat plane of skin, and my insides burst to life as though to help him along.

He repeated the motion until his knuckles felt so close to my navel that I thought he'd dipped one in. Little pyres of fire dotted the backs of my lids. I squeezed them tighter, pulled in breath after breath, huddled closer to the hulking angel, desperate to hold on and hold still.

"Almost out." His voice slipped over my pebbled skin like soap.

I felt myself swoon.

He must've felt it too because the arm around my back tautened. "So, tell me, Feather . . . who's Jarod?"

The shock of his question made the world temporarily stop churning.

"Your boyfriend?" His fingers kneaded my pounding skin with

such force, I started to think that if he failed to get the explosive out, he'd succeed at removing an organ.

After sucking in a breath and releasing it, I managed to ask, "Why?"

"Because you moaned his name all night."

Had I? How embarrassing. Almost as humiliating as admitting Jarod was the name I called the dark stranger who haunted my dreams.

Besides Mira, I'd told Raven and Eve about him. Where Raven had rolled her eyes at my theory that my recurring dreams were premonitory and that I may be destined for this Jarod, Eve had listened raptly. She'd even gone so far as to suggest I might meet him someday but warned me to stay open-minded about his looks and name. At least, she hadn't scoffed like Mira.

I had no doubt Adam would, though. He didn't strike me as the romantic, mystical type. He struck me as the exact opposite of that type. "I don't know any Jarods."

My shoulder blades jerked together, and although I didn't think it was possible to feel anything over the insistent ache at my waist, I felt the distinct twinge of a falling feather along with a hefty dose of antipathy for the ishim. How unfair that they'd punish me for a man I hadn't yet met. A figment of my imagination!

Unless they were punishing me for another Jarod. Had one of my sinners been named Jarod? A fellow fletching? An ophanim?

Out of the corner of my eye, I caught the shimmer of my collapsed down. Before I could warn Adam it was sailing straight for his foot, the feather collided into his toes. His knuckles froze on my stomach, and he sucked in air.

I sighed against the hard ridge of his collarbone, preparing myself for a bout of annoyance that he'd been towed into one of my memories, however accidental it was.

Adam came to with a harsh shudder and a harsher exhale. He didn't speak a single word as he resumed his unpleasant knuckle-massage, but the roughness of his fingers spoke volumes.

"Which one of my missions were you privy to?"

Three punitive strokes later, he grumbled, "The hockey schtick. Anderson."

Ah. Anderson. *The college student hooked on performance-*

enhancing drugs. "I think he may have been my longest mission. He kept promising to stop but didn't."

"Of course he didn't. He was obsessed with you, and his little pill-popping got him your attention. Why would he stop?"

I gritted my teeth at the excess force Adam was using. "Anderson wasn't obsessed with me. He had a girlfriend."

"Because that's never stopped a guy . . ."

My head reared back, thumping against the warm stone. "Maybe it's never stopped *you*, but Anderson never tried anything on me."

Although Adam's knuckles still rested on my middle, they no longer moved against me. I'd definitely hit a nerve. Which was probably not the smartest thing I could've done at a time like this, but I was not in the mood to let him judge my sinner unjustly.

"The same way Junior didn't try anything on you? The same way he didn't suggest having his way with you in Caracas?"

I held his narrowed stare. "You said there was no feed inside the bedrooms."

Averting his gaze, he said, "Your earrings are equipped with mics."

"What?" I shrilled, my insides twisting from the abrasive breath it took to cry out the word. "When were you going to tell me?"

"Never."

I shook my head, then blinked back tears that didn't entirely have to do with the wound in my abdomen. When I opened my mouth to call him a jerk, my stomach lurched and expelled something that went plink against the stone. Before the shower spray could wash it away, I clapped my palm over it.

"It's out," I said dully.

I closed my fingers around the chickpea-sized contraption and cocooned it in my shaking fist, before spreading my fingers open, careful to keep my hand cupped.

I waited for the pain to subside, but my insides shuddered, and a rope of tainted blood gushed from my navel, filling the damp air with the stench of decaying flesh.

Bile rose, colors swirled, lines curved. When my head spun this time, not even the strident sound of the silly nickname Adam had given me made it stop.

35

ADAM

ANGELIC FACT #363
IN ORDER TO FLY, YOU MUST DARE TO FALL.

"Naya? I brought you some water. You need to drink." Noah's voice was soft but insistent, like his eyes, like his contorted features.

Tying a towel around my waist, I watched him hold the glass to the girl's pallid lips.

They didn't part.

Naya didn't wake.

It had been a full twenty-four hours since I'd carried her broken body out of the shower and back into the king-size bed.

Twenty-four hours of Noah and I taking shifts to change her blood-soaked bandages and swap the towels we used to keep the bedding somewhat clean.

Twenty-four hours of the room smelling like cooling fire and the inside of a tin can.

Her body would wake when she was ready. Worrying was a waste of our time and energy. She was immortal after all.

And yet, for all my pretense to the contrary, I was worried because I'd never seen an injury like hers. I'd never seen so much blood. What if the explosives never completely dissolved? What would happen to her body then? I'd dialed Dov. He hadn't answered, the same way he still hadn't stopped by or answered my text message about the cost of murdering Triples.

I'd called Apa next but hung up before he could answer. Even though I needed reassurance and Dov wasn't delivering any, I couldn't betray the ishim.

"We need to bring her to a guild." Water sloshed out of the glass Noah banged against the nightstand. "She'll heal faster and—"

"No." I stared at the angel lying in sheets as colorless as her skin, a corpse in a shroud.

I pushed that thought away. *Far* away.

"Adam . . ." There was a tightness to Noah's tone, as though his mood was a rubber band about to snap.

"She's immortal."

"She's in pain."

"She's peaceful."

"She's not forking peaceful! She's burning up! Since when does our kind get a fever?"

"Dov said she'd bleed it out."

"What if he's wrong! Ishim aren't omniscient. You know who is though? Seraphim, that's who!"

"We're not calling her father."

"For fork's sake, Adam, we can't just sit around and do *nothing*."

Noah and I had never fought before. Not over toys when we were kids. Not over girls when we were teens. Not over missions when we'd joined forces. We didn't compete and we didn't disagree. And yet here we were, competing over who was in the wrong and disagreeing over what was right.

All over a girl we barely knew.

"The plastic explosives are tainting her blood, probably heating it as they burn off. Thus, the fever." A load of crap, even to my ears, but she was immortal.

Immortal.

Immortal.

The word bounced around my skull, refusing to settle and imprint. I balled my fingers around the knotted towel at my waist, willing it to stop being fickle and just root itself in already.

"When did you become such an expert on Semtex, huh?" Noah's brown eyes, six shades lighter than Naya's, shone ten shades darker.

"We're out of clean towels and running low on gauze." In other words, *get out of here. Go for a walk. Go clear your head.*

"Are you telling me or ordering me?"

"She'll need both soon."

"Why don't you go play errand boy for once?"

"Because I'm not the one about to lose it." I unknotted the towel and dragged on a pair of jeans Boone had lugged over from Chicago when he'd come to retrieve the device.

Noah jerked a hand over his fade hairdo. "How are you so calm when a girl is bleeding out in our care?"

Sometimes, to do the sensible thing, one needed to be a little heartless. "Not a girl, an angel."

"I swear, Elysian quartz has *nothing* on the hardness of your head," Noah growled.

In any other circumstance, I may have smiled at his lyrical insult, but I had no smile in me.

"I'll go, but I'm not happy about how you're handling things, Adam. Not happy at all." His pink wings bristled as he stormed toward the door, U-turned to grab the pile of towels, then spun around and exited with great fanfare.

Did Noah think keeping Naya here was making me happy? Because it wasn't. It would've been far easier to dump her in a guild and let the ophanim deal with her. Not to mention that, although Galina insisted she had things handled in Chicago, the team had come together for a reason.

Sure, the serial killer case had evolved, and only one human needed protection instead of countless others, but allowing Calliope to carry out her vengeance plan held a crapload of risks. For the angels guarding her. For the grandfather who refused to leave her side. And for Calliope's soul, if the police force got through our defenses.

Our revenge killer and every Circle Girl would benefit from me placing Naya in someone else's care, because, on top of Chicago, a trip to Venezuela was in order.

My crowd-cheer chimed. I dug my cell phone from underneath the itchy plaid blanket that had kept me semi-warm during the night.

LEVI: *Hey. Got news about the girl who died on the plane.*

Her death was ruled a drug overdose. Dunmore sent parents his condolences and promised to ferry the body home and foot all funeral bills.

I gripped my phone so tight I expected it to collapse on itself. Drug overdose, my ass. More like a Semtex overdose.

ME: *I doubt the body will ever make it back onto British soil.*

LEVI: *That's my guess too.*

ME: *How's Calliope?*

LEVI: *She and Galina just took a road trip to get the next one. The one that left town. Galina thought it would be better if C. got out of Chicago, which is crawling with law enforcement.*

ME: *Probably smart.*

ME: *Any word on when Junior's planning his coup?*

LEVI: *Trying to tap into his cell phone but he has some high-tech scrambler in place on that thing. If I can't get through, Boone's going to head over in person and plant a mirror virus on the phone so I can pilot it remotely.*

ME: *Not alone.*

When he didn't immediately shoot me a reply, I added: *Understood?*

LEVI: *He says he won't do anything without consulting you.*

ME: *What about the eSIMs? Can you deactivate them?*

LEVI: *They're not activated.*

I huffed in frustration before rewording my question: *Can you destroy them remotely so they CAN'T be activated?*

LEVI: *To permanently delete them, they have to be activated.*

ME: *So how do we activate them?*

LEVI: *With a QR code.*

ME: *Do it.*

LEVI: *I don't have the QR code.*

ME: *And where is this QR code?*

LEVI: *On the servers of the telecom company.*

LEVI: *Still running the digital SIM's ID through the system. As soon as I get a hit, I'll let you know.*

LEVI: *When are you coming home?*

ME: *When Naya pulls out of this.*

LEVI: *You can't leave Noah with her?*

My gaze slid over her motionless form, over the long sweep of lashes, over the bow-shaped pink mouth.

ME: *She's my responsibility.*

ME: *Send updates as soon as you have any.*

I was contemplating calling my fathers, when the rustle of sheets drew my gaze to the tumble of blonde curls fanned around a face that seemed carved from a block of quartz.

"Don't leave me," Naya murmured.

"I'm not going anywhere."

I was walking over to her bedside when she added, "You promised, Jarod."

A chill wrapped around my spine. Jarod again. Who the Abaddon was this guy? A human, a fletching, a fully-feathered prick?

Ouch. I rubbed my sore shoulder.

The feather hadn't come from there, but the pain had radiated far and wide. If gambling were allowed, I'd wager angels had set up their punitive system to incite us to seal our feathers to our wing bones as swiftly as possible. To think a day would come when I could curse to my heart's content and feel zilch.

"No!" Naya's heartbreaking cry stilled my hand and stopped my heart. "Nonononono!" She'd pretended not to know him, but her distress was too palpable for this person not to be real.

Sweat glossed her forehead. I pressed the backs of my fingers against the fine sheen. *Fire.*

Noah was right, she was burning up. I tossed the comforter off her body, then pushed up her T-shirt to look at the bandage. Soaked.

I grabbed the dwindling roll of gauze on the nightstand, unwrapped it, then peeled away the edges of the one we'd pasted onto her skin, not two hours before, and replaced it with the fresh one. As I taped down the edges, her thin fingers shackled my wrist.

"You can't leave me."

I stared at the galaxy of blue veins marring her clenched lids. Did she mean me this time?

Her fingers towed my hand up to her cheek, flattened it there. "Please, Jarod. Please."

Ah. Not me.

Instinctually, I hadn't liked the guy, but grasping their history strengthened my distaste for him. It also made me realize why she'd pretended not to know him when I'd mentioned him in the shower. I was going to go out on a limb and guess Jarod had abandoned her.

I disengaged my hand from her quivering fingers. "I'm not going anywhere, Feather."

Yeah, I knew she didn't mean me, but I couldn't resist reminding her that I wasn't the fickle jerk. The same way I couldn't resist using that silly nickname that always sparked her temper.

I wanted to kindle that spark.

I wanted her dark eyes to open and telegraph her dissatisfaction.

I flopped down on the side of the bed that still sported the imprint of Noah's body, even though he hadn't lain there in hours, and pulled out my phone, meaning to check the news, when Naya whimpered.

I turned onto my side, crooking one arm under my pillow, and touched her cheek. "You're going to be okay. I swear it on every Elysian star in the firmament. You know, all the ones you're named after?"

A tear slipped from her eye and raced across the length of my middle finger.

Crap. I was so not equipped to deal with tears. Especially when I didn't understand their origin. Was she crying from the pain of the dissolving Semtex or because of the dream she was having of her bastard ex?

"Naya"—I brushed my thumb over her cheekbone, the callused pad of my finger skidding across her dewy skin—"what can I do?"

I didn't expect an answer.

And yet, I got one. She opened her eyes and fixed me with that obsidian stare of hers that reached straight into my soul. "Don't leave me this time." A breath later, her lids sealed, and I wondered if I'd hallucinated her piercing stare.

Was she confusing me for the dumbass she'd dated, or was she calling me out on having left her in the Dunmore manor the night we'd come to get her out?

NAYA

The soft patter of rain against shingles pounded against my nebulous skull.

"She'll heal faster in a guild," Noah was saying.

"We can't bloody bring her to a guild. Her father will rip out our wing bones." *Adam.*

"She's been unconscious for two days, and she's still bleeding."

"As long as she has Semtex inside her, she'll bleed." This was a third voice. Boone's, I thought.

"What if she has Semtex in her system for the next two weeks?" Noah asked. "She doesn't eat and doesn't drink—"

"It won't take that long." I hoped Adam's confidence was borne from actual facts.

"The ophanim could purge it from her system faster," Noah insisted. "They have ways—"

"We cannot plucking bring her to a guild!"

"You can be so selfish sometimes, you know that? *So* selfish."

"This isn't me being selfish, this is me trying to save all our asses!"

"Yeah. Keep telling yourself that."

Maybe Adam was being selfish, but he was also being smart. Carrying me into a guild would ruin everything. I was immortal; I'd eventually make a full recovery. Unlike the Circle Girls.

Had Adam's team found a way to help them? Was that why Boone had come? Had they managed to deactivate the SIMs?

"I promised my parents I'd spend the day with them. It's Ama's birthday." Noah's words were punctuated by sporadic huffs. "I'll be back in the morning. If Naya isn't better by then, and Dov doesn't offer us help, I'm not giving you a choice, Adam." And then the door slammed shut.

Complete and utter silence reigned after Noah's brusque exit. Had they all left? My pulse ramped up at the possibility. I may have been indestructible, but I didn't want to be alone. Since my eyelids were determined not to lift, I listened for sounds.

A heartbeat. A sigh. Anything.

My dread festered and my lungs cramped. They were gone. They'd—

Adam's gravelly voice pricked my eardrums. "You sure you're up to going there on your own, Boone?"

"If you're free to come with, I won't say no."

"Can't."

Warmth spread through my chilled body at Adam's refusal. Maybe my fragile health wasn't his reason for staying, but I couldn't help but feel touched that he was still here when he could've never come at all.

I tried to croak, "Go," but the word stuck to my tongue as my mind turned as fuzzy as the feathers keeping me alive.

NAYA

A hiss made my eyelids flutter. "What happens if he shows up at Emmy's, huh?"

"He won't. I just messaged him that she's on a trip with friends."

"You honestly think her overprotective father will buy that?"

Like puzzle pieces, the room came together before my eyes, interlocking, and the two shapes towering over my bedside filled out with color.

Adam and Noah.

My two faithful nurses.

They didn't notice my opened eyes, much too concentrated on each other's slitted ones.

"I don't have friends I'd go on a trip with," I murmured, voice thick with sleep and disuse.

"You see?" Noah flung one arm out in an *I-told-you-so* gesture before freezing. His head jerked in my direction. "Naya! You're awake!"

I grimaced at the intensity of his pitch.

"Sorry." He cinched his bottom lip with his straight, bright teeth. "Didn't mean to yell."

"That's okay." Although I wanted to stretch, I was much too afraid of angering the dull ache gripping my stomach. "Am I still bleeding?"

"You stopped at dawn." It was Adam who answered.

His voice was so flat that I couldn't help myself from saying, "Contain your excitement."

Noah snorted and smiled, but not Adam.

His pinched lips didn't even bend. "Glad to see your coma didn't do away with your sense of humor."

A phone buzzed. When both Adam and Noah stared at the nightstand, I realized it was probably mine. I reached out for it. The name *Apa* flashed on my screen, along with a picture I'd taken of him after he'd attended Lyla and Arden's "beauty salon" and they'd bedazzled his blond locks with sparkly barrettes.

I smiled until I remembered the reason he was calling. "Where did you say I went?"

"The English countryside." Adam's cheeks hollowed, then filled. "I stayed vague."

I nodded, steeled my spine, and then swiped my finger across the screen to accept the incoming call. "Apa, hi."

"Since when do you take vacations in the middle of your missions?" His voice was so loud, I peeled the phone away from my ear. "And who are these friends?"

"I needed a little break." I glanced up at Adam and Noah. "As for the people I'm with, they're just fletchings I met recently."

"What are their names?"

"Apa . . ." I tried to sound chiding instead of thoroughly apprehensive.

"Names, Naya."

"Why?"

"Because I want to know who my daughter hangs out with."

I sat up, wincing a little. Noah rushed to help, fluffing my pillows.

I whispered a *thank you* that was overpowered by my father exclaiming, "Who—"

"Apa, if I give you their names, you're just going to scare them away the same way you do with all the boys I befriend."

"These friends are boys?" His roar drilled my temples.

"Yes."

"Plural?"

"Yes."

The dimple in Adam's cheek appeared. Clearly, his nerves had loosened, and he was getting a kick out of my cross-examination.

"But they're just that. Friends. And I'd like them to stay this way, since I no longer have Raven." *So, stop* . . .

Even though I didn't utter my request out loud, my father must've gleaned it from my tone, because he breathed through the phone like the horse I'd galloped on before my mission hit the proverbial fan.

"You lost three feathers," he finally said.

I rolled the comforter between my fingertips, staring at the neatly piled logs in the round fireplace. "I'm aware."

"Do your new *friends* have anything to do with your fallen feathers?"

"Haven't you ever lied, Apa?"

Silence. It stretched out for so long that I checked my screen to make sure the call hadn't dropped.

"If you feel the need to lie to these new friends, then they're not people you should be hanging around with, Starlight."

I pinched the soft fabric, flattening it between my thumb and index finger. "It's my fault. *Only* mine."

No longer smirking, Adam crossed his forearms in front of his chest.

"I want to see you." My father's voice was infinitesimally gentler. "I'll pick you up for dinner tonight. Tell me where you are."

My pulse spiked, in time with a bolt of surprise that he couldn't track my phone's GPS. I was assuming Levi had somehow deactivated it. "As soon as I get back, I'll call you."

"Naya . . ." My father sounded exasperated, which was a nice change from his previous livid tone.

"I'll call you as soon as I get back, I promise."

"I don't like this."

I fathomed as much. "Apa, I'm safe and I'm—" *Having fun* would've been a stretch and surely knocked a feather off my wing bones. "I'm safe and I haven't lost track of my purpose."

That would appease him since those were his two biggest concerns. Absurd, considering how ahead of the game I was. Sometimes, it felt like my parents suffered from selective memory loss, like they forgot I'd earned over nine-hundred and forty feathers in half the allotted time I had to build my wings.

"*Ni aheeva ta*, Apa."

He sighed, long and loud. "Not as much as I do, *Kalkohav*."

Regret absconded with the warmth his declaration kindled. I hated not being able to tell him everything. I hated not being able to run to him and hide in his arms until all was well with the worlds again.

When a tear rolled down my cheek, I scrubbed it away. "Give Ama and Lyla a big kiss from me. And Nitznootz. He's still there, right?"

"He's still there."

"Has Mira forgiven Tobias?" I looked over at Adam then. His arms were still crossed, but his shoulders had lost their serrated edges.

My father released a soft snort. "She's prohibited him from gift-giving for the rest of her tenure as ophanim, but she's allowed him to stop by and visit *the pet*, as she calls the poor creature."

"Whom she loves to pieces."

"You know Mira." I was glad to hear the smile that limned my father's words. "She made Nitznootz a bed in her office, even though she claims the blanket on the floor has always been there."

I laughed, and it hurt, but it also felt so good to laugh. After telling my father that I loved him again, I hung up.

Adam was staring at me as though I were part *haccoul*.

"What?" Self-consciously, I patted my hair and cringed. I tried to smooth down the roots and untangle the knots, but my fingers got jammed.

"Thanks for not giving us up."

Oh. I lowered my hand, shifting my gaze over to Noah, who was crouched in front of the fireplace, and nodded as the flickering flames wobbled, spreading over the logs. "Thanks for not giving up on me."

The haze of drugs, the weight of the swamp, the stab of the needle . . . What Robbie and Pablo had done to me came back in such sharp focus that a shudder raced through my body. I blinked the past away and settled on the present.

On the two angels who'd spent countless days and nights holed up in this oddly-shaped bedroom.

I swallowed to moisten my parched throat. "The girls . . . are they still alive?"

When Adam's biceps flexed, I was already jumping to the horrid conclusion that I'd slept through the massacre. "They . . . are." Why had he hesitated? "But Boone overheard a conversation between Robbie and his mother about King Perez's birthday celebration. Robbie was encouraging his mother to leave the country before then."

I spotted a glass of water on my nightstand and reached out, my fingers closing around it with difficulty. "And when is that?" My arm muscles shook as I lifted the drink to my mouth and took a sip that burned as it moistened.

"In three days."

Three days? It was all at once too little time and more than we could've wished for.

"No." Adam's interjection startled me out of my thoughts.

Had Noah asked him something?

He dipped his chin into his neck, pinning me with a pointed look. "Don't even think about it."

Ah. So that's what he'd said no to. Tough luck. "I'm seeing this mission through."

Noah dusted his hands against his jeans as he stood, his metallic wing tips outlining his broad frame like glitter glue. "We've got it handled, Naya."

Hope flared behind my breastbone. "You managed to deactivate the bombs?"

"We're working on it." The ball in Adam's throat rolled.

"In other words, you guys are handling it, but it's *not* handled." I tossed the sheets off my legs. Discovered I was wearing a pair of briefs that weren't mine and that purple pub shirt that was. I decided not to wonder how either got there.

"You're far from healed." Adam's gaze traced the line of mauve skin between the hem of my shirt and the waistband of the briefs.

"I stopped bleeding."

"Just because your wound sealed doesn't mean you're in any state to go gallivanting through South America."

My mind stuck to the word *gallivanting*. Not a word I'd expect to hear drop from Adam's mouth. "You got shot in the leg and still went *gallivanting* through the British wilds, so you're really the last person who should be advising me to sit still."

"Told you your logic was flawed." Noah smiled as he stuck his arms through his leather jacket and shouldered a heavy bag. "Off to launder these in the guild so the hotel personnel doesn't think we murdered anyone during our stay." Noah halted at the door. "Unless you prefer *I* stay, and Adam plays housekeeper for once. Come to think of it"—the bag skated down to the crook of his elbow—"that'd probably do his sullen ass a bunch of good."

Adam flicked his head toward the hearth. "Toss'em into the fire for all I care."

After a lengthy pause, Noah sighed and slid the bag back up his arm. "We're not burning thousand-dollar sheets."

After he dragged the door shut, rattling the forest of glass bottles littering the coffee table, I asked, "What did Boone learn from studying the device inside of me?"

"That it works with an embedded SIM card."

My pulse leaped at the news. "So the bombs go off with a phone call?"

"Once the eSIMs are activated, yes."

"They aren't?"

"No."

"That's . . . good. Right?"

"Yes and no. They need to be activated in order to be permanently deleted. Activation requires a QR code, which the telecom company will send Pablo at his request."

"Can we pose as Pablo and request the QR code?"

"Once we figure out from where the virtual chips were bought, maybe. Levi's started going through all of Dunmore's recent purchases, since Robbie's the one who purchased them, but the Triple uses cryptocurrency for most of his transactions, which makes getting information plucking difficult."

"I'm surprised you haven't been able to pick up anything useful from those nifty earrings Boone made me."

Adam grew very still. "I was hoping you forgot about that."

"I can't believe you were eavesdropping on my conversations." I willed an apology to flutter from his mouth.

"Crypto's hard to trace because hacking the blockchain's virtually impossible."

If he thought we were done discussing the earrings, he had another thing coming. I let it go for now. "Grayson explained the system's complexity to me."

A flicker of annoyance tightened Adam's eyes.

"Maybe he could help us," I mused aloud.

"We're *not* involving humans."

I canted my head to the side. "I thought you worked with law enforcers and experts on *all* your cases?"

His jaw ticked. And ticked. "That may have been a stretch."

Yet, he hadn't lost a feather when he'd gone on and on about it. It had probably been his wording. Cleverly articulated lies flew beneath the ishim's radar.

"Is Grayson out of the hospital?"

"He is." Adam's dismal tone made one of my eyebrows rise.

"Why do you dislike him so much? Did he do something to you when you were dating Emmy?"

"You can't like or dislike someone you don't give a pluck about."

I scrutinized Adam's narrowed stare, then the carpet beneath his sneakered feet. "Regardless of your non-feelings and your rules, Grayson knows blockchains. He could be an asset on the case. Plus, he hates the Dunmores and since he faked an illness, he's already aware of our involvement."

"You should have more faith in Levi."

"I do have faith in him, but I don't see how getting one more person on this case could hurt. We have three days to save forty-nine girls."

"Forty-eight."

"I didn't count Emmy."

"I didn't either."

My heart held very still.

"One of the girls died during the flight."

I sucked in a breath that singed the lining of my throat.

"They're claiming she ODed in the bathroom of the plane. Got the local ME to run a bunch of tests to confirm the presence of drugs in her system. Needless to say, the tests came back positive for heroine but not for Semtex."

I pressed my hand against my banging chest. "Who? Which girl?"

"Does it matter?"

"To me, it does." I'd met all of them.

"Your roommate Natasha."

My body went numb, as though I were being doused in that sleeping gas all over again. "You think she died because of the Semtex or because of me?"

The fact that Adam didn't ask what had made me jump to the latter conclusion told me he was asking himself the same question. That maybe, just maybe, Natasha had heard something that night. That maybe she'd asked questions or refused to believe I'd just up and left.

"Semtex is highly noxious," he said slowly.

In other words, *don't guilt-trip yourself.* How could I not? I may have caused an innocent human's death.

"Naya . . ." Adam sighed. "Even if it's because she heard something, you're not the one who killed her."

I thought of Natasha's bright smile and luminous eyes, how her soul was probably in Elysium. I could ask Eve to seek her out and apologize on my behalf, but that would require explaining what I was apologizing for, and although I considered Eve a confidant, I couldn't very well explain. The quartz walls of the guilds had ears and eyes everywhere.

The fire grew more ravenous in the glassed-off hearth, devouring like my guilt. "What a guardian angel I make . . ."

The knot of Adam's arms loosened. "Without you, we wouldn't have found out what they'd injected inside the girls."

"You tapped into the Dunmores' surveillance equipment. You would've found out with or without me."

"I told you. All we saw were syringes. We wouldn't have learned what was in them without you."

"You're just saying that to make me feel better."

"I'm not."

Our gazes held.

And held.

And then I glanced at the carpet, expecting to find a black feather, but none had fallen. When I looked back up into his face, it seemed alive with a thousand and one contemplations.

"To think a malakim collected her soul. To think our people know and won't intercede." I eased my legs over the side of the bed until I was sitting. Although my insides still felt clapped in a vise, and my bones creaked, and my muscles quivered, my head was clear. "We can't afford to waste another night here."

My comment thinned Adam's full lips.

Before he could dismiss me, I said, "My mission. My call." I pressed my palms into the mattress.

"*Our* mission."

"Fine. But my participation in *our* mission remains *my* call."

"You are so plucking stubborn."

I smiled. "Must be a trait that comes with the color of our feathers."

His nostrils flared with a soft snort. "Or being born on the same day."

"That's right. We are, aren't we? If we looked at all alike, I may have wondered if we were related."

My observation snuffed out what little amusement had lit up his green eyes, apparently horrified by my speculation.

"Don't look *so* disgusted. According to Lyla, I'm a terrific sister."

That didn't smooth out the sharpness that had reshaped his jaw. "I'm of Middle Eastern descent. You, Naya Moreau, are most definitely not."

"What gave it away? My extreme pallor?"

"You are alarmingly pale."

"You should see my bestie, Raven. Her hair's snow white, and her wings and eyes are the palest shade of blue you've ever seen. Like icebergs."

I missed her terribly, but the more I thought about it, the more I realized her absence was a blessing in disguise. Raven would've had a lot to say about my recent decisions.

"Where does it hurt?"

I cleared my throat. "What?"

He gestured to me. "Where does it hurt?"

My guilt must've made me grimace. "Oh. A little everywhere."

His nostrils flared as though angry on my body's behalf.

"You're lucky to have an open-minded best friend like Noah." I left it at that as I pressed myself up.

I stayed standing for all of two seconds before my knees turned to soft rubber and my eyesight, to fine grains of sand. I swayed, but instead of falling backward, I listed toward Adam, who whipped out his arms and caught me. That wouldn't help prove I was in any shape for what was to come.

My vision realigned first, followed by my skeleton, and then my sense of smell. Angels, the boy smelled good—fresh and sweet with the slightest hint of musk. "My blood sugar's low. A little food, and I'll be good to go."

His grunt told me he disagreed about calories being my only issue.

After another moment of using Adam as a crutch, I pressed away from him. Well, tried to. His arms were unyielding.

I turned my face up toward his. Found him glaring down at me with such vigor that it compressed my veins. "I swear I'm going to start pulling my weight."

His eyebrows lowered some more, saturating his vibrant eyes with shadows.

Yes, I'd been diminished, and yes, I'd found myself at the mercy of nefarious men and then at the bottom of a marsh, but not again.

Never again.

As I pressed my palms against Adam's chest to free myself of his grip and prove I was capable of standing on my own two feet, his face loomed closer, so close his breaths nipped my nose before nipping my mouth. Well, the corner of it.

I startled.

Had he just . . . had he just *kissed* me? No . . . Adam would never . . . he'd never kiss me. His mouth must've slipped or— "What was that?"

"What was what?" Irritation deepened his timbre and scowl. Was he irritated with me? With himself?

My pulse whooshed against my eardrums as I raised my fingers and touched the spot his lips had grazed. "Um . . ."

His glaring intensified, making a blush soak my face. I must've imagined the kiss.

Sudden clapping and whistling erupted from his pocket, putting an end to the awkward parenthesis in the life and times of Naya Moreau. Adam's arms loosened like a snipped rubber band as he fished his phone out.

When I wobbled backward, attempting to put some distance between us, his palm smacked the base of my spine to keep me upright. Although I was glad for the support, it forced me to stay near him, which didn't help my body cool off. Thankfully, though, his attention was on his screen and not anywhere in the vicinity of my face. Suddenly, his eyes slitted, and his fingers crimped the back of my T-shirt, fisting the material.

"What happened? Did they detonate the girls?"

He angled the phone screen toward me. As I read the news article, I felt like I was back in the marsh, the icy water enveloping my limbs and filling my lungs.

My fingers shackled Adam's wrist and jerked the phone closer, because I couldn't be reading the words right.

Grayson couldn't be . . .

EVAN.

"Grayson Evan." I read the victim's full name out loud before tapping my index finger against the screen. "Not Rogers. This isn't Emmy's . . ." My voice shriveled back into my throat as my finger inadvertently dragged the article lower, to the headshot of the young Brit who'd gotten struck by a car while crossing a busy intersection in South Kensington. I slapped my mouth. "They claim it's an accident," I croaked through my shaking fingers. "But it wasn't, was it? They targeted him because of what I—what I asked you—Oh, angels . . ."

"Not. Your. Fault." Adam's fingers spread wide on the small of my back. He didn't shake, but his stiffness betrayed how shaken he was. "I should've known. Should've thought my plan through."

"We need to call Emmy." Even though I knew Grayson's soul was safe in Elysium, she didn't. "She must be devastated."

If Dunmore and Pablo had taken out an outsider, what would they do to someone who'd been on the inside?

Adam's grim expression told me his mind had hooked onto the same consideration. In slow-motion, he scrolled through his contacts until he landed on her number and dialed.

It rang and rang.

Went to voicemail.

He tried again.

Voicemail again.

When I gazed up at him, he wouldn't meet my eyes.

Although we angels knew that good souls had a future, seeing mortal life come to an end still affected us, still made our hearts ache.

As his fingers paced across his screen, I traced the pattern of the shoeprint marring the cream wool carpet and thought of the prints each one of us left behind on people and on things.

How considerate Grayson had been by cooking for his busy mother. How gentle he'd acted with Emmy after her benders. How generously he'd behaved when I'd found myself alone in a new city.

Tears for his brief life trickled out. What a loss his passing was for this world.

"She's alive." Adam's voice broke through my little Grayson slideshow. "She's alive and currently flying over the Atlantic."

I palmed my tears. "She's on a plane?" I sucked in a breath. "She's on a plane!"

He didn't have to tell me her destination. I knew it in every fiber of my being. What I didn't know was whether she'd boarded it willingly or had been forced onto it at gunpoint.

ADAM

ANGELIC FACT #76
ONE LOOSE COG CAN COLLAPSE
AN ENTIRE STRUCTURE.

"How do you know?" Naya asked. "That Emmy's alive? Noah just checked her profile on a holo-ranker. That she's headed to Venezuela? From Grayson's last text message."

Dunmore had contacted Emmy to check up on Grayson's health. After she'd told him that he was home and astoundingly fine, Robbie told her there was an airline ticket with her name on it in case she felt like joining them in Caracas, effectively luring her back.

Where grief consumed Naya, rage swallowed me whole. Everything we'd done, we'd done it in vain!

And the collateral damage...

I stabbed my fingers through my hair as I thought of what Emmy had gone and done! Of what she'd set into motion. If she hadn't joined the Circle Girls, Naya wouldn't have ended up at the bottom of a marsh and Grayson wouldn't have been silenced by car tires.

It was wrong of me to blame her for everything, though, 'cause I was the one occupying the highest rung of the onus ladder. After all, *I'd* signed up to Emmy and subsequently dated her to get a foot in

London and observe the Dunmores. And then *I* was the callous ex who'd spurred her desire to leave the city and who must've idiotically dropped the Dunmore Foundation name at some point during the time we'd spent together. As for Naya, she'd signed up to Emmy to meet *me*.

"Show me."

"Show you what?"

Naya nodded to my phone. "Grayson's last—" Her voice caught, held. A ragged breath later, she said, "text."

The girl was distraught, and she'd known the guy what? A week. I'd known Grayson two months. I was admittedly bloody furious he'd passed away, because Emmy's stepbrother had been a decent guy, but his soul was safely tucked in Elysium, so tears were excessive. I avoided reminding Naya that she'd see him again, and soon at that, considering her wing density.

The realization chafed.

Jealousy, that's what it was. Jealousy that Naya was so close to ascension when I was, *by choice*, far from it. That's all it was. I wasn't jealous of Grayson.

The lie detectors grafted on my back thrummed. Okay, fine. I may have been a tad jealous of how into him she was and how into me she was *not*. The look of horror that had crossed her expression when she'd lifted her head and our mouths had sort of accidentally brushed flooded my vision anew.

I swallowed, compacting my annoyance into a ball of spit that I jammed down my throat. "Here." I shoved my phone into her hands, and as she read his final words, snatched my hand off her back and rubbed my pec almost raw.

"Emmy probably doesn't know that Grayson died." Naya's voice was barely above a whisper. "At least, when she lands—when she learns about it, she'll fly home." Tears clumped her lashes, deepening the darkness and shimmer of her stare. "He won't have died in . . . vain." Her brow scrunched.

"You do realize he's living it up in Elysium, what with his single-digit score?"

The darkness of her eyes seemed to ebb and flow right out of her and into me. "You can be so insensitive sometimes."

"How was *that* insensitive?"

"*He* may be all right, but in what state do you think his death left his mother? Or his stepfather? How do you think Emmy will react when she finds out she'll never again get to talk to him or hug him?"

"She probably won't find out. They'll scramble her phone and cut off her access to the internet, and since the untimely death of a nobody won't get international news coverage—"

"Grayson wasn't a nobody!" Color streaked across Naya's cheekbones and jaw, painting her face in more color than I'd ever seen it.

"I didn't mean it like that." I gritted my molars, and my jaw emitted a hollow pop. "I just meant Grayson Evan won't make the Venezuelan papers, so she won't find out he's gone until her soul gets shepherded up to Elysium. And realistically, that'll probably happen sooner rather than later."

Naya's puffy lids pulled up high. "Why do you sound like we've already lost?"

"Because false hope creates false expectations."

"Well, no hope creates *no* expectations," she fired back.

"Glad to see you've fully recovered your wit and fighting spirit."

"Good thing, since you're sorely lacking both." Naya looked around the room before taking a step toward the nightstand. "What time does she land?"

I stuffed my phone into my pocket to be ready in case gravity, again, got the better of the archangel's daughter. "Why?"

She checked the clock on her cell phone's screen. "So we can be there in time to tell her and help her board the next flight home."

"I never thought I'd say this, but Emmy's ticket to surviving is by being an obedient Circle Girl. If she goes home to London, you really think they'll hesitate to off her?"

Naya looked away from her string of notifications, mostly missed calls from her parents. "You think they already injected her with the explosive?"

I shrugged. "Possibly. But if they didn't, they'll probably do it the minute they collect her from the airport."

Naya's phone-laden hand arced toward her thigh, which seemed worryingly frail after her three-day coma, even defined as it was with muscle. I hunted around the room for food, found a bag of crisps on the coffee table. I popped it open and handed it over.

She thanked me and swallowed down a few, wincing after each bite. I seized her glass of water and pushed it into her hands. She drank. When she was done, I took the glass to the bathroom to refill it.

Over the sound of the running tap, I heard her say, "I should never have asked you to bring her home."

I turned off the water, finding Naya in the bathroom doorway. Now that the healing process had started, she was recovering at lightning speed. "Don't."

"Don't what?" She tipped her head back as I strode toward her.

"Play the blame game." *Like me.*

The packet of crisps crinkled. "How can I not blame myself for what's happened? Robbie wouldn't have pursued Grayson if Emmy—"

"Gray's dead because *I* involved him. He's dead because I left him to fend for himself the minute Emmy was on her way home. Want someone to blame, Naya? Blame *me*. Blame the person who came up with the shoddy plan. Who didn't plucking think things through."

Admitting my fault—*faults*—out loud felt like hammering a nail through plaster, subsequently cracking the wall surrounding it. My guardian track record had been spotless, but not anymore.

I banged the water glass down on the sinktop. "Galina got you some clothes. Can't guarantee the fit, but your father will probably like them a lot more than my briefs."

Her cheeks flamed as her gaze dropped to the hem of the T-shirt that barely covered my borrowed underwear, the waistband of which Noah had had to fold a few times.

"Don't look so disgusted. They were fresh out of the guild-hamper."

"I'm not"—she cleared her throat—"disgusted." Since she didn't lose a feather, I supposed she wasn't.

"Just perplexed as to how they got there, then?"

She scrunched up her nose. "I'm *actively* trying not to think about that."

The bastard that I was grinned at her discomfiture. "I'll go get those clothes."

She stepped aside so I could walk past her. "Galina didn't send over a hairbrush by any chance?"

"No, but there's a comb in one of those drawers." I gestured to the cupboard beneath the sink as I returned with an armload of clothes. After depositing them on the rim of the bathtub, I lumbered back over the threshold. "Need help getting dressed?"

Her gaze flipped up to mine, her complexion pinkening again. "No."

"All right then. I'll go tidy up the room. Just yell if you change your mind. I'll be right outside."

As her dark stare spilled across my face, my shoulders itched. Perhaps, I should've admitted Noah had been the one to dress her, that I'd been too shaken to do it, but would it appease her? Noah was as much of a stranger to her as I was and just as heterosexual as I was. I doubted having his eyes and hands on her would make her any less flustered.

I lifted my hand to scratch my itch when my fingertips met feathers. I tried to banish my wings, but for some reason, failed. Naya's cheeks were still rosy, but her gaze was no longer on my eyes. They were on my wings that were stretching and stretching—

I shut the door.

And then I stood there, outside the bathroom, palm flush against the lacquered wood, blood tunneling through my body as though trying to reach the farthest extremities of my body, presently my outstretched wing tips.

I wanted to swear, but my mouth was pinned shut in shock and my mind was whirring, trying to come to terms that I'd just winged someone.

And not just anyone.

Naya Moreau.

A girl who'd either been unconscious, mad at me, or fantasizing about some other guy during the extent of our companionship.

A girl who'd recoiled at the inadvertent touch of my lips.

I hung my head and breathed as the shower spray hit the tiles. I imagined her clothes had come off too, and picturing her naked made another part of my body grow as rigid as my wings.

Pluck. Me.

I never lost control. I was a control freak. What was this girl doing to me?

I forced myself to think of unpleasant things and unpleasant people until my wings no longer felt like rotary blades and my dick, like solid stone. Minutes passed before I even began to cool off.

When I realized it was silent on the other side of the door, that

Naya must've been done with her shower, I snapped into movement, magicking my damn wings away and rushing around the room, tossing stuff haphazardly into two large duffel bags. By the time she stepped out of the bathroom, a pair of jeans hugging her lean legs and a long-sleeved tee hanging off her too-thin upper body, I was zippering the bags closed and panting harder than when I'd fished her out of the swamp.

She carried over the purple shirt and black briefs and held them out.

"Toss'em." I nodded to the trash can besides the oval desk propped against a wall. "They'll just remind you of this place."

"Good." When my eyebrows bent, she said, "I'm not looking to forget what happened to me here."

Slowly, I took the clothes from her, and although cotton held no magical properties, the second my fingers closed around the material, I heard her pained whimpers and breathy moans spurred by a man named Jarod. Even though I wanted to shred the clothes, I hauled the zipper back open and stuffed them inside the bag.

When I looked up, I caught Naya staring at my white-knuckled grip, a frown denting the creamy expanse of her forehead. She'd caught me winging her. She must've. Before she could suggest discussing it, I pointed out the shoes I'd ordered online after I'd measured her feet.

I'd selected something bright, since that was the type of footwear I'd spotted in her wardrobe. Abstract roses decorated the outer sides of the white-soled sneakers and red laces adorned the front.

After opening the box, Naya stared at the contents for a full minute before raising her attention to me. "Galina picked these?"

I tried to glean from her expression whether she liked them or thought they were hideous. Unable to tell, I shrugged a shoulder. "They're the only pair you currently own, so better put them on."

My evasion made her frown, but she sat on the couch and laced them. Before standing, she ran the tip of her finger along the geometrical petals of the rose. "They're gorgeous."

That buffed my ego right up. I still didn't fess up to having bought them, though. I didn't need gratitude or for her to think I had some sort of foot fetish, because I didn't, even though the girl admittedly had pretty feet, as far as feet went.

"I'll let Noah take care of checking out of here when he gets back." I fisted the two duffels as she retrieved her cell phone from the nightstand. "Ready?"

She stared around the room, as though looking for something of hers she may have missed, but the Dunmores had destroyed all her earthly possessions. She combed her fingers through her damp golden locks that were already starting to curl and nodded. "Oh, I'm ready."

She sounded ready for more than just leaving this makeshift infirmary.

She sounded ready to take on the world, or at the very least, the Triples prowling it.

NAYA

*I*t was silly, but I couldn't keep my eyes off my shoes.

After I'd gazed lovingly at them for the thirtieth time since I'd sat down for lunch with my parents in my home guild, Ama cocked an eyebrow. "You and your obsession with shoes."

I startled. "I'm not obsessed with shoes. I just really like them."

"Honey, you're obsessed."

Okay. Maybe I was, but the reason I couldn't stop staring at this pair was because they were so *me*—unlike the jeans and black T-shirt that could've been anyone and everyone.

Where Ama was chirpy as always, Apa had barely said a word since landing in the New York guild after I'd texted him that my schedule had cleared up and I was free for lunch. Guilt-ridden as I was about my undercover mission, I'd barely held his gaze.

My parents were so perceptive that I once asked Ama if the ascended possessed X-ray vision that allowed them to look straight into souls. She'd laughed it off and guaranteed that no one, not even seraphim, could see through flesh and bone.

"Why are you so skinny?" he finally asked.

Ama cocked her head to the side. "Huh. You do look like you've lost a little weight."

I tugged at the hem of my T-shirt, suddenly worried they'd get a glimpse of my mottled abdomen. "I just haven't had much of an appetite."

"Why?" Apa's eyes had turned a frightening shade of teal.

The geometric petals on my sneakers went a little hazy as I evaluated how to best answer that question. "I've just—"

A ball of lime-green fur streaked through the cafeteria and leaped straight onto Apa's lap.

Awesome timing, Nitznootz. I reached over and scratched the *haccoul* behind his tiny, perky ears.

"Naya?" *One-track-minded father of mine.*

I shifted in my seat. "My sinner's surprisingly harder to reform than I initially thought. Not to mention she joined this humanitarian organization in Venezuela, and I guess what with relocating to Caracas, my mind has been on other things than food."

Even though I kept my gaze locked on the purring creature in my father's lap, I could feel my parents eyeing each other, then me, then each other again.

Ama finally sighed. "Tobias's son reformed her right before you did. Maybe we can ask him how he went about achieving it."

"Just took him two months to do it," Apa grumbled.

"Maybe he wasn't in a hurry." I realized, only after I said it, that jumping to Adam's defense may look suspicious. After all, my parents still weren't aware that I knew him, and the last thing I wanted was for them to learn about it. So I added, "Most fletchings aren't in a hurry to reach Elysium. I mean, look at Ama. She used up *all* her allotted time." I wanted to pat myself on the wing for how subtly I'd slid the spotlight over.

Ama held out a green bean to Nitznootz who gobbled it right down. "I did. Almost paid for it dearly though."

Apa's lips flexed, the memory of how close the love of his eternal life had been to failing still fresh in his mind.

I wrinkled my nose. "Sorry to have brought it up."

"The outcome is what's important." Ama patted my hand. "Not what could've been. Now tell me, I hear you're going off on weekends with boys."

I could almost hear all the bones realigning in Apa's jaw as I toyed with a surprisingly tame curl. Raven had been right about combing my hair only when it was wet. It'd probably poof up in no time, but for now, it looked sleek and pretty.

"Naya?" My mother raised an expectant brow.

"I'm making friends. Is that so bad?"

"Of course not, *levsheh*, but these friends must have names?" She and Apa sounded like broken records.

"Doesn't everyone?" I quipped.

She rolled her amber eyes. "You know what I mean, Starlight."

I did. "When I'm ready to introduce you, I will."

My sister arrived then, slicing right through the stilted air with her joyful voice and happy coos directed at her furred bestie. "You know who fell in total love with Nitznootz?"

"Mira?" I suggested.

"Well, duh. Everyone knows that."

I ruffled her hair. "Since when do you say *duh*?"

"It's her new favorite word." Ama sighed, which almost made Apa smile.

Actually, that was me being hopeful. Until I revealed the identity of my new friends, he'd probably wallow in his grumpiness.

"So, who else's heart has Nitznootz captured?"

"Raven's!"

"Did Nitznootz have a vet visit in Elysium?"

"A whatta?"

"Vet? Veterinarian? Forget it. Angelic creatures probably don't need doctors. So, why did Nitznootz go up to Elysium?"

After smacking a loud kiss on the *haccoul*'s head, Lyla peered at me over his flattened ears. Apparently, Nitznootz was still concerned by my sister's expansive affection. "He didn't. Raven came here."

Her avowal sent a lick of pain through my chest. "Raven . . . Raven got her channel key?" I stared between my parents. "Why didn't anyone tell me?"

Ama folded her legs, then refolded them, smoothing out her already smooth leather leggings. "We didn't know about her trip until after she'd returned to Elysium."

Okay . . . but why hadn't Raven at least called me? She'd promised I'd be the first person she'd phone when she returned. "When is she coming back?"

"I don't know, Starlight, but I can find out when I go up tonight. I promised Mimi to have dinner with her." When that failed to lift my spirits, Ama leaned over and captured my hands. "The first time we're allowed to leave, we're not given much time to stay."

I supposed I was taking all of it too personally.

But she was my best friend. *And* she'd promised me.

If the tables had been turned, I never would've broken my promise.

"Is it Chen?" my father asked, severing my train of thoughts.

"What?"

"One of the boys you *vacationed* with? Is it Chen, Akio's son?"

I vaguely remembered the malakim's son from a guild party in Kyoto last year. He'd been super chatty, up until Apa showed up. "I'm not going to tell you so quit trying to find out." I yawned nice and wide before they could cross-examine me some more. "I'm going to bed."

"Already?" Ama glanced up at the sky beyond her mural, still blue.

I kissed my parents and Lyla's cheeks. "Jetlagged." After scratching Nitznootz between the ears, I started toward the dorms.

Apa's gruff voice drifted to me, just as I turned the corner. "You saw her reaction. I bet you it's Chen."

I couldn't help but snort. *Poor guy.* But my amusement tipped and tumbled when I passed by Raven's old bedroom and was reminded of her broken promise.

ALL NIGHT, my mind pinged from Raven to the Circle Girls to Adam, before circling back. When dawn brimmed over the inky darkness, I rolled out of bed and peeled off my sleep shirt on my way to the bathroom. The denim shade of my abdomen had been replaced by a yellow one as bright as an egg yolk bobbing in lavender soup. We really did heal faster between quartz walls.

The skin was still tender to the touch, but at least, it no longer throbbed with a pulse of its own. I showered quickly, then packed the dregs of my closet—items I either hadn't worn in a long time, because the colors were drab, or Elysian frocks I'd never worn at all. I only brought one other pair of shoes, patent black stilettos Ama had bought me because "black went with everything." I'd sighed and mumbled, *"Don't I know it."* After all, I had a black accessory grafted to my back.

Once I'd zipped up my bag, I typed out two messages. One to Adam asking where to meet, and one to Dov asking *to* meet. I hadn't had any contact with the ascended handler, since Noah's introduction two weeks ago. Well, besides his impromptu check-up at the Dunmores, but that didn't qualify as contact since we hadn't spoken.

It felt like months had blinked by since I'd run into Noah in Sweden. Like I'd grown years older, stepped . . . no, *leaped* from childhood into adulthood.

I slid my phone into the back pocket of my pale blue jeans, hoisted my bag off the bed, and stepped into the still-quiet dormitory hallways. Even though I wasn't particularly hungry, I stopped by the cafeteria for a muffin, which I ate beside the fig tree. As I chewed, lost in thought about Emmy and the mission, I closed my eyes and inhaled the forever ripe fruit's fragrance.

Like always, my heart stuttered at the smell, as though someone were reaching through my ribs and flicking the organ. Such a strange reaction. I was about to open my lids and step away, when an image consumed my mind, that of a masked man with dark, glittery eyes. The man I called Jarod.

He reached out and painted the shape of my parted lips with his thumb, his irises color-changing to a shade that rivaled the leaves of the fig tree. *"Tu es ensorcelante, Plume."*

My fingers sprang open around the muffin, and it tumbled to my feet. And then my lids flipped up, and air scorched through my parted lips that tingled from Jarod's phantom caress.

Actually tingled.

Jarod's words—or I guess, *my* words, since hallucinated men didn't speak—skipped against my skull: *You're enchanting, Feather.*

I didn't like Adam's nickname, yet was lending it to my dream man? And what the Abaddon was up with that oil-spill stare of Jarod's veering to green?

Yesterday, the black-winged grump couldn't dump me at the guild quickly enough, yet now I was hallucinating his face over a man I actually liked? I rubbed at my temples. I was losing it. Completely losing it. Exhaustion and stress were taking their toll on my mental wherewithal.

"Who's Jarod?" he'd asked me.

Someone I dream about. Someone who makes my heart ache. Who smells like fig leaves and shadows.

A little like you . . .

Maybe that was why I'd merged the two men. Because Adam's scent reminded me vaguely of my dream stranger's.

I tried to stomp down my troubling lunacy and ease my spiky breathing before it could wheedle my heart any farther up my throat.

"Naya?"

I spun on my pretty sneakers, the red laces blurring like blood smears against the abounding quartz. "Hi, Mira."

Her eyes moved from my bag to my fallen muffin. "Leaving again so soon?"

"I'm not done with my mission."

"I heard."

Had she heard or seen? Ama told me Mira checked the progression of her fletchings' missions on holo-rankers religiously.

"Any chance you could give me a lift to the Caracas guild?" I added a smile to sweeten my request, just as Nitznootz galloped through the cafeteria and pounced on my tumbled breakfast.

Mira's entire face pinched. "At the speed *the pet* eats, he'll grow into a lion."

I laughed as he tore through the breakfast treat, barely leaving the wrapper unscathed. Once he'd licked away every crumb, Nitznootz pranced over to Mira and threaded his lime-green body over and over around her ankles, purring louder than the engine of Adam's bike. Although Mira admittedly made a brave attempt at remaining indifferent, every line on her face softened as she peered down at the streak of pure, furry love.

"Good thing the guild halls are wide enough to accommodate a pride of *haccouls*."

"A pride of—" Mira's attention flipped back to me. "If Tobias brings another one down, I'll—"

"Have to make Nitznootz's bed under your desk wider?"

Her cheekbones became swathed in a color that closely matched her red wings. "Didn't you need to be somewhere, Fletching?"

I grinned, taking such pleasure in ruffling Mira's feathers. "I did. Can you take me?"

"Yes. Let me just—Oh, there you are, Pippa." Mira reached down and scooped up Nitznootz. "Please see that the pet doesn't eat everything in the cafeteria." Mira's fingers stole briskly through the soft pelt before Pippa whisked him into her arms.

As she walked away, the ophanim murmured through a smile, "What do you say we go wake the children, little twinkle?"

Mira huffed. "He won't *say* anything, Pippa. He's an animal, not an angel."

Pippa waved her hand to shush her colleague.

Mira huffed again, but from the way her gaze strained toward Nitznootz, I could tell she considered him far more than an animal, the same way she considered her fletchings far more than her students.

Every inhabitant in this guild, be they furred or feathered, constituted Mira's family.

Even though I hadn't given much thought to my birthmother since discovering her identity, I realized that trying to meet her would be pointless—she'd never fit into my world, the same way I'd never fit into hers. It wasn't so much that I thought we needed to stick to our kind, but the pain of separating from someone you loved had to be excruciating, even if the separation lasted only a couple decades.

"Have angels ever given up their wings for love?" I mused aloud.

Mira's head reared back, sending her blunt, silver-threaded black bob swishing around her ears. "Excuse me?"

"I was just thinking how hard it must be to fall in love with someone you have to leave behind and was wondering if it ever factored into the decision of wing removal."

The blood deserted her face, making her complexion undistinguishable from the wall behind her. "Such drab wonderings for such a lovely morning."

"It's always a lovely morning in Elysium." I lifted my gaze to the skylight that extended the length of the hallway.

"Sometimes, it rains."

"Even when it does, there's sunshine." I squinted into the blushing sky, marbled with veins of pink and lavender. "You know, Mira, people usually discuss the weather to avoid touching upon deeper subjects."

She halted at the entrance to the channel. "That subject is one I dislike immensely."

"Love, or becoming a nephilim?"

"Becoming a nephilim *for* love." Was it the effect of the Elysian light, or were her dark eyes uncharacteristically shiny?

Although I sensed I was tiptoeing upon her last nerve, I pushed my luck. "Why would an angel choose to give up their wings when they could wait a few decades for their beloved's soul to ascend?"

"Enough, Naya." Mira stared over my shoulder at the sparkling channel vapors. "That's enough."

But I had *so* many more questions.

As she tugged me into the Elysian light that carried us thousands of miles away in the blink of an eye, the chilling answer laced around my bones like a skin-tight corset. They gave up their immortality because their beloved's soul would not, *could not* be collected by a malakim.

How veritably tragic.

Perhaps that was the reason my parents were so adamant I hurry on up to Elysium . . . so that I didn't fall in love with a human bound to annihilation or a fletching incapable of completing their wings.

Inexplicably, my mind veered to Adam.

Not inexplicably, *per se* . . .

His wing-score was particularly low for someone who'd been out in the world for four years. But then I recalled Ama's wing score before Apa walked back into her life and she walked into mine. If she'd managed to earn seven-hundred feathers in three months, then surely Adam could collect the same amount in six years.

Not that it mattered to me what became of his soul.

My wing bones tightened. And tightened.

When the pressure released, I peered past the billowing smoke twirling over the channel floor and winced.

40

NAYA

Mira tracked my gaze and gawked. "What in the worlds? Is that yours?"

"Adam's not around, so I'm guessing, yes."

Her gaze bulleted back to mine.

"You know . . ." Heat billowed up my neck and jaw. "Since he's the only other fletching with black wings." *Ugh.* Why did I have to go and mention him?

I pressed my palm to the base of my neck in an attempt to cool myself off. Thankfully, the channel brightened then, and pulsed so much sparkly smoke that it veiled my blush. I stepped out to give the travelers room to land and to put some distance between myself and Mira before she could pepper me with any more questions on the subject of my feather's collapse.

I preferred not to lose another. "Thanks for the ride, Mira." I started to retreat when I caught sight of swooping blond locks and retracting golden wings.

"Ophan." Dov inclined his head in greeting.

"Dov." Mira's tone was as dry as the Arizonian heat.

Dov smiled at her; she didn't smile back. Not unusual for Mira, who wasn't one to wear her heart on her wings.

He turned that smile on me. "Fletching."

When he didn't tack my name onto my title, I took it he was pretending that we hadn't met and went along with the ruse. "Good morning, Ish." I allowed myself to speak his title. After all, he was wearing the customary gray ranker uniform.

Mira stared daggers at his angular jaw covered in neat scruff. "What brings you down from Elysium, Dov?"

"Must I have a reason to visit Earth, Ophan?"

Even though most angels referred to Mira as *Ophan Mira*, my professor was staunchly opposed to the use of titles among ascended because she believed it added to the manifest segregation between hybrids and verities.

"Yes." Mira was all angles. Even the red down of her wings seemed to have grown points. The last time I'd seen her this tense was when Seraph Claire had stopped by the guild to congratulate me on my first successful mission and to catch a glimpse of my much-talked about, odd-hued plumage.

"Even though I outrank you, I'll indulge your curiosity just this once. I've come to iron out the rebellious streak of a misbehaving fletching since the ophanim are failing at their duty to oversee our young."

His hostility toward Mira made me bristle, but I reasoned Dov's caustic words were intended to confound Mira as to his true reason for coming to Earth.

"Have an auspicious day, Ophan." Without casting her, or me, another glance, he strode out of the channel.

I started to go after him, when Mira muttered, "Self-righteous prick."

"Mira," I gasped.

She lifted her pointy chin a notch higher. "Whatever you do, Naya, you stay away from that man."

I wrapped my fingers around the straps of my bag and heaved it up my arm, my blood pumping faster. "Why?"

"Because he"—she wet her lips—"because your father wouldn't like you spending time in Dov's company."

Oh. The pressure in my veins deflated as swiftly as it had increased. I almost smiled but forced myself not to. I didn't want to appear disrespectful, especially since Mira was trying to protect me.

"I'll see you in a few days." I smiled as I backed away from the frothing channel.

"With new growths."

"Yes. Promise."

"What about the fallen feather?"

"I don't feel like walking down memory lane." Before she could suggest I do so to make sure I didn't lose track of my purpose, I whipped out an, "I love you."

She harrumphed as though the sentiment was ludicrous.

"I'm expecting you to say it back to me someday, you know."

"Complete your wings, and I might."

"I'm holding you to it, Mira." I blew her a kiss and hurried away.

As I trekked through the guild, I crossed paths with two fletchings on their way to breakfast. They gave me a cursory glance. Had my wings been on display, the once-over would've been interminable, but I'd learned early on to keep my odd wings magicked away outside my home guild.

After the guild door banged shut behind me, I looked up and down the city street for a pair of golden wings but caught no ethereal sparkle among the thready crowd of early-morning risers.

"Care for a ride, Fletching?"

I craned my neck.

Dov hovered just out of reach, wings pulsing the pale dawn. "It'll be quicker to reach the hotel."

I'd only ever been airlifted by my father and had loved every exhilarating minute of it. "Sure."

He banded his forearms around my middle and hooked my sneakered feet with his booted ones. I winced as he shot upward and his ulna compressed the bruise yellowing my abdomen.

I was about to suggest turning around but decided I'd rather suffer than have my front pressed against his. To forget about the pain, I concentrated on my bird's-eye view of Caracas, a city built from as many skyscrapers and as much asphalt as the one I'd left behind.

The warm wind kissed my cheeks and whisked my hair into a frenzy as we sailed past buildings silvered by the rising sun. Although the flight was short, it filled my veins with a cocktail of adrenaline and energy. I clung to this heady feeling as we touched down in front of a high-rise hotel manned by men in cream-colored uniforms.

None of them blinked at our sudden apparition, probably because Dov had sprinkled his angel dust to camouflage us. We stepped through a lobby dripping with a surplus of gilded items that reflected my haggard face from twenty different angles.

I wasn't vain but cringed at the sight of my insipid complexion and tousled whorls of hair. As Dov led the way to the bank of mirrored elevators, I smoothed my locks out.

"Everyone's staying here. The Dunmores. The Circle Girls. The Prince. I've got dust concealing you for now, but you may want to keep promenading through the hotel to a minimum, since your body's supposed to be resting with the fishes."

The crisp memory sent a shudder through the fingers unsnarling my hair. As though I were underwater again, my lungs gripped my exhale, only freeing it once the elevator dinged and opened on a high floor. We walked to one end of the carpeted corridor, and Dov knocked.

A second later, the door opened, and Galina all but squealed, "Naya!" engulfing me in a hug. "You scared the soul out of us, love." She pressed away from me and ogled my stomach. "You're healed, yeah?"

"Almost like new."

Dov nodded to the room, and I stepped inside. Once the door shut, he whisked away his gold appendages.

"This place is sick, Big D."

"Glad it's up to your standards, Galina." He tipped her a curt smile as he stepped into a room twice as vast as the bedroom I'd shared with Natasha and Emmy back in the Dunmore mansion.

Navy velvet framed a bay window that stretched the length of the space and overlooked a manicured public park.

"*El Jardín del Príncipe.*" Adam's deep voice startled me out of my botanical contemplation.

I lowered my bag to the chocolate marble flooring. "It's truly Pablo's private garden or it's just named that way?"

"Truly his garden. His hotel too, for that matter." Still studying the mandala-shaped pathways snaking through lush vegetation forty stories below us, he asked, "How's the bruising?"

"Fading."

He side-eyed me.

Did he think I was downplaying my injury? "The guild's magical air works wonders."

His mouth thinned, and I bit my lip as I remembered Noah and him fighting over whether to bring me to one. Before I could tell him I wouldn't have wished he'd done anything differently, hands clapped.

"Shorhim, I don't have much time. Walk me through your grand plan."

I turned away from the window and took in the rest of the room. The brothers sat on a couch. Where Boone waved hello, Levi didn't. Noah, looking comfy in an overstuffed armchair, sent me a wink just as Galina dropped down beside him and nestled into his side.

It had been months since I'd sunk against another person. Well, besides Adam. Sinking into him hadn't been out of comfort, though, but out of necessity.

"Our plan depends on the answer to the question I texted you, Dov." Adam crossed his arms, and his elbow grazed the side of my biceps, leaving behind a streak of heat.

"What question is that, Adam? You ask many."

"Can we kill Triples without consequence?"

NAYA

*D*ov's gray eyes set on Adam's emerald ones. "By answering your question, I'd be infringing Elysian law."

Adam's jaw flexed. "By being here, you're infringing it."

The ishim's eyes narrowed a fraction, clearly not appreciating the reminder. "I suppose you're right."

"So?"

"Yes."

"Yes, there are no consequences to killing Triples?"

He nodded.

The collective exhale that ensued was so loud it thumped against my eardrums.

"Then there's your plan."

"Adam," I gasped, "we can't just go around killing humans."

He glanced down at me. "Not mere humans. Triples. And Dov just confirmed we *can*."

My shock didn't dwindle. "We're supposed to be guardian angels, not homicidal ones."

"Although I also prefer peaceful resolutions," Dov said, "killing Dunmore and Perez will save a lot of humans."

I gaped at the ishim, stunned he was on board with Adam's plan.

"May I suggest you divide and conquer, though? Adam, no one knows Robbie Dunmore as well as you do. And, Naya, Pablo seemed quite fond of you. You should concentrate on him."

"Pablo believes I'm dead. *You* even told me to lie low."

"Imagine his surprise, and pleasure, when he finds out you aren't."

Adam took a step forward, and his wings unfurled, as though to shear me off from Dov's sight. "No."

"No to what?" the ishim asked.

"We're not using Naya to trap Junior." After a beat, he added, "As long as I'm killing one Triple, I may as well kill two."

"That's far from your wisest plan, Adam."

"I agree. It's epically *stupid*." Noah removed his arm from around Galina and scooted forward on the seat cushion.

"Tell me how you really feel, No," Adam grumbled.

"Get Robbie to turn on Pablo!" Noah slapped his thighs. "They can take each other out."

"How do you suggest we do that, love?" Galina had sprawled out over the space Noah had vacated and draped her legs over the tufted arm.

"The Prince is superstitious." Levi glanced at his tablet that had just sounded with a notification. It mustn't have been all that important, because he didn't click on it. "He believes in our kind and all. Naya can pretend to be a ghost that came to warn him of Robbie's duplicity."

"What part of *we're not involving her* wasn't clear?" Adam all but growled, leathery-black wings extending and retracting in time with his chest.

Beyond the bulging ridges of his body, I caught Levi sandwiching his lips, cowed that his idea hadn't appealed to Adam.

"I was just trying to help." He sounded like the kid he was then.

Dov rubbed his mouth, and the tiny action reminded me of Grayson. Since Dov wasn't hiding crooked teeth, I wasn't certain what he was trying to conceal. His disagreement with Levi or his enthusiasm at the idea of turning me into a wraith? Even though I wasn't crazy about the young angel, I wasn't completely opposed to his scheme.

I leaned back against the picture window. "What do you think, Dov?"

Adam's shoulders tensed along with his wings, and then his neck was twisting, and his eyes homing in on mine. "You can't seriously be considering this?"

"I'm immortal."

Adam's arms untangled and shot skyward in exasperation. "Just a day ago, you were bleeding out!"

"And I healed." I kept my tone calm, hoping it would soothe his temper.

He stared at me in loaded silence for a full minute. Then his head jerked back around. "Noah!"

Galina jumped from the intensity of Adam's voice, but not Noah.

Sighing, he cupped his kneecaps. "Yeah?"

"You agree with me, right?"

"Of course, man. Of course I agree with you." He stood, walked over to the chocolate-marble bar in the corner, then crouched to retrieve a water bottle from the built-in fridge.

"I think we should *all*"—Boone ferried a look Adam's way—"stay inside the suite until Levi finishes creating the deepfake aural bytes to get the SIM card provider to send us the QR code."

My pulse ticked faster. "You managed to find the telecom provider?"

Boone nodded.

Dov's eyebrows bent. "You lost me, Boone. A deepfake what?"

"Deepfakes are fakes that are so well made they seem real." Levi's answer was a grumbly mutter. Clearly, he was still miffed about Adam's reaction to his idea.

"And why do you need a QR code?" The furrows carving Dov's brow indicated he wasn't up to date on Robbie and Pablo's scheme.

"To activate the SIMs in the detonators," Boone said.

Dov's eyebrows jacked up another inch. "I thought you wanted to save these girls."

"In order to do so, Big D, we need to make the SIMs visible by activating them. Only then will we be able to delete them. Sounds counterintuitive, I know."

"And by activating them, you don't chance detonating the humans?"

"The bombs can only be triggered by a phone call." Galina twisted her diamond nose stud. "As long as no one dials, they're safe."

"And one QR code will activate all of them?" Dov inquired.

"Yeah." Boone cracked his knuckles. "They're all connected."

So Pablo was planning on detonating us all at the same time . . . *One, big, bloody splash.* "How did you find out?"

Boone scratched a stain on his jeans. "The pearls. Susan Dunmore's been wearing them." Was it me, or did he sound sheepish? "She asked Robbie how the bombs would go off. That's also how we got the telecom company's name."

Dov clapped to get everyone's attention. "Sounds to me like you have a lot of leads but no unanimous plan of action."

"Retrieving that QR code *is* our unanimous plan of action," Noah said. "Right, guys?"

Adam was the only one who didn't nod.

"Your team leader doesn't seem on board." Dov stared at Adam who stared right back.

"King Perez's birthday is in two days." Was Adam reminding us or informing Dov? "If by tomorrow night, we haven't made any headway in dismantling the SIM cards"—a feather dropped from Adam's wings—"I'll take care of both Junior and Dunmore."

A chill webbed my skin. "I know they're Triples, but how can premeditated murder be penalty-free?" I gestured to the fallen feather seesawing on the russet stone. "I mean, Adam lost a feather from just thinking about murdering them."

Dov shook out his wings as though dust had accumulated along his golden plumage. "It's penalty-free, because angels don't care about truly despicable souls."

"If our people don't care about them, then why are they in the system in the first place? Why do we even try to reform them?"

"Because all human souls are in the system, Naya." Dov fluffed his wings again. "Even the worthless ones. That being said, I preferred Noah's plan of getting Perez to dispatch his friend's vile soul. Considering how expeditiously the Prince murdered his own cousin when he learned of your demise, I doubt he'd hesitate to put a bullet through his childhood friend's skull."

I curled one arm around my stomach as though Luis stood in front of me, armed with his big syringe.

"What about the Prince?" Galina asked. "Who takes him out?"

"You could ask his father." Dov stared over my shoulder, at the awakening city beyond the picture window. "I'd wager he'd have no objection."

Horror and shock basted my tongue. "How could you suggest such a thing?"

"There are rumors the King bathes in the blood of his enemies." Dov's gaze shifted back to me. "They aren't rumors. I've seen him do it. He's a monster, Naya. The truest one you'll ever meet. Dunmore and Perez are choirboys compared to him." He shook his head as though to clear it of the memory of the monarch steeping in a crimson pool.

"Then why are we concentrating on the son? We may as well help the Prince get the throne." Galina mused. "In exchange, we'll ask him to remove the explosives he packed in the Circle Girls."

Dov sighed. "You'd merely be switching one tyrant out for another."

"Our objective is to save the Circle Girls, Dov." My voice barely carried through the room. "And we have two days to do it."

"The only way you'll save them is by getting rid of Robbie, because as long as he's here, he'll be whispering in his friend's ear. Once Dunmore's dealt with, you could try and haggle with the Prince. Might work. Might not."

"If we get the QR code, we don't have to interact with anyone," Boone said.

"*If* you get it. In the meantime, you don't have it." Dov's gaze cycled around the room, before stilling on the youngest shorhim. "I think Levi was onto something when he suggested Naya return from the dead..."

Levi sat up.

"You could surprise the Prince in his apartment tonight, Naya. I could fly you up there, and—"

"Out of the plucking question!" Adam's vertebrae stood out in sharp relief between his wings.

I laid my palm over his arm, felt muscle, sinew, and bone roil beneath my touch. Adam looked at my hand, looked at me, then stepped away as though disgusted I'd touched him.

I rolled my fingers into my palms. "I could call him. Or text him, if you guys have his number."

"Without proof of life, he could assume you're a... What is it you children called it again? A profound fake?"

"A deepfake." Galina's gray top rode up her carved stomach. Even with all my training, I'd never achieved abs like hers. "The

Prince and Dunmore are organizing a party in the garden tonight. In honor of the Circle Girls. Maybe you can make a cameo, Naya."

Dov's eyes shone like foil in his tanned, chiseled face. "Perfect!"

"Perfect?" Adam spat out the word. "You call *me* reckless, but you're okay with Naya prancing around a park full of trigger-happy Triples? And guards! Have you forgotten how much security the Prince has?" Adam's hand slashed the air. "Levi can doctor the hotel's security feed and send some stills to Junior."

"Technology's useful, Adam, but there's nothing more convincing than reality. Besides, there'll be a crowd. They won't open fire. Can you imagine the chaos that would ensue?"

Adam's jaw clicked. Audibly clicked.

"Excuse me if I'm slow on the uptake, but how will Naya's ghost motivate Pablo to kill Robbie?" Boone asked.

"If the Prince thinks Robbie lied about Naya being dead to keep her for himself," Dov explained, "it will anger him."

I slipped my arm off my waist and let it settle back along my ribs. "Except Robbie doesn't like me, Dov."

"But Pablo isn't aware of that. And whose word is he more likely to believe?"

Levi swept his fingers through his disheveled hair. "His friend's."

"Wrong, Levi." Dov's voice sliced through the strained atmosphere. "The girl who traveled all the way to Caracas for him, that's who. The girl over whom he killed his own flesh and blood."

"Seriously?" Levi eyed me, as though trying to figure out how a girl like me could possibly incite men to kill each other.

I had to admit, I was wondering the same thing. My conclusion was that Pablo was *that* unhinged. Or that he'd used me as an excuse to get rid of someone he hadn't fully trusted.

Adam tossed his hands in the air. "I think you're all out of your effing minds!"

"Says the person who wants to go all Rambo on their asses," Galina muttered to no one in particular.

"Naya, what would you prefer? Sit back and have Adam eliminate them, or go out there and sow confusion and distrust?"

When Dov put it that way . . . "Obviously, the latter."

"Good." Dov walked to the door. "I have a lot of work up in Elysium with the onslaught of new ishim trainees, but I'll try to travel down to check my phone time and again. Text me if you need anything. And as usual, charge anything you need to the room."

I bit my lip, released it. "Dov?"

His hand closed around the doorknob. "Yes, Naya?"

"How did you hear about the Prince's cousin? Did a malakim recover his soul?"

"No. The man died a Triple."

"Then . . . *how*?"

Dov nodded to Boone, then wished us good luck, before letting himself out.

The tinkerer shifted around on his seat cushion before tucking a long strand of hair behind his ear and peeping up at me. "I'm really sorry we didn't tell you the pearls were equipped with mics. It wasn't cool of us."

No, it wasn't. "At least, you're getting priceless intel from Susan wearing them."

He swallowed, toyed with his hair some more. "Yeah. Anyway, we should, um . . . get to work. Adam?"

Adam's rigid form thawed at being called upon. "How long do you still need to polish the audio, Levi?"

"Couple hours."

"I want you to concentrate only on that. Boone, map out the cameras in the hotel. I want to gather footage of Naya walking around after Dunmore and the Circle Girls leave for their daily outing. What time are they heading out to the slums again, Galina?"

"Eleven."

Adam magicked away his wings. "Be ready then, Naya. We'll head down to the lobby together."

"What about the garden party?" I asked.

"If Levi isn't done by tonight, then we'll go. But only if he isn't done."

"It's cocktail attire." Galina got up from the couch. "Did you pack any dresses, Naya?"

"I did."

She leaned over and grabbed my duffel. "You're sleeping in my room by the way. Let's get you set up."

"We'll need dinner jackets to blend in," I heard Noah say, as I followed Galina toward an open doorway. "Mine's at the guild."

"*We?*"

"If we crash the garden party, we do it as a team." Noah's tone brooked no argument.

Adam's answer was slow to come, but eventually he said, "Fine. I'll grab them from the guild this afternoon."

"Bring me one?" Boone asked. "Unless you prefer I stay with Levi..."

"No, I prefer you come with us. The more backup, the better. In case Naya's *ghost* becomes too real." He added loudly so that his words carried into my latest bedroom.

I tried not to let his stress and disapproval get to me. After all, if our plan worked, if we managed to turn Pablo against Robbie, it'd keep Adam from spilling blood.

Murdering Triples may not have harmed our wings, but it couldn't possibly leave our consciences unscathed.

42

ADAM

ANGELIC FACT #559
ANGELS AREN'T GODS EVEN THOUGH
MANY ACT AS SUCH.

I plugged my ear and pinned my cell phone to the other. "You don't make your move until we get back. Got it, Calliope?"

Two girls walking arm-in-arm, wearing bikini tops and micro shorts, rammed into me as I crossed the busy street. They both exclaimed apologies and then one of them proceeded to stroke my biceps as though to mitigate a potential bruise. I cinched her wrist and, as politely as possible, flung it away.

Where did people get off thinking that petting a stranger was acceptable? If I'd done it to them, they would've slapped me with a lawsuit.

"I took care of them on my own before you." I barely heard Calliope's response over the aggressive honks of merging traffic.

How I missed the silence of autonomous vehicles, but they'd yet to become the norm in countries where people had trouble affording basic commodities.

"The FBI wasn't sniffing up your trail then." Levi had gotten that information off a tap he'd put on the detective's phone. The man had been pissed the case had been turned over to the Feds and had begrudgingly conveyed his findings. One of which had been the Big Sister program that had led us to Calliope.

"If I wait, they'll give my last target a new identity, and I'll never find him."

"They won't. Not yet anyway. They'll use him as catnip to trap you."

Calliope got so quiet I wondered if she'd hung up.

"Don't step out of the safehouse, okay?"

"Okay. Fine." She sounded as sullen as I used to when I misbehaved as a child and my fathers sat me down for three interminable minutes in front of the boring quartz wall to contemplate the error of my ways.

"Put Gregory on the phone. I'd like to talk to him."

"Why?"

"Because I've got something to ask him." It chafed that she was still suspicious of us after all we'd done for her, but the humans we guarded usually were. Gratitude came with hindsight, once it hit them how close they'd been to losing their lives.

"Ask me."

"No."

She expelled a disgruntled sigh.

"Please," I added.

Another sigh. Slightly less irritated. Then a door creaked. "Pops, Adam wants to talk to you."

"Who?" Granted, Galina and Boone had spent the most time with the Underwoods, but was I truly *that* forgettable?

"You know, one of the guys helping us."

"Oh." Springs creaked, and then Gregory yawned.

I tried to feel bad about having woken her old man up, but truth was, I needed to hear him confirm he'd rein in his granddaughter in order to focus fully on the Circle Girls case.

"Hello?"

"Greg, my team and I are going to be out of town until Monday. I've already had a talk with Calliope about lying low, but I need you to make sure she does."

The scrape of a palm across buzzed hair rustled through the receiver. After a brief pause, he sighed. "I'll make sure she stays put."

"Jesus, that's what you wanted to ask him? I told you I'd wait," Calliope huffed from somewhere nearby.

"Just wanted to have an extra person holding you to it. And, Calliope, since you can hear me, don't forget that if the cops catch you, they catch Gregory."

Silence.

"I didn't forget." Calliope's usually blunt voice was sanded down. "I would never compromise him."

I was glad she was fully aware that her fate was tied to his. "Or yourself."

"Or myself," she confirmed.

"You've got enough food to last you the weekend?"

"Yeah."

"Good. If you need anything, call Galina. Otherwise, we'll see you next week." And then I disconnected, pushed my baseball cap farther down to shade my face, and entered the hotel.

When a voice I knew only too well assaulted my eardrums, I ducked behind one of the gold columns in the expansive lobby.

"I'm so glad I didn't miss this trip," Emmy told one of her new girlfriends.

Yeah . . . She'd probably think otherwise if she found out about Robbie and Pablo's intent. The temptation to tell her about Grayson itched my throat, but a freak-out wouldn't work in her favor. Or, in ours.

Emmy's voice drifted toward me again, louder this time, like nails against a chalkboard. Estimating it was coming from my right, I went left, skirting the column until all I saw of her was her brown ponytail swishing excitedly over a teal jacket that looked familiar.

Wasn't it Naya's? Silver wings were embroidered on the silk. Definitely Naya's. Here I thought I'd helped Emmy overcome her kleptomania, but apparently not.

Pity imbued me as Emmy retreated. Not regret. Not desire. Not even anger. Pure pity for a girl who aspired to be someone she wasn't because she hated the person she was. To think I used to look forward to crawling into her bed after I returned from prowling the London streets to stop crime. To think I used to get hard at the sight of her. My dick didn't even twitch. Not at the sight of her or of her leggy friends. I scanned the busy lobby, my eyes pinging from one pretty body to the next. Not a single person's physique lit up my blood.

I told myself it was because I was wound too tight and not because I was inexplicably obsessed with a girl I had no business being attracted to.

I pivoted, my sneakers squeaking against the buffed floor, and walked to the bank of elevators, blood lashing my veins as the face I'd pictured in the shower that very morning came into crisp focus inside my mind.

I jammed my finger into the elevator call button and banished the sight of Naya's blonde mane and soulful eyes.

She wasn't even my type. My type was no wings, no hang-ups on other men, and no blood relation to archangels.

I punched my thumb into the call button because the damn elevator had still not shown up. Had our room not been on the forty-eighth floor, I may have taken the stairs. I probably should have, considering my sudden excess energy.

The doors finally ground open, and a small crowd outfitted in suits and fancy dresses spilled out. I gaped for all of a second at the head that bobbed above the others like an orange reed—Robbie Dunmore. When his gaze flicked to my shadowed one, I stepped into the space that reeked of too many perfumes and cast my attention on my phone, pretending to be engrossed by an email from the vehicle dealership back in Chicago, asking if I wanted to extend the lease on my bike.

I typed out a *YES*, then scrolled through the rest of my messages. The ride up took mere seconds but felt excruciatingly slow. Thankfully, it didn't stop on any floor since everyone was headed to the hotel gardens.

We'd cased the glitzed-up area where they were throwing the event earlier with Noah and Boone, adding cameras to blind spots. Although I was still hoping Levi'd come through with the audio files, I wanted to be prepared in case he needed more time.

I let myself into the suite that vibrated with loud electronic music—Boone's favorite. Levi was propped at the bar, sipping Coke through a glass straw, while his brother and Noah were seated at the six-person dining table, noshing on room service burgers.

"We got you one too." Noah nodded to a plate covered by a cloche.

"Had dinner with the dads, but I'm sure I'll have room for it after." I tossed the garment bag holding our dinner jackets on the couch. "Any luck on that audio, Levi?"

He speared his hand through his fluffy hair, which he'd visibly been messing with for hours, and winced. "I'm still missing two key words. I'm really sorry, Adam."

"It's fine." We were ready for operation-ghost anyway. "Where are the girls?"

"Galina went to find a mask." Noah waved to the room Galina had elected as hers, the largest of the three bedrooms in the suite. "And Naya's getting ready."

"A mask?"

Noah dabbed at a glop of ketchup on the side of his mouth. "She thinks Naya should keep her face hidden."

"Smart. Earpieces?"

"On the bar," Boone said around a mouthful of food.

"I spy two."

Boone swallowed, before gulping down some water. "Galina and Noah already have theirs. The remaining two are for you and Naya."

My eyebrows spiked. "What about you?"

"I think I should stay up here to monitor the cameras. There are a lot of them." He twisted a fry in the ketchup he'd puddled on the side of his plate. "Unless you really want me down there . . ."

"No. Stay up here. It's better." Since I was on my way to check up on Naya, I pocketed the two earpieces. Deep down, I was hoping she'd changed her mind.

I strolled toward the girls' bedroom and was about to knuckle the gaping door when my hand froze in midair. Naya stood before a mirror, slicking crimson lipstick over her parted lips, body gloved in black sequins, and hair—

I clutched the doorframe. "What the Abaddon are you wearing and what have you done to your hair?"

She startled, stamping lipstick on the cleft above her mouth. "Galina straightened it, so I'd look like myself . . . but not." She lowered the wand, rolled it back into the tube, and headed to the bathroom. "As for what I'm wearing, it's called a dress." A moment later, she returned, stain gone, lips impeccably filled out.

The urge to tell her to change into something with a lot more fabric seized my tongue, but what right did I have to comment on the way she dressed? She wasn't my girlfriend. When she turned to grab something from her nightstand, my ears began to ring and my fly to dig into my swelling cock.

In a spectacular display of observational skills, I said, "Your hair's long." It hit her tailbone.

As though I'd made her self-conscious about it, she gathered it in her fist, drawing my gaze to her fully exposed spine.

The buzzing in my ears grew brassier, and my cock, thicker. I was either going to burst a coronary or my fly if I kept gawping at the backless frock that dipped so low, I spotted dimples at the base of her spine as well as a heart-shaped sequin holding two black strings.

Pluck.

Me.

Was that her thong?

"Aren't you going to change?" She nodded to my black jeans and black T-shirt as she slipped her feet into a pair of shiny stilettos.

I hoped Galina would bring back an ankle-length shapeless coat along with that mask.

"Adam?"

"What?" I snapped, every cell in my body and nerve ending on high alert.

Naya crossed her arms. "I know you hate this plan, but don't take it out on me, okay?"

The plan currently rated number two on the list of things I hated, number one being how gorgeous Naya looked. I hauled my gaze away from her barely-there dress and set it on the illuminated gardens beyond her window. My body was tingling, twitching, my wings angling to make an appearance and stretch out.

I needed air, preferably not drenched in her sweet scent, and distance before my wings sprung out and ridiculed me once again.

I shoved away from the doorframe, when something glittered outside. Instead of backing out of the room, I plodded forward, searching the darkness for an explosion. Or fireworks. Or—

A soft gasp made my gaze zip off the glittery glass.

My pupils and veins dilated at the sight of Naya shimmering from wingtip to fingernail. When the influx of syrupy blood hit my heart, it, too, puffed.

Her wings had materialized, and although she'd curled them around her shoulders, they did jack to hide her splendor.

She lifted her hands and twirled them in front of her wide eyes, and my wonder turned to confusion. She swallowed and tucked her chin into her neck, sending her wheat-gold strands cascading forward.

I willed her to raise her face and push her hair back. To wear her attraction to me with pride. Hypocritical of me, considering I'd been so ashamed of winging her, I'd shut the door in her face.

"Wow . . . that's—" She cleared her throat. Peeked at me through lashes so thick and long they cloaked her brilliant stare. "A strange sensation."

It took a moment for her voice to reach my brain and then another to register. "Wait . . . this is the first time you've smoldered someone?" I kept my voice low so the rest of the team wouldn't be privy to our conversation, even though I doubted they could hear anything over the music pumping through the living room.

Naya dented her red-red lips and nodded. My mind blanked, focusing on the point of contact between her white teeth and trapped flesh. I was going straight to Abaddon for all the ways I pictured her using that mouth on my body.

I hauled my mind out of the gutter, and then the rest of my body. "You're telling me you've never smoldered *Jarod?*" His name tasted foul and tainted the moment. It also turned off her skin's tormenting glitter.

A masochist, that's what I was.

I wanted to talk about her ex as much as I wanted to watch Junior lay his sleazy gaze on Naya tonight.

She finally picked up her head, dainty fingers wrestling back her golden locks, and fixed me with her bottomless stare. "Why are you so obsessed with Jarod?"

"Why am I—" I let out a sound between a snort and a chortle, even though I was anything but amused. "Oh . . . maybe because you kept calling out to him back in England, then lied about not knowing him. Which honestly makes me wonder why you're smoldering *me.*"

She shook her head. "You really want to know who Jarod is?"

"No." I grimaced when the ishim fleeced my wings. Stupid lie detectors.

She trailed my feather's collapse before lifting her gaze back to mine. "He's this guy I dream about. A guy I've dreamed about my entire life. A figment of my imagination who feels so real, I lose feathers when I claim not to know him." Her chest heaved, her pulse thudding wildly in her neck.

Out of all the excuses she could've made up...

"I can tell you don't believe me."

I refused to check the rug for a fallen feather, because it wouldn't matter. "I'm not interested in being a placeholder for someone else. Real or not."

Her lids closed and her nostrils flared. "Good, because I'm not interested in dating you."

"Because you're holding out for your fantasy lover?"

"Yeah. That's why," she hissed, just as a door slammed somewhere in the suite.

"I found the perfect—" A lacy black mask swung from Galina's fingers. "What's with the standoff and the shedding?"

Naya snatched the prop with a muttered *thanks* and tied it on.

"Party's in full swing outside. We should get going." Galina peered at the two black feathers littering the rug—one sparkly, one dull—before cocking an eyebrow at me. I didn't offer an explanation and neither did Naya.

"Let's go," I murmured roughly.

Galina gave my outfit a pointed look. "You're not even dressed."

"I will be in a minute." I tossed Naya her earpiece, and although I'd given her zero warning, she caught it. Good reflexes. "You know how it works?"

"Boone gave me a tutorial." After fitting it into her ear, she adjusted the mask until her eyes were perfectly aligned with the almond-shaped openings.

Forget Abaddon. My soul would be incinerated long before it could reach our version of Hell if her father could see even a single one of my indecent thoughts, most of which featured Naya, wings and legs spread, wearing only her mask, thong, and lipstick.

Get an effing grip of yourself.

Breathe.

Galina clapped the air in front of my face.

My head reared back. "What the pluck, Galina?"

"Stop staring at Naya, and get your suit on." A small smile curved her lips, as though she could see the dirt flying around my mind.

She probably could. Like Noah, Galina was starting to know me too well.

Toying with the bill of my cap, I grunted and stalked back out into the living room, but not before I caught a blush staining Naya's cheeks and ears.

43

NAYA

"You're sticking out," I whispered to Adam from where he and I stood in the shadow of a tall palm, close to where the waitstaff had set up their HQ.

Although he'd added a jacket to his all-black outfit, he'd kept his white sneakers and ball cap.

"Says the girl wearing a sequined napkin and a mask fit for a masquerade ball." He'd barely looked my way since we'd left the suite, yet had insisted on staying at my side while Noah and Galina wandered through the crowd.

Not that I wanted his attention. I was still trying to get over the fact that I'd smoldered him. Angels, how humiliating.

Galina's voice erupted against my eardrum. "Robbie's gearing up to make a speech. I think that'd be the perfect time to make your presence known, Naya."

I tapped my earpiece twice so my voice would register. "Okay." Then tapped it again to cut the broadcast.

Adam's arms were crossed so snugly in front of his chest, I kept expecting to hear the seams of his jacket rip.

"I'm very tempted to write Susan a message in blood on a cocktail napkin," I murmured. "Along the lines of: *I know what you did.*"

He side-eyed me.

"Let me guess. You think it's an awful idea?" Under my breath, I added, "Like all my ideas."

"I don't hate *all* your ideas."

"Oh, come on." I rolled my eyes. "Name one you didn't think was stupid."

"You just seem to enjoy putting yourself in harm's way, that's all."

"Always evading my questions..."

"I actually think writing Susan a note is a terrific idea." He hinged to face me. "If you do, I'll deliver it."

This time, I was the one who side-eyed him.

"But preferably not in blood." His conciliatory tone was a nice change to how curt he'd been since he'd shown up at my door and grimaced at my appearance.

Here I'd been convinced Galina was the reincarnation of Pygmalion, because she'd made me feel so pretty. And then he'd come along and squashed the soft clay figure she'd fashioned before it had any chance of drying. Now, I felt underdressed and overpreened, and wanted nothing more than to wipe off my makeup and pitch my dress in a bin.

Adam intercepted a waiter carrying a platter of bite-sized cream puffs. While he asked if he could borrow a pen and stole a napkin from the stack in the man's hand, I eyed the pink choux, my stomach growling. I'd been so anxious when room service had delivered dinner earlier that I hadn't been able to stomach more than a bite of my grilled cheese.

And yeah, I was still nervous, but since no one had swung a gun my way or beamed a spotlight on my face, my anxiety had receded. Not that one needed an appetite to consume desserts.

Right before the waiter could backpedal to get us the pen, Adam seized his tray. "I'll hold on to that for you."

The man startled, but then whirled, retreating the way he'd come.

Adam pushed the platter my way. "Eat."

I blinked at him, then at the tray, which I'd assumed he'd lifted to help out the waiter. "Maybe I'm not hungry."

"Your stomach's louder than the band."

Had he really heard it over the brass band's rendition of Adele's newest song?

Unable to resist, I pinched a cream puff and popped it into my mouth where it melted into a delectable puddle. *Oh, angels* .

. . That was— "Amazing," I said out loud. "You should try them."

"I hate sweet things."

"How unsurprising."

He grunted as I filched another.

I must've moaned, because he shook his head, as though taking pleasure in sweet things was totally absurd.

"Noah needs to try them."

"I'd suggest you pocket some, but you're all out of pockets." He gave my scrappy dress a disdainful look.

"What did my poor dress ever do to you?" I asked, grabbing two last puffs.

His eyes gleamed like mined emeralds in a face otherwise impeccably expressionless. Because I was unfortunately not immune to his inscrutable stare, a blush stole across my cheeks.

I pitched my attention off him and on a jovial cluster of Circle Girls. A familiar wheezy-laugh made me squint, and then I squinted harder, because—Was that . . . ?

Was Emmy wearing *my* bomber?

One of the girls from the group she'd nicknamed Circle Bitches stepped between us, curtailing my view. I leaned to the side to see past the tall socialite, whose name I'd forgotten, jerking when a hand scraped the bare skin along my back.

"Your pen." Adam brandished it between our bodies.

I'd been so concentrated on the teal jacket Emmy was wearing that I'd missed the waiter returning.

I nicked the pen, then the proffered napkin. "You really did a bang-up job reforming Emmy."

He flinched. If he was curious as to why I'd just gone off on him, he didn't ask. Wise man.

I flattened the napkin against my palm and scribbled:

I want my pearls back. –the girl from the marsh

If that didn't give Susan's conscience goosebumps, I didn't know what would. "Are you delivering it yourself or are we asking a waiter to do it?"

"I'll take it." As he tucked it into his jacket pocket, he canted his chin low, trying to catch my attention, but I didn't meet his eyes.

Perhaps it was unfair to take my anger out on him, but the jacket Emmy wore meant so much to me.

"What's going on?"

I gnashed my teeth when the supermodel-tall Circle Girl shifted, and the light from the lanterns strung to the tree branches over their heads splashed the silver embroidery.

Adam pinched my chin and tilted my face, forcing my eyes to his. "What is—"

"Your ex stole my jacket," I hissed, twisting my head free from his fingers.

He sighed. "I'll get it back."

"Yeah? And how exactly are you planning to do that? Will you stroll over and tap her shoulder?"

"I'll have Galina get it, all right?" His lips thinned. "Or I'll buy you a replacement."

"You can't buy it." The backs of my eyes stung. "Mimi had it specially made for my mother, who entrusted it—" I closed my eyes to block the tears.

A warm, rough palm skated up my spine. "I'm sorry, Feather." His breaths warmed the skin not covered by black filigree.

I inhaled deeply, squashing down my resentment, because this wasn't Adam's fault. "No, I'm sorry. I shouldn't—shouldn't have snapped at you." I lifted my lids, my lashes grazing the edges of the mask. "It just—that jacket means a lot to me."

"I'll get it back." His voice was as rough and dark as the scruff lining his jaw. "And you're right about me having done a piss-poor job. I don't even understand why the ishim awarded me any feathers for Emmy." He pressed his lips together, flattening their fullness. "I was so concentrated on nailing Dunmore that I didn't put in the work and effort I should've."

"Too concentrated on nailing Dunmore or Emmy?"

His fingers stiffened, and his pupils tightened. "We all have a past, Naya." He removed his hand and pivoted but didn't stalk off into the night.

Loud clapping resounded around us, and then Noah's voice drilled my eardrum. "Robbie's got the mic."

In other words, *showtime*.

44

ADAM

ANGELIC FACT #897
DARK WINGS AREN'T DIRTY, BUT THE MIND
OF THE BEING BEARING THEM MIGHT BE.

*N*aya raised her hand to her mask's ribbon and pulled it free.

I'd been mulling over the dodgy choices of my past, but the second the material slipped off Naya's face, my full focus fell on the angel standing before me.

"Like you so aptly pointed out earlier, I don't have any pockets. So hold on to it?" She dangled the mask between us.

"Why are you removing it?"

"So both Robbie and Pablo can get a clear view of my face. I'll put it back on as soon as they've both seen me, and we leave." Her dark eyebrows—twenty shades darker than her pale-gold hair but ten shades lighter than her eyes—slanted. "We discussed this in the elevator. Weren't you listening?"

I'd been way too concentrated on the heart-shaped sequin winking at me from the base of her spine to catch the mask-plan. Just the thought of it swamped my veins with lust.

"Adam?" She shook the mask.

I took it. "Walk me through your grand plan."

"I'm going to stride around the perimeter of the crowd until I catch Robbie and Pablo's attention. Once they've both gotten a lasting eyeful of my face, Galina and Noah will provide a distraction, and I'll fade into the crowd."

Naya couldn't fade even if she tried. Especially not wearing what she was wearing on her body and lips.

I pushed the mask back into her hands. "Put it back on."

"But—but I want them to recognize me," she sputtered.

"They will."

"My hair's different, and—"

"Trust me. You still look like you but with flat hair."

Her eyes widened in shock, and it hit me that she honestly thought Galina had transformed her into another woman.

"Please," I added gruffly, in case that was why she still hadn't reclaimed her mask.

Her fingers jerked and bumped into mine as she seized it.

"Guys, did you miss Noah's—" Galina broke through the line of partygoers, who all had their backs turned to us, much too enthralled by Robbie strutting around the makeshift stage. "What are you doing?" she asked Naya who was refastening the mask.

"Adam thinks I should keep it on."

"They'll recognize her just fine with it," I grumbled.

Galina frowned but thankfully didn't butt heads with me. Good thing, 'cause I was in no mood to debate the merits of my decision.

"Hey, Gee." I dug out the napkin. "Make sure this ends up in Susan Dunmore's hands." I wasn't sure why I'd agreed to deliver it in the first place since I didn't plan on letting Naya out of my sight for an angelsdamn second.

Galina nodded, one finger in her ear. "They're ready. Are you in place, Noah?" Her voice resounded against both my eardrums.

"Yup. Just tell me when."

I tapped the earpiece twice. "*I'll* give the signal. Boone, what do you see?"

"Most of the guards are congregated around Pablo and the stage, but four are standing along the perimeter, blocking off the footpaths. Your safest bet will be to pass through the thicket on your right."

"Got it. Naya and I will head there once she's done."

"I'm going to go woman the fuse box. See you back at the coop, loves." Galina dashed away in the boots she'd worn with her yellow dress.

I glanced down at Naya's shoes and grumbled, "Why didn't you wear sneakers?"

"Because sneakers aren't very cocktail-y. Besides, I can run fine in heels."

"Guys, he's almost done talking," Noah hissed. "What are you waiting for?"

Naya backed away, then spun and skimmed the tight arc of guests, keeping a few feet of space between her and them.

I lowered the bill of my cap, grabbed a glass of something from a passing waiter's tray, and moved in parallel to Naya, close enough to reach her in a heartbeat, but far enough that the Triples she was trying to spook wouldn't see me and realize we were working together.

I wanted . . . no, I *needed* to stay under their radar so I could move around the hotel and this city freely, because stalking monsters in broad daylight was far easier than stalking them from the shadows.

I stared around me to map out the whereabouts of the Prince's security detail, my gaze snagging on the decadent hotel that glowed like a beacon in the night.

To think that more than half the inhabitants of this city couldn't afford electricity. Now wasn't the time to seethe about human inequalities and iniquitous monarchies, but angels, how it ticked me off.

My grievance faded to white noise when Boone yipped, "On your left, Adam. One of the guards is watching you. Remove the cap. You'll look less conspicuous."

My fingers set on the bill, but then a familiar voice injured my eardrums, and I lowered my hand. Yeah. The cap was staying on. If Emmy stopped eye-screwing Junior, who stood by the stage, looking up at his buddy, she'd recognize me in a heartbeat.

She leaned toward her new friend. Although I didn't hear everything she said, I did catch the mention of the words "Prince" and "condom." Probably the same ones she'd offered Naya back in England before advising the archangel's daughter to carry Junior's baby.

When I'd read over the pearls' transcript, I'd wanted to punch something. Still did. I rolled the hand not holding a wine glass into a fist and steered away from the girl of my past and nearer to the one of my present.

Naya had stopped walking, and her shoulders had squared.

I hadn't realized how quiet it had gotten until I heard Boone say, "Robbie saw you, Naya."

Not only had he seen her, but he'd stopped talking.

In slow-motion, or possibly my mind slowed it all down, Junior turned to look at what had made his freckled friend go as white as the button-down peeking from between the velvet lapels of his dark dinner jacket.

NAYA

*A*dam was right. Robbie recognized me through the mask, and his ensuing shock spiked his eyebrows and stapled his mouth.

Pablo, too, saw me, but his brow stayed bent far longer. Perhaps because his vantage point wasn't as ideal as Robbie's bird's-eye view.

I glided to the side, slipping behind a group of tall men in bespoke suits, as Robbie attempted to cover up his snafu with a comical tale from his boarding school days.

"Now!" Adam's voice hissed through my earpiece.

Next to the stage, a table full of drinks tipped over, causing a great ruckus. Susan screeched, something about a wine stain on her bouclé Chanel dress. Had Noah been the one to bump the cloth-wrapped high table?

My breath snagged, because Pablo had seen my fellow shorhim back at the manor, the night he'd spilled water over my lap. Hopefully, Galina had triggered Susan's meltdown, but wasn't she handling the lights?

Although tempted to look over my shoulder at the stage, I kept my gaze on the outlying shadows, raking them repeatedly for the tall, broad male who'd promised to stay at my side.

Adam was feathering nowhere.

My heart began clapping faster, dowsing my tongue with the taste of metal.

Had the guards caught him? Had he run back to the hotel and left me?

I reasoned with my panicked brain that I knew where to go. I didn't need him.

I spun, about to dash for the grove of tropical plants, when a muted scuffle made my steps falter. I squinted, making out two bodies, both dressed all in black. One upright; one keeling over.

Ice filled my stomach, until I noted the ball cap and white sneakers on the man still standing. After dropping the guard, Adam ticked his head toward our exit route.

I darted forward and made it to the palm tree, behind which Adam and I had lingered earlier, when a man stepped into my path. My heart jounced, but settled a smidgeon at his attire—crisp suit and open-collared white shirt.

Just a guest, Naya.

I tried to sidestep him when he asked in broken English, "You are Circle Girl?"

Crap. "Um . . ."

Adam stalled, and although his face was steeped in darkness, the annoyed glint in his eyes was unmistakable.

"Yes." I refocused on my interlocutor and smiled, so he wouldn't grow suspicious and click his fingers to summon a guard.

"I like *tu máscara*." He swept his fingers over his face to indicate he was referring to my mask and not my makeup. "Very . . . How you say? Intriguing."

Through the crowd, I noticed Pablo speaking to two guards. As though my stare prickled his cheek, he started to turn. I took the suit's arm and spun him, so his body blocked the sight of mine.

The man smiled, apparently not put off by my strange move. If anything, he seemed . . . entertained? "Can I offer glass of—" The suit wheezed, and then his lids were clapping shut, and he was listing backward, right into Adam's arms.

"No, you cannot," Adam muttered, propping the man's collapsed frame against the base of the palm tree. "Done flirting, Feather?"

I blinked away from the incapacitated male. "I wasn't—"

The lights went off. All of them. Galina must've pulled the wires.

A hand grabbed mine. Adam had touched me often enough that

I recognized the scrape of his calluses and the breadth of his fingers. "Hold on."

Oh, I held on. So tightly, I probably cut off circulation to the rest of his body.

Adam steered us through the moonless darkness, his strides never faltering.

Leaves rustled, then grazed my cheeks, arms, legs, and back as we squeezed into the thicket. When the branches snapped closed behind me, sealing us in a mound of green darkness, he came to a stop.

Guards were running amok on the path we were supposed to take, barking at each other, phone beams splashing the cement.

When their light scraped our lair, Adam whirled and pressed his index finger to his lips. *Wow . . . really?* He thought I was about to pick that moment to carry out a full-blown conversation with him?

The beam swung away. When no one charged us, I let out the breath my lungs had been clutching since the lights had sputtered off. Although concealed well, we were wedged in tight, with nowhere to go until the guards returned to the party.

"Boone?" I felt Adam's murmur more than heard it.

I swallowed, then swallowed again, because my heart had begun to scale my throat.

"Hold your positions." Boone's voice bounced against my skull. "Too many guards in your sector."

"Holding." Adam dragged his thumb across my knuckles in slow arcs. "You're not claustrophobic, are you, Feather?"

I shook my head as yelling continued to echo around us. Suddenly, the pressure of his fingers vanished, and I inhaled a harsh, panicked breath.

"My jacket. Put it on."

"I'm not cold," I whispered.

"No, but you sparkle like a disco ball." He guided my arms through the silk-lining, ensnaring me in his body heat and irksomely delicious scent.

Each whiff of him agitated my blood. Why did he have to smell so good?

"Are you sure you're not cold?" His fingertips skimmed my collarbone as he adjusted the lapels, flicking more of his mouth-watering fragrance my way. "Your skin's full of goosebumps."

I bet it was. Between the adrenaline rush and the nearness of his body and his scent...

"No need to be scared." Adam's blunt nails bumped the side of my thigh, pebbling my skin some more. "Everything's going to be just fine," he murmured so close to my lobe that my body quaked. "I promise you, Feather. Just fine."

Another tremor stirred my body.

And then...

Ugh.

Not. Again.

NAYA

My skin set the darkness ablaze.
No, no, no, no, no.
Now was really not a good time for smoldering.
Now was an epically terrible time.
I begged my body to quit flashing. But did it listen? No.

A corner of Adam's mouth quirked. "Guess you're not cold *or* scared," he murmured.

"Shut up," I hissed, moving my gaze to the sharp apple in his throat.

A soundless chuckle shook his chest.

"Not funny." I pushed my mask up because it was scratching my sparkly face.

Loud chatter buzzed behind us as the party organizers urged guests to settle. Although a few squeals pierced the air, they were more often than not followed by peals of laughter. Apparently, people were enjoying the blackout.

"That's twice now," Adam breathed against my forehead.

"Twice?" I lifted my eyes back to his, my stubborn shimmer highlighting his vivid irises.

He pushed aside a strand of my hair, his nails scraping my heated skin, and leaned over to pulse out his answer, "That you've smoldered me."

Great. He was keeping score.

I wet my lips. "It's just physiological." I moved my mouth closer to his ear to make sure no one would hear us talk, even though I doubted our voices carried over the hubbub. "Doesn't mean anything."

"Doesn't it?" His fingers threaded through my hair, and my disloyal body reacted to his slow touch with another shiver. "When I—"

"They're working on the lights. I estimate you have five minutes of darkness left." Galina's voice scored the eardrum not being branded by Adam's words. "On my way back to the coop. Noah? Position?"

Noah's voice crackled through the earpiece a second later, "I'm at the personnel entrance. Just got through the doors."

Even though I wanted to ask Adam, *When you what?*" I kept my lips sealed.

"Ready to run, Sparkles?"

I glowered at him. "Sparkles? Really?" My body *finally* stopped flashing, but the damage to his retinas and my ego was done.

The infuriating fletching grinned. He pressed the long sleeve of his coat up to fish out my hand, his palm warm and solid around my chilled fingers.

He started to turn to lead the way when Susan's affected voice breached our leafy hideout. "She telephoned someone that night, Rob. Someone who knows what we've done. Someone who must be here."

"Keep your voice down, Mum."

"Keep my voice down? You're not the one who received a threatening missive!"

"For God's sake, *be quiet!*"

My eyes widened because both Dunmores stood inches away. If they beamed their telephone light at the rubbery leaves, they'd make out my outline. Dread chattered my teeth anew.

Adam hooked my waist beneath the jacket he'd loaned me and pulled me flush against his front, probably to quiet my trembling before I rattled the branches and gave us away.

"Guys, you've got to move. Pablo's head of security just radioed Naya's description to the rest of his team and gave the order to have all park gates and hotel entrances sealed." Boone's voice pounded to the beat of my teeth. "Four are coming up on your right. Go left."

"One of Pablo's guards will escort you to the suite, Mum. Stay there until I've fixed the situation you and Henry botched."

"Don't you dare blame me! I'm not the one who left early. I'm the one who got on that goddamned plane with those goddamned girls."

The arm Adam had curled around my waist slid away as he turned, but the hand he'd wrapped around my own tightened. He turned, and although his footfalls were silent, his body bent the branches, which snapped closed around me. Thankfully, the Dunmores' screaming match absorbed the soughing creaks and murmurous swish of our escape.

I stepped gingerly, careful to balance my weight on the balls of my feet so that my skinny heels didn't sink into the dark soil. As I lifted my arm to press away a branch swinging back toward my face, I froze. Something moved against my arm.

Something with small, glassy eyes and a coiled reptilian body. I mashed Adam's fingers as a scream clambered up my throat.

He whirled, surely expecting the Dunmores.

The snake hissed.

Adam's hand shot out, and he grabbed the snake. Just grabbed it.

"Did you hear that?" Susan asked.

A beam carved through the leaves.

"Rob, there are people—" Before she could finish her sentence, Adam flung the snake at her. It must've landed on her or near her, because she shrieked.

He yanked on my arm, and we burst out of the serpent's nest, my mask snagging on a branch and slipping off my head.

I was immortal. *Immortal!* Not even venomous snakes could harm me. I reasoned I'd flipped out, because the creature had caught me by surprise.

When my heels hit the cement path, running became easier but also louder.

"*¡Por ahí! ¡Por ahí!*" *Over there!* Narrow beams licked the path and dappled the shadows around us, and then boots pounded.

It sounded like a stampede of hooved beasts was descending upon us.

Adam cursed under his breath, then almost dislocated my shoulder as he booked a sharp right, driving us back off the path. My heel got stuck, and I flailed forward, my foot slipping free. Thanks to Adam's death grip, I stayed upright.

"My shoe," I mouthed as the yelling and footfalls increased in volume.

Adam's fingers crushed mine. "Leave it."

"They'll find it," I hissed.

He mustn't have cared, because he propelled us forward, right into another thicket.

My skin crawled, my shoe long forgotten.

"Kick off the other."

I stared down at the only thing between my skin and the myriad of creatures creeping around the fertile soil. Since I couldn't very well hop back to the hotel, I toed off my remaining stiletto right before we emerged from the tropical grove.

My wings sprouted. How I wished I could flap them and fly.

If only Dov were here.

Or any ascended.

If only—

The bollard lights flared and drenched the park in so much brilliance, it felt like the sun had bumped the stars out of the sky.

Bulbs illuminated the glossy foliage and the rows of parked vehicles in the service lot, that sprawled at the base of the short but steep hill on the crest of which Adam and I stood.

They also haloed the guards standing by the personnel entrance, heavy artillery strapped to their chests, gazes narrowed on us.

"Fuck," Adam whispered. Or had he said, *duck?*

ADAM

ANGELIC FACT #7
ANGELS, LIKE SIRENS, MAY LEAD YOU ASTRAY.

I spun and hooked the back of Naya's skull, ready to dive sideways, when Noah's battle cry shredded my eardrum. I glanced down in time to see him and Galina charge the guards. In seconds, they'd incapacitated both.

"Forkin' hurry up, you two." Noah grunted as he grabbed his unconscious guard by the ankles and dragged him through the sliding glass doors, right behind Galina and her guard.

It took my soul several seconds to peel itself off my spine. I unthreaded my fingers from her hair and fished out her hand from the sleeve of my jacket.

Naya trembled so hard, her wings sparkled furiously at her back. Her complexion was as white as my shoes, and her eyes as round as the reptile I'd tossed at Mama Dunmore. I hoped the thing had coiled itself around her throat.

If I lost a feather for wishing her ill, I didn't feel it, wound way too tight.

Adrenaline pumping, I turned toward the grassy hill and lunged forward, tugging Naya back into motion. The grass was so brittle and untended, we skidded.

When Naya let out a soft whimper, I dug my sneakers into the rough terrain and flipped around, lungs pumping hard, heart pumping harder. My fingers balled, my elbow bent, my muscles coiled. I was primed to pounce and punch, but no one stood beside her. No one had touched her.

She hopped, trying to remove something from her bare sole. "Stepped on something," she whispered.

My breaths jackknifed up my rigid neck. *Pluckin' A.*

I climbed up a step to swoop her into my arms and carry her the rest of the way, when yelling erupted right behind the bend in the cement road. I eyed the glass doors Noah and Galina had vanished into, eyed the pathway. We wouldn't make it.

"Your wings," I hissed.

"What about them?"

I clasped the back of her head and shoved her to the ground. Her eyes widened as we went down, and her wings . . . they thankfully evaporated. The second our bodies smacked the ground, I draped mine over hers and hiked her leg up. Hopefully, Pablo's men were still looking for a lone girl in a sparkly dress, not a fornicating couple.

"Adam," she gasped, eyes glistening as wildly as the sequins on her dress. "What are you—"

"Just go with it." I jammed my cap on top of her head and framed her face between my forearms to hide the rest of her blonde hair.

She got with the program quickly, hooking her foot around my thigh. She even went a step further, pressing her mouth against the column of my stiff neck. The warm, damp feel of her lips shepherded the blood away from my brain.

Bloody Abaddon. I needed it in my head. Not in my dick.

The guards erupted onto the path, their shouts dying at the sight of us. They peered down at where we lay rutting like animals, weapons aimed at our heads.

When they crept closer, I muttered, loud enough for them to hear, "*Fisgones.*" Before barking, "*Váyanse de aquí!*" *Scram!*

They froze, clearly not expecting to be called filthy voyeurs in their native tongue. I made sure not an inch of Naya's face was visible as I glowered at our four-person audience.

One of them looked toward the hotel. My lungs held still. Had Galina or Noah stepped back out?

"Antonio and Carlos. Weren't they supposed to be guarding the South entrance?"

"Do you mind?" I growled at them, as Naya's hands trembled toward the base of my spine.

One of the men flicked on a flashlight and beamed it into my eyes. "Stand!"

She knotted her fingers into my black T-shirt, as though scared I'd actually abide by the bastard's orders.

One of their walkie-talkies crackled, "Twentieth floor. The girl just got off the elevator."

Levi must've planted the footage we'd filmed earlier of her entering a bedroom we'd paid cash to have on hand for the weekend.

"This is private property." The guard, who'd asked me to get up, tried to squeeze the beam of his light over Naya's face, but I kept her fully cloaked. "Screw your girlfriend elsewhere."

"Aye aye." I flicked him a two-finger salute, making sure my middle one was more prominent.

He grunted, finally pivoting away. The second his boots slapped the service lot, I murmured, "Noah, Galina, guards are coming through the staff entrance. Stay out of sight."

"Roger that."

"Boone, there were four guards. Are they all getting on a lift?"

"They've called one."

"Let me know when they get on it. Galina, Noah, positions?"

"We parked the guards in the spa locker rooms. We were going to take the elevator from there. Unless you want us to come back—"

"No, go up."

"Guards are in the elevator," Boone announced.

"Any more heading our way?"

"No."

"'Kay. We're coming up." I tapped my earpiece, then blew out the mother of all breaths and let my forehead sag into the crook of Naya's neck.

"That was close," she murmured.

"Too close." I inhaled deeply, in an attempt to quiet my careening heart, but her sweet skin only spurred the erratic tempo.

I picked my head off her throat, meaning to pry the rest of me off her, but I stilled at the sight of her quivering lips and slick eyes. "Hey." I picked a strand of hair off her cheek. "They're gone. We're safe."

Her nose crinkled, and a tear slipped free. "Why did I think this would be a good idea?"

I ran my thumb along her temple. "Because Dov seconded it."

Her clumped lashes fell against her colorless cheeks. "I should've listened to you."

I sighed. "At least, I got to toss a snake at another snake. Such poetic justice."

Although her lids didn't reel up, one corner of her bow-shaped mouth tucked up.

To think it had been on my neck minutes ago.

So soft. So red. So plump. So damp.

Between the memory of its shape and the wash of adrenaline leaving my system, my blood turned sticky and hot, and my dick . . . it swelled, grooving the inside of her thigh.

Her eyes opened. Fastened to mine.

Up. Get up, you sleazeball. You're probably scaring the poor girl.

I pressed my palms into the poorly-maintained lawn, managing to boost my torso, but her arms and leg were still wrapped around my lower half. She probably wasn't even aware she was holding on to me.

Or was she?

"Naya, we should . . ." I started to tick my head toward the hotel when she rolled her lips, and holy cherubs, the sight cut off what little brain power I had left.

My wings snapped out. I tried to rein them back in, but to no avail. My feathers strained outward, lengthening and hardening like the beast in my pants.

She sighed as she glided her leg off me, the soft pressure of her heel burning a path down my unyielding thigh, the soft whoosh of her breath blazing another path down my face.

When I didn't push off her, her eyebrows bent. "Adam? Are you okay?"

My limbs were unresponsive, as though a concrete mixer had dumped its load over my body.

"Adam?" She wriggled her hips, which honed my feathers into

blades. I bet they'd impale anyone who tried to approach, angel-blooded or not.

"Minute. Give me—a minute." I grimaced as though I had a cramp, so her eyes wouldn't stray to the trellis of feathers on my back that were desperate to catch her attention. To think I'd picked at her when she'd smoldered me. I was a prick through and through.

"Why?" Her breaths fanned across my mouth, and although I was stiff as a board, a shudder stole through me.

"Shove me off."

Her crimson mouth thinned. "If you're trying to test my strength, now's really not—"

"No test. I just—can't move."

"Why?"

"Why?" *Was she kidding?* I wet my lips. "Can't you see my plucking wings?"

Her hands sprang off my back.

My ego took a hit, because, evidently, she hadn't. "They may be mangier than what you're used to, but they're not that fucking mangy."

The ishim jabbed my wing bones, carving out a feather, and although its loss pissed me off, the ensuing pain slackened the web of cartilage keeping them erect.

"They busted down the door of room 221." Boone hissed inside my ear. "Levi's planting another video of Naya. Where are you guys?"

I'd never been gladder that he didn't have eyes on us and that I'd had the prescience to shut off my end of the broadcast.

I rose to my knees, and then to my feet, vanquishing my winglets. Sure, I hadn't wanted Naya to catch my impromptu winging, but the fact that she hadn't smooshed my ego.

I tapped my earpiece. "We're coming." I kept my eyes on a clump of dried grass instead of on the twin stilts poking out from the hiked-up hem of her dress.

Naya patted the dry soil around where she sat.

"What are you doing?"

"I lost my earpiece."

"Doesn't matter. Let's go." I turned and started for the service lot, but halted when she sucked in a breath.

Although she was upright, she teetered. I was about to ask what was wrong when I remembered her saying she'd stepped on something. Apparently, it hadn't come out.

Because we'd wasted enough time out here, and only because of that, I strode back up the hill and scooped her up. She settled with a soft gasp but no fight. Once through the sliding glass doors, I headed right, to the bank of service elevators and jammed my elbow into the up button.

"You can put me down." Her voice was as pebbled as the skin beneath my palms.

I did, but only after entering the lift. "We're in the elevator, headed up." I leaned against the wall opposite Naya and dug my earpiece out.

"Are you—are you mad at me?"

I rolled the toe of my sneaker to loosen a clump of dirt stuck to it.

"You are, aren't you?" A pause. "Is it because I touched your wings?"

We rose at the speed of a narcoleptic snail. *Plucking cheapskate Prince.* Couldn't even give his staff machinery worthy of the ones in the lobby.

The elevator jerked and then stopped inching up altogether. What the—

I was about to retrieve my earpiece from my pocket and stick it back in when I noticed Naya's palm flush against the emergency stop button.

"I'm sorry, okay? Your feathers are black, and between the baseball cap and the fact that it was night—" She bit off some of the bright color on her lips. "I'm sorry."

Salt in my wounds. "I'm not mad because you touched my wings, Naya."

"Then what are you mad about?"

"Can you just drop it?"

"No. I can't just *drop it*. We're not done with this mission. Which means we're going to be working together for at least another day or two, so explain what I did"—she pressed her mouth shut, then eased it back open—"so I don't do it again . . ."

I rubbed the back of my head, messing with the hair matted from too much time crammed beneath a hat. I almost wished the Prince's goons would shoot up the ceiling of the lift and slingshot themselves inside, so I could cut this agonizing soul-to-soul short.

"You do realize we aren't safe until we get to the suite?"

Her eyes tapered. "You're prevaricating."

"I'm stating a fact. Junior's entire fleet is hunting you."

"Spit it out, and I press the button."

I growled low in my throat. "I'm sore about my shortcomings, all right? Now press—"

"Which ones? You have many."

Was she for real? I lowered my hand and crossed my arms. "Didn't your parents ever teach you that it was rude to kick a man when he was down?"

"S-sorry." The beginnings of her smile crumbled. "I was only—only teasing you."

Her stuttered apology compelled me to explain myself, angels only knew why. "Look, I've never had a hang-up about my wings, but apparently, you've managed to give me one. I'll get over it, though."

"A hang-up?" The space between her eyebrows dented. "You have less feathers than I do, yet your wings look fuller than mine. Which are almost complete, in case you've forgotten. If anyone should have a complex, it's me."

I hadn't forgotten how close she was to leaving this world. "I winged you, Naya. Twice now. I winged you twice, and you didn't even notice."

Her fingers rolled around the metal rod screwed into the elevator wall at her back. "When?"

"Back in England. At that inn-hotel."

"Doesn't count if I was unconscious."

I let out a faint snort. "You were very much conscious."

"Then why don't I remember?"

"Probably because I was so shocked, I shut the bathroom door in your face."

She was quiet for a moment. "And the second time was . . . when you asked me to push you off?"

I stared at her knuckles that poked out of my jacket sleeves. "Yeah."

Another beat of silence.

"Two for two."

My gaze lurched up to hers. "Two for two, what?"

"I've smoldered you twice; you've winged me twice. Thought you were keeping score."

Oh. The reminder that she was attracted to me, even if she wasn't attracted to my dinky wings, blew air back into my ego.

"I'm sorry I didn't understand what you were doing tonight. It's never happened to me before, so I didn't . . . you know?"

"Not sure I do, actually."

Her gaze dropped to the apple in my throat. "Our skin emits light; you guys, your wings just spread. Our form of PDA is impossible to miss; yours is subtle. And since it was my first time being winged . . . well, second—"

"Hold up." My eyebrows pushed off each other in surprise. "Are you saying you've never been winged?"

Her cheeks pinkened.

"How's that possible?"

The pink turned red. "Overprotective parents. An archangel father." She shrugged. "Or maybe it has nothing to do with Apa, and everything to do with me not being"—she averted her gaze—"very *wingable.*"

"I assure you, Feather, you're *very* wingable."

What I could see of her black irises through her lowered lashes shimmered with so much uncertainty that it tenderized my toughened mood. Did she honestly believe she wasn't attractive? She hadn't lost a feather, so I was guessing it wasn't false modesty.

Before I could debate the merits of what I was about to do, I pushed off the wall and poured myself into her space. Her neck cranked back, eyes alight in spite of the shadows cast by my cap.

I raised my hand to the side of her face. Wrapped my fingers lightly around her neck, threading them through the mass of gold silk at her nape. I rested my thumb on the edge of her jaw that quivered with her pulse, as though by levering her face, I'd levered her heart into her cheeks.

I slowly, hesitantly stroked the sharp bone, and her breaths quickened. "Your father's a terrifying man. Which, I guarantee, is the *only* reason you've never been winged."

"Does he terrify you?"

"Not enough." I slanted my head and leaned into her, hovering my mouth over hers, but not going any farther. I was giving her time to twist her head and push me away.

She broke out into pinpricks of light, as though her skin was pavéd with diamonds. Her tongue darted over her quivering lips, wet the red, made it sparkle harder.

My lungs, veins, throat . . . all of me was wound so tight that my timbre dropped a full octave. "Does glitter mean go?"

She pulsed out a soft, amused breath that curved up the corners of her candied mouth.

I wanted her to paint that mouth crimson every day.

Nah. I wanted to bite it raw and turn it red without artifice.

I wanted to lash my tongue against hers and stroke every dark, glittery corner of her mouth, then move on to other dark corners and glittery slits.

Holy Abaddon, I was well and truly plucked.

I was not passing GO and collecting a thousand feathers.

I was going straight to soul jail for all the dirt collecting in the crevasses of my brain.

Her hands rose to my chest. Good. She was going to push me back. Her palms skated higher, hooked on the shelf of my shoulders.

"Yes, Adam." She rose on tiptoe, bridging the gap between our bodies, and spoke the tail end of her answer against my aching tongue. "Glitter means go."

48

NAYA

*A*dam and I jolted apart as the elevator jerked to life.

Both his hands were on my body, so he hadn't pressed the emergency button. Which meant—Which meant someone had activated it remotely. Who would greet us? Pablo's guards? The hotel manager? Robbie Dunmore?

Adam released me and pivoted toward the door. His body seemed to expand, the line of his shoulders stretching, his rib cage broadening, his spine lengthening. "Stay behind me."

When the elevator dinged, my heart emitted a shrill chime of its own.

The doors parted.

Feathers.

I saw feathers. Pink tipped in gold.

My lungs stopped spasming.

"Pluck, Noah," Adam grumbled. "You scared the crap out of us."

"*I* scared . . . ?" Noah stood with his arms bent over his head, elbows touching, a small pile of pink down at his feet. He raked his palms down his face, which glistened like lacquered wood. "Oh, that's fresh. We thought they'd caught you, you . . . you . . . ." He flapped one hand around as though trying to coax the right word from the air. "What happened to your earpieces?"

"I lost mine," I said, stepping around Adam. Well, hobbling.

Noah's nostrils pulsed. "And *you*? Did you lose yours, too?"

Adam's dimple pressed into his cheek. "Mine was itching my eardrum."

"Itching his eardrum . . ." Noah rolled his eyes so hard that it dragged his whole head back. "Itching his forking—"

"Stop muttering like a bedlamite, No."

Noah's head straightened, and he glared at his friend.

"Oh, hey. It's our floor, Feather." Adam extended his hand. I looked at it, looked at him. Was he offering me support because of my injury or did he want to hold my hand because we'd kissed? His eyebrows dipped. "You molest me in the elevator, but now you object to holding my hand?"

My cheeks flamed. "I didn't . . . molest you." I darted a glance Noah's way.

The pink-winged verity stopped talking to himself.

I twisted my lips. "And for what it's worth, I'm really sorry that we caused you so much stress, Noah."

"Uh-huh." He didn't look accepting of my apology.

"Was I right, or was I right?" Galina's voice zipped down the hallway. She was leaning against the suite's open door.

Noah grunted in response, then whirled and trounced the runner toward her, wings shaking.

She nodded to the camera. "It's off."

Adam's hand was back at his side, curled in on itself. "Can you walk?"

I took his hand and towed it around my waist. "I wouldn't mind a little help." His arm was slow to relax, but once it did, it locked around me. I leaned into him as I limped toward Galina.

She frowned at my foot. "What happened?"

"Stepped on something. Not sure what, though."

When the suite's door closed behind us, the air vibrated with a collective exhale. Even I sighed.

Adam led me over to the couch. I didn't think it had ever felt so good to sit. I may even have moaned when my thighs met the plush cushion.

Adam crouched and picked up my foot. "Looks like you stepped on a cactus. Gee, you got some tweezers?"

"Yeah. Be right back."

"White glue works best." Boone uncapped a beer, which Noah

stole right out of his hands. "You have to let it airdry, but it gets all those pesky things out in one go."

"Get it."

"I don't have any. I could buy some tomorrow."

Since our bodies rejected foreign objects, the needles would probably all have fallen out by then.

The glower Adam tossed Boone's way was formidable. "Don't suggest solutions you can't follow through with."

Boone seemed nonplussed by Adam's outburst, much too busy staring between us, probably wondering what had delayed our arrival. Or maybe, he knew and was wondering if it was a one-time thing or a many-time thing.

Or maybe, I was projecting my own thoughts.

The angel I'd made out with was far from angelic, known throughout the guilds as the *sinnerizer*. Yes, even I'd heard of his nickname. Kinder and nobler than I'd given him credit for when we'd first met, but I wasn't his first and had no illusion I'd be his last.

Adam straightened. "Naya and I apologize about going dark. Thanks for covering our asses."

They all nodded. Except Noah, who was too busy guzzling down his beer.

Adam walked over to the fridge and grabbed a water bottle. He downed half of it on his way back to me, before offering me the remaining half.

Galina drifted out of our shared bedroom with a small towel and the tool that would give my poor insole and heel quick relief. I held out my hand for it, but she plopped down at my feet, spread the towel over her lap, and took my dirt-smeared foot.

"Galina, you don't have to—"

"Shush. I've been on edge since the elevator stopped on the twenty-ninth floor. A mindless task is exactly what I need." She started unearthing the needles but paused to cock a brow Adam's way and then mine. "So . . . is this something we should get used to?"

Hopefully, the baseball cap on my head camouflaged my blush. "Um . . ."

Adam sank onto the arm of the couch beside me. "Get used to it."

Galina grinned.

Levi frowned. "What do we need to get used to?"

"Naya being around," Noah answered vaguely.

The look Levi sent Adam was equal parts shock and dismay. "You made her part of the team?"

"No, knucklehead." Galina smirked. "They hooked up."

Levi blinked, and I wondered if he'd have preferred if Adam had inducted me onto the team.

Although I didn't want to drive a wedge between them, I also didn't want Levi to drive a wedge between Adam and me. I was sure time or one of Adam's future sinners would accomplish that anyway. This wasn't me being pessimistic, merely realistic.

"What's our next move?" Noah stepped up to the window overlooking the sprawling park, the tension in his body reflecting in the dark glass.

"You mean, now that half of Venezuela's looking for Naya?" Boone uncapped a fresh beer. "We should probably move out of the hotel and into the guilds."

I sighed, because Boone had a point. We were compromised. Or at least, I was, but by being here, I was compromising them. I kept my gaze on the vase overflowing with stargazer lilies in the middle of the coffee table, my fingers combing through the gold tassel on the throw pillow behind my back.

"Not a good idea, Boone. We'd be surrounded by ophanim, and we can't have them sticking their wings into our business." Adam shook the foot he'd hooked over his opposite knee. "What's the status on the QR-code retrieval, Levi?"

"It would've been ready, if I hadn't needed to stop working on it to run interference."

"Hey . . . Naya playing ghost was your idea, Levi." Galina drew out a cactus needle as long as a porcupine quill, and holy moly, that did not feel good . . . "So partake in the blame like a big boy."

A blush streaked his cheeks. "They were only supposed to wonder if she was alive, not know for sure that she was."

I clenched my teeth as Galina fished out another mammoth needle. Why couldn't I have stepped on a normal-sized cactus? I wrung the poor tassel and breathed through the discomfort.

"What's done is done." Adam stole my hand off the pillow and clasped it. "How long do you still need before we can attempt to call the telecom company?"

"A half-hour."

"Pablo asked his men to bring Naya to him unharmed." Noah's breath fogged up the glass. "I heard it on the walkie-talkie of the guy I incapacitated. The Prince threatened to kill anyone who so much as touched one of her hairs."

"No," Adam gritted out, and I wasn't sure what he was saying no to. Unless he was calling Noah by the nickname he sometimes used.

Clamping the neck of his beer bottle between his middle and index fingers, Noah turned. "I'm not suggesting she head to Junior's penthouse residence to discuss his evil associates."

Adam's fingers tensed around mine. "Then what are you suggesting?"

"I'm suggesting she call him to explain what Robbie did and to ask him to rein back his hounds. I'd prefer not feeling like a sitting duck."

"Won't Pablo be able to track where my cell phone signal's coming from?"

Boone took a seat beside his brother at the bar. "Not with the jammer I brought with me."

"Guys"—Levi squinted at his screen—"Susan's active."

Boone read over his little brother's shoulder: *Jay, we've decided to shorten our trip. Robbie and I will fly home tonight.*

So Robbie was running away . . . How predictable.

"*What do you mean Henry sent you to Los Angeles? To do what?*" Boone transcribed in real-time. Long seconds ticked by. "*Him and his whores. Well, change of plans. Get back here immediately.*"

"How long does it take a plane to fly from LA to Caracas?" I asked.

Boone glanced away from the screen. "About seven and a half hours, depending on tailwinds and aircraft."

"Nine." Levi gestured to his screen. "She just phoned Henry to yell at him and mentioned the next nine hours were going to be the longest of her life."

"How nice will it be to have two less Triples to contend with?" Galina quipped.

Adam had mentioned the Dunmores were untouchable in England. I didn't want mother and son to get away with what they'd done, which meant I had nine hours to find a way to keep them in Caracas.

"I'd like to call Pablo now."

Adam released my hand and stood. "First, the QR code."

My protest transformed into a hiss as another large needle slipped free. How had I *missed* this cactus?

"Show me what you've got, Levi. Maybe we have enough to give it a go."

The deepfake audio bytes were eerie. Levi typed, and Pablo's mellifluous voice would trickle out of his tablet's speaker. Adam pointed out a few words that sounded too robotic, and Levi chiseled them until the team leader was pleased with the result.

Galina ran a finger over my dirty, bleeding skin to check for protrusions. "All done." She smiled as she wrapped up the towel and stood.

"Thank you."

"Please. I'm sure you'd have done the same for me."

I would, because Galina had been kind to me from the get-go. She'd never replace Raven, but she felt like a friend.

"Boone, check if Junior's activated the SIMs," Adam ordered.

Boone grabbed his phone and clicked open a search page. After about a minute of scrolling, he popped out the word, "Nope."

"I wonder what he's waiting for?" Galina mused as she returned from the guest bathroom, drying her hands on her flouncy black dress. "His father's birthday's in two days. You think he's having second thoughts?"

Could Pablo's soul be in turmoil?

"He's a Triple," Adam said, as though Triples were incapable of changing their minds.

I sucked in a quick breath. "What if he isn't anymore?" When no one said anything, I added, "We should check. In case"—I licked my lips—"in case his score went down."

Adam cracked his knuckles. "If we're unsuccessful, we'll go check, but until then, no one leaves the suite. Understood?"

Everyone nodded.

As Levi put the finishing touches on his lines of code, I stared out at the city ruled by a tyrant, at the golden dome in the distance that shone like a manmade sun. While straightening my hair, Galina had explained it was part of the palace and had been named after the former Queen, which had led me to ask about her, but Calliope had phoned Galina then, and my query got lost underneath a long-winded conversation about the Chicago serial killer.

"What happened to Pablo's mother? Is she still alive?" The silence that followed my question was so considerable that I dragged my gaze off the palace to check whether Dov had swooped in and carried everyone away.

Boone shook his head. "She died in a fire. Her son tried to save her, but he was just a kid. Got third-degree burns on his hands."

I gasped.

"Don't go pitying him." Adam's jaw ticked. "Junior doesn't deserve your pity."

"He lost his mother, Adam."

"Lots of people lose their mothers. They don't all turn into monsters."

He was right. Deep down, I knew it, but it still pained me. "Was the fire accidental?"

"No. One of the King's political rivals instigated it." Noah kneaded the nape of his neck. "A lot of people say that's what made the old man ruthless, but he was a sicko before his wife's death. Used to head the ex-President's army. His specialty was torture."

Dov's words from earlier clanged through me: *the King bathes in his enemies' blood.*

Adam's eyes tightened on me. "Has it already slipped your mind that Junior planned to blow you up?"

"No." The same way Pablo's hand on my boob hadn't slipped my mind. I removed the cap from my head and laid it on the couch, then shrugged out of Adam's jacket. "But if Pablo ran through fire to save his mother, then maybe he has a shred of humanity left inside of him. And if he does, then maybe we should exploit it." I got up and limped toward my bedroom. "We should check his score before we write off his soul as unsalvageable."

No smoke leaked from Adam's nostrils, yet he seemed to be undergoing a complete system meltdown. "Next thing you'll suggest is signing up to him." The crispness of his tone made everyone but me gape. "Can you imagine? You'd get to leave this angelsforsaken world in no time."

Instead of playing into his little game, I said, "I've already told you, Adam, I'm not in any hurry to ascend."

Adam's neck was so corded I could count each tendon and vein.

Galina rested her hand on Adam's arm. "Let's trounce his plan, so Naya doesn't need to interact with him at all."

I slid my lips together as a harsh truth set in. "We can trounce his plan all we want, but he'll just plot something else if we don't succor his soul."

"Our objective is saving the Circle Girls, Naya. You seem to have forgotten that."

I didn't like that Adam had used my real name. How ironic, considering there'd been a time when I'd disliked all his nicknames. "I haven't forgotten."

"Are you sure? You're acting an awful lot more like a fletching than a shorhim right now."

I needed to walk away. Our tempers were too brittle, our nerves too high-strung.

As I reached my bedroom's threshold, he added, "As for future schemes, there won't be any, since dead men can't scheme."

Our eyes locked. To think an hour ago, we'd been kissing. I doubted there'd be any more of that in our future.

"Better check his score before you off him," I advised him, before hobbling out of sight and smacking the door shut.

My chest ached as much as my foot, as though it, too, had been poked by cactus needles. I closed my eyes and sidled against the door. The darkness behind my lids lit up with a cobbled courtyard, a statue with broken wings, a little boy with an upturned face. My anger at Adam was replaced by a yawning sadness for this child.

I pried my lids up. Slowly, the dusky bedroom with its pillowy queen-size beds came back into focus, and yet the hallucination continued to haunt and hurt me.

I'd dreamed of that courtyard and of that statue, but in all my dreams, a man stood in the place of that boy.

A man named Jarod.

Was my subconscious trying to remind me that Adam and I weren't meant for each other? That I needed to find Jarod?

ADAM

ANGELIC FACT #200
CLOUDS ARE DECEPTIVE MASSES, SOLID IN APPEARANCE YET INTANGIBLE IN CONSISTENCY.

Naya's desire to save Junior's soul bothered me, and the fact that it bothered me chafed my already raw nerves.

"Should we call the telecom company?" Levi's voice snapped my attention off her locked door.

I tried to speak, but my jaw was not having it. I nodded. I wanted to end this case, and Junior, and Robbie, and get out of Venezuela with my team.

If Naya insisted on reforming the Triple, I'd make sure her father found out. If anyone could keep the girl away from a man who murdered for sport, it was the doting archangel.

Levi clicked on his tablet, and a dial tone knelled through the suite like a clocktower marking someone's last hour.

Then the line clicked, and a clear, feminine voice swept across the tense air. "This call will be recorded for quality assurance. Please state your full name and date of birth after the beep."

"Pablo Rivas-Perez, born December 4th, 2011."

"Our automated system requires a voice identification. Please say YES to proceed."

Levi hit enter on the word *yes*.

"Please repeat after me: *The world is a wonderful place*."

I snorted. Yeah, *wonderful*. Made even more so by your customers.

Levi quickly tapped out the sentence, then pressed enter, and Junior's mix of British and Spanish flecked words rang out.

A little jingle played. "Your voice has been authenticated, Mr. Perez. Stay on the line while we connect you to one of our representatives."

Noah pumped a fist in the air.

The line clicked, and then a man's voice dribbled through the tablet's loudspeaker. "How may I help you today, Señor Perez?"

Levi cued up the answer: "I'm calling to activate the eSIMs on my account."

I shifted on my sneakered feet as the sales consultant replied, "Wonderful. Let's get those set up." *Click click click.* "May I have your password?"

"Password?" Noah mouthed.

Of course the prick had protected this account . . . I would've done the same.

Levi slung his wide gaze in my direction. The others did as well.

My nerves jangled. What password could Junior have chosen? I tried to climb into his head. Lord of Caracas? King of the world? *Dios*, to suit his God-complex? And in what plucking language?

"What was his mother's name?" Noah murmured, even though the guy on the line couldn't hear us. All he could hear was whatever words Levi typed.

Boone rubbed his jaw. "Azucena."

Noah cocked an eyebrow. "Should we try that?"

Levi cued it up but didn't press enter, waiting for my approval.

What happened if we got it wrong? Would the telecom company signal the disturbance to Junior? Would Levi's screen fill with a virus that erased all the data we'd collected?

Rapid keyboard clicking sounded through the tablet speaker. "Do you need another moment to retrieve your password, Mr. Perez?"

"Should we ask him for a hint?" Boone looked up at me.

They were all looking at me. Oh, how I wished Dov was here, because the weight of this responsibility was suffocating.

I shifted from one sneaker to the other. "That'll raise an instant red flag." Already our lag in answering was problematic. "Pretend you had another call to explain the wait."

Levi cued up: "My apologies. I had another call."

"Not a problem, Mr. Perez. I'm here to assist *you*, so just let me know once you have that password."

Levi joggled one knee, looking from Noah to me to Galina to his brother.

"What about *Circle Foundation*?" Boone suggested.

Levi froze before whipping his fingers across the digital keypad to type it out. He looked up, waiting for my green-light.

I decided to ferret out the most logical password by using process of elimination. Robbie Dunmore had set up Pablo's account. Azucena Perez died the summer before Pablo was sent to boarding school in England. Even though he'd surely heard of her, Robbie had never met her. Her name couldn't possibly have been *his* first choice. Not to mention, it seemed too easy to crack, and for all my wishing the two Triples were dimwits, they sadly weren't.

I steeled my spine. "Go with *Circle Foundation*."

"In what language?" Levi murmured.

"He's speaking English, and the company's British, so let's go with that."

Levi pressed enter, and our deepfake Pablo articulated the five syllables.

Silence ensued, the type that was so loaded it crawled over flesh and sank into bones.

Then, "Thank you, Mr. Perez. That password is correct." *Click click click.* "I'll have that QR code generated immediately and placed inside your secure dashboard. Unless you'd prefer it emailed?"

"No email." The words rushed out of me, before Levi made them rush out of his tablet.

"That's what I thought." *Click click.* "May I help you with anything else today?"

"No. That'll be all. Thank you."

"Have a lovely day, Mr. Perez. And please don't hesitate to call back if you need assistance with anything else."

After another *thank you*, Levi hung up.

It got so quiet, we could hear the gurgle of pipes in the wall, the creak of Boone's barstool, the rise of Noah's chest, the rush of Galina's breaths.

"I can't believe we got it right . . . ." Noah murmured, as we all continued to gape at each other like trouts who'd collided while swimming. And then his face cleaved into a huge grin, and he whooped.

Boone and Galina high-fived.

Relief prickled my skin but didn't penetrate. *Too easy.* It had been too easy. I didn't like easy.

"Check his dashboard." I wouldn't rejoice until the labyrinth of black pixels appeared.

Levi blew up one of the windows on his screen and worked his magic in the login area. A second later, we were in, and there, on the screen, sat the most beautiful QR code I had ever seen.

Emotion careened through me at the sight of those tiny broken lines. We'd plucking done it!

"Now what?" Noah asked as Levi climbed off his perch and shakily drew the minibar door open to grab a bottle of iced tea.

"Now we activate the SIM cards and delete them." My shoulders finally dropped, my stress level plummeting right along with them.

My gaze flicked to Naya's door. I was itching to bang on it and bellow our success. Would it change her mind about reforming Junior, though?

I refocused on Levi's glowing tablet and the geometrical code. "How long will it take from this point forward?"

"It should be quick." He held his phone out to the code until his camera captured it.

The words, "*Activating eSIMS*" materialized, along with a throbber.

Quick was unfortunately not instant.

"Let me know when it's done." I marched over to Naya's door and knocked.

No answer.

"I'll go talk to her," Galina offered.

"No." My word was a tad abrupt, but Naya and I had a lot of unresolved issues to iron out. "Can you text Dov to find out Junior's score?" I looked over my shoulder at her. "Please?"

She sighed at my pretext to dismiss her, which wasn't entirely a pretext. I did need the information. Although I doubted the guy's soul had become any shinier, if anything went wrong, and I had to resort to offing him, I wanted to make sure my wings didn't suffer.

I was about to rap again when pride got the better of me. I tried the handle, which gave way beneath my palm. I reasoned that if Naya had wanted to keep me out, she would've locked herself away.

Besides, I *had* knocked.

Without glancing at the others, I entered the dimly-lit room and shut the door quietly. The shower was running, and it triggered the memory of another shower, one where Naya's blood had been all over me.

My stomach clenched and my fingers balled.

Forget reforming Junior . . . I wouldn't even allow her to call him. Especially now that we'd foiled his grand plan.

50

NAYA

"It worked." Adam's voice startled me so much I almost dropped the towel I was still securing around my body.

"What worked?" I didn't bother asking him why he was sitting at the foot of my bed, shoulders rolled forward, hands crushing his kneecaps. I'd suspected he'd seek me out.

"We obtained the QR code from the telecom company." Adam looked away from the navy rug. "Levi's activating the SIMs as we speak."

My fingers froze on the back of the clip holding my hair up. "So . . . so . . . ?"

"So, we win."

I must've squeezed the clip because my hair poured over my shower-dampened shoulders. "That's . . ."

"Sensational news? I couldn't agree with you more." His mouth quirked at the corners, his dimple pressing in. "Our job here is done. As soon as Levi deletes the SIM cards, we're leaving."

"Without the girls?"

"They can't explode."

"They have explosives in their body. Those aren't going to come out by themselves."

"We'll leak the information to the British press. The King will execute his son for treason and save the girls, because that'll be the diplomatic thing to do."

I tried not to flinch at how unmoved Adam sounded by the idea of a father murdering his own son. "What about Robbie and his mother?"

Adam rubbed his palms up and down his thighs. Up and down. "There was a crapload of skeletons in the Dunmores' marsh. We'll pull a few out and identify the remains, then locate their families and let them avenge their dead."

Ice. My blood became ice. Even though Adam's plan was solid, I didn't want to dwell on the marsh and the cadavers it held.

"It's game over for all of them, Naya. We're leaving tonight." Adam clapped his thighs and rose, as though our discussion was over. "*Everyone* goes."

"Did you find out Pablo's score?"

"Galina's finding out." His mouth flattened.

"If he's no longer a Triple, Adam, then I object to your decision of informing his father."

"If he's no longer a Triple, then his soul will get collected, and in a few decades, he'll get a second shot at being a better human."

"You're talking of letting someone perish because it's more convenient than saving him." I walked over to my dresser and fished out a tank top and jeans, both plain and functional. All my fun clothes were still at the Dunmore manor. Unless Emmy had taken more than just my jacket. I almost wished she had because I wanted Ama's collection of T-shirts back. And my shoes. Angels, I'd had such nice shoes.

"Your heart makes you blind."

My vertebrae stiffened. I turned to face him, squeezing my little pile of clothes to my chest. "My heart makes me look for what you don't care to see."

"You really think someone who's killed hundreds of humans has a conscience? Come on, Naya. Grow up."

I balked. Where did he get off speaking to me as though I were a rambunctious child? "If you have no encouragements or tips for me on how to help a Triple, then please show yourself out." I glared at the pair of sneakers with the roses on them. After thanking Galina for them earlier, I'd found out she had nothing to do with them, that they were all Adam. I'd been meaning to thank him but no longer felt like it. The same way I didn't feel like wearing them.

Palms settled on my bare shoulders. I'd been so busy seething, I assumed Adam had heeded my demand, but I should've known better. My fellow black-wing obeyed no one.

"I'm sorry, all right?" His body dwarfed mine.

"Well, I'm sorry, too." When his eyebrows bent in confusion, I added, "I'm sorry you said what you did because it makes me regret having given my first kiss to someone who thinks so poorly of me."

He hissed. "I don't. Don't say that."

"By *that*, you mean what I'm thinking? Sort of ironic you'd ask this of me when you have no qualms sharing each one of your thoughts."

"Feather..."

"Don't. Don't call me that." I shrugged off his hands by leaning so far back into the dresser, the frame bit into my spine. "And don't touch me."

His pupils dilated as though my dismissal had bruised his very irises. I tried to walk away from him, but his arms came down on either side of me, caging me in. "Stop. Please."

"Stop what exactly?"

"Pushing me away."

I craned my neck back. "Were you expecting a hug after your half-assed apology? Maybe that's what you're used to, but I have enough self-worth to know I deserve someone who doesn't think I'm an impetuous kid with no acumen."

His lids closed, squeezed, crinkling their outer corners. With what seemed like Herculean strength, he jimmied his body away from the dresser. "I don't think of you like that at all. I'm just bloody worried. I know you're immortal but—" His tongue scraped his lips. "But you bleed. You bled all over me. I can still smell it." His eyes opened. "If that man hurts you—"

"I'll have deserved it, and I'll find my way to a guild and let the ophanim deal with my injuries."

"No one deserves to be hurt. But that's beside the point, because if he hurts you, I will murder him, whether his score is ninety or a hundred." Adam's eyes were unfocused, as though he were picturing himself ending Pablo's life. "And I'll make sure to draw his death out."

Soft down brushed against my shin, dissolving the bedroom and the boy looming over me.

Suddenly, I was sitting, my hand—not mine... Adam's—on

some girl's bare thigh. Jealousy spiked and engulfed me so fast I couldn't focus on what he was telling her.

I wanted out of this memory.

Out of this dark club and away from this human he'd clearly reformed by seduction.

When I finally snapped back to reality, my palate burned with annoyance and grief. I managed to swallow back both. What I didn't manage to stifle was my body's shaking.

I pushed away from Adam and dropped my clothes on the bed. Their sharp hems blurred, stitching into the white sheets.

It was an old memory, yet I felt so betrayed. Unreasonably so since Adam wasn't mine then, and he wasn't mine now. And the more I thought about it, the more I realized, we should never be together. We were too combustible. A spark, and we'd catch fire, and fires torched everything they touched. Especially celestial fire. We'd end up destroying each other: wings, bodies, and souls.

The scent of charred flesh and ashen feathers snuck up my nose and turned my stomach. My shoulders smarted. Was this phantom agony a premonition? I gripped the sides of my face, trying to shut down my runaway imagination.

"Naya, baby, what's wrong?" Adam clutched my waist, turned me. His eyes were so green. So bright.

Like his scent.

Green, bright, with a hint of sweetness.

I inhaled deep lungfuls of him, needing to repel the reek of charred feathers.

"Which mission of mine did you see?"

His words tossed me back into the chasm of jealousy from which I'd just emerged. "Does it matter? Don't you seduce all your sinners?"

His grip slackened. "Not all." He surprisingly didn't lose a feather, which meant it must've been true.

Although, it would only take one sinner to make it true . . .

"You're mad." Not a question.

"I'm not mad, Adam; I'm wary."

"About?"

"About being one of so many women to fall under your charm."

"I have to compete with Jarod."

An annoyed breath streamed out the corner of my mouth,

blowing back a renegade strand of hair. "He's an imaginary man. All those women . . . they exist."

"Existed."

"Did they all perish from heartbreak?" I fingered the knot on my towel, making sure it was secure.

His mouth hooked to the side, making that horribly beguiling dimple of his appear. "What I meant was, they existed before you. And that's where they'll stay. In the past."

"What about your next sinners?" My stomach roiled at the memory of the girl whose thigh he'd stroked.

He sighed, and his hands rose to my cheeks, landing gently. "I'm going to confess something that'll hopefully change your mind about us. Swear not to make fun of me?"

Curiosity rumpled my resolve to point out there was no *us*.

"Swear it."

I expelled a sigh. "Fine. I swear."

"Okay. Here goes." He breathed in and out a few times, as though readying himself for a cliff dive. "Noah thinks you're my soulmate."

My lashes rose so high I thought they'd collide with my hairline. Out of all the things he could've confessed, I hadn't expected *that*.

"I grumbled at him when he said it, but I'm not grumbling anymore, because you make me feel—" Adam's lips shut, opened, and then his forehead puckered. "You make me feel so much."

At his confession, my fingers drifted back down to my sides, shivering like my pulse, because he, too, made me feel so much. *Too* much. It was as though my soul came alive when he was close. Like he electrified it. I supposed that, in a way, he did. After all, I'd smoldered him three times in one day.

The furrow on his forehead grew more pronounced as my silence dragged, but admitting I felt the same felt dangerous. Like handing someone a loaded gun with which he could take you out at any moment. Yes, he'd handed me a weapon, but Adam was a master at seduction. It's what he did for a living. Outside of guarding select humans.

"I'm infatuated with you, Naya." He dropped his forehead to mine. "Since we've met, all I see is you. All I think about is you. And it's driving me bloody insane, because I don't know how to make it stop."

My chest tightened. "Why do you want to make it stop?"

"Because even if you're not in any hurry to ascend, you're sixty feathers away from Elysium."

A rope of emotion coiled around my throat, around my chest, winding itself so snugly I could hardly breathe.

He nosed my cheek, and my lids slid shut. "Do you feel anything for me? Besides wariness and annoyance?" There was an edge to his tone, a tension that exposed his insecurities.

That was what ended up carving through my defenses and flattening my walls. Not his pretty words or his distressed admission that I may be his soulmate.

His vulnerability.

"I smoldered you, Adam. And not just once."

His head straightened, and his gaze held mine.

"How can you wonder about my feelings when I wear them on my skin?"

Although I didn't ask my body to prove my point, it must've felt Adam needed extra convincing, because the narrow darkness between us began to spangle with my soul's light.

NAYA

*A*s my body continued to serenade his with flickering light, his earlier declaration twirled inside my mind.

Soulmates...

Even though the ophanim claimed it was a human fabrication, Ama insisted souls had mates, more than one actually, and it had always made sense to me because it explained why we sometimes felt so much for a complete stranger.

Even if Adam hadn't always inspired love, he'd unfailingly inspired emotion.

A lot of emotion.

He canted my head up, then picked a strand of hair off my lashes and tucked it gently behind my ear. "You're blinding me, Feather."

His whispered words jolted my heart, transported me out of this dusky hotel room and into a temple of marble and gold, where they echoed anew against my cheek in another man's voice, in another language.

I blinked away the abounding splendor and Jarod's voice, and returned to my bedroom and the boy with the jeweled eyes. Trying to calm my racing heart and conceal my glitching mind, I croaked, "I'll get you sunglasses in the morning."

Adam smiled. "And dim the sight of you shimmering for me? Bring on the third-degree burn to my corneas." He grazed my lips with the rough pad of his thumb, parting them, wetting only the tip of his finger before gliding it over my mouth.

It was only my mouth he touched, yet I could feel phantom fingers stroking another seam, one that heated and dampened as he dragged his finger back across my cheekbone.

"I'm starting to wonder if you were made for me." His murmur filled my stomach with sparrows, and my blood, with their aria. "Because there isn't a thing about you I don't find captivating."

They were just pretty words, but Elysium, how sweet they felt upon my skin.

He cupped my jaw and slanted his head, replacing the lingering scrape of his calluses with the feather-soft pillow of his mouth. The contact made the light that darted over my skin sink into my pores and crackle in my blood.

So much for nipping this in the bud.

Adam had spoken about infatuation, but if anyone was infatuated, it was me, the girl whose skin skipped with glitter with a mere flick of his breath.

Instead of resisting, instead of pushing him away, I slid my hands up to his neck and towed his head lower, closer. I tasted his heartbeats, greedily made them mine before surrendering some of my own. He licked them off my tongue as he imprinted the shape of his body against mine, branding himself into my smoldering flesh.

I'm starting to wonder if you were made for me.

His words reverberated against the great scarlet muscle in my chest, bloating it so precipitously, I worried my ribs would perish like my will to stay away from such a sweet-talker.

Adam drew one of his hands down the slope of my neck to the point of my shoulder, then dipped his roughened knuckles along the bare skin of my arm. Everywhere he touched burned, the fire spreading, catching on all the places he hadn't touched yet. I was a gathering inferno, a glittering cosmos. I was energy and heat.

The friction between our bodies untangled the precarious knot holding my towel, and it slipped. I broke our kiss with a shallow gasp, reaching out for the scrap of cotton, but it slid past my outstretched fingers and pooled at my feet.

The cool air redistributed the heat in my body, sending most of it inside my cheeks. I banded one arm around my chest as Adam panted out harsh, ragged breaths. Although I wasn't ashamed of my naked form, my wings sprouted out and curled around me.

"Don't!" Adam's palms jerked up to block my downy screen. "Don't hide from me."

I froze at the feel and pressure of him on a part of my body that no one had ever touched. Eyes on mine, he coaxed the glittery black expanse back open, and then even more gently, he lowered my arm from my breasts.

His throat rose and fell ten times before his gaze finally dipped beneath the point of my chin toward my pink, peaked nipples. Then lower, to my taut stomach, still a little yellowed. Eyes weren't hands and yet I could feel them scrape over each curve and toned muscle, before settling on the tangle of blonde curls at the juncture of my thighs.

His Adam's apple bobbed sharply in his throat as his blazing irises finally returned to my face. "I understand why your father hid you from me." His wings unspooled, stretched. *Stretched.* "He knew you'd become my obsession."

My father had hidden me from *all* males, and I hardly inspired obsession in any other, but I took Adam's declaration and stored it atop all the other honeyed lines he'd fed me tonight.

His fingers brushed across my feathers, and a thrill shot through the fine webbing. When he reached the lowest ridge, his hands stilled, along with my breathing. "May I?"

Lungs clutching the breath I'd taken, I nodded, and he traced the inverted V of my wings, his gaze back on mine. I exhaled and gulped in a new breath as he pursued his exploration, the weight of his gaze and fingers reawakening the smolder that had died off when my towel had deserted me.

"I can't believe *you*, of all people, believe in soulmates," I rasped.

"Trust me"—his fingers hit a spot that made my back arch and my breath hitch—"I can't either." His fingers combed back down through my feathers, his caress so excruciatingly slow it pulled a moan from my lips. "But I don't have any other explanation for how plucking drawn I am to you." He dropped his mouth to the crook of my neck and suckled the soft flesh.

I tipped my head back to give him better access and gripped his shoulders. "I've never touched my wings. Well . . . *there*."

He blew warm air against my damp skin. "Don't tell me it's because you find the spot hard to reach."

I smiled. I supposed it was a little, but that wasn't why.

Shivers paced up and down my spine with each languid stroke. "No. I never touched myself, because I didn't want to lose control and become a slave to my body's whims."

He picked his head off my neck to peer at me. "Then I assume you've never touched yourself"—one of his hands dropped from my wing, and I felt its absence like a fallen feather, but then it slipped between my thighs and drew a slow line across my wet folds—"here either?"

A breathy whimper spilled from my lips. "Clumsily, and without much success."

The rough pad of his thumb circled my tight bundle of nerves, and I gasped, my vision starting to dissolve along the edges. "Oh, angels. Adam. What are you doing?"

"Learning you," he murmured, returning his mouth to my neck before dragging it lower.

I squeezed his shoulders, probably leaving imprints of all ten of my fingers.

When he latched onto the pink bead of my nipple, heat flared through my core, and his name seared my lips.

I wasn't sure how long I burned with bliss, but it struck me that I wanted him to burn with me. I skated my hands off his shoulders and dragged them over the outline of his thick, long feathers.

A low growl built in his throat and shook the air between us, and his hands turned clumsy. He lifted his mouth off my breasts and narrowed his eyes on mine.

I didn't remove my hands but did pause. "Want me to stop?"

"*Never*," he all but snarled, the vein along his temple becoming so engorged it stood out starkly beneath the dark sweep of his hair.

I drew my palms lower, stroking each raven vane from tip to quill. When I started the ascension toward his inverted V, his gaze turned ferocious, then smoothed, then pained again, as though he were teetering between pure agony and complete ecstasy.

Even though watching the play of emotions made for a spectacular show, I leaned forward to taste him again. My lips glided over the rough stubble lining his jaw to the velvet-softness of his lobe. I caught it between my teeth, nipping it gently, before releasing it and drawing a line of kisses toward his mouth.

His lips were as hard as tanned hide and didn't soften. I wasn't sure any part of Adam's body was capable of softening.

"Naya . . . Feather . . . baby."

I didn't quicken my touch on his wings the same way I didn't stop stamping kisses across his face, marking him like he'd marked me. I wanted to drag out this gentle torture until his heart pounded out of alignment.

This wouldn't be the first time he came, but it would be the first time he came *with me*, and I wanted him to remember it. I wanted it to become his only memory. I wanted my fingers to replace all the others that had traveled across the valleys and hills of his burnished skin.

"Have you ever been with an angel?"

He grunted. Hummed. "No!" His answer was as much a shout as a whisper.

"So no one else's fingers have ever been where mine are now?"

He released another throaty, almost pained croak. "No. First. Oh, pluck." He panted. "Holy . . . Feather." More words streamed out at intervals, but they didn't make much sense. And then he stopped talking, and his body went alarmingly still.

I almost stopped moving my hands, but one look at his sealed lids and parted mouth spurred my fingers' slow dance, and I played Adam until a shudder shook his rigid body and another shook his wings, and a spot of warmth bloomed over his jeans, dampening my palpitating stomach.

I drew my fingers down one final time before letting them fall away.

He stared and stared. And I couldn't tell if he was happy, mad, in shock.

As the wrought silence endured, I remembered how naked I was and gathered my hair over my shoulders, finger-combing the strands until they lay flat over my breasts. "Was that—okay?"

"Okay?" His hand came up to my face. "You just ruined me for humankind, Feather."

I wanted to revel in the compliment, but couldn't help but wonder: *what about for angelkind?*

His eyes roamed over mine, hunting their depths for a reaction.

Was he expecting me to grin smugly because I was endowed with the ability to see and touch the appendages that made us different? Hundreds of thousands of supernaturals had that ability. All four fletchings outside this door could do what I'd just done. It was no accomplishment, merely DNA.

"I should get dressed." I twisted around and sidestepped him to grab my underwear. After yanking it up my legs, I pulled on my tank top, then my jeans. As I zipped them, I glanced over my shoulder.

Adam was watching me with both eyebrows bent, as though trying to solve a puzzle. "Why did you pull away?"

"To get dressed." I nodded to his pants. "Want me to get you a change of clothes?"

"What I want is for you not to ice me out. Do you think I was lying when I told you that you'd ruined me for humans? Because—"

"I know you weren't lying." I stared at the rug where a black feather would've lain had it been a lie. Only mine from earlier shivered on the rug beside my nightstand.

"Then what the Abaddon have I done now?"

"It's stupid, Adam." The more I dwelled on it, the more I realized how stupid it was.

"Nothing that makes you angry or sad is stupid." He took a tentative step toward me, wrapped a tentative hand around my hip. His stance and grip both firmed when I didn't retreat. "Please tell me."

I lowered my gaze to the chipped pink polish on my toenails and rued my insecurities. "I just assumed *I'd* ruined you, not my ability to touch your wings." I looked back up at him, discovered that his eyes had become crushed-velvet instead of stained glass. "And not just for humans." I licked my lips and murmured, "I warned you it was silly."

"I've never had an interest in our kind until you. As for humans, you ruined me for them the night you appeared on that sidewalk and thrust yourself into my life."

"I didn't thrust—"

"You did."

I wrinkled my nose. "It sounds awful."

"It sounds like a woman who knows her mind."

I did know my mind. It was my heart I was currently having trouble with.

"If anyone should be feeling insecure at the moment, that person should be me. I tell you I think you're my soulmate, and I get nothing in return. Well, besides a spectacularly wet crotch." His dimple tucked into his cheek, but the indent vanished almost as swiftly. "Do you—Do you *not* believe in soulmates? Is that it?"

"I do believe in them."

Hesitantly, he asked, "Do you believe I could be yours?"

The vision of the French man with the haunting dark eyes swept across my mind. "Ama says we have many."

His pupils seemed to sharpen. "Many?"

"Mates means friends."

Although his hand was still on my hip, his grip had slackened considerably. "So, I could be one of your *many* soulmates?"

"Yes, but—"

His hand fell from my body. "You really know how to make a man feel special."

"That's not—Adam . . ." I reached out for him but, this time, he was the one who pulled away.

"I'm glad to hear we have many. Immortality's a mighty long time to remain faithful to just one person."

My fingers balled around air, even though it felt like they'd balled around my heart. "Wait."

He didn't. He flung open my door and barged out before I could add that I didn't think every soul connection was the same, that some ran on different frequencies. The bond that tied my parents was evidently different than the one that tied me to them.

A door slammed shut, and the thwack resonated beneath my ribs.

52

NAYA

An hour after Adam's temper tantrum, I was sitting in the hotel bar, nursing a glass of sparkling water, waiting for Pablo. I'd phoned him, partly because Galina had found out from Dov that the Prince's score had dipped beneath the hundred bar, and partly because the others—excluding Adam who was MIA—had become edgy about the QR code they'd downloaded. It still hadn't activated the SIMs, which, according to Levi, wasn't normal.

Noah had been against me meeting with Pablo, but the Prince, who hadn't been surprised to hear my voice, had insisted on talking face-to-face or not at all.

"It's a ploy," Noah had hissed.

"He can't kill me."

"What if he puts the bomb in you again?" Galina had bounced her leg.

"It'll come out. Again."

The Dutch brothers had kept quiet; one concentrated on his screen, the other on his thoughts.

Noah had jumped from the couch and started pacing the chocolate-marble. "We'll remove the devices from their abdomens tonight."

"How? We're not surgeons." I was already fitting my feet into my shoes, my insole smarting from my cactus collision. "If we nick a blood vessel, they'll bleed out, and these girls aren't Triples."

In other words, we'd lose our wings.

I'd called Pablo back. He'd suggested his suite. My father had instilled enough of a survival instinct in me to insist meeting in a public space. The hotel bar had felt like a good option, since the team could monitor me from the surveillance cameras Boone had stuck around the room.

"If you think he's a lost cause, Naya"—Galina had walked me to the suite door—"play with your earlobe and say you're feeling jetlagged, and we'll enact Plan K."

Plan K was phoning up the King and warning him of his son's deceit.

Plan K would save the girls but doom the Prince.

My gaze had strayed to Adam's closed door but only my gaze. The rest of me had drifted out the suite, past the pile of Noah's shiny pink feathers, into the elevator, and across the lobby.

I checked the time. Thirteen minutes late.

Was Pablo hoping his tardiness would make me antsy or was he still making his way out of the garden?

Listening to the two women seated at the table beside mine discuss the Prince's single status, I ran the tip of my index finger over the curved petal of the stargazer lily sitting so proud and pretty in a slender, handblown turquoise vase.

"I heard all those British girls were brought so he could have his pick of a bride," one of the women gossiped.

"They're a little young, no?"

"Azucena was eighteen when she married King Pablo."

Azucena . . . Lily. Pablo's mother. It explained the name of the hotel and why these blooms were strewn across every surface. Although I hadn't forgotten Pablo's wandering hands or his ploy to wield innocents as weapons, my soft heart wept with empathy at how violently his mother had been torn from him.

A ruckus sounded outside the bar. A second later, four conspicuous bodyguards streamed through the double-wide entrance, making the thirty or so humans crowded around the smattering of mahogany tables and the backlit glass bar sit up straighter.

"¡*Fuera*!" they yelled. "¡*Ahora*!" Out! Now!

The women jerked out of their seats, along with the rest of the patrons. Never before had I seen people scatter so fast. Once the place was emptied of everyone but me and the young, ponytailed bartender, who'd served me my water, three of the guards swept the room for stragglers or explosive devices, while the fourth made me stand to pat me down.

An all-clear rang out from the other guards as I sank back into my padded seat, which was as wide as a small throne and carved just as extravagantly.

As the massive man, who'd just searched me, spoke into the black device on his wrist that resembled a high-tech watch, my gaze slipped to the backlit shelf of alcohol bottles, toward one of the surveillance cameras. Was Adam watching me from the suite? Had he even emerged from his bedroom?

Footsteps resonated on the marble outside and then Pablo appeared in the doorway. Bracketed by two more guards, he strode over and pulled out the purple velvet armchair in front of mine. After he sat, his guards took up residence by the bar.

Pablo scanned my face, as though running my features through his memory to make sure they matched the girl he'd met back in England. "You look different."

His gaze lingered on the hickey Adam had left on my collarbone and which I'd, unfortunately, only noticed when I'd tied my hair up in a ponytail in the mirrored lift. I doubted Pablo was referring to my neck, though. I suspected he was referring to my disposition.

I spun my glass of water slowly, leaving a wet ring on the wood. "Almost dying will do that to a person."

I caught the subtlest downward tug to his mouth. I hoped it was sympathy. "What brings you to Caracas, *mi sol?*"

The nickname felt ironic, considering he and Robbie had snuffed out my sunny spirit and turned me into a ray of pitch-black, made even blacker by my newest misunderstanding with Adam.

I was about to tell him not to call me by anything but my name, but checked my temper. I was here to talk him out of blowing up innocents.

"You," I finally said.

His posture seemed to change, stiffen; his gloved hands on the armrests, to still. "You came all the way here for me?"

"Yes."

"I'm flattered."

"Flattery wasn't my intent."

"What was?"

I dragged my finger over a drop of water and dragged it across the smooth tabletop. "I heard my friend Natasha passed away on the flight over."

He studied me as though trying to glean just how much I knew. "Drugs are an unfortunate pastime."

"They are, but they weren't one of hers." I hadn't known her well but well enough. I leaned forward as though to impart a little secret to him. "Her older brother died of a drug overdose six years ago, and she never forgave him for it."

Pablo's single pupil shrank, making his pale iris all the more luminous. "Are you implying there was foul play in her death?"

"I'm not implying it, Señor Perez; I'm telling you. In case you weren't aware. I hope you weren't. I hope only the Dunmores are the monsters in this story." I slid my gaze over the socket covered by the leather patch. "The Dunmores *and* your father."

A vein titillated the freshly shaven skin of his jaw. "How did you survive?"

"You mean how did I not drown in the swamp Susan and her eldest son tossed me into?"

His nostrils flared as the account of the Dunmores' nighttime activities settled. "Susan and Henry did *what?*"

"They tried to drown me. On Robbie's command. They tied my wrists and ankles to cinder blocks and tossed me inside that marsh we cantered by. Thankfully, the rope binding my wrists came loose, and my body rose."

He leaned forward, and the heavy wooden frame of his chair creaked. He dropped his forearms on the table, his fine navy suit creasing at the elbows, revealing an extra inch of bright white cuffs speared through with faceted rubies that resembled drops of fresh blood. "All by itself?"

I eluded his question by pandering to his ego. "You strike me as a man who appreciates justice." My gaze traveled off the cufflinks and onto his black leather gloves. "Isn't that why you decimated the family of the general who stole your mother from you?"

Silence dropped like rain, drumming the air between us.

"I want justice for Natasha. For Emmeline Rogers' brother. For myself."

"Are you asking me to murder people for you, *mi sol?*"

"No. I'm asking you to keep Robbie and his mother from flying out of your country tomorrow morning. I'm asking you to have them tried for their crimes and locked in jail."

Unlike Adam, I wasn't after their deaths, because dying was the easy way out. They wouldn't even have to face Abaddon. Their souls would just cease to exist. Especially now that Susan's attempt on my life had given her a Triple's score.

"You cared enough to murder the man you thought had ended my life with his poor medical skills. Your own cousin. Won't you do something about the one who outright tried to eradicate me?"

Pablo didn't move a single muscle, but his eye twitched, and that twitch made the bodyguard parked nearest us dig under his suit jacket, probably for a gun. The seated ones shoved their chairs back to rise. Pablo lifted one hand to calm them.

"Is it asking for so much that you put them in jail so they can't harm another person?"

"No, but I unfortunately can't do that."

"Because they know too much?"

"They're apparently not the only ones who know too much." He leaned back in his chair, folding his legs as though we were having the most relaxed conversation. "What's stopping me from putting a bullet inside *your* head?"

My pulse didn't leap because if he wanted me dead, he'd have given his guards the order to shoot. "I'd have said your conscience, but you're at war with your conscience. And you'll stay at war with it as long as innocent lives are in play. I understand you want your father gone, but don't take him out the coward's way. Don't take him out Robbie's way." I was fishing, but my sudden realization felt accurate. "Am I mistaken that using the Circle Girls as weapons was his idea?"

Pablo didn't confirm or deny it, but his Adam's apple bobbed up and down in rapid succession.

"Besides, ending my life won't solve your problem. I'm not working alone, and everyone on my team knows what you're planning to do. If you shoot me, they'll inform your father of the *coup*." I punched out the word, hoping I hadn't played my ace too soon.

He glanced down at my phone, which was lying flat on the table.

I grazed the screen to show him no one was on the other line. "He's not on the phone, and I'm not recording this conversation. I have no need for a confession, not when the device you put in me is in my possession." My phone screen went dark again, almost as dark as Pablo's mood. "I'm here, Pablo, because I believe you're not the monster your upbringing turned you into." I let my hand fall flat on the tabletop. "I believe there's still some goodness in your heart, but for it to shine through, you need to either lay your political aspirations to rest or find another way to impeach your father."

Pablo snorted. "Kings cannot be impeached. The only way to remove them from power is by killing them."

"Will killing him make you happy? Is ruling this country truly what you want?"

"Yes."

I wished he'd hesitated because taming someone's desire for revenge was easier than forcing them to turn away from a dream. "Then don't start your reign of power by executing innocent women. Start it by putting those snakes you call friends behind bars and gathering a group of true friends. True supporters."

His mouth puckered, smoothed, puckered, the wheels spinning inside his head.

"Wouldn't you want your mother to be proud?"

"My mother's no longer here." Although far from tender, his voice had lost a degree of its steel.

"You're a spiritual person, aren't you?" Ama's favorite expression was: *go big or go home*. I chose big, but if big didn't work, then I'd go home. "Do you believe in the afterlife?"

His gaze flicked to his bodyguards, to the bartender mopping his brow behind the bar, before returning to me. "What's your point?"

"What if I told you that if you go through with your assault, your soul will perish for all of eternity? That you won't be reunited with your mother?" My tone hitched as the ishim punished me for disclosing one of our people's closely-guarded secrets.

"I'll have my whole life to atone for my sins."

"Your whole life won't be long enough," I said, glancing over at my feather, which shimmered like spilled diamonds on the stained ebony floorboards.

"Why? Are you planning on cutting it short?"

"If I wanted you dead, you'd already be dead."

He laughed. "You're truly something, *mi sol*."

"Something that could get you to change?" *Come on, Pablo. Prove to me you still have a conscience.*

He sobered, his expression turning so grave I sensed I was losing him. "A man can only fail so many times before it strips him of his pride. I'm not failing again." After a beat, he added, "Their families will want for nothing."

"For nothing? Money doesn't repair broken hearts."

"My father knifed my eye the last time I tried to remove him from power."

I stared at the one he had left. "So you think it's fair forty-nine young girls pay for your mutilation with their lives?"

"What is fifty lives compared to all the ones I'll change once I'm in power?" Forever trying to justify his intent.

My hope that this Triple's soul could still be salvaged shriveled. "Those girls have families and friends. They have prospects and dreams. Their lives *matter*. Maybe not to you, but to those who love them, they matter." I lifted my hand to signal the waiter for the bill. "I guess I was wrong about you."

I could just hear Adam say: *I told you so.* That was, if my fellow black-winged fletching ever deigned to speak to me again.

The ponytailed bartender hurried over with a leather sleeve, trembling as he tendered the bill.

Pablo snatched it before I could and tossed it back at the guy as though it were a bone and he a dog. "Charge it to my residence."

Nodding, the bartender jolted backward, tripping over his own feet and knocking into the table beside us. The impact tipped over the turquoise vase. He quickly righted it before mopping the water with the corner of his belted apron.

"Tell me, Naya, who do you work for?" Pablo's voice was deceptively silky. "I can't imagine it's a government agency, because government agencies don't train their agents to feel. They train them to kill, and you aren't even armed."

My wings materialized at my back. "You're right. I wasn't trained to kill. I was trained to save."

He smiled. Actually. Smiled. "A true guardian angel."

"A true guardian angel who's jetlagged and done talking." I flipped my ponytail over my shoulder and touched my ear, activating Plan K.

ADAM

ANGELIC FACT #15
NEVER LET DREAMS GUIDE YOUR FLIGHT.

The tentative knocking at the door turned to brutal pounding. "Adam! Come on, man, let me in." Noah sounded desperate.

I was too pissed—physically and emotionally—to get off my perch and let him in. Why the Abaddon had I listened to him and his big mouth? More importantly, though, why the Abaddon had I spouted all that bullmush about soulmates to Naya?

Because she'd bared her body, and I'd felt compelled to bare my soul to even things out?

I downed the last of the beer I'd snatched from our bedroom minibar, then dropped the bottle on top of the medley of others. It didn't shatter, probably because it landed on one of my fallen feathers, but it still clinked satisfyingly as it rolled toward the base of the stone railing and settled amid the hotchpotch of glass recipients and black feathers.

The pounding resumed.

I swung my gaze toward the door I'd locked. Had Naya come to apologize?

"Adam, come on. Open up, man."

Yeah. Not Naya. The girl was probably on her way to reform the big bad Prince. Maybe she'd even call *him* her soulmate. *Ha.* It would be so like Naya to have a Triple as a soulmate.

I glanced back out over the city cloaked in night and stuck out my thumb and forefinger, shut one of my eyes, then pinched a star and imagined squeezing the light out of it. And then I visualized doing that to all the stars, so the twilit sky stopped glimmering like Naya's wings.

"I'm going to bust down the door if you don't forking open up!" Noah hollered.

I smirked. "Hope you don't bruise too many of your pretty verity feathers."

The pounding stopped. "Glad to hear you're alive."

"Can't die, remember?" I stared at the park down below. Imagined my body listing. My fingers breaking away from the stone. The air slashing my face. The gravity slurping down my weight.

All of me would shatter. Except my heart and ego, but both were already nice and injured, like my wings. How many feathers had I dropped since I'd met the seraphim's daughter?

More than she deserved.

Should've kept my distance from Asher's girl. The man was right to keep us apart. He must've known his daughter would screw with my head.

I lifted my hand, thinking I had a bottle wedged there, but all I held was a fistful of dark air and mocking stars.

"*Hola, guapo.*" *Hi, handsome.*

I looked to the side. Found two women leaning against the railing next door. No, three. By the looks of them, they were triplets. I squinted. *Wait, wait, wait.* There was just the one. "You got a minibar?"

"Why don't you come over and check?"

I stood, feet poised like a tightrope walker's.

"*¡Cuidado!*" *Careful!*

I snapped out my arms and my wings for balance and teetered over to the woman, stopping on the edge of my balcony. I stared into the dark void that separated it from hers, hated how it twinkled like the starlit firmament above. Why did every plucking thing have to shine?

I batted away Naya's smoldering body, bent at the knees, and jumped.
 Landed. Or thought I did.
 The world shifted beneath me.
 I stumbled.
 The woman screamed.

54

NAYA

The guard stationed closest to Pablo leaned over and murmured something so close to his lobe, I failed to hear the rapid-fire Spanish words. Were the King's men coming? Was that the news he was delivering?

Pablo nodded.

As the guard backed away, returning to his original post, I tucked my wings into my spine and started to rise.

"Sit, *mi sol*."

I didn't.

"I said, *sit*."

His guards moved closer.

My chest filled with wild battering. Adam had been right. There was no changing this man.

"You seem agitated, *mi sol*."

"Merely disappointed. I thought you were a better man." Although I was no longer in the mood for his pet name or his company, I magicked away my wings and sat back down. Since I was forced to wait for the King to storm the hotel, I decided to make the best of it. "Why do you hide your hands? Does your melted flesh remind you too much of your mother?"

His jaw became bladed. "Scars make a man look weak."

I draped one arm over the back of my chair and folded my legs to display my total lack of fear. "Funny. I personally think scars make a man look invincible."

He studied my face, my relaxed posture, either hunting for the truth of my words or wondering why I wasn't trembling. "My ex preferred me with gloves."

I flicked my ponytail. "And you cared about her preference?"

"You have me pegged for a heartless man, *mi sol*, but I can be tremendously considerate."

I dropped my hair. "I do find that hard to believe, considering your refusal to save the Circle Girls."

His eye tapered on the slope of my neck mottled by another man's kiss. "I was going to save you."

I'd inferred this from the decrease in his sinner score. "Good thing my father taught me to save myself."

"Is that what you're doing at the present moment? Saving yourself? Because if you were my daughter, I'd have told you asking the devil on a date was a surefire way to get yourself killed."

"This isn't a date; it's a meeting." I leaned back toward him to offer him an unobstructed view of my complete confidence. "Which I will walk away from."

"You are so unflappable in your optimism, Señorita Tremblay."

"Moreau not Tremblay."

"*Hmm.*" His fingers curled into his palm, stretching the leather. "I beg to differ. You see, I mourned your death. Until Robbie informed me I was mourning a ghost. Naya Moreau does not exist, but a girl sharing your DNA named Valentine Tremblay did. Not for long, though. She died minutes after her birth. I called your mother to tell her how deeply regretful I was about her daughter's passing."

So he knew which Céline Tremblay birthed me . . . I almost asked for the information but bit my tongue. He'd use it as leverage, and leverage was power. Besides, if he'd unearthed her identity, so could I.

"I wanted to send her flowers and a check. She asked if this was some sick joke because *her* Valentine has been dead for eighteen years." His face loomed so close that the faint scent of peppermint and gin permeated the air between us. "And yet, here you are. Which leads me to wonder if you are part cat."

I smirked. "I assure you, Señor Perez, I am no cat."

"Then how is it you are still alive?" His words smacked the tip of my nose, but still, I did not flinch.

"I told you, the rope was loose."

"What about when you were two minutes old? Was the rope loose then, too?"

"You'd have to ask the man who raised me, and trust me when I say this, you do *not* want to meet him. According to most, he's quite terrifying."

"My benchmark for terrifying is assuredly not the same as yours."

Even though I kept my gaze on his, I listened for sounds beyond the closed doors. Had the King not taken our warning seriously or were the Prince's men waging a battle with his outside the hotel walls? I wasn't sure how much longer I could keep the man entertained and my body bullet-free.

If they didn't show in the next minute, I'd have to fight my way out of the bar. Not impossible, but dangerous, because if I accidently caused the death of any of these men, I risked losing my feathers. The safer option would be to allow them to shoot me and escape whatever grave they stashed my body in, hoping it wouldn't be too deep or difficult to claw out of.

Come on, guys.

Come through for me.

Just as I was settling back to wait, the doors burst open.

Relief thrust back the unease creeping up my spine.

Until I heard a soft whimper.

Until I caught the flash of tears in a set of bright blue eyes.

55

NAYA

"I thought you were going to dispose of the rats, not bring them to me." Pablo frowned at Emmy, whose cheeks puffed with labored breaths and glistened with tears.

Robbie tensed the forearm he'd locked around her neck as he stepped forward. "The others are all dead. Just brought this one down here."

My heart stumbled. *The others? What others? The Circle Girls?* Had they set their bodies off?

"She claims she isn't part of the blonde's little posse." Robbie narrowed his hazel eyes on me.

Posse? Did he mean—

"So, what?" Pablo snapped. "You wanted confirmation that she was before ending her life?"

Emmy whimpered, hands wrapped around Robbie's forearms, knuckles white. "I don't know anything. I don't. I swear. I don't."

I blinked past the quaking bartender who had his back smooshed against the backlit rows of bottles, right into Boone's surveillance lens. If only it was a two-way mirror.

"I thought we could use her to interrogate the girl," Robbie said. "Find out where she stashed her *device*. We searched the suite, and it wasn't there."

The suite...

My ears began to buzz.

They'd ambushed my team.

That's what they'd meant by my *posse*.

"How?" I whispered, the news clanging through my head like an incessantly battered gong, the vibrations gathering volume and power, spiking my levels of adrenaline. Had they gotten footage of them in the auditorium or in the gardens? Was that how they'd known?

I swallowed, tasting the metallic tinge of my rising horror. I should've listened to Adam and kept myself out of the spotlight. How could I have thought, for even an instant, that I could outsmart Triples?

"How what, *mi sol*? How did we find your associates? You gave the telecom company the wrong password."

My mouth went dry.

"The second you downloaded the QR code, the manager himself called to inform me someone had hacked my account and offered me your coordinates on a silver platter. It took us a little while to find the right room, what with the location being the hotel."

No, no, no. This couldn't be happening.

Everyone on the team was trained and cunning. I'd watched Galina spar with Noah and Boone just that afternoon. I'd seen Adam in action. Had fought him. They were incredible . . . Far more skilled than I was. They must've been caught by surprise or not fought back for fear of killing someone and losing their feathers.

I forced myself to spot the silver lining. We still had two days to sabotage Pablo's coup. The second my friends woke up, the second their bodies rid themselves of the bullets, they'd get on the phone with the King. Maybe they'd even involve our people. At the very least, Dov. I swallowed back the lump swelling in my trachea and linked my fingers together so they'd stop displaying my shock.

"I have nothing to do with Naya's plan. I don't even know her. Not really." Emmy shook her head, blue eyes phosphorescent from all her crying. "I rented her a room. That's all. That's—"

"¡Por Dios, cállate, mujer!" Pablo roared.

Emmy quieted for a full second before a great big sob lurched out of her.

Grief that she'd gotten caught in the crossfire softened my heart. Even though she didn't care what happened to me, I cared what happened to her. "She's telling the truth. She has nothing to do with this. The same way the boy you had murdered, Robbie, had nothing to do with this."

Emmy's puffy eyes rounded. "They murdered Adam?"

Funny how her mind had gone straight to him. "No. They murdered Grayson," I said this gently, even though anger throttled my insides.

Her jaw dropped as far as a jaw could drop when propped up by a forearm. "What? Gray's . . ." Her bottom lip wobbled. "Gray's dead? Oh God, how? When? And why hasn't Mum called and—Oh God, oh God, oh God." More tears streamed out. Snot, too.

Wanting to ensure she didn't incur the same fate as Grayson, I catalogued all objects in my proximity. The vases on the tables, the glass of water in front of me. Both would make lethal missiles or improvised blades. My gaze alighted on my phone, and the sight of it steadied my heart.

I'd be in a world of trouble if I called my father, but Emmy would be safe. The poor bartender trying to become one with the liquor shelves would be safe. Keeping my gaze affixed to my former landlady, I palmed the slender device, the screen cool beneath my clammy skin.

I'd programmed Apa's number as my emergency contact. A long press of my phone's power button, and the red button to call him would appear.

I pressed.

Pain detonated inside my hand, and I released a wet gasp.

"*¿Qué demonios?*" *What the hell?* Pablo's gaze swerved toward my torn flesh.

The bodyguard, parked beside our table, lowered his gun. "The girl was trying to call someone, *su Alteza*."

Blood oozed from my perforated flesh, trickled between my knuckles, and dribbled onto the tabletop. I jerked my hand off the smashed phone and reeled it into me, cocooning it against my chest with my other hand.

Pablo went off on his guard. "*I* give the command to shoot!" He reached into his jacket pocket and swung out his own gun, which he raised, aimed at his guard, and fired.

The man sputtered, gaped at his boss, then down at the blood gluing his black shirt to his pecs. And then . . . and then he buckled.

Emmy shrieked.

"Fetch me a towel!" Pablo roared.

Two of his guards scrambled toward the bar, while I just blinked between the corpse and the Prince, trying to understand why he'd punished the man for incapacitating me. Wasn't *I* the enemy?

"What the hell did you shoot him for, Pablo?" Robbie gave voice to my question.

The Prince's eye set on me as he slipped his gun back into his jacket. "I have plans for her."

Dread momentarily dulled my physical pain.

"Besides, if anyone gets to damage her, it's me."

A breath skated past my lips. Damage me? What sort of torture was he planning?

The guard nearest the bar returned with a neatly-folded cloth napkin.

Pablo took it, drove his chair back, then rounded the small table and crouched. He stole my hand off my tank top and wrapped up my wound, securing the napkin with a firm knot. "I'm sorry, *mi sol*."

What sort of demented mind game was this? Not any I wanted to play, that was for sure. He ran a gloved knuckle along my cheek, then down my neck. When his fingers reached the hickey, he paused, then pressed down on it. I didn't wince, but my throat bobbed.

One of the first lessons our self-defense ophanim had imparted on us was that immortality wouldn't safeguard us from everything, that there were worse fates than death and we needed to prepare for those. And she *had* prepared me for them, but angels, how I'd hoped to never have to defend my body from a person's ill intent.

I suddenly wished Pablo's score hadn't dipped. Had he still been a Triple, I would've shattered my glass and sliced his carotid. If the ishim punished me for the thought, I didn't feel it. I felt nothing over the burn radiating up my wrist and the wash of adrenaline flooding my body.

"*Su Alteza*, what should we do with Franco's body?" the guard, who'd toted over the napkin, asked.

"Store him in the suite with the four others," Robbie suggested. "Easier cleanup."

"No." Pablo eyed his felled guard. "Drive him back to his house, so his family can give him a proper burial. And wire them the usual sum."

He had a usual sum? *Oh, Pablo . . . your soul is doomed.*

The guard grabbed his fallen brother's hands and dragged him across the room, slaloming around the tables still covered in half-empty cocktail glasses and hammered silver bowls of nuts.

I shut my eyes and breathed through my mouth, my stomach rumpling from the coppery stench of blood. Angels, I was going to be sick.

Emmy's fresh cries of anguish made my lids flip open. "I don't want to die. Please, no."

"Not up to me, Miss Rogers." Robbie's nasally voice rolled through the dusky space. "*That* is up to your tenant. If she gives up the location of what we need, I will set you free."

"Naya, please! Please tell them! I'll do anything. Please."

My heart ached at her naiveté. Did she really think her freedom hinged on any confession of mine?

I turned to Pablo. "Is one inside her?" I remained purposely vague because if I spoke the word bomb, not only would she freak, but neither man would let her leave this room with her vital organs intact.

"No." Even though Pablo was a lot of things, he didn't strike me as a liar.

My tongue darted over my parched lips again. "Put her on a commercial plane back to London, *alive*, and I'll tell you."

Emmy mouthed a *thank you*.

Pablo smiled gently, ran his knuckle back up the curve of my neck, then stood. "Such a kind heart you have, *mi sol*. Another woman would've demanded her own freedom."

Because another woman would've been worried she'd never break free. I had many worries, but that wasn't one of them. "Oh, and I'd like my jacket back." I gestured to the teal bomber Emmy was still wearing.

"S-Sorry. I don't know how—"

I lifted my palm to silence her apology. Her kleptomania was the least of my current concerns.

Pablo extended his gloved hand toward me. "Done and done."

"Have you lost the plot?" Robbie tightened his grip on Emmy's throat. "She'll rat us out the minute she lands."

"I won't. I swear. I won't." She kept clawing at his arm.

Pablo yelled at one of his guards to relieve Robbie of his charge and get my jacket, then ticked his head toward his outstretched hand. "Come."

"Where?" My skin crawled at the idea of going anywhere with this man. However lenient he was proving, as long as he didn't change his stance on the Circle Girls, I couldn't trust him.

"Why... to my residence. We have much to discuss."

"I'm not risking my reputation, my life"—spittle flew out of Robbie's mouth as he backed up toward the wall, heaving Emmy along—"because of some whore who's bewitched you."

Emmy's complexion purpled, like the chairs, like Ama's wings. *Oh, Ama, how did I get myself into such a mess?*

I wanted the King's army to charge in here. I wanted justice to be meted out, even if it was inflicted by more unjust men. But the army wouldn't come, because they'd cornered us before we could corner them.

Irritation heated my blood and dimmed the sting of my hand. "I'm neither a whore nor a witch, Mr. Dunmore." I said this calmly, even though I wanted to scream it for the world to hear. I wanted my voice to echo in the guild halls and rise to Elysium, so angels would intercede and punish these vile humans who'd put bullets inside my friends.

Something struck me as I finally took Pablo's hand and stood on rickety legs. Robbie had mentioned *four others*.

That meant...

Someone had escaped!

"I'll go with you, but I want to stop by my suite first."

Pablo cocked his eyebrow. "I can have your clothes—"

"I want closure or I'll never be able to get over the fact that my friends are gone."

"It's a trick, Pablo! She probably has a weapon stashed up there, and—"

Pablo tilted his head to the side. "I never knew how deeply you underestimated me, my friend."

"You are blind when it comes to her," Robbie shouted. "You shot your own bodyguard. You shot him when all he was doing was his job!"

Pablo's mouth pinched. "*¡La chica... sácala!*" *The girl... get her!*

Two of his men walked over to Robbie, who whipped a pistol from his velvet dinner jacket and aimed it at me.

"Put the gun away, Robbie," Pablo said calmly.

He didn't push me behind his back, though. Why would he? For all his desire to play with me, he'd never sacrifice himself for another person. After all, his life was worth so much more than anyone else's.

"Put. The gun. Away." Pablo's clipped words sailed through the air like bullets.

Tears squeezed out of Emmy's eyes and raced down the sides of her nose. Her hands were still on Robbie's arm, still white-knuckled. I was proud of her for fighting.

"I risked my fucking life for you!" Robbie shouted. "I refuse to sit back and watch you act like a goddamn idiot."

Pablo's fingers clenched around mine, and although he wasn't squeezing my bullet-riddled hand, my palm began to ache.

"I'll compromise." He swerved the barrel into Emmy's temple. "I won't shoot your whore, but this one's not walking out of here."

"NO!" I tore my hand from Pablo's and reached under his jacket. The second my fingers closed around his gun, I whipped it out and leveled it on Robbie's head, steadying my bobbing hand with my throbbing one. "Let her go. Or-or I'll shoot you." Even though my attention was on Dunmore, I caught Pablo's guards raising their weapons in my direction.

Robbie snickered. "Look at that, Pablo. She has your gun."

Pablo's stillness pressed into my skin. "If I hadn't wanted her to have it, she wouldn't be holding it."

Even though my grip was shaky, my confidence wasn't, and although I had no doubt he would've put up a fight, I'd be holding his gun whether he'd wanted me to hold it or not. I raised my hand a mere inch and hooked the trigger. The glass sconce above Robbie's head burst. Shards rained down over him and Emmy like a handful of glitter.

The Brit jerked, mouth no longer stretched into a smug smile.

"The next one goes between your eyes if you don't let Emmy go, Mr. Dunmore."

The fact that Pablo didn't even try to disarm me told me he was on board with his friend dying. "Better let her go, Robbie." His tone was dulcet, *amused*.

Angels, they were all so sick.

Robbie growled, "Shut up," at Emmy, who seemed about ready

to shatter like the sconce. "Are you sure it's your eye your father removed and not your balls, Pablo?"

Wow. I hadn't pegged Robbie Dunmore for a suicidal idiot. Then again, I hadn't pegged him for a terrorist either. I was woman enough to admit when I was wrong, and boy, had I been wrong.

Pablo wrenched the gun from my hands, the cold twist to his mouth destabilizing my grip and tripping up my heartbeats, making them drop even more erratically.

He raised the gun.

My knees softened. I readied to crouch and sweep his legs out from under him, certain he'd finally had it with me, when he pivoted and leveled the gun on Robbie.

He squeezed the trigger at the same time as Robbie.

Two shots rang out.

Two bodies thudded.

NAYA

I gasped. Or maybe I screamed. Or maybe I didn't emit a single sound. But inside, I wailed as loudly as Emmy had before Robbie silenced her.

My sinner was dead.

Dead.

I'd seen humans die, but never like this. Not with such violence.

The terror that had lit up her eyes, rounded her mouth and discolored her face.

The gunshots echoed again between my temples.

Bam, bam. Bam, bam. Bam, bam. Bam, bam.

They multiplied and intensified, matching the thump of my pulse.

The reek of spoiled bodies punched up my nose, and I gagged. I spun around just as vomit flowed out of my mouth and landed on the innocent lily.

My eyes stung from the smell, propelling anguished tears down my cheeks that dripped off my chin and onto the pink-and-white petals. The air stirred as Pablo barked orders that his guards enacted.

I'd wanted Robbie gone, and he was.

Robbie's gone. Unreal. Everything that had happened to me since I'd set foot in the Dunmore manor felt unreal.

"I'm sorry about your friend, *mi sol.*" Pablo had ended his friend's life with such aplomb, I doubted he cared an iota about Emmy.

Still hunched over the table, palms biting into the wood, I blinked away my tears and angled my face sideways to look at the sinner. Since he wasn't a fletching, no feather confirmed or denied the shape of his conscience.

I pressed away from the table, my torn palm screeching from the effort, and raised the wet napkin to my mouth, soiling it some more.

Pablo watched my mouth, probably reddened with blood. "One monster down. One to go."

Was he speaking about himself?

I licked my lips. Sure enough, the faint taste of copper lingered over the burn of my revulsion.

A guard walked up to us and extended a rolled piece of fabric. His mouth opened, but my mind couldn't latch on to anything he was saying.

I'd failed Emmy.

I'd failed her, and she was dead.

My heart folded upon itself for these parents who'd just had to bury a son and would now need to shovel the earth to make room for a daughter. If only I could tell them that their children's souls continued to exist, that they'd return, in some other form and with no memories, but that they weren't completely gone.

Pablo pushed another napkin into my hands, a wet one this time. My fingers trembled as they lifted it to my mouth and patted my skin.

The only thing that kept me from screaming was the realization that a malakim would come for her soul. I needed to be there when the harvester came, so I could get a message to Dov. Or to my father.

Oh, how furious he'd be. But I'd take his fury if it came with his help, because there was no way I was letting one more innocent soul rise before its time.

"*Su Alteza*, the girl has a pulse." One of Pablo's men was crouched before her body, knuckles on the rim of her throat. "What would you like us to do?"

I sucked in a breath, and then my legs were carrying me to the two bodies the guards had rolled off each other and lain parallel. I dropped to my knees beside the guard and replaced his fingers with mine, aching to feel the muted thump-thump.

There was so much blood. It caked her brown hair and covered half of her face. How could she still be alive?

Somehow, her pulse fluttered against my fingertips.

Even though there was hardly enough light in this room to create shadows, one fell over me. I looked up to find the Prince's eye running down the length of my friend's body before skipping to Robbie's.

"What would you like me to do? Put her out of her misery or have her sent to the hospital?"

Put her out of her misery? Had he really just suggested shooting her? "The hospital, Pablo."

"Her chances—"

"Her chances are better than any she'd get from a second bullet."

He nodded, and phone calls were made. The doors of the hotel bar were finally opened, letting in a gust of welcomed air.

I stayed with Emmy, whose eyes flitted open, watery and blue, but vivid. "Fight, Emmy. And don't you dare stop. Grayson would want you to live." After a beat, I added, "Adam, too."

Her lips quivered but emitted no sound.

A stretcher was brought in, and she was hoisted onto it.

As they rolled her out, I rose from the viscous pool of her blood. "What will happen to Robbie's mother?"

"Hmm." Pablo took my arm, and even though I'd have much preferred he didn't touch me, I let him because I preferred not to end up in a body bag of my own. "What do you suppose she'll do once she finds out I killed her favorite child?"

"Hurt you."

"And what do you think would hurt me the most?"

"Disclosing your plan."

Pablo patted my arm. "Smart girl." And then he turned to one of his bodyguards, spoke Susan's name, followed by the single word: "*Mátala.*" Kill her.

Goosebumps sprouted over my bare arms at how calmly he'd requested her death. How many people had this man killed or ordered to kill? Did he know or had he lost count long ago?

"She stole my pearl earrings," I murmured. "Could your guard bring them back to me?"

Pablo's gaze slunk over my lobes before dipping to the bruise on my neck. "The ones your lover bought you, *correcto?*"

"No. A friend."

"The same friend who kissed your neck?"

"No."

"You are a woman of such mystery, *mi sol*." After a beat, he ticked his head toward another one of his men and told him to retrieve Susan Dunmore's pearls.

I tried to calm the relieved jump of my pulse by concentrating on Robbie's body, which was being zipped up in a body bag, his orange hair and blood-coated forehead the last spots of color to vanish before he became a dull stain on the shiny ebony hardwood.

"*Tu mano.*" *Your hand.* Pablo nodded to my napkin-wrapped hand as he led me to the bar and helped me onto a stool.

A uniformed woman—EMT? The hotel's on-call medic?—laid a first-aid kit on the bar top, then unwrapped the napkin. She squirted so much alcohol my eyes watered, then took out a syringe. I snatched my hand away, dribbling blood onto the backlit glass.

"So it not hurts when I sew up hand." She spoke in broken English, assuming I wasn't from around here.

"*No quiero puntos*," I said. *I don't want stitches.*

Her surprise at my fluency rounded her eyes briefly, before she launched into all the reasons a wound like mine required suturing. I shook my head. The foreign thread would only give my immune system more work and would extend my healing time instead of reducing it.

She looked toward Pablo, who held my gaze. I shook my head some more, my ponytail slipping and sliding over my shoulders. He sighed and instructed her to put butterfly strips and swaddle it tightly. With a huff, she complied.

Once my hand resembled a football, Pablo escorted me out of the bar, curling my good hand around his biceps and cementing it there with his gloved palm as though we were a couple strolling home from a date. Had my legs not felt like cotton candy, I'd have pulled it away.

The lobby had been cleared of personnel and guests but was crawling with armed men. All glanced toward their boss and the girl with the blood-soaked jeans and soiled tank top.

In front of the bank of elevators, he asked, "Are you certain you want to visit your suite?"

I nodded.

"Very well." He punched the appropriate button.

I'd held out hope he'd hit any other floor, even though it would've been a cruel twist of fate if he'd rained bullets on mortal innocents, instead of on my immortal crew.

Several of his guards filed into the wide lift and shadowed us down the carpeted hallway, trampling over Noah's pink feathers. A keycard was held to the lock. *Click.*

The first body I saw was Galina's, lying supine beside the door, a bullet hole oozing blood between her glassy eyes.

I pressed my bandaged hand to my stomach, held it there as I took in Levi, hunched over the bar, face free of blood but oversized blue T-shirt soaked. Boone lay prone beside his brother's stool, blood coursing from his nose and temple and dripping onto the brown marble. Noah was crumpled against the door of his bedroom, legs outstretched before him, eyes closed as though he'd fallen asleep with his head tilted at an odd angle, white button-down saturated in blood.

As the massacre imprinted itself on the back of my lids, my eyes stung anew.

They're not dead. Not really. I repeated this to myself silently but firmly.

I dropped Pablo's arm and wobbled over to Noah, blotting my eyes with my knuckles, then peeked into his room for another body. The beds were made and corpse-free.

My hope that I wasn't the only one walking around firmed, alleviating some of my grief. I'd have been glad that any one of them had escaped, but knowing it was Adam . . .

"Was that one your lover?" Pablo stood over Noah, chin tucked disdainfully into his neck.

"No."

"Which one, then?"

I turned on my heels and plodded to my bedroom.

"I asked you a question, Señorita Moreau." The sharpness of Pablo's voice made me pause in the doorway of my bedroom.

I stared around the suite darkened with gun-slinging men and women. Mostly men. "I wasn't involved with any of them."

"Then, who?"

I still wasn't sure what his plans for me were, but the feral gleam in his eyes told me he was primed for a manhunt. "A boy I barely know." Hopefully, he'd assume it was a hotel guest or someone back in England. "I'm here with you now. That's the only thing that should matter."

I stepped past my threshold to retrieve my bag from the closet. Two guards followed me. One stood framed in the entrance while the other trailed me around like a dog as I dumped armfuls of clothes inside my bag.

In the bathroom, I lingered by the mirror, twisting and untwisting my tube of scarlet lipstick, debating whether to paint Adam a message so he'd know where to find me. One glance at my gun-toting shadow, and I chucked the lipstick in my toiletry pouch.

Even if a guard hadn't had eyes on me, I would've forgone leaving a note. I preferred Pablo to keep thinking he'd smothered my entire team than to be on the lookout for a rogue member.

ADAM

ANGELIC FACT #743
ANGELS AREN'T IMMUNE TO ALCOHOL.
OR TO STUPIDITY.

My brain rattled, clanging with a voice that was too loud, too shrill, and completely unfamiliar.

What the ever-loving Abaddon?

I reeled up my lids and groaned as the bright white ceiling seared my corneas. I started to shut my eyes and roll over when a leathery face swam into focus over my face.

Pluckin' A!

My heart jolted into my throat, then seemingly farther up, into my brain, which began to pulse. Although debilitating, the ache combined with a hefty dose of adrenaline, cleared my vision right up.

I blinked, and the person's features sharpened—a woman with a square, puckered face and lips painted the same powdery pink as Noah's wings.

As she murmured a string of prayers, her minty-fresh breath iced my nose and her overstated citrus perfume upset my stomach. "*Gracias a Dios.*" Thank God. "I thought I'd never be able to rouse you."

I was sprawled out on a rug beside a bed that looked a lot like mine, but where there should've been a door in front of me, there was only taupe-colored plaster. I tucked my chin into my neck and hefted up my head, hefting up my stomach in turn. Relief that my pants were buttoned-up rolled through me at the same time as a wave of nausea. I shoved the woman aside, sat, then stumbled out onto her balcony and emptied my stomach's contents on the stone.

Minutes that felt like a bloody hour later, I dug my fingers into the banister and straightened. The sun blinded my watery eyes while the woman behind me hissed her disgust at my uncouthness.

After several steadying breaths, I turned around and squinted at her past the morning glare on the glass. "How did I get here?"

The woman paused mid-rant, brown eyes growing square as though to match the shape of her face. "You leaped off your damn balcony, that's how." She nodded to the stone guardrail a body-length away.

Pride that I'd made it across overwhelmed most of the other thoughts in my brain. But then I remembered the reason I'd jumped. To get more liquor to mend my bruised ego. Mend was probably not the correct word. Drown.

Yeah... *drown*.

I'd been on a mission to smother my pissed-offness. And I'd smothered it, all right. But just like Naya's immortal body, it was resurfacing, along with a hefty dose of annoyance and a side of humiliation.

Although my bedroom window was still open, I no longer felt like turning my bones to confetti, so I flipped around, thanked the woman for letting me crash on her rug, which finally pinned her mouth shut, and let myself out of her bedroom.

I banged on the door of the suite. When no one opened, I shoved my hands into the pockets of my jeans. All empty. Damn it all to Abaddon.

Muttering to myself, I started for the elevator, but the thought of carrying out a conversation with a concierge to replace my key shuffled my feet back to my square-faced neighbor. I rang her doorbell.

She opened up, her mouth forming an eloquent, "¿Qué?" *What?*

"Forgot my key."

The skin on her forehead pleated as I blustered past her, climbed on the railing, and sprang. My relief at landing my jump morphed into a grunt when my left foot hit a bottle and I flopped onto my ass.

Instead of hitting stone, I hit a school bench in a ginormous gymnasium. Beside me, Starla, a cheerleader I'd had a thing with when I was fifteen, the year before I met Dov, burst into giggles, then shoved me with her yellow-foil pompoms.

"*You are such a flirt, Adam.*"

I heard myself answer something slick that had her giggling some more. The girl resembled a cute pixie yet had single-handedly destroyed the reputation of most of her fellow sophomores.

Just as swiftly as she'd appeared, she vanished, and I was back on my terrace with a throbbing tailbone and brain. I beat down the temptation to lie back and wait out my hangover by sunbathing. I had things to do and a team to see. I heaved myself up, avoiding the duvet of black feathers pillowing a cluster of empty glass bottles. No wonder my insides felt like compacted trash.

Holding one arm out for balance, I toddled over the threshold and pressed the glass balcony doors wider.

All the air left my lungs at the sight before me—my best friend, slumped, bloodied, lifeless.

In my most gruesome imaginings, *never* had I pictured my team getting caught in actual crossfire. I staggered toward Noah, pressed my fingers into his bent neck. Even though his skin was ice, the barest hint of a pulse pricked my fingertips.

My brain stopped wriggling around like a hooked fish and all my senses sharpened. I backed quietly onto the terrace, grabbed the largest bottle by its neck, then tiptoed into the living room.

My pulse froze at the stench of blood and then my body followed suit at the sight of three more silenced friends.

Heart detonating, I raced over to Galina, vindictive thoughts flashing behind my lids like the neon signs above stripper clubs. Maybe because my deliberations weren't aimed at any particular person, the ishim didn't reprimand me. Not that I would've given a flying feather if they had.

Ire coated my tongue as I moved deeper into the suite, readying myself for the sight of Naya haloed in blood. Stomach as hard as my fists, I penetrated the bedroom, my reddened vision swinging around the dim space.

No Naya.

I charged toward the bathroom, hit the lights, and peered around every square inch of marbled tile, my heart drumming so hard it made my tee vibrate.

Where the Abaddon was she?

I retraced my steps and flung open the closet doors, found nothing but half-empty shelves and swinging hangers. I walked over to the window and all but ripped the curtains off the rod. The glass doors were locked, the balcony vacant.

I was about to return into the suite and check the guest bathroom when my gaze landed on the top dresser drawer. Ajar and empty.

I returned to the closet and pulled down a pile of T-shirts—all Galina's. The lone leather jacket on the hanger was Galina's too. Where were Naya's clothes? Where was the bag she'd arrived with? I searched under the bed, in every damn drawer.

Not an angelsdamn thing.

Had she packed up and left Caracas after I'd walked out on her?

Fucking Abaddon.

A feather fell. Before it had even settled on the rug, I was back in the living room, checking every nook and cranny for the culprit. When I found no one lurking with a smoking pistol, I bolted the suite door shut and set the bottle I was still carrying down on the bar. Guilt gnawed at my insides as I stared around the room.

How had they found us? And why wasn't Naya among the bullet-riddled bodies?

She'd gone to meet Pablo!

The memory of Noah begging me to talk some sense into her made my molars grind down to stumps. My pride had gotten in the way. Plucking pride.

Had Junior threatened her, and she'd divulged the team's whereabouts to save her ass?

Didn't sound like Naya, but people behaved unpredictably under duress. Not to mention, she knew they'd all come back from the dead. I didn't want to think like this, but the alternative, that we'd been sloppy and clued them into our location, ticked me off even more. I was petty enough to prefer thinking she was the weak link instead of myself, but who was I deluding?

I'd drank my weight in brain-numbing fluids.

I'd failed them.

Even if she'd divulged our whereabouts, I hadn't been there to protect the team. I had no one to blame but myself.

Fueled by guilt and anger, I got to work feeling their bodies for exit wounds, and when I couldn't find any, I finagled tools to dig the bullets out while sandwiching my lips to avoid hurling on them.

Once I was done fishing out metal casings, I laid my friends in a row on the girls' beds, sopped the excess blood off their horizontal bodies with wet towels to spare them the gory sight, then grabbed a shower.

And then, dressed all in black like the devil himself, I went hunting.

NAYA

"Want some help with the clasp?" The saleslady asked through the curtain that kept me hidden from Pablo and the slew of bodyguards he'd brought along to make sure I didn't make a run for it.

Or try anything funny, like steal his gun and spring a bullet between his eyes.

After a late breakfast on his rooftop terrace, during which I'd picked at my food, too edgy to ingest much of anything, he'd explained the terms of our arrangement, and I'd finally understood why he'd spared me and how he planned on damaging me.

Up till then, I'd considered myself the puppeteer, but I'd gotten myself so entangled in this man's web that I'd all but handed him the strings to make me dance as he pleased. Brain humming from all the ways the deal I'd struck with the Prince could go awry, I'd followed him into his private elevator down to the lobby and climbed into one of the four identical SUVs idling in the driveway.

While the Circle Girls enjoyed a spa day to keep them distracted from their notably absent expedition organizer, I was dragged into the glitziest boutique on the glitziest boulevard of the capital for a dress *that would distract the King while I assassinated him.*

Pablo's stipulations: that my gown was royal-blue, since that was his father's favorite color, and that it was sheer, so that the man wouldn't fret about hidden weapons.

"It's a complicated dress. Let me help you."

When the curtain began to retract, I whipped the fingers of my good hand and seized the velvet screen to keep the woman from barging in. "No!"

I didn't have many pet peeves, but changing rooms made me break out in cold sweats. I avoided them like the plague and had only let myself get hustled into one today because the alternative, trying on designer gowns in front of Pablo and his guards, made my already raw nerves fulminate.

When the pressure released on the partition separating us, I let go, but never took my eyes off the heavy folds of fabric. After hooking my head through the halter top, I secured the bodysuit bikini bottom, then tugged up the skinny zipper running from an inch below my crotch to an inch over my navel, just covering what was left of my bruise.

Still holding the curtain shut, I peered down at myself to make sure my breasts weren't spilling out from the elongated triangles that smooshed them against my rib cage, then finger-combed my still straight hair for extra coverage.

Between the barely-there top and the sheer, pleated tulle skirt, I felt even more naked than in last night's get-up. Thank Elysium I was too preoccupied about what I'd agreed to do to care much about what I'd be wearing to do it.

In truth, if I had to stand in front of all of Venezuela in a thong and pasties to save the Circle Girls, I would.

I pushed through the gathered fabric, careful to keep my bad hand curled into my chest, so it didn't graze anything on the way. Although no longer swaddled in a boxing-glove amount of gauze, my palm burned as though skewered by a fiery poker.

I strode over to the center of the amber-hued boudoir. "Will this one do, Señor Perez?"

His jaw stiffened when I called him by his last name, which was exactly why I was doing it. I was no longer scared of the consequences since I'd agreed to be his weapon. I was now officially too necessary to be eliminated.

I stared at him through the six-paneled mirror, and he stared back. Not at my face. He was staring at the gown Eve would've picked out for me in a heartbeat had she come shopping with us. Thinking of Eve got me thinking about my mother. Without a phone,

I felt untethered from my home, but I supposed it was for the best, because it saved me from deceiving my parents.

A little more than a day until I was home. Until the curtain closed on this nightmare of a mission. As the blue fabric blurred into my white skin, I pondered whether I'd have the nerves to take on another mission that drove me to act like a ruthless god instead of a petrified fletching. I shook my head to clear away my corrosive train of thought before it could strip me of my willpower to save any more souls.

Focus on that, Naya. On all those hearts and lives you're about to spare. Besides, the King is a terrible man.

To convince myself I wouldn't be eliminating a soul with the potential of redemption, I'd asked Pablo to show me visual proof of his father's crimes, which he'd done immediately and exhaustively. The articles I'd scoured on his tablet had curdled the few bites of arepitas dulces I'd managed to swallow.

Pablo stalked around me like a predator. "I'll want your lips painted red like last night."

I was about to make a quip about not being aware cyanide came in such brilliant hues but kept quiet about his plan of murder-by-kiss. Just the idea of slicking poison over my lips and then kissing a man old enough to be my father threatened to upheave the contents of my stomach.

Although Pablo had promised to supply me with an antidote as soon as his father's heart stopped, I didn't care about the antidote, immortal being that I was. All I cared about was that he upheld his end of the bargain, which was to delete the virtual SIMs, and then reoperate on all the girls that very night, once they returned from the party.

As he went to browse the display of shoes with the saleswoman, my mind wandered to my friends. Pablo had promised to leave their bodies in the suite and cordon it off to hotel personnel, so I could collect them myself the moment his father was declared dead.

I was secretly praying Adam had found them, even if he'd yet to find me.

At the rumble of a motorcycle, my gaze strayed to the glass façade beyond the mannequins decked in gowns worth more than the yearly salary of the average Venezuelan.

I didn't expect Adam to be sitting astride the purring ride. And he wasn't. The rider had a sleeve of tattoos, and ink didn't take to our skin, the same way dye didn't take to our hair.

Not to mention Adam wasn't as thick and beefy as the man; he was taller, with leaner muscles. A lot like the scowling guy on the other side of the boulevard, who was drawing a black baseball cap low over his eyes. The fine hairs on my nape rose, and I blinked, expecting it was a trick of my desperate mind, but it wasn't.

The man standing across the wide road was none other than the one occupying my mind. I jerked my hand to my ears, bumping the pearls I'd speared through after Pablo's guards had retrieved them from Susan's cold, dead body, and I'd disinfected them.

Was that how Adam had found me?

Gloved fingers clicked in front of my face, snapping my attention off my fellow fletching. "Naya, your shoe size?"

"Um." I caught a lock of hair and twirled it so my fingers didn't shake. "Seven."

When he conveyed my size to the saleslady, I peered past him, past the mannequins in the window, past the line of bodyguards, past the bumper-to-bumper traffic.

Adam was gone.

ADAM

ANGELIC FACT #901
TO DO THE RIGHT THING, YOU MUST DO
MANY WRONG ONES.

I'd felt many emotions during my brief lifetime, but never such blinding disgust. At least, not toward a fellow fletching.

Naya was a traitor.

I'd feared it when I'd heard Junior's guards discussing their boss's blonde obsession, the girl he called his sunshine and whom he'd moved into his suite. I'd even caught them wagering on whether a marriage proposal was in the works, because, apparently, the Prince hadn't moved a woman into his home since his British supermodel-ex, who'd ended up shacking up with his father the second the King had taken an interest in her. Their affair had lasted all of a month after which she'd run back to the son.

The girl was never seen or heard from again, and although some assumed Junior had sent her away with a stipend, I knew—from casing her guild profile—that she was dead.

Watching Naya in that store, getting dolled up by a Triple, had felt like a slap on the heart. Pablo was just as vile as his father. Why couldn't she open her angelsdamned eyes and see his putrid soul?

What more proof than a triple-digit score did she need to grasp a person's wickedness?

As I stalked the sidewalks of Caracas toward the guild, I took out my phone and pounded out a message to Dov that consisted of two acronyms: SOS *ASAP*.

I added that I was on my way to the ranking room of the male guild.

Instead of burning off my excess anger, I grew progressively more pissed off with every mile and progressively more determined to carry my team home and leave Naya to deal with Junior and the Circle Girls on her own. At this point, I didn't see how we could save them anyway, not without access to that phone number, which I had no doubt Pablo had activated and put on several devices to remove any chance of his coup failing.

I flung the door of the guild wide and stepped through the fountained atrium, not sparing a glance for my fellow fletchings or acknowledging the ophanim. The curved glass doors of the round ranking room had barely any time to part before I pushed my way inside and slapped my palm on a glass panel.

The second the holo-ranker identified me, I traced Junior's name. His score: **100**.

So much for his score dipping.

I traced Robbie's name next, my eyebrows drawing together when his profile appeared with a large, red holographic stamp that read: **DECEASED**.

No effing way. Robbie was gone? Why hadn't I heard the bodyguards discussing this? Had the dayshift guys not been brought up to speed by the nightshift?

Of their own accord, my fingers traced the name: *Susan Dunmore*. I sensed there'd be a stamp across her holographic profile image. And there it was.

Did Naya know? Had *she* killed them?

I traced her name next, my palate and tongue pummeled by my chaotic pulse, my skin clammy with fear that she'd appear with zero feathers to her name, even though Dov had sworn ending Triples was cost-free.

I didn't expel my breath until her score materialized—**941**.

For all my disappointment with her, I would never wish her

wings harm. And then, because I was a masochist, I checked my score. The substantial shrinkage made my jaw spasm.

My crowd-cheer chime went off, extracting my attention from the seedy number. I half-expected it to be my fathers, calling to find out why I was molting, their exasperation fueled by both intense dismay and acute worry. As I readied a plausible excuse and a plan to comfort them, I extricated the device from my black cargo pants and shut off the holo-ranker.

DOV: *I'm here.*
ME: *At the hotel?*
DOV: *No. Across the street from the guild.*
ME: *Be right out.*

Shoulders tense as steel rigging, I rose from the stool, trotted out through the fountained atrium, and shouldered open the guild doors.

Conspicuous as always in his gray ishim uniform, Dov was leaning against the façade of a wine shop.

I crossed the road, skirting the throng of honking cars and flux of bicycles. "Let's walk and talk."

In the fifteen blocks it took us to reach the hotel, I filled him in on all that had happened.

"You understand why I can't fly them into a guild, right?" he asked, when the tower of glass and stone shimmered before us, reflecting the neon smear of sunset.

"I understand." At the same time my gaze rose to the forty-eighth floor window, my stomach dropped. Had I really jumped between two balconies? I'd been out of my angelsdamn mind. "Just heal them with your fire and—"

"No."

My neck straightened as I turned to look at our silent partner. "Why not?"

"Because I'm compromised. Ever since I crossed paths with Naya, the nosy ophanim who carried her through the channel has been sniffing around, itching to uncover something to report to Asher."

I shut my eyes for all of a second, wishing, not for the first time, that she hadn't run into Noah. "I should've found a way to keep her out of this."

"What's done is done." Our celestial handler sighed. "I'm glad

Susan and Robert Dunmore have been eliminated, but, Adam, this mission will be the team's last if you fail to succor the Circle Girls."

My pulse halted as Dov's words dispersed through my brain. "Why?"

"Because if you fail, it'll prove us wrong. It'll prove fletchings aren't equipped to be shorhim."

I turned on him. "We've saved hundreds of lives already!"

"Hush."

I balled my fists, in no mood to be told to shut up by an ascended.

His gaze traveled to a cluster of passersby that were all looking at me funny. Since not a single one peered at Dov, I assumed he'd used dust to conceal himself. "You think Elysium cares about statistics? Our world has a one-strike policy. For everything. You strike out now, and that's all they'll see. All our other missions will be prescinded."

I swallowed hard. "More than half the team is nonoperational, and the birthday party's tomorrow night."

"Naya's still in play." His eyes rose to the penthouse as though he knew where she was.

"Naya's either a traitor or a coward," I muttered.

"Are you sure?"

"She was out shopping with Prince Charming today!"

"Why are you jumping to the conclusion that she betrayed you? Maybe she has a plan."

Yeah. Seduce the phone number out of the Triple. My pulse knifed my eardrums as I pictured her in bed with Junior. I was going to strangle the sleazebag to death with his plucking eye patch.

"I think that's unfortunately your last solution."

I hadn't realized I'd spoken my homicidal thought out loud, but I must've. Unless it was the flutter of black down around my legs that had alerted Dov to the murky direction of my mind.

"You need to talk to Naya. She may be better placed than you to deliver the final blow."

My knuckles whitened, tugging on the scabs peppering my knuckles but not splitting them. "How do you suggest I do that, considering she moved in with Pablo, and his residence is more guarded than the palace?"

Dov smiled and extended his palms.

60

NAYA

I hung up the garment bag and tucked the shoes beneath it in the walk-in closet of the bedroom Pablo had moved me into last night. It was ridiculously expansive, almost as large as the entire suite my friends were convalescing in.

Although I'd been tempted to go check on them after my shopping trip, Pablo had stuck me with four bodyguards—either he really feared me or feared something would happen to me—while he went to have tea with his father to gush about his new girlfriend in order to set our plan in motion.

Before we'd left the privacy of his penthouse, he'd explained why he was certain his father would accept a kiss from a complete stranger. Not only did the King have a thing for blondes, but he also had a thing for his son's girlfriends, which had instilled equal parts contempt and disgust inside of me, while firming up my decision to end the monster's life.

Nothing precluded Pablo from becoming like his father in the future, but that would be for another shorhim to deal with, because I'd have ascended long before any children he might have grew old enough to have girlfriends.

When I shut the closet door, my wings snapped out of my spine, and I let out a little shriek that was instantly muffled by a large palm.

"Shh."

Heart in my throat, I dragged Adam's hand off my mouth and hissed, "How did you get up here?"

Adam ticked his head toward the darkening sky beyond the balcony doors.

"You scaled the hotel wall?"

"No. Dov gave me a wing up."

A knock at my bedroom door startled me again, but this time, I didn't gasp.

"¿Señorita Moreau, todo bien?" *Miss Moreau, all is well?* one of my babysitter's called out.

"¡Sí, gracias!" Thankfully, I'd locked the door. Not that I thought a lock would keep any of them out if they really wanted in.

I dragged Adam into the bathroom, so I could get another door between us and them. "Is Dov still out there?"

"No."

"How are you getting back down?"

"In such a hurry to get rid of me, heiress?" His tone was as dark as the shadows pooled beneath the bill of his cap.

"That's not why I'm asking." I shook my head. "I was asking because what do you think will happen if Pablo finds you here?"

"You tell me. He's *your* boyfriend."

I jerked back from the vitriol in his tone. "Not my real one. It's just an act to get his father to take an interest in me."

Adam's brows gathered low over his eyes. "Does Junior know it's an act?"

"Of course he knows. It was his idea. Geez, Adam." I tucked a lock of hair behind my ear and pushed out my lobe. "I took these pearls off a dead body so you could stay in the loop. I even pointed them out to you in the shop. Are they no longer transmitting?"

A nerve feathered his jaw.

He'd completely missed the fact they were on my lobes! How had he located me then?

Before I could ask, he said, "Been a little busy fishing bullets out of the friends you abandoned."

I sucked in a breath. "*I* abandoned? Where were you last night when we were back-hacked by the telecom company after *you guys* gave them the wrong password?" I poked his chest with my good hand. "Where were you when the team was ambushed, huh?" I poked his chest again, driving him back into the outsized porcelain sink top.

He gripped my fingers and towed them off his chest, mouth thin, pupils mere dots. "Yeah. Okay. I get it. I failed everyone. No need to rub my face in it."

My nostrils flared. "Do you want to know the plan, or did you just come up here to complain about my lack of team spirit?"

His Adam's apple went up and down twice before he finally separated his lips. "Tell me the plan."

So I told him all he'd missed and all there was still to come, which led him to bellow, "Are you out of your plucking mind? The King may be vile, but it's Junior we need to get rid of!"

"Keep your voice down." I went to the bathtub and twisted the gold faucet handle, then returned to Adam. "Pablo's score dropped, so it's not exactly like we can take him out anymore."

"His score didn't drop."

My jaw softened. "But Galina said—Yesterday . . ."

"Guess killing his own guard and his best bud put him right back where he started. Or maybe it's organizing his new girlfriend's death, since how exactly do you suppose a real girl would survive cyanide poisoning, huh?"

My pulse jumped, thudding against the fading bruise of his kiss.

"You do realize he thinks you'll die too, right? Two enemies. One kiss."

"He told me he'd give me an antidote."

Adam snorted. "Yeah. It's called a bullet."

My feathers bristled at my back. "His score decreased, which means he's capable of kindness. But that's beside the point. I don't care if he kills me, as long as he saves the girls."

"Really think he'll uphold his end of the bargain and delete those SIMs?"

"He'll be in the ballroom with us, so yes, I do think he's going to uphold his end of the bargain. Getting blown up would really put a dent in his coup." I hissed this, annoyed by Adam's condescension. "You may not love this new plan, and if you have a better one, I'm all ears, but I haven't been able to come up with anything better."

"How about stealing his phone? You *are* living with him after all. You could lift it after he tucks you in tonight."

I glared at him because he was being incredibly petty about my forced living arrangements. Did he think I was enjoying this situation? "He's outsourced the call, so getting the number won't exactly help us. Guess I can sleep soundly beside him. All. Night."

Adam's eyes burned the crispest shade of green. "I thought it was a farce! He's making you sleep with him?"

"Got to make it look real for his guards." Magicking away my wings, I spun to check on the bathwater temperature.

Although I hadn't planned on taking a bath, now that it was run, I'd soak. I held my fingers beneath the tap, hissing at how hot the water was. As I adjusted the temperature, Adam gripped my wrist and spun me back around.

"Tell me you're kidding?" Adam had blanched, his deep olive complexion rivaling my pearly one.

Okay, that was a stretch, but he'd definitely gone a shade or two lighter. "Of course I'm kidding." I tried to shake him off, but his two hands were on me now, grinding my hipbones. "What is wrong with you?" I pressed my uninjured palm into his chest to create a little space, caught the frenzied kicks of his heart beneath his black T-shirt.

"Really?" There was a manic edge to his voice. "I bloody drank my weight in alcohol to nurse my bruised ego, then slept off my hangover in some stranger's room, and you're wondering why I'm reacting the way I am to the news that you're sleeping in the apartment of another man?"

My mind caught on the middle part, and my heart unmoored itself and tumbled into my fisting stomach. "Wow. You don't waste a minute."

"Doing what?" His head reared back an inch. Not the rest of his body, though.

That would've been too much to wish for. "Let go."

"Not before you tell me what you meant by me *not wasting a minute?*"

I looked to the side, hating everything about this conversation. The gold fixtures blurred a little. I blinked. I was not shedding a single tear over this fickle boy who'd jumped into someone else's bed before his lips had even dried from my kiss.

"We're not a couple. You do your thing; I'll do mine. Now let go before I knee you, because that'd surely put a damper on your next random hotel hookup."

Silence.

Then . . . A throaty chuckle carved through the steam-filled white and gold bathroom.

I lifted my searing gaze to his, wondering how he could laugh. Did he find my jealousy amusing?

"I passed out on the woman's rug on my way to her minibar."

So he hadn't had time to screw her? I still didn't see how that was any better.

He sobered up, but his eyes kept glowing beneath his baseball cap. "I didn't go looking for another warm body, Naya. Just more alcohol, 'cause you banged up my damn heart last night," he added, barely above a whisper.

I raked his expression before raking the floor, hunting the slabs of marble for a disturbance in the veined pattern, because I couldn't imagine any of what he'd just said to be true.

I found no feather.

I returned my gaze to his cautiously.

"I may not be it for you forever, but I'm hoping I could be it for now." He kept ahold of my hip with one hand, moving the other to my face to tilt my chin up.

I shook my head, not because I was saying no, but because his *Jekyll and Hyde* personality was giving me emotional whiplash. When the corners of his mouth turned down, I said, "You didn't let me finish what I was saying last night. You just walked out." I tossed one hand in the air. Unfortunately, it was my bad one, and the abrupt movement made the wound throb. "If only you'd heard me out."

His gaze hardened. "I'm listening."

"Maybe I don't feel like talking about it anymore." I wasn't one to pout, but I'd had a night and a day, and another one of each to *not* look forward to.

"Talk." At my scowl, he added a placid, "Please."

"Can we do this tomorrow? After—"

"I won't leave until you tell me."

I sighed. "Fine. But after that, call Dov, because I'm operating on zero sleep and fried nerves."

He dipped his head, which I took as a nod.

"According to Ama, we have many soulmates—"

"I heard that loud and clear," he muttered.

"Stop interrupting, and maybe you'll hear the end of that thought."

His lips sealed.

"All those soulmates, they don't all mean the same to us. The way Ama sees me and the way she sees Apa are evidently very different. The way your fathers love each other, and the way they love you . . . it's not the same love." I licked my lips, trying to compose my thoughts better because he was still frowning. "What I'm trying to say is that our souls connect in different ways. And"—I swallowed—"although Ama changes the topic each time I corner her with specific questions, I think that among all those *mates*, there's one we connect with on a deeper level. I mean, how else do you explain that some angels stay together for centuries?"

When light scored his irises, I assumed my skin had lit up, but a glance at my arms showed my skin wasn't aglow. I guessed it was my explanation, and ultimately, my belief in a supreme mate that had cleared the shadows obscuring his eyes.

"I'm sorry, Feather."

"For walking out? For assuming I was a hussy? Worse . . . a traitor? For having spent your night in someone else's bed?"

"Rug, not bed."

I rolled my eyes.

"And yeah, for all of the above. I'm sorry for failing the team and contemplating walking away from you for good." His eyes dropped to my neck. To the small mark he'd branded me with.

"In a way, you not being there was an angelsend, because if you'd been shot too . . ." My voice broke. "If they'd gotten you too, then I'd be all alone right now. All alone tomorrow." My lids swept away the heat clinging to my lids. "I'm scared. I'm so scared."

His hand came off my hip, caught his cap and flung it off, and then he palmed my cheek and pressed his forehead against mine. "I'm right here. And I'll be right there tomorrow. You're not alone, baby. I'm right here."

He kissed my mouth to prove he was, then kissed the tears snaking down my cheeks as my heart gave a hard shudder.

Of relief and anguish.

Of gratitude and love.

The velocity and force at which I'd fallen for a complete stranger cemented Adam's romantic claim that we could be soulmates. What other explanation was there for how deeply connected I felt to this boy? How quickly I forgave him?

"I wish you could stay here with me until tomorrow," I murmured.

"I can and I will."

I leaned back, unhooking my face from his. "Pablo's going to come back."

"So what? You're allies, not lovers."

"What if he knocks and suggests dinner?"

"You'll tell him to bugger off. Or better yet, I'll do it."

"Adam, I need you *alive*."

"Can't die."

I scrubbed the wetness off my cheeks. "You know what I mean."

"Your work for him begins and ends tomorrow, Feather. Tonight, you're mine. Only mine." His thumbs arched beneath my lash line.

"What about the others? What if they wake up?"

"I left them a note to stay put, and Dov promised to drop off new cell phones, so they'll call when they wake up."

My gaze dropped to my bandaged hand. "They shot my phone. When they shot my hand."

Adam's eyes blackened as he scrutinized the bandage. "That guard's lucky he's already dead or I would've made sure to perforate all his extremities before separating his spine from the rest of his body."

I hissed but not Adam, not even when a feather loosened from his invisible wings and landed on . . .

"Shoot!" I turned around, my sneakers squeaking on the wet marble, and skidded toward the jacuzzi-sized bathtub, which had managed to overflow.

"Hope it's hot."

Um, what . . . As I opened the drain, I looked over my shoulder at Adam who was peeling the T-shirt off his chest.

Holy angels . . .

My pulse droned against my eardrums as I absorbed the sight of his bare chest.

Smooth olive skin notched by bricks of muscle tapering into narrow hips. Curved pecs tipped with dark nipples, chest hair sprinkled evenly, funneling down the runnel of his abs before flaring between the carved structure of his waist. Rangy forearms thickening into veined biceps and rounded shoulders.

He stalked closer, covered my hand with his, and twisted the drain knob to prevent me from emptying the bath. "Was I being too forward in assuming we could share the bath?" He towed my hand off the rounded gold dial, helping me straighten. "Especially since we've already shared a shower..."

I wrinkled my nose at the memory because that shower had been anything but romantic.

"Sorry." He rubbed the side of his neck. "Probably shouldn't have reminded you of that."

My teeth sank into my bottom lip as I evaluated the reasonableness of bathing with this man when another was bound to knock on my door.

Completely unreasonable.

Not to mention, bathing implied full nudity.

Adam's hands dropped to the button of his pants, and my mind blanked, whitewashing my thoughts and apparently the remainder of my levelheadedness, considering I walked back into my bedroom and unlocked my door.

To the first guard standing there, I said, "I'm going to turn in early. Since I don't have a phone, please inform his royal Highness that I'll see him in the morning and not before."

The guard frowned slightly but nodded. "*Buenas noches, señora.*" Good night, Madam.

I locked my door, shut my curtains with a flick of a switch, and returned to the fletching standing in my bathroom doorway, brow grooved, probably assuming I'd made a run for it.

Unlike some people, that wasn't my MO. When I cast off my shirt, his forehead smoothed and a pleased smile dimpled his stubble-roughened cheek.

ADAM

ANGELIC FACT #2
TRUE BEAUTY IS SOUL-DEEP.

I didn't deserve her.

But did I refuse her when she unwrapped herself for me?

Heck, no.

I was taking what I was being offered before the angel snapped out of her magnanimous daze and wondered why in the worlds she was giving an unworthy bunghole like myself a second chance.

Naya suddenly stopped advancing, stopped unzipping her jeans. I shut my lids, readying myself for a change of heart. I'd merit it. "Do you think there are surveillance cameras in here?"

My eyes opened, and my confidence billowed right back up. I'd have said like the rest of me, but the rest of me hadn't gone down. I spared the walk-in closet a cursory glance, aware that hunting for cameras would be pointless, since most were the size of ladybugs.

Even though this wouldn't be our only night, I was not spending it worrying about an audience. "Let him watch." I walked into her space, driving her backward into a wall of drawers, and replaced her motionless fingers with mine. I unzipped her jeans and pushed them down the legs I wanted to wear around my neck for the better part of the night.

She'd mentioned sleep. I hoped she wasn't too impatient to get some.

"Adam..." A deep coral stained her cheeks.

"Yeah, Feather?" I dropped to my knees.

When I hooked my thumbs in the waistband of another black and beautiful thong, she inhaled sharply and gripped my shoulders with both hands, but only one held me. The other, the bandaged one, hovered, light as a feather. I twisted my neck and kissed her trembling fingertips, then tipped my head back and locked eyes with her as I drew down the skimpy piece of lace.

Her breathing hitched, a shallow, quick nip that had my blood beating harder against my tight skin. I couldn't wait to hear her exhales growing ragged when I spread her thighs and teased the sweetness off her skin with my tongue.

"What are you doing?" she murmured.

"Contemplating my next meal." Angels, she smelled sweet.

Her blush spread down the delicate column of her throat and across her collarbone.

Chuckling at her wide-eyed innocence, I lifted her ankle to rid her of her pants and underwear, then repeated the jig with her other leg, until she stood before me in only a black lace bra and pearl earrings.

Crap. The earrings. Oh, well. I'd edit the transcript before the others woke up. And if I couldn't, at least it'd give them a little inspo for their next hookup. Or ammunition to use against me till the end of days. Didn't much care really.

All I cared about was getting the angel before me to relax into my touch and trust me with her body. With her heart, too, but I was guessing that would take more than a few orgasms.

Naya stared down at me in silence, throat dipping with slow swallows. She was nervous. I could feel her tension as I spiraled my hands back up her taut calves and toned thighs. Her muscles thrummed beneath my roughened palms, and goosebumps sailed across her smooth skin.

Even though the apex of her thighs called out to me, I kept my eyes fastened to hers, waiting for her twilit gaze to mellow, for her lashes to sweep low, for her jaw to stop quivering. I stroked up the frame of triangle blonde curls as flaxen as the ponytail draped over one of her breasts.

I reached up and flicked it off the lace-covered pink bud, wishing I could reach the elastic binding her long, white-blonde locks. I wanted to tear it off, to watch her hair stream down her spine like melting wax, to run my hands through it to create chaos where she'd put order. For all my complaining, I was entranced by its wildness that contrasted with her serene disposition.

I curved my thumbs back down the trenches of her pubic bone and eased her legs open. "So beautiful," I breathed as I shouldered her legs farther apart.

Just before I could trace the seam of her pale lips with the tip of my tongue, her skin broke out in glitter, and the sight . . .

I had no doubt Elysium would pale in comparison

Naya wasn't beautiful; she was magnificent.

And mine.

Tonight.

Tomorrow and for the rest of her angelgiven life, because I'd beat back anyone who so much as dared prostrate themselves at her feet.

Mine.

Driving her scent so deep it permeated my very soul, I finally closed the thin divide between us with a soft kiss.

So sweet. And so tight I had to thumb her folds apart so I could flatten my tongue against her and properly revere her. As her heat basted my palate, I groaned, regretting not having shoved down my pants before kneeling, because my zipper chafed.

I'd never come from going down on a woman, but as breathy moans slipped from her mouth, my cock swelled . . . and swelled.

Pluck.

I draped one of her legs over my shoulder and undid my pants before I could ruin another pair, then shoved them down along with my briefs and fisted myself. Although I'd just meant to free my erection, I gave myself a few pumps but let go fast, because a few more, and I'd climax before her.

Pleasure building down my spine, I lashed at her, my tongue delving deeper, mapping the creases of her glittery center. She gasped my name. Tugged at my hair. Pressed my head against her as though worried I'd want to be anywhere else.

I smiled as I continued my assault, my clasped lids dancing with her light.

Two swirls of my tongue, and she cried out. I wrapped my arms around her and cupped her ass as she shuddered. When she tried to squirm away, I locked my arms tighter, caging her so she wouldn't deprive me of a single drop of her essence.

I wanted it all.

I wanted to be full of her and steep in her spun-sunlight scent until soaked to the bone. To the soul.

NAYA

Oh, Abaddon, I finally understood why humans spent the better part of their lives contemplating sex. It was magical. A communion between the heart and body. To think Adam had only penetrated me with his tongue. What would remain of me once he penetrated me with that beautiful, and slightly daunting, part of him that smeared a trail of damp up the inside of my leg as he stood?

"How does this not cost us feathers? It's so . . ."

"Extraordinary?" He licked his curved lips.

I latched on to one of the drawer handles biting into my spine as my body gave such a harsh shudder, I suspected that if his tongue darted over his shiny mouth once more, I'd climax from the sight.

"Wicked," I croaked.

After kicking off his shoes, pants, and briefs, he coasted his palms up the sides of my body as delicately as a potter shaping a vase. "And yet, celestially-approved."

As a flotilla of goosebumps descended upon my skin, guilt wormed itself through me. Seeking pleasure when our friends were on the mend was indecent and wrong. "What are we doing?"

"Getting to know each other." His swollen, purple tip poked my abdomen while his hands curled around my rib cage to undo my bra.

I tried to calm my breathing since I was failing at calming my pulse.

My bra released my breasts, but Adam didn't slide it down my arms, simply let it hover like sandpaper over my hardened nipples, abrading the sensitive peaks.

His hands returned to my hips, and he stepped back, removing the leaking weight of himself from the yellowed bruise on my abdomen. "But we can stop anytime."

"Problem is, I don't want to stop," I rasped.

"Why is that a problem?"

"Because, our friends were shot, and we're inside a stranger's home. Because I don't deserve to feel anything but guilt right now." I shuddered. "I've conspired to kill a man, Adam."

His eyes grew hard. His grip, too. "Except, you won't."

"What other choice do we have? We can't let those girls die."

"They won't die."

"If I don't take out the father, the son will—"

"They. Won't. Die," he repeated in a voice that was as soft as velvet yet harsh as shrapnel. At my frown, he glided one of his hands to the column of my neck and wrapped his fingers around it, his touch mimicking his voice. "Feel my hand?" He applied almost no pressure, and yet, when he forced my neck back, the conduit between my mouth and lungs seemed to snip.

"I feel it." I didn't try and pull off his wrist, because I knew strangling me wasn't the point of his little demonstration. In truth, I wasn't yet sure what was.

"I can snap a neck faster than you can blink," he whispered against my ear, making my heart hammer out a trillion beats.

"You've never killed a man, so how can you know that?"

"Because I've trained, Naya. I've trained on immortals. The first time I tried the move on my martial arts ophanim, I didn't mean to sever his vertebrae, but I did. It took him several days to recover. Days during which, to my fathers' great concern, I failed to feel guilt, too proud by what a natural I was. Can you imagine?" His thumb stroked the brim of my raised jaw, the rough scrape of his calluses dragging heat across my face . . . but also lower. "Feeling pride for such an unangelic accomplishment."

He released the pressure, and I gasped, but not so much from the sudden influx of air as from the feel of his palm skating down my chest, bumping into my bra. He carried it so low, one strap dipped over my shoulder and down my arm. On his way to ease off the other, his palm brushed against my exposed breast again.

"Until we arrived in Caracas and Dov told us about Triples, I'd always been careful not to touch monsters, worried I'd inadvertently kill one and it would cost me everything." He rid me of bra and breath. "But now"—his fist balled over the black lace as though it were a Triple's neck—"now I itch to slay them."

My nostrils flared at his confession. To crave inflicting pain and death was a dangerous sentiment. It went against everything we'd been taught. But as I searched his gaze for the darkness that tinted the eyes of all the Triples I'd met, I realized that what Adam craved wasn't murder; it was justice.

"Tomorrow, *I'll* end the vile King's life." He finally tossed aside my bra. "Not you. Me. And not because I don't believe you're capable of it, but because I want to spare you and your sweet conscience. Besides"—he lowered his face to mine, slid his skilled tongue over the seam of my mouth, the same way he'd slipped it over another seam—"these lips are mine now, and angels help any man who so much as contemplates them."

A heady warmth dispersed through me at what was essentially a threat. Who was I?

"Understood?" He trailed kisses from the corner of my mouth to my ear.

"That my mouth is yours? I understand. What I don't understand is how you plan on getting close to a man who has more security than the President of the United States and the King of England combined."

"How did I get into this bedroom undetected?"

My throat constricted around a shallow swallow. *Dov* . . . "What if he refuses to get involved?"

Adam straightened, removing his warm mouth from my already cooling flesh. "He can't." His bloodlust transformed into moroseness. "He said this would be our last mission if we failed, so it's in his best interest that we don't." He pushed a hand through his hair, wrangling back the glossy brown waves. "All I need is for him to dust me. Make me invisible to the human eye. It's not that big of an ask."

"You really think he'll agree?"

Wasting no time, Adam crouched to retrieve his phone from his discarded pants, then dialed, putting the call on speakerphone.

Surprisingly, Dov answered on the second ring. "Ready for that ride down?"

"You were right. Naya had a plan, but I thought of a better one."

As he walked him through his strategy, I nibbled my bottom lip while studying the puffy garment bag holding the dress I'd bought to lull a man into a false sense of security. The mere sight of it made my palms grow clammy, because, for all my desire to save lives and eliminate evil souls, I hadn't been eager to end a stranger's life.

"I don't know, Adam," Dov said. "Naya's plan sounds better to me."

It's not my plan, I wanted to scream. *It's Pablo's.*

Adam, who was pacing the length of my closet, halted.

"Not to mention, from what I understand, the Prince won't hesitate to detonate the girls if she suddenly backs out and fails to show."

"I'll be there." My voice was entirely toneless. "I'll even slick on the cyanide if I need to." The show would go on.

"And while everyone's distracted and in their seats, you'll sprinkle me with some of that cosmic dust of yours, so I can creep around the palace."

"There's one fatal flaw in your plan." Dov paused, as though to build anticipation. All it achieved was to grow my annoyance. "Necks don't break on their own."

Adam stared at the phone screen as though he could see Dov through it. "Fine. Then I'll stop his heart. I'll make it look natural, okay?"

The line went so quiet that I wondered if Dov had hung up, but then he released a sigh that curled out of the receiver and permeated the walk-in closet like the humidity from the brimming tub. "Fine. We'll do it your way, but I could lose my wing bones for using magic to aid and abet a murderer, Adam. If you so much as breathe a word of my involvement to the others, to *anyone,* I will take you down with me. You, too, Naya. Understood?"

His threat resonated inside my marrow and made my neck ache from how straight I was holding it. The ishim had never inspired love, only respect. By threatening us, he was displaying a side of himself that raised my hackles and abolished my admiration. Not only was creating the undercover team *his* idea but so was the homicidal turn of this mission.

Mira's warning clanged through my skull. I wanted to rip the phone from Adam's grasp. I wanted to tell Dov to butt out of our lives. Besides covering costs and bringing Adam to me tonight, what had he done to help us?

He hadn't been the one to retrieve me from the marsh.

He hadn't been the one to minister to me while my body ejected poison.

He hadn't been the one to create smart gadgets or doctor camera footage.

The only reason I kept my mouth shut was the possibility that he'd helped the team out more than just financially in the past.

The second Adam hung up, I said, "I don't trust him."

Adam tossed his phone on his pants and sighed as he stepped back toward me. "As long as you trust me." His arms wrapped around my waist.

"You, I trust."

"Then trust that I have everything under control." He hefted me off the ground, which shot the air from my lungs into my mouth and made my legs curl around his narrow hips. "Even though he's terrified to tarnish his good name and lose his position, his heart's in the right place."

"Are you sure?"

"He's the one who wanted to save humans."

"Yet he sends others to do the dirty work."

"Can we stop talking about Dov?"

"He *threatened* us, Adam!"

The corners of his mouth flipped up.

"Why are you smiling?"

"I didn't expect such sharp claws on such a tender body."

I rolled my eyes. "I'm not tender."

"Feather"—he hovered his mouth over mine so I could feel the shape of each word—"you have the kindest heart and the most forgiving soul."

I shook my head, because my heart wasn't always kind, and I held grudges. I was still peeved at Raven for having returned to Earth without telling me.

"My perfect opposite," he added.

"My wings are black like yours."

"They shimmer. Light, meet dark." He gave my ass a light squeeze that drove my soft front into his rigid one. "Tender, meet hard."

I flicked a lock of hair out of his eyes. "You believe in soulmates. A grim, tough man wouldn't."

"I believe in *one* soulmate. I'm still not sold on the existence of several," he whispered before bridging the gap between our mouths.

What started as sweet turned torrid, and when he slipped his hardened length between his stomach and my center, I instinctively rocked my hips.

His mouth tore away from mine. "Careful. I'm ten seconds away from coming all over you, and I'd much rather come inside of you."

I held still, cheeks flushed, chest on fire.

When my throat dipped with a slow swallow, his expression softened. "But I can wait. We have our whole lives to—"

"Do you have a condom?"

His irises ignited with surprise. Or was it anticipation? "I . . . um. No." His Adam's apple slid up and down. "But I've been taking that male contraceptive pill for a few years now. I've never—not without a condom. It was just—you know . . . ?" His forearms tautened beneath me, the muscles so dense they dug into my buttocks. "For added protection."

I chose not to linger on the few years part, because a few years meant many partners, and although I was aware he wasn't a virgin, I still preferred not to picture him with anyone else. "Is it a hundred percent effective?"

"Ninety-nine point something."

Ninety-nine point something seemed safe. "Okay."

He stilled. "Okay?"

Instead of explaining what I was agreeing to, I levered my body a little higher so he'd slip out from between us. When I felt his engorged tip graze my entrance, I lowered myself. I may have dropped a little fast, because the burn and stretch was . . . *whoa*. My breath frayed, like my hymen, and possibly other inner tissues.

I didn't dare move.

Adam, apparently, didn't dare either, clearly as shocked as I was by how hastily I'd done away with the remainder of my innocence.

"Are you okay?" he finally asked.

I hummed, because in all honesty, I wasn't totally sure I was. I had no point of reference, but I suspected that Adam was rather generously endowed, what with his tip currently poking my stomach lining.

As he readjusted his hold on my backside, shifting inside of me, I hissed.

"I may have gone a little fast," I finally admitted, still trying to recover.

He blinked; brow creased as though he were the one in pain. Maybe he was.

"Is it uncomfortable for you, too?"

A chuckle fell from his mouth, which was unfortunate for my shredded lady bits, because it made the dagger lodged inside of me judder and carve me up some more. When I cringed, he sobered and swept a lock of hair off my perspiring brow.

"No, Feather"—he propped his forearms a little higher, propping me higher in turn, which lessened the tightness—"it feels like I just found my way home."

To think this man didn't consider himself sweet.

He pivoted on his heels, kneeled, and with the utmost care, deposited me on the plush rug, still buried deep. "How about we take it a little slower, though?"

"That sounds wise."

His eyes, usually the hardest shade of emerald, turned soft as moss as they raked over my face. Bracketing me between his forearms, he rolled his hips, and my core spasmed. He held still, slanted his mouth over my own and snuck his tongue inside. I latched on to that point of contact, and when he rolled his hips again, I didn't tense, and it felt . . . *better*.

I lifted my good hand to his back, felt the planes of muscles shift beneath my fingertips, his vertebrae spool and unspool with the measured grace of a wild cat. I moved my hand lower, to the firm hills of his ass.

When I crimped the cheek to capture the magnificent power sculpting him, he groaned. "Your body," he rasped, chest and brow growing slick with sweat. "It feels . . . like sunshine and starlight." His wings appeared and unfolded over us like a canopy of black satin, extending to bladed points.

I traced their outline toward the sensitive V, eliciting words that sounded like thunderous raindrops and incandescent lightning against my flushed skin.

Adam stopped moving and braced himself over me. His half-lidded eyes locked on mine, and in a voice so deep it seemed to billow out from his very soul, he murmured something that sounded like, "Made for me."

I lifted my gauze-swaddled hand to brush away a sweat-dampened lock of hair that had gotten caught on his long lashes. "What did you say?"

He flexed his buttocks, driving himself deep, and I gasped. We'd become so slick that his silken rod glided against my walls, filling all the empty space inside me to the point where it was now his absence that hurt.

"I said that your body was made for mine. That *you* were made for *me*."

My chest clinched with emotion, and I carried his face down to mine, his lips to mine. As his words penetrated my heart, his strokes quickened, deepened, and it was my core that clenched.

I breathed in deeply, and his scent, so crisp, so green . . . it transported me to the guild. To the tree forever bursting with ripe figs, which had always scattered my heartbeats.

A brush of his lips, and I was carried away from my celestial home and returned to this new one made of musk and salt and feathers, to this fearless pillar of a man, who stole my breath with a mere look and my heartbeats with a simple touch.

I skimmed my palm over the solid expanse of his wing, before returning it to the feathers wreathing his spine.

Adam bruised my lips with his kiss, bruised my pubic bone with the punishing rhythm of his hips, yet I clung to him, my fingers alternately dancing over the indent of his wings and the dip of his spine.

Heat blustered beneath my veins, spreading . . . spreading.

I skated my mouth off his so I could draw in a breath, but the air seemed laced with fire. "Adam, I'm . . . *Oh*." My spine arched off the floor as a comet shot to the juncture of our bodies and detonated, flinging me into an ocean of stars.

He curled his hand beneath my knee and drew my leg up, and, *oh* . . . Another thrust, and the stars brightened, erupted, and spread their luminous dust through the web of muscle and bone and blood barely holding me together.

Adam grunted while I floated. And then he guzzled in a strangled breath, and his body shuddered over my buoyant form, liquid heat ribboning against my engorged walls.

"Naya," he murmured, "Feather." He dropped his face into the crook of my neck, and groaned long and deep, like a man awakening from years of slumber.

I flattened my palm against the burning skin at the small of his back, and I could've sworn it was beating with the same frenzied pulse as his chest. "I think you're right. I think we're not a coincidence."

He turned his face toward mine, one eyebrow slung low.

"You and me, Adam. We're not a coincidence."

I'd known his scent before I'd known him. That had to be magic or fate or *something*.

He finger-combed my hair, eyebrow lifting in time with his reddened lips. "Finally catching up with my theory on soulmates, huh?"

Was that why I'd known his smell? Could we recognize our soulmate from the fragrance of their skin? Or did this scent run deeper than our flesh? Was it his soul that smelled like rainstorms and ripe fruit?

Oh, the questions I'd have for my mother once this mission was over...

63

NAYA

"I almost forgot." Pablo dug through his tuxedo jacket as the SUV rolled through the grid of streets that had been cleared of traffic to facilitate travel to the palace. "I brought this back for you last night." He tossed a small velvet box onto my lap, over the hand buried in the folds of electric-blue tulle. "Wear it on your ring finger."

My ribs tightened at the depth of our sham. "We're engaged now?" I untangled my hand from my poofy skirt to open the box. A cushion-cut diamond as large as my thumbnail shimmered inside.

"We are. Had to make it more . . . believable." He studied my crimson lips, before his eye lowered to the hickey that had already faded to the palest shade of denim.

Thankfully, Adam hadn't left any more traces of his visit behind, and although he'd gotten a lift from Dov long before Pablo's return, I'd still feared my ungracious host would find out I'd entertained a guest in my room.

Why? Because, even if he didn't want me for himself, merely wanted to use me, hubris made men rash.

Pablo reached over my armrest, grabbed the ring from the box, and jammed it over my knuckle with such force that I felt the echo of his brutality inside my ruined palm. I stifled the gasp behind locked teeth.

Soon.

It'll be over soon.

I gave the enormous stone a cursory glance, then returned my gaze to the street festooned with garlands as blue as the Venezuelan flag, as blue as my dress.

"Had a pleasant evening?" Pablo asked.

My skin went cold, but the same way I'd forced back my gasp, I forced back the shiver. "I slept well. Thank you." Since I had, I lost no feathers. "Did you sleep?"

"Don't pretend to care."

I glanced away from the street and into the blue eye clinging to my glossy curls. Although I hadn't meant to wet my hair last night, sharing a bath with Adam had trashed my attempt to keep it dry.

Thankfully, though, Pablo had had a stylist stop by my room to doll me up, and the man had managed to tame my wild locks. In spite of my protests to keep my face makeup-free, with the exception of mascara and lipstick, he'd dusted my lids with a mix of silvery blue powder that ended up adding depth to my fathomless irises.

Pablo's gaze snapped back to the road. "You'll sing *Happy Birthday* during the cocktail."

His mood whipped up my pulse. "I thought I was singing when everyone sat down for dinner?"

"Plans change. Adapt."

I squared my shoulders, not appreciating being talked to this way. I was doing *him* a favor. The least he could do was show me some respect. "Is it your nerves that are making you so rude?"

"What should I be nervous about? Even if you fail tonight, I'll get my way."

"Then why are you biting my head off?"

He tugged on the white cuffs that glimmered with those rubies that resembled vials of blood. "Pardon me, but I wasn't aware whores deserved to be spoken to with respect."

My fingers crimped the tulle, the diamond vanishing beneath the bolts of blue. "What did you just call me?"

His eye twinkled as he removed his phone from the inner pocket of his navy silk tux. "Tell me . . ." His voice was barely louder than the tap of his gloved fingertip on the black screen. "Which one of my guards helped you smuggle in the kid you fucked"—he flipped the phone around so I could see the video footage running over his screen—"on my rug . . . in my bath . . . in my bed?"

Liquid metal submerged my tongue. If I'd already applied the cyanide, I would've worried it had breached my skin and was poisoning me. "None of them."

"You expect me to believe the kid's Spiderman come to life? I mean, he's well-built, I'll give him that much, but my hotel is built *better*."

The air sliding down my throat did little to ease my harshening lung cramp. "In a few hours, I'll be out of your life. What do you care who I have sex with?"

"It is not the men you screw I care about. It is the ones who screw me." He leaned over, fished my ringed hand from the depths of tulle, and squeezed my palm between his thumb and forefinger. "Give me a name, or I will shoot *all* the ones who were on duty last night."

When blood seeped into the flesh-colored bandage, I snatched my hand back, tears of horror and pain swelling my lids. "I told you, none of them betrayed you. Just check the cameras inside your home since you apparently have them *everywhere*."

I suddenly wondered if he had more than visuals. I was guessing no, or he would've asked what sort of technology we possessed to make ourselves invisible and would've asked about Dov.

I ripped my hand from his.

"Just remember, *mi sol*, that if you or your boyfriend try to hurt me, your little friends will go . . ." He mouthed the word KABOOM, flourishing his fingers to mimic an explosion.

I kept my hand raised to staunch the blood flow. "I haven't forgotten."

"Oh, and don't take this personally, but I put out a kill order on your boyfriend, in case he shows his face at the party."

How had this man's score ever dropped? Had Galina misread Dov's message?

As the palace appeared before us, golden dome burnished by the setting sun, I decided that once the devices were out of the girls, I'd return for Pablo, and I'd put an end to his reign of terror before it could even begin.

How I would enjoy seeing the life leak from his eyes . . . A feather drifted from my invisible wings, onto the dark gray carpet between our seats.

Although the pearls weighed heavily on my earlobe, I couldn't help but raise my uninjured hand to make sure they were well and truly there. When I felt the smooth curve, I breathed out a shallow breath that hardly relieved me.

"So, at what point during the cocktail will I be singing?" *Adam, please be checking the transcript.*

As our SUV barreled past ridiculously tall golden gates, Pablo readjusted his blue bowtie. "After my toast."

"Which is . . . ?"

"When I take the microphone."

Was Pablo being purposely vague to confound me or because he didn't trust me? "So when should I apply my lipstick?"

"I'll take care of that for you. All you have to do is take care of my father."

The car lurched to a stop in front of the domed structure the King had built after he'd seized power through his military coup.

"Don't move," Pablo barked, hopping out his side of the car just as paparazzi raised their cameras. He came around to my door and unlatched it, then held out his palm, the perfect gentleman.

To think I'd once fallen for that act . . .

I gave him my uninjured hand, too afraid he'd drain the other of blood, and stepped out in my pair of six-inch golden heels that put my face level with his. I was glad for the added height. I didn't care to look up at a man like Pablo.

He drew me into him, and before I could react, kissed me. Flashes detonated around us as the rabid press ate up the photo op. My lips parted around a surprised gasp but firmed up immediately, forbidding his tongue entry. My wings poured out from my back and curled around my shoulders, and although they couldn't shield me from humans, they reminded me that I belonged to a better race, one where beings didn't plot vengeful schemes to eliminate others.

Sure, Elysium was full of power struggles, but not violence. Not deception. Not bloodthirst.

Nausea roiling through me, I counted the seconds until the curtain closed on the show I should've seen coming—after all, I'd agreed to play someone's fake-fiancée. I hoped Adam wouldn't be privy to the kiss. Not because he'd believe I had any affection for the man using me, but because of what he'd said. Too many innocents would suffer if the Prince fell before the King.

The pressure of Pablo's mouth finally slackened. When he

straightened and took my arm, a camera-ready smile was already flexing his slightly-reddened mouth. "Smile, *mi sol*. The world is watching."

I smiled, not for the world or for this man; I smiled to hide the rising thirst for retribution this man had conjured within my soul. I failed to hide it from the ishim, who pilfered my wings yet again. Although my spine flinched at the hot jab, my smile remained intact.

After we'd passed through metal detectors and guards who patted us down, Pablo took my arm again. I tried to pull it away, but he merely clamped down on it harder. "Would it kill you to act less frigid?"

As we penetrated into the gargantuan-domed space lit by garlands of light wrapped around suspended orchids and faceted-crystal chandeliers reminiscent of French castles, I murmured, "No, but it might kill you, Pablo. My boyfriend isn't into sharing."

He grinned. "Your boyfriend couldn't enter the palace, even concealed inside a Trojan horse."

Oh, the irony. Even though Dov was no Trojan horse, his magic would serve the same purpose.

"Are you certain?" I replied sweetly. "He did enter your residence undetected."

The Prince's biceps turned to plaster. When his gaze began gyrating over the tide of partygoers garbed in sequins, velvets, and silks, I patted myself on the back for having instilled fear in a monster.

My pride quickly took a back seat to my nerves, though, when I caught sight of the silver-haired tyrant sitting atop a throne whittled from solid gold, on a dais rimmed by a fleet of armed guards.

As we got in line to greet the King—apparently, the son had to wait his turn—my gaze cycled around the throne room. If the people of this country had been well-off, I may have admired the carpet of twinkling gold-and-blue mosaic, the stone-encrusted brocade papering the four walls, and the sea of tables sagging beneath glass candelabras and hand-painted porcelain, but the slums, that had existed under the President, had proliferated under the King.

My festering annoyance at the gaudy display came to an abrupt halt when Pablo leaned in and whispered, "To think all of this could've been yours, *mi sol*."

He'd planned to wed me? Why? To keep me under his thumb?

"Here I assumed killing me would be more your style . . ."

"I would've wed you first. A family man makes for a more respectable king."

"I doubt the people would've respected a man who'd married his father's"—I dropped my voice—"killer."

"Darling, no one would ever believe a girl like you"—his eyes ran down my very bare front, making me feel even more exposed—"could premeditate murder. Which would've made you the perfect queen. Too blindingly innocent to spot the intelligence and darkness lurking within." When he ran a gloved finger down the edge of my cheek, I pulled away. I got a full inch before he tightened his arm around mine, pinning it to his side. "You and I have so much in common."

"You and I have nothing in common."

"We both want what's best."

"You only want what's best for *you*. That isn't even close to what I want."

How could my people stand to stay on the sidelines? How was my father, one of the most generous and powerful beings in Elysium, not campaigning to restore order in the human realm? Was the celestial one so difficult to regiment?

Although I'd promised Dov and Adam to keep their endeavor quiet, this world needed so many more guardians than six measly fletchings and one anxious ishim.

Right before we reached the steps that led onto the raised platform, I spotted the Circle Girls clustered together, doe-eyed and underdressed amid the preening throngs. When they caught sight of me, a few of them waved; others whispered. Had they noted Emmy's absence? Robbie and Susan's?

"Do they know what happened to their hosts yet?"

"No." Pablo smiled at them, falsely gracious man that he was. "Most of these girls are hysterical enough already."

I was almost surprised that he'd used the word girls instead of sacks of flesh, since clearly, that's all they were to him. Vessels for his bombs. "They're young and impressionable, Pablo, not hysterical."

He pulled me up one step. "The more into me you appear, the more intrigued he'll be. Which is what you want and what *they*"—he jutted his lotion-smooth chin toward the Circle Girls—"need."

"I agreed to put on a show, but not *that* sort of show."

"And you call yourself selfless?" His hand threaded into my hair and gripped my skull, turning my head until our noses collided. "Your false sense of modesty might cost hundreds . . ." His eye gleamed with savage promise. "*Thousands,* their lives." Before I could recoil, he stole another kiss from my stiff mouth.

Glass splintered, followed by a high-pitched squeal. I spun, untethering the fingers clutching my scalp. Mere feet away, beside a woman whisking droplets of champagne off her ample bosom while a waiter apologized emphatically for having overturned his platter of drinks on her, stood Adam, eyes lambent with fury.

I whipped my head toward the Prince, expecting to find a gun already raised, but the only thing Pablo had raised was an eyebrow and a bored smile.

Which meant . . . which meant Adam was cloaked to the human eye.

Although my thundering pulse pounded against my neck, knowing Adam was here eased the disquiet rolling through my stomach.

I glanced back at where he stood, listing forward, one wrist clasped between the fingers of an angel with solid gold wings. From the play of muscle in Dov's bare arms, I guessed he was employing all his energy to keep Adam from charging toward us.

The ishim whispered something into Adam's ear that must've been effective, because, although his nostrils never ceased to flare, he rocked back onto his heels, and once set free, didn't attack the Prince.

"Our turn." Pablo grabbed my ringed hand and squeezed so hard a little yelp fled from my lips. "Make sure to show off your ring."

"My ring is attached to my bleeding hand. You really think your father will enjoy the sight of how his son hurts his bride-to-be?"

"My father loves nothing more than to play hero and make me look like a dolt," Pablo murmured beneath his breath, right before we were both patted down *again*. Did the guards think we'd picked up some knives from the dining tables on the way?

Huh . . . Not a bad idea.

Right before we reached his father, Pablo snuck his arm around my waist and pressed his mouth to my ear. "Everything I do, I do it to benefit our endeavor."

Your endeavor, Pablo.

My endeavor was to save forty-eight souls.

64

NAYA

The King, who hadn't budged off his throne for anyone yet, rose when his son and I approached. Even if he had no love for his flesh and blood, appearances were everything.

"*Feliz cumpleaños, Padre.*" Happy birthday, Father. Pablo's smile was all smoke and mirrors.

The two men embraced as though there existed real affection between them, as though the father hadn't removed his son's eye and the son wasn't plotting his father's slow and painful execution.

Once they separated, the King turned his attention to me, and his eyes, the same icy blue as his son's, scraped over my dress, or rather over the body beneath it. "I understand why my son succumbed to you after one glance, Señorita Moreau. You are most exquisite." His gaze caught on my ring. "I hear felicitations are in order."

I felt the Prince's stare on the side of my face, as heavy as a gun barrel.

I lifted my hand to display the diamond and the son's brutality.

The King inhaled sharply. Although he wore no crown, his hand went to his silver hair as though to push one back. "Whatever happened to your hand, *querida*?"

I deferred to Pablo for the answer.

"My fiancée is a beauty but entirely too clumsy. So much like

Mamá. Do you remember how many injuries she'd get when she tried to cook us meals?"

His father's expression hardened, and the faintest glaze sheeted his eyes, but then he blinked, and the emotion vanished, and his full focus fell heavily back on me, instead of on whichever memory the Prince had stirred.

He snapped his fingers, barking orders to get fresh bandages for his *nuera*.

Yeah. I was not and never would be his daughter-in-law.

"Show me your hand." He held out his palm, and I reluctantly gave in. As he unwrapped the bandage, he asked, "Did you not notice she was bleeding, *hijo*? I mean, you do still have one eye."

The faintest twitch made a nerve beside said-eye jump. "I was too busy taking in her angelic face and her . . ." He gave me a slow once-over. "Sinful curves, to pay much attention to her hands."

My skin crawled as though I were lying in a spider-infested bed.

"Even though those hands are marvelously skilled. Almost as skilled as that very red mouth."

My stomach revolted at his implications.

The King shook his head. "Excuse my son. I entrusted his education to boarding schools and grasped too late the error of my ways."

The medic arrived and although the man tried to redress my hand, the King insisted on doing it himself. He was so gentle that if I hadn't known his sinner score and witnessed all the crimes he'd committed, I may have been duped.

He taped up the gauze. "How's that?"

"So much better. Thank you."

He smiled at me, and the fine wrinkles around his mouth and eyes crinkled like on the face of a concerned parent.

He's a murderer, Naya. He took out his son's eye. Stop pitying men who don't deserve it.

Although he released my hand, his attention lingered on my body. "Is your hair—"

"Naturally pale and curly? *Sí, Padre.* Exactly like Mamá's." It struck me that Pablo referred to his father formally, but not his mother.

If only the woman had survived . . . How different their relationship would be. How different *they* would've been.

I briefly wondered what had become of her soul. Whether it had made it to Elysium or was it in Abaddon? Unless she, too, had been a Triple. I doubted it, but my gut had proved a very lackluster barometer these last two weeks.

The King's hand was suddenly in my hair, and I jumped, effectively dislodging the unwelcomed touch. "You remind me so much of my Azucena."

"Doesn't she?" Pablo's arm glided around my waist. "Except she's *mine*. Please don't steal another woman from my bed, Father, or I will have to stop introducing you."

The King didn't react to his son's taunt, too busy running me over with his gaze.

"We've kept your guests waiting long enough." Pablo's arm tightened as he turned me. When he pulled me down another set of stairs, this time, set behind the throne, he whispered, "Your uncanny resemblance to my mother was what caught my eye the first time, as well."

I grimaced, utterly disgusted by his confession. No wonder Pablo wasn't quite right in the head with all his parental issues.

He raised his eye to the domed ceiling that was as luridly gold on the inside as it was on the outside. "May she rest with the angels."

As he stared upward, the temptation to reveal our secrets bit at my tongue. I'd tried to sway him in the past with hints, but not facts. Maybe facts could still sway him.

Maybe—

He jerked me to a stop. "He's looking. Make it look real this time."

Before I could understand who was looking and what I was supposed to make look real, Pablo jammed his mouth over mine. When he pinched my ass, I reared back. "I already caught his eye, so don't you dare touch me again."

"I watched you last night. Watched it all." His pupil shrank to a dot, and then his arms banded around my waist, pressing me so harshly into his front that each one of his ruby buttons imprinted themselves into the deep V of skin between my halter top. "I've known whores with more virtue, little girl."

"Fuck you."

I may have lost a feather for my insult, but Pablo's insult cost him more.

It cost him the truth about our world.

ADAM

ANGELIC FACT #666
AVOID STRIKING DEALS WITH MORTAL DEVILS.

"Let. Me. Go. Dov." My bare hands itched to close around Junior's throat and tear it clean off his shoulders. I was so pissed, I knew I'd be capable of it.

"People are staring." The ishim cinched both my biceps.

"I thought your dust blocked our voices?"

"It's not your voice they're hearing; it's your body they're feeling. You've knocked into ten people already. One more, and I'm airlifting you, and you'll have an ascended's-eye view of your girlfriend."

I ground my molars as I tried to fucking calm down.

He sighed, probably at the sight of another one of my feathers. "Don't lose sight of your objective."

My objective was to paint the room red with blood. The father's first, but the son would bleed.

Oh . . . *how he would bleed.*

If I lost a feather, I didn't feel it over my sweltering rage. If only I had fire of my own. Or dust. I'd scorch the rest of Junior's body and steal Naya right from under his nose.

When I'd suggested Dov do just that—both the funeral pyre and the cloaking-Naya part—he'd threatened to strip me of his dust and went so far as to tell me to quit my tantrum.

If I hadn't needed to remain invisible for Naya's sake, I would've told the verity to take his dust and shove it where the Elysian sun didn't shine.

"In an hour, this'll be over. You and Naya will be done. For the love of all that is angelic, contain yourself one more hour."

An hour that would feel like a century.

"We should've waited at the hotel." Dov sighed. "I shouldn't have let you sway me into bringing you earlier."

"How can you stand to let humans harass our kind, Ish?" My voice was thunder. My words lightning. "How can you let them get groped without their consent? How?"

"Because our kind is equipped to deal with such base creatures."

"We're not! If Noah and I hadn't fished Naya out of that swamp, she'd still be there." Maybe because she heard my shouting, Naya looked my way. When I glimpsed her calmness and strength, I ground my feet and—somewhat—settled.

"Granted, but she wouldn't have died."

"For another five years. What if no one collected her by then?"

"That's why our world has ophanim. Besides, Naya has a father who loves her. A mother who would, without a doubt, toss celestial consequences aside and illegally exit a guild to help her daughter."

Celeste would. In a heartbeat. She'd sacrifice herself for Naya. The thought of Celeste becoming a nephilim chilled me. Out of all the ascended I'd met, she was one of my favorites. A spitfire of a woman with wing bones of steel.

What a loss it would be for Elysium.

Asher would fight it. This, I had no doubt. Which would surely win him the same fate as his beloved—burned crescents and a soul vowed for extinction.

With her two parents gone, Naya would follow.

My stomach bottomed out.

If Naya lost her immortality . . .

If she ceased to exist . . .

The throne room faded, and I was propelled onto a stone terrace lashed by rain.

I'd have attributed the vision to one of my downy flyaways colliding into a patch of skin, but it wasn't a memory, because this faceless girl was in it, and she was being carried into the sky by Seraph Asher of all people.

A shuddering blink later, the room came back into full focus and surround-sound.

What the—

I rubbed at my chest. Was the faceless girl Naya? Was my anxiety causing me to hallucinate Asher taking her from me? Although it'd crush my plucking heart, the hard truth was that Naya would be safer far from the likes of me.

NAYA

Every chance I got, I stared at Adam over Pablo's shoulder. My fellow black-wing managed to calm himself down, even though the vibrations of his temper rippled across the room.

"What is it you find more fascinating than your fiancé, *mi sol*?"

I averted my eyes but not before Pablo followed my line of sight.

"Ahh," he said.

My heart tripped.

What did he mean *ahh*?

Could he see Adam?

I reasoned that if he had, he'd have alerted one of the two bodyguards he'd been allowed to bring, and they were both stationed like gargoyles just far enough away to give their boss privacy, while he schmoozed with various heads of state, but close enough to intervene in case of an attack.

"The wall covering. It is quite spectacular, isn't it? One million tourmalines were handstitched into the brocade to make up the outlines of the stargazer lilies."

"Sounds expensive."

"My father wanted to build a mausoleum grander than the Taj Mahal to celebrate the love of his life. And so he did."

I stared at the mosaic beneath my golden stilettos, not so much in horror as in shock. "Your mother's buried here?"

"You weren't aware? This edifice *is* called Azucena's Dome."

I lifted my gaze back to his. "You forget I didn't come to your country as a tourist."

"Of course. Silly me." He studied the elongated pistils spilling out from one of the lilies.

"Your father really loved your mother."

"The only person he ever did. Well, besides himself."

Keeping my gaze on the patterned wall, I tossed back what he'd told me earlier. "Guess you two have a lot in common."

"He and I have *nothing* in common. Nothing." He'd have lost a feather had he been a fletchling.

Instead of wasting my breath to disprove him, I said, "That's the last of the guests. Time for your speech."

"Observant little thing."

"Impatient." I glared at him, while he stared back with just as much contempt. "Have you logged into your phone provider's account?"

"*No pones el carro delante de los bueyes, mi sol.*"

How could I not put the cart before the horses? I didn't trust the man I'd struck a deal with.

"I promised to do it in front of you, and I will. The same way I promised you the antidote." He patted his breast pocket as though to prove the vial was tucked in there. "But you are right. It is time." He reached inside his jacket.

I couldn't help myself from taking a step back, totally counterintuitive, since, had it been a gun and not a tube of lip-gloss, proximity would've been the only way to disarm him.

He handed me the tube. "Once I thank everyone for coming and announce that my fiancée has prepared a song, roll it on thick."

My fingers locked tightly around the gloss, relieved that he hadn't insisted on slicking it on my mouth himself.

"To the Circle Girls." He raised his untouched champagne flute in a toast but didn't drink, then pivoted, handed his glass to one of his guards, and returned to the dais where a woman was already waiting for him with a mic.

As his gloved hand closed around it, another hand closed around my hip.

ADAM

ANGELIC FACT #948
DON'T TRUST THOSE WHO SPILL
OTHERS' SECRETS.

The second my arm went around her waist, I stopped feeling as though I was about to set the human realm on fire. And then, once she realized it was me and reclined against my chest, the rest of my tension fizzled out.

"I missed you," I murmured into her flaxen curls, drawing in their silken scent.

Only a day since I'd held her, yet it felt like a lifetime. Who was I kidding earlier? I would never let her father carry her away from me. Just the thought was unbearable.

"Me too." Her low whisper caught the attention of a woman standing beside her.

The older lady raised an over-blackened brow in our direction before returning her attention to the makeshift stage where Junior had just started his little speech.

I splayed both my hands on Naya's front, one on her sternum, the other on her abdomen. I momentarily wished my hands were visible, so I could hide all the skin Junior had made her put on display, but if I'd been visible, I couldn't have held her, so I contented myself with my lot.

"I've decided what to do about him." Her heart palpitated beneath my palms as robustly as mine against her spine.

"The King?" she murmured.

The white-haired lady glanced over again.

"No, Junior. I'm going to carve out his lips before carving out his heart."

If she hissed, the sound was absorbed by the crowd's chuckling, because Junior was apparently a real showman.

Naya craned her neck to look into my face, probably to check if I was kidding. But then she surprised the Abaddon out of me. "I'll help."

I searched the velvet darkness of her eyes for the innocent fletching who'd come to me for a job. That girl was gone, and although I felt responsible for her demise, I also felt proud of Naya for having withstood such a trying mission and grown fiercer for it.

Before I could stop myself, I breached the distance between our mouths.

"You may want to stop that," Dov grumbled. "People are already looking at Naya as though she broke out of the local asylum."

When Naya skated her mouth off mine, I sighed. "Remind me why I can't just grab someone's gun and shoot both of them now?"

"Because we need him to delete the SIMs." This time, Naya's response was drowned out by a sea of clapping.

The lady next to her, though, must've heard Naya's murmur, because she inched away. Oh, the irony that she was applauding two monsters, yet feared the innocent blonde in my arms.

A spotlight fell over me, freezing the smirk on my lips and the air in my lungs. I'd already mapped out the exits and was about to haul Naya to the closest one when my lashing pulse made way to Junior's dulcet voice.

"My lovely fiancée has prepared a song in your honor, Padre." He waved Naya over, and it was clear from the smile dangling from his mouth that he wasn't seeing me. "The stage is yours, my sun."

My whole body sharpened into a mother-plucking blade, because she wasn't his angelsdamned sun.

"Let her go, Adam," Dov murmured.

Naya had turned to ice between the cage of my arms, but then she sighed, and it percolated from her body straight into mine. Where it relaxed her, it had the opposite effect on me.

"Adam..." Dov growled.

I shut my eyes and sprang my arms wide. When she stepped away, I felt like a layer of my skin had been removed. I wanted to reach out and snag her waist, reel her back into me. Hold her there for all of eternity.

My throat rolled with a swallow as her black wings unfurled from her rigid spine, like the windblown sails of a pirate ship warning its enemy of an attack.

Walking away from her last night had been painful.

Watching her walk away from me now . . . it fucking shredded my soul.

NAYA

*A*s I climbed onto the stage, I tucked the lip-gloss beneath my skinny zipper, right against the hardened knot of my stomach.

"Ready?" Pablo held out the mic to me.

My throat was spasming too hard to speak, so I nodded and grabbed the microphone as he trundled back down the stairs. To think I'd need to sing soon. Angels, how I didn't feel like singing. Thankfully, Pablo had asked me to prepare Marilyn Monroe's version of *Happy Birthday*, so it was neither challenging nor long.

Just two stanzas.

As the string quartet launched into the melody, and the notes swirled up into the dome and bounced along the gemmed walls, I kept my gaze on Adam, who propelled himself through the crowd like a shark. When he neared the Prince, he stilled and his hands fisted at his sides.

I gave the smallest headshake. *Remember the girls.*

Pablo must've thought I was trying to back out of our arrangement because he slid his cell phone out of his tux pocket and held it up. To anyone else, it would look as though he were about to immortalize his fiancée's performance, but I read his gesture for the threat it was.

Dov must've hissed something at Adam, because he glanced over his shoulder before slinking around the Triple, elbowing the arm holding the phone. Pablo startled, and the phone almost slipped out of his gloved hand.

My heart stopped when he looked at Adam.

Started again when his gaze slipped over the encroaching crowd, a dip forming between his eyebrow and eyepatch. He returned his phone to his pocket, just as Adam reached the tight fence of guards stationed around the dais.

I must've missed my cue, because the crowd cheered encouragingly.

Heart clocking my ribs, I inhaled slowly and turned toward the King lounging on his throne, one elbow propped on the armrest, chin cradled on his fist, gaze so oily it greased my skin. "It's daunting to sing before a king."

That earned me a few chuckles and some more jovial encouragements.

"I'm ready." I nodded toward the string quartet, then added, "I think."

More laughter, and a wide grin from the King.

The string quartet looped back to the beginning. This time, I didn't miss my cue. The breathiest *happy birthday to you* lurched out of my mouth, eddying across the mausoleum, silencing the crowd.

A second one.

At the third repetition, I substituted the *Mr. President* line with, "Your Majesty."

A commotion by the dais stairs pulled my gaze there. Adam must've jostled a guard, because two were hissing at each other. As I sung the fourth birthday line, Adam marched toward King Perez's throne.

Although Dov had warned him against breaking the King's neck, the ishim had given him the green light to choke him. People would assume he was either having a stroke or that someone had spiked the shot of rum he'd poured for his son and himself from a sealed bottle after the Prince's syrupy speech.

One stanza to go.

"*Thanks, Your Majesty.*" I never broke eye contact with the King, even though my full awareness was on Adam. "*For all the things you've done; the battles that you've won.*"

Two more steps, and Adam would be in position.

"*The way you treat your foreigners; and your people's problem by the ton; we—*"

A shriek sliced across my voice, making the orchestra falter and the King's guards rack their firearm slides.

"Watch out, Your Majesty!" someone yelled, pointer finger bobbing.

Adam froze as the beam, which had been on me, swung to him.

NAYA

My fingers clamped so hard around the microphone that my knuckles marbled. Although I wanted to search the Queen's burial chamber for the golden-winged ishim, who'd just failed us, I couldn't tear my gaze from Adam's rigid shoulders.

His hands came up, along with a hiccup. "Just came to get a closer look at Singing Beauty," he slurred, tipping his head toward me and staggering in my direction.

"¡*Mata al idiota!*" the Prince hollered. *Kill the idiot!*

Adam swayed, stumbled. I gasped, certain he'd been shot, but no blood matted his dark T-shirt.

Guards poured onto the stage.

Four circled the King.

One strode toward me. I thought he was going to cuff me, but he merely said, "Follow me, my lady."

"Dov!" I shrilled, using the mic to amplify my voice before my guard snatched it from my hand. "Wait. Wait." I shrugged him aside to keep Adam in my field of vision. "Take care of your king. I'm fine."

I wasn't fine.

I was a wreck.

Although Adam was still pretending to be inebriated, he was outnumbered.

Where the Abaddon are you, Dov?

I raised my gaze to the golden dome, sucking in a breath when I saw a piece of it crashing down. But it wasn't the ceiling falling; it was the pure verity. Dov soared toward Adam, sprinkled dust, and fished him out of the circle of guards.

His disappearance caused a grander upheaval.

The shrieking crowd streamed out toward the exit, a groundswell of disjointed limbs and bobbing colors.

"NAYA!" Adam struggled to break free from Dov, who was flying him out of the mausoleum.

Oh, Elysium, if he broke loose and fell . . .

"FEATHER!" His rage pounded against my heart as he vanished into the dark night, sneering like a crazed animal.

As my attention swung back to the pit of darkness encircling me, I caught the Prince's eye.

His jaw flexed.

His phone came out.

A split-second. That's how long it took me to react. Breathing out an apology to the guard, who'd only meant to help me, I elbowed him in the throat to stun him and swiped his gun. And then I marched through the throng of armed men surrounding the monarch.

No one noticed the little girl in blue until she was standing before the King.

No one noticed the gun clutched in her hands until it was too late.

But they all noticed when the bullet rippled the air and embedded itself inside their ruler's chest.

The mortal god blinked at me, a trickle of blood dribbling from his mouth.

And then he collapsed.

The world held still for one second.

Two.

Three.

And then all Abaddon broke loose.

My spine arched as bolt after bolt of fire shredded the skin on my back. I'd expected punishment for assassinating a king, but had prayed the new one would intervene. When would I learn that prayers were useless. After all, God didn't exist and angels didn't listen.

Another tongue of fire licked up my spine, sending me to my knees with a violent gasp.

ADAM

ANGELIC FACT #496
STICKS AND STONES CANNOT BREAK
OUR WING BONES.

My fist collided into Dov's jaw with a satisfying thwack. "Turn the fuck back!"

Dov spat out a string of garbled words that sounded like, "Good for nothing nephilim."

"Turn around, Dov!" I reeled my arm back, prepared to smash it into his throat this time, when he released me, dumping me straight into one of the trees planted around the mausoleum.

Yelling obscenities at the ishim, I pinwheeled through the branches and ate so many plucking leaves I had to quit cursing out the useless clump of downy dung. I braced myself for the final drop, yet wasn't prepared for the skeleton-rattling impact.

Groaning, I blinked up into the moonlit branches, waiting for my brain to catch up with my body and land.

Guttural shouts vibrated the air and a stampede pulsated the ground, flushing my bones with steel. I pried myself off the grass and took off, but my gait was rickety, and I teetered like a toddler, zigzagging and swaying. When my sneaker hooked a root, I went down face-first.

Nose gushing blood, I heaved myself onto my knees. Determination to get to Naya made me stand and put one foot in front of the other.

From how plucking high had the winged prick dropped me?

I thought I heard Apa shouting my name.

Papa, too.

I was guessing *high* if I was hallucinating my fathers' voices.

What I wouldn't give for the aural mirage to be real, though. For them to have come.

Because I fucking needed them.

The girl I'd failed needed them.

Blinking the sting out of my eyes, I took another step, stumbled again. The world swam in and out of focus, a mutiny of color and screams.

I inserted myself into the pandemonium, shoving against the current, managing by some bloody miracle to reach the golden doorframe.

I gripped a giant hinge and hefted my battered body between the cool metal and the human riptide. A man bumped into me, and I tottered sideways, thudding into the wall, the faceted stones scratching up my cheeks.

"Feather!" I croaked, scraping my palms over my eyes to clear my brow of sweat and blood and twigs.

I heard my dads again.

If plucking only...

But then...

But then I heard Naya's father.

I snapped my head back, almost blacking out from the rash movement.

Elysium must've opened its floodgates because angels were everywhere.

My gaze locked on the umber-winged one diving straight for me, golden wing tips sparking with the same fury flashing behind the clear blue irises.

Apa had come.

Elysium had come.

Dov must've alerted them.

Although I still bloody hated the guy for having made me

abandon Naya, gratitude he'd called for backup supplanted my animosity.

Arms curled around me, dragged me into a solid chest, and although I didn't cry, my head flopped against my father's shoulder. "I messed up, Apa. I messed up so badly."

"Shh." His palm stroked my hair. "Shh, my boy. It's all right."

"It's not . . . Naya." I pushed him away. "I have to get to—"

I swung my gaze toward the dais, and my heart . . . it didn't only hold still; it stopped beating entirely.

NAYA

"*N*AYA!"

That voice. I knew that voice.

My father's earsplitting roar shredded the darkness that churned with powerful wing beats.

I tried to look up, but my neck wouldn't bend. How it held my head at all was a miracle. The ache radiating down my spine made me certain the guards had embedded bullets into each one of my vertebrae.

I attempted to stand but only managed to sag further, then attempted to scrub my slick lashes, but when I lifted one arm, the other gave out, and I drooped beside the King's polished shoes.

Footsteps thudded as the guards scattered, barking and shouting. One bumped into me, sent me sprawling onto my side.

The domed mausoleum faded.

I was back in Berlin.

In Phnom Pehn.

In Tokyo.

In Melbourne.

In Paris.

In Nashville.

My past missions swarmed through my mind, a dizzying kaleidoscope of faces and sound.

Was I dying? Was that why I was seeing my whole life flash

before my eyes? Because a malakim was extracting my soul to prepare it for its next life?

In a corner of my brain, I remembered that angels didn't get *next lives*, so that couldn't be it.

Plus, I was immortal . . .

"Starlight. *Levsheh*."

I blinked my eyes open. Found Apa hovering over me, his golden hair cascading around the whittled frame of his face.

"Oh, Starlight."

"I didn't imagine you. You're really here . . ." I murmured.

Gently, he uncurled my fingers from around the gun, extricated the black killing contraption, then, snarling like a caveman, tossed it so far away I didn't hear it thud. His turquoise eyes swung back to me, so shiny they looked like stained glass.

I bit my lip. I was aware he'd be disappointed, but not to the point of violence and tears. I pressed my limp palm to his wet cheek. "Apa, you can yell at me after, but first, you need to find Pablo. The Circle Girls. You need to make sure he deleted the—" Nausea roiled through my stomach, pinning my mouth shut. "The—"

"Feather?"

I turned my head toward the source of my croaked nickname, swallowing with relief when I saw Adam. He was all right. Well, bleeding from everywhere, hair sticking up like Levi's, and pale as a ghost, but he stood.

Tears smudged the borders of my vision. I tried to blink them away, but the shimmering darkness remained, and I realized it was because my wings had materialized beneath my broken body.

"Pablo. Find Pablo," I rasped.

Adam neither nodded, nor spoke. He just stared and stared and stared, a haunted look glazing his beautiful emerald eyes.

A guttural sob cracked like thunder through the throne room. A sob that had come from my father's lips. My father didn't cry. At least, not in front of me. And yet, tears were gliding around my knuckles and rolling down my wrist.

He kissed my fingers, then gently placed my hand on top of my chest and lurched off the dais with one powerful swoop of wings. "You!" he growled, pounding toward Adam. "I should've known you were behind this!"

Tobias lunged between them, pushing my father back while

Gabriel wound a protective arm around his son's shoulders. "Calm down, Asher."

"Don't fucking tell me to calm down! Look at what he's done! Look at what your son has done to my daughter!"

"Apa, stop. It's not Adam's fault." I tried to roll onto my side, but my body wasn't having it.

"I should never have brought you back," he roared. "I should've let your soul rot—"

Tobias slapped my father. Although his head didn't fly to the side, the assault shut him up.

"Stop it! I know you're hurting but stop it," Tobias hissed. "You're only going to cause our children pain."

"Don't fight," I croaked. "Please. I'm okay." To prove it, I gritted my teeth and rocked onto my side, the effort almost knocking me unconscious. The golden dome dipped, bounced back, dipped, reminding me of those colorful human toys Ama had bought me during one of her last outings into the human world.

My father looked over his shoulder at me, his gaze so wet it made an ache blossom beneath my ribs. I hadn't meant to disappoint him. I really hadn't. I'd only ever hoped to make him proud.

For several quiet heartbeats, he watched me, like the rest of the angels in attendance, but then his great shoulders rolled forward and began to shake with such grief I wanted to rewind, not just tonight, but the last few weeks.

If I hadn't bumped into Noah . . .

If I hadn't signed up to Emmy . . .

No.

I wouldn't want to unmeet Adam.

Our eyes collided. His were packed with such pain and guilt that I smiled through the ache lancing up and down my back.

I was about to ask my father if he could remove the bullets, when another sob lurched out of him.

Tobias slung one arm around his friend's hunched shoulders and pulled him into a hug. "Five years, Asher," he murmured, his voice carrying through the empty mausoleum. "She's got five years."

I did. Although my father would probably force me to complete my wings in five days and stick to me like raw cookie dough.

Adam broke away from Gabriel and started for me.

"Don't," Apa warned, his tone so full of rancor it iced my veins and grounded Adam's feet.

My father shot away from Tobias and flew back onto the dais. I tried to tuck my wings in, to magick away my feathers, but my wing bones throbbed as though they, too, had been shredded by bullets.

Oh, well. Droopy wings it is.

Lines creasing his forehead, he landed beside me.

It struck me that he was standing on my wing. Curiously, it didn't hurt. Then again, my back was in so much pain that it eclipsed everything else.

He crouched and scooped me up.

I grimaced when his arm touched my tender skin. "Apa, you need to—" I breathed through the hurt. "To find Pablo before he— before he detonates his bombs."

"What I need, Starlight, is to get you home."

I palmed his stone jaw. "If you don't find him, then everything I did will have been for nothing."

No smoke leaked from my father's nose, but angels, how his nostrils flared. "What is she talking about? Who is Pablo?"

"The dead man's son." Adam nodded to the silver-haired king bathing in a crimson pool. "He blackmailed Naya into killing his father."

Apa's heart seemed to skitter to a stop.

"Take her home, Asher. We'll find him." Tobias nodded to the angels hovering in the dome between the chandeliers or standing to the side, keeping a respectable distance as though not to intrude on our rather catastrophic family reunion.

"I'll help you." Adam stepped toward his father, even though his eyes stayed riveted to me.

"You're done helping for a while, *vehnleh*." Tobias's voice brooked no argument.

Adam flexed his jaw, probably knowing there was no point fighting his father on this and returned to the tall man with yellow wings and blond hair who'd raised and loved him as his own, like Ama had raised and loved me.

Oh, she was going to be so upset with me.

"Once you find him, you come and find me." My father's timbre vibrated with such murder that I feared Pablo's soul would spark out of existence this very night.

"The Circle Girls, Tobias. Adam, tell your father about the Circle Girls, so he can round them up and take out what they have inside of them."

A tear pitchforked down Adam's bloodied cheek. He scrubbed it away fast, but I'd seen it.

Horror prickled my skin. "They were blown up?" I hadn't heard the blast.

His throat dipped. "I-I-I . . ." His body gave a violent shudder. "I don't—I don't know," he murmured. "I don't know."

Then why was he crying?

Gabriel spoke quietly into his ear, which only made Adam's head sag and shoulders stoop, then he seized both sides of his son's face and lifted it to press a kiss against his forehead before entrenching him in a hug.

I wished I could give him a hug, too. Take away his sadness and stress.

I willed him to look back at me as Apa lifted off, but the boy I'd given my heart to didn't watch me leave. Sighing, I rested my cheek against my father's thundering torso, my gaze falling to the dais, to the bleeding king and—

I picked my head off my father's chest. "Apa, my . . . Are those my . . . ?"

The blood drained out of my body so fast that I half expected it to ribbon out of me and splatter the twin fans of glittery black feathers dispersed beside the King's corpse.

It couldn't be.

It was probably just an imprint. Or an illusion. Or . . . I licked my lips, urging my feathers to pour out around me, but try as I might, no velvety darkness swathed me.

"I . . . I lost my wings?"

Apa didn't look at me.

He stared straight ahead, at the glimmering city unspooling beyond the palace gates.

He said he was taking me home.

Home was the guild.

Was I still allowed inside celestial dwellings?

"Apa, do I still have wing bones?"

His golden hair whipped around his face, sticking to the wet tracks of salt. "Yes, *Kalkohav*." His lips pressed tightly before parting around a ragged exhale. "Yes, you still have wing bones."

"But I lost all my feathers?"

Although his head didn't dip, his throat did. I took that as a yes.

"Oh, angels. He wasn't a Triple."

My father's brows slung so low they dyed his aquamarine irises an inky blue. "Who?"

"The man I killed."

"The man you killed was a Triple."

"Then . . . Then I don't understand . . . Dov said killing Triples was cost-free."

My father stopped flying so brusquely, my body rocked in his arms, which lit up my spine with little fires. "Dov?"

"The pure verity with the solid gold wings . . ."

My father purpled.

"What is it?"

"What did"—he swallowed—"what did Dov say?" He sounded calm, yet shook like a volcano about to erupt.

"He said we could kill Triples without it harming our wings."

The trembling stopped.

"I'm guessing it isn't true since . . ." I grimaced.

A normal person would've lamented the demise of five years of hard work, but I was too shocked to grieve. Not to mention, worried about the Circle Girls, and angry at Dov, but also at myself for having been so easily duped.

My father shouted something in Angelic to a white-robed erelim bobbing beneath us. All I grasped was the barked name: Dov.

"What will you do to him?"

"Don't you worry, Starlight." He gritted out in a way that made me do just that.

"Don't handle me with kid gloves, Apa. I just lost my wings because of that man. I think I deserve to know what will happen to him."

My father set his jaw. Raised his eyes toward the pinpricks of stars. "I will eradicate that stain from our worlds."

ADAM

ANGELIC FACT #861
SINNING ISN'T ONLY A HUMAN PASTIME.

"How did you know where to find us?" I asked Papa as we touched down in front of the Caracas guild.

He hadn't spoken a word to me during the short flight, well, besides the *yes* confirming that Naya still had wing bones, but I didn't think his silence was due to anger as much as shock.

Angels, that sight . . .

Naya kneeling in the glittery puddle of her feathers.

It was scored across my lids. Scratched into my heart.

"It could've been you," he murmured, his voice breaking. "Oh, Adamleh, it could've been you."

My bones felt as though they were sharpening beneath my skin, shredding me from within. "I wish it had been me."

Papa's eyes, almost as dark as Naya's, grew wide in horror.

"It should've been, Papa." I drew in a harsh breath. "So how did you find us? Did Dov send you?"

"Dov?"

"You know, the pure verity ishim?" When his forehead stayed grooved, I went on, "Dov like the bird but with no -e?"

"Seraph Claire's paramour, Dov?"

"What's a paramour?"

"Is that the Dov you're referring to?" He gripped my shoulders, fingers so tight they awakened a bruise I must've gotten on my way down through the tree. "The male with the golden wings?"

"Yes." I frowned. "I didn't know he was involved with the seraphim."

"Oh, Adam," he whispered.

"What, *oh*?"

My father pinched the bridge of his nose and shut his eyes. "I need to call Tobias. And Asher." He took his cell phone out and dialed the second number on his favorites list: Apa.

I was the first contact on both their lists. I'd often joked they'd put me on top to make reaming me out swifter, but truth was, my name was up there because my fathers always put me first.

"Tobias, Dov's behind this."

The street was so silent, the Venezuelan people probably grieving their king's passing—or celebrating it in secret—that I heard Apa's response: "I know. Asher's got people looking for him."

Although they both stayed on the line, their silence grew into a tangible thing.

When Papa muttered, "I'm going to kill Claire," my mouth dropped open.

"Wait, you guys think they conspired to hurt us?"

Papa's dark gaze fanned over my face. "Did you find the Prince, Tobias?"

"I did." Apa's voice was hard. "Just waiting for Asher to get here."

I took the phone from my father's fingers. "Did he delete the eSIMs?"

"Oh . . . he was most obliging."

"Did you round up all the girls and—"

"We're in the process. They'll be fine." Apa sighed hard. "*Vehnleh*, we'll talk when I get home. Can you put Gabriel back on?"

I had so many more questions, but I understood I was being dismissed. Before disconnecting, though, I told him about the rest of the team.

"How do you think we found you?" Apa let out another breath. "Noah phoned us. He was worried you and Naya were in trouble."

Well, at least I got *one* answer. Only a couple hundred to go.

"He should be at the guild. He didn't want to go back to Vienna without you."

"And the others?"

"Levi and Boone were collected by their parents and brought home. Galina was brought to the female guild. Adam, can you—"

"Yes. Here." I tendered the phone to Papa.

He nodded to the nondescript wooden door. "Why don't you go inside and find Noah? I'll be right in."

There was something they weren't telling me.

I was about to protest, when Papa said, "Go."

I reluctantly pushed open the guild door. Although Papa had cleaned my face up with his fire, I could still feel streaks of dried blood on the underside of my jaw and along my neck.

There were four people in the fountained atrium. Noah, his father Malak Smith, his mother Malak Lyssa, and the head ophanim of the Caracas guild. When my friend spotted me, he sprang up surprisingly lithely for someone who'd sustained multiple gunshot wounds to the chest and slugged my shoulder.

I hissed because he'd definitely hit a bruise. "Hey . . . what was that for? Aren't you happy to see me?"

Noah shook his head, pink wings shaking too. "That was for scaring the soul out of me, you . . . you idiot."

I smiled.

"Glad you're amused because I'm not. Not even a little."

That only drew my lips wider. Naya had mentioned I was lucky to have a friend like him. She was right. I was damn lucky. It struck me that, if we did indeed have several soulmates, Noah must be one of mine. He'd just love that.

I almost dropped it in casually, but then he just had to go and blow my eardrums out. "You and Naya went after the King? The forking King? Are you crazy?"

Naya surrounded by her wilted wings flashed behind my lids, absconding with my good humor. "Not crazy. Misled." I swallowed, my throat growing as tight as my skin, as tight as my guilt. "She lost all her feathers."

"What?" It was Noah's mother who shrilled this.

I stared at the garnet-winged verity, at the sharpened tips

silvering each feather like arrowheads. "Dov lied to us, Noah. Killing a Triple isn't cost-free."

"That forking donkeyhole!" Noah growled.

"Noah." His blue-winged, golden-robed verity father chided him, or I thought he was chiding him until he put his arm around Noah's shoulder and added, "That soulless, lowlife piece of Elysian scum with shit for brains."

Lyssa tsked. "That's way too kind, *aheevaleh*." She strolled up to me, her golden eyes glowing like a cat's in her deep-brown face. "I think *Seraphim kaskaseem tobahat* suits the man better."

Smith smiled. "Can you tell your mother really doesn't like him?" he asked Noah.

"What does *kaskaseem tobahat* mean, Ama?"

His mother hissed, hunting the air around his legs for a loose feather. I was guessing it was a really bad word—words.

Noah tipped his head to the side. "So?"

"Rectum dandruff," she admitted. "How come that didn't cost you a feather?"

"Because our children are not supposed to know Angelic until they ascend," the hybrid ophanim manning the guild said on a sigh. "Noah, Adam, I expect you two not to share this loophole with your peers. As well as the colorful new words you just learned." He narrowed his eyes on Lyssa's curled mouth.

"Adam, sweetheart, can you maybe keep my son, and yourself, out of trouble from now on?"

Papa came in then, the door rattling as he closed it behind him, sealing us off from the human world.

"I'm sorry, Lyssa." I grimaced. "And I swear, no more—" I'd been about to say *playing guardian angel*, but I wasn't ready to stop, so I switched that out with, "doing anything behind your wings."

She palmed my cheek and squeezed it like she used to when she visited us between soul harvests, making me feel like I was eight instead of eighteen. "Good. Now, let's go."

I stared at the door that felt like an electrified fence. I didn't want to go to Vienna; I wanted to go to the female guild. I wanted to see Naya. And Galina, but especially Naya.

Papa must've read my intent, because he draped his arm around my shoulders and steered me through the aisle of fountains toward the channel. "Home. We're going home."

I must've twitched or maybe it was the longing look I cast over my shoulder that made Papa add, "You'll see her soon."

My lids lifted. How had he known whom I was thinking of?

"It's not like we can keep you apart anymore," he murmured.

"Anymore?"

"Not now, Adam."

"When?"

"When Tobias comes home, and Asher's ready."

The sensation that they were keeping something monumental from us gunned my pulse. Knowing my father would just shut me down if I pushed for an extra scrap, I bit my tongue, but my mind began to whir.

NAYA

*W*hen Apa opened the door of the Caracas guild, someone stumbled into us.

Ama.

She must've just broken away from Mira and Eve, because their arms were outstretched as though to lasso her back and their cheeks puffing as though it had taken everything in them to keep her from exiting the guild.

I caught Apa and Mira exchanging a look that spoke a thousand words, but Mira's face was quickly blocked out by Ama's.

My mother was wailing, the whites of her eyes so red her irises looked orange and her freckles like polka-dots sprayed across her colorless face. "Naya. Oh, Starlight." She crushed my body between her thin arms, crushed my heart with her sobs. "Oh . . . baby."

Eve pressed her lips together as though to stifle a sob, but Eve didn't cry. She was probably trying to keep herself from passing judgment on my decidedly *not very judicious* stint, but then her bottom lip wobbled, and although she snared it with her top teeth, I realized that she, too, was on the brink of weeping.

I hated that I'd caused so many people so much distress.

"You think you can stand, Starlight?" Apa asked. "It's not that I can't carry both you and your mother, but I'm worried she'll smother you."

Ama raised her head, shot my father a droll look that was quickly washed away by another deluge of tears. Apa set my feet on the ground and then gently levered my body. When I sucked in air, his arms tightened.

Before he could sweep me back off my feet, I palmed his giant forearm. "I'm okay."

A stretch, but it wiped a little concern from his brow. I was surprised when I didn't lose a feather, because I was *far* from okay, until I remembered I had none to lose.

Ama's agonized howl quieted the chanting sparrows. "When we—the call—holo-ranker—your score—all your beautiful—all of them."

I sighed, studying the graceful swoop of the birds brightening the atrium with their pretty chants and rainbow feathers. How I'd envied their colorful plumage, especially after I'd learned my feathers were black. Now, I'd give anything to have all my black feathers back.

"I'm so sorry," I murmured for the tenth time that night.

Ama was trembling so hard that when she clutched my cheeks, it made my face wobble.

She pressed her forehead to mine. "*Kalkohav*, why? Why did you—why?"

"Because Dov told our daughter it wouldn't harm her wings to kill Triples."

"Dov?" Ama gasped.

At the same time as Mira growled, "I knew it. I knew the ishim was up to no good. I knew it."

Eve's hazel eyes slitted. "Dov, as in the wannabe scumbag my mother's screwing?"

Whoa. Whoa. Whoa. "Dov is involved with Claire?"

Eve scoffed, shaking her head so hard, her black hair fanned out around her oval face. "I. Will. Kill. Him. That murderous . . ." And then she snarled a bunch of Angelic words. Did she detest Dov because he'd come between her parents or because of what he'd done to us?

My mother had gone alarmingly quiet, yet her eyes danced with fury.

"What is it?" I looked between my parents.

My answer was met with silence. A whole lot of it. Even Eve had quit growling all the words she knew in Angelic. When she hauled in a hissing breath, I got that something was being thought by the four ascended, something I wasn't privy to.

"Will someone please tell me what's going on?" I rolled my aching shoulders, which shot so much fire across my back that the atrium fractured. I blinked away my lightheadedness. For all my desire to go lie down and sleep this day away, the desire to understand what the Abaddon was going on was more pressing. "Please?"

Apa's phone rang. "Yes, Tobias? . . . On my way." He slid his phone back into his tunic pocket. "Celeste, take Naya home. I'll meet you there as soon as I'm done."

Ama's arm slid around my waist, replacing my father's.

"Apa," I called out, stopping him at the door. "I will win them *all* back. I swear."

"Not only do I know you will, but I'll be there every step of the way, Nayaleh."

I wrinkled my nose. "At every mission?"

"Every. Single. Mission. It'll be just like the good old days." He gave me a most glacial smile.

I bit my lip, not because having my father spy on me while I helped sinners was *that* awful a memory, but because I had a boyfriend now.

Or maybe I didn't . . .

Maybe Adam would be too disgusted by my bare wing bones to date me. Or he'd listen to my father's threat and stay away. Or—

"Apa, why did you tell Adam that you shouldn't have brought him back? Brought him back from where?"

My father ironed out his lips. "Amsterdam."

"Amsterdam? What happened in Amsterdam?"

He exchanged one last look with my mother, then left.

"What happened in Amsterdam, Ama?"

Her gaze jolted to me. "What?"

"Okay, what's going on? Clearly I'm missing something."

"Naya?" Galina's voice made my gaze swing to the arched entrance of the atrium. Although pale as the quartz beneath her feet, she was smiling. "I thought I heard you! Are we—um—did we um—"

"Just say it, Fletching." Mira turned, red wings looser against her spine than they'd been when we'd walked in. "It's not as though we're not aware you kids have been wreaking havoc on Earth."

Galina's features contorted apologetically, which made her piercings catch the light of the fire-lit stone. "Sorry?"

Mira huff-grunted.

"So? Did you manage to save them?" Galina pushed away from the doorway, and although her back was hunched and one of her hands was poised on her forehead as though she had a migraine, she was upright and walking.

"Save who?" Eve asked.

Apparently, they were aware we'd been breaking a few laws, but they didn't know why.

"Fifty human girls." I thought of Natasha. Almost asked Ama about her, but decided to broach the subject of ferrying an apology up to her later. "And I don't know if we did."

Galina came to a stop in front of me, and although I noticed her fingers twitching, they remained fastened to her temple. "What do you mean, you don't know?"

A flash of her prone, bloodied body layered itself over her healed, lively form. I shook the chilling sight away.

"It got a little . . . chaotic."

"A little?" Eve scoffed.

I sighed. "A lot." When Galina frowned, I said, "Dov lied to us."

Galina's eyebrows jacked up. "About what?"

Probably about everything. "About the cost of murdering Triples."

"No way. Why would he do that? Can you imagine if one of us had—" She stopped talking, gaze swinging over the three women's faces. "Adam lost his wings?"

"No." I tried to paste on a smile to soften the news that it was my wings that were gone.

Oh, angels, my wings were gone . . .

My eyes began to burn. Galina's face to blur.

Oh, angels, oh, angels, oh, angels.

I lost my wings.

I inhaled a shaky breath, let a shakier one out, then lifted my hand to my chest and massaged the aching muscle, the immensity of what I'd done and all I'd lost finally catching up to me.

Over nine hundred and forty feathers gone. *Gone. All gone.*

My heart spasmed with despair and misery.

When tears popped out, understanding rushed across Galina's face. "Oh, Naya... no."

Ama reeled me into her armored hug, and I rested my cheek on her bony shoulder.

She whispered soothing words that did little to pull me out of my rabbit hole of pain. I closed my eyes, tears spilling over, soaking her belted sweater. I thought about her jacket, told her I lost it. Told her I also lost all her T-shirts and many of the dresses Eve had given me.

"All replaceable," Ama said.

"Like my feathers." *Look at me, being so optimistic.*

I heard Eve snort. Or maybe it was Galina. I doubted it was Mira. Then again, she was known for using sounds when words eluded her.

"I just thought of something." Ama pressed me away. Her eyes were still red as traffic lights, but she'd shed a little of her pallor. "You're going to dethrone me as *fletching who's earned the most feathers*." As always, using humor to paste together our tattered souls.

"Ha." I knuckled away the dampness clinging to my lashes.

"Actually. Maybe not." Ama's tongue darted out the side of her mouth in thought. "Mira, how many feathers did I net in total?"

Mira's thin throat bobbed, and her nose rose just the slightest inch. "I've decided to eliminate irksome memories to make room for nicer ones."

Ama rolled her eyes. "You're not a hard drive, Mira."

Eve smirked. "I doubt Mira knows what a hard drive is. She wasn't born this century."

Mira huffed. "I'll have you girls know that even though I am of a mature age, I am also a modern woman."

Eve's smile strengthened as she walked toward the guild matron, who'd raised her like she'd raised Celeste and me, and hooked her arm, drawing her toward the hallway. "So, what is it?"

"It's ... something that is hard and—"

Eve burst out laughing, which made my heart lighten a little more. "Uh-huh. Want me to explain it?"

I didn't hear Mira's response, because they'd turned the corner, but I had no doubt the prideful woman would turn her down, change the subject, and then research the heck out of it in the privacy of her office.

When I focused back on Ama and Galina, I caught the name

Dunmore and Pablo and realized my friend was explaining what had led us to Caracas. I was glad, because it saved me from speaking about the hateful humans.

Once Galina grew quiet, I asked, "What are you going to do now?"

Her eyes flicked to my mother, then back to me.

"No more secrets, girls."

Galina nibbled on her bottom lip. "Well, I need to go to Chicago."

When she scratched her neck, Ama said, "What's in Chicago?"

Galina ended up telling her.

"Uh-huh." Then, "Sweetheart, why don't you let the ascended deal with this Calliope-girl?"

"Because the ascended don't care about guarding humans, Ama."

I was certain my comment would earn me a reproof, but Ama surprised me by saying, "It's time they do. Tell you what, as soon as your father's done burning the soul of the blue-blooded limp noodle, we'll fill him in on Calliope."

"She's a Triple, Ama. Apa hates Triples. He's never going to get behind her revenge killings."

"Your father's going to be all about revenge killings for the foreseeable future." She stared at the water spurting out from one of the seven fountains.

"Starting with Ish Dov?" Galina asked.

Ama blinked away from the water and nodded. "Starting with him before scaling up the Elysian chain of command."

I was guessing she meant Claire. "Ama, why would Claire ask Dov to lead us astray?"

A breath. Two. I waited for the words: *not now*. Instead, I got, "Because she wants you and Adam to fail."

I jolted, which rattled my poor wing bones, but . . . *what?* "Why?"

"Because . . ." Ama sighed. "Your father would want to be here. No, not would want . . . needs. Your father *needs* to be here for this conversation."

Galina's eyes widened.

"Does it have to do with the color of our wings?" I whispered.

Ama closed her eyes, her chest lifting with sorrowful breaths. "Yes. Yes, it has to do with the color of your wings, Starlight."

74

ADAM

ANGELIC FACT #199
GOOD THINGS COME TO ANGELS WHO WAIT.
OR SO I'VE BEEN TOLD. REPEATEDLY.

I spent the next three days taking out my anger and impatience in the guild gym. I wore my sparring gloves, because Papa didn't give me a choice, and I punched that bag until I tore a hole in it.

"I think I just heard your father." Noah set the twelve-pound dumbbells he'd been lifting down on the rack. He hated the gym, yet had spent the better part of the last three days holed up inside with me, filling my ominous silence with his effervescent babble.

I swiped my forearm across my sweaty brow. "Probably wants to make sure I put on my gloves."

"I meant Tobias."

That got my attention. I hadn't seen nor heard from Apa since the night Naya lost all her feathers.

Each time I thought of her, my whole plucking body shook. With rage. With need. With grief. But mostly with need.

To see her.
To hear her.
To touch her.

To kiss her.

To hold her.

I'd tried negotiating with various ophanim to carry me through the channel to her home guild but none accepted. Papa had made sure to warn everyone that I was not to leave Vienna. At some point, I hesitated to contact Levi for a fake passport, so I could book a commercial flight, but decided against involving him in another one of my schemes. He and Boone were in enough trouble already.

All because of me.

Tearing open the Velcro straps of my sparring gloves, I strode out of the gym, coming to a dead stop in front of the cafeteria entrance.

Apa was home and he hadn't returned alone. Asher was also there.

Naya's father eyed me; I eyed him right back.

I still hadn't figured out the meaning of those throwaway remarks he'd made back in Caracas. How he'd known I was behind his daughter's misfortune, and how he shouldn't have brought me back.

Even though the cafeteria entrance was wide, I made sure to stand smackdab in the middle so that neither he nor my father could slip past me.

I wanted answers.

And I wanted them now.

"How was *Dov*-hunting?" I asked crisply.

Purple circles rimmed both their eyes. I was guessing neither man had slept much.

Apa sighed. "Successful."

"Is he a pile of golden ash?"

Asher let out a soft snort that did nothing to soften the lines on his face. "No."

I raised a brow. "You let him live?"

Apa speared his fingers through his dark hair. "What Asher meant, is that he incinerated Dov's ashes instead of executing my plan, which was to sprinkle them over a cesspool."

"Would've been poetic," Papa said, sidestepping me to reach my other father.

As they embraced, I narrowed my gaze on Asher. "Ready to explain why you've kept me away from your daughter, Seraph?"

A muscle feathered his jaw. "No."

"No?" I squared my shoulders and lifted my chin. "You're not ready to explain your reasons to me, or you're not planning on telling me?"

Asher's wings bristled behind his broad back. "Don't you think you've hurt her enough, Adam?"

His answer made my fathers pull apart, and Noah, who'd parked himself beside me, let out a low hiss.

My reaction was silent and invisible to the naked eye.

My reaction was my heart decomposing anew.

"I meant—before." There was no more bite to my voice, because guilt sat too heavily on my lungs.

"Let me go home tonight and see my girls. Tomorrow, I'll come back here and"—his eyes fell on my fathers, before returning to me—"and I'll explain everything."

"You'll come back with Naya?"

His eyes darkened as though I'd suggested marriage instead of a supervised playdate.

Apa shrugged. "Might as well, Asher."

The seraphim didn't nod, but he also didn't reject the suggestion.

I moved aside to let him pass and didn't avert my gaze until his coppery-turquoise wings melted into the channel.

NAYA

 I never thought I'd relate to those humans who lost limbs yet were convinced those limbs were still attached, but every morning since getting home from Caracas, I woke up with the distinct impression that my glittery black feathers were all still there.

My phantom wings.

The need to go back out into the world and start earning them anew was eating at me, but what was eating at me more was the need to see Adam. We hadn't even been able to communicate using the holo-ranker phones, and my cell phone—

I'd asked Mira for a new one. She told me to ask my father, but my father had come home late last night, so exhausted I hadn't had the heart to bother him. And this morning, over breakfast, just when I was about to ask, he mentioned Vienna and Adam, and my cell phone flew straight out of my mind.

"Ready, Starlight?"

I dropped the pink marker I'd been using to play tic-tac-toe with my sister and vaulted to my feet, then leaned over and kissed her puckered forehead, before streaking toward my parents, who looked as though they were heading into battle.

Ama was standing beside my father, her small hand cocooned in his large paw. She reached out to me. I took her free hand and didn't release it until we landed in Tobias's guild.

My nerves felt as raw as my stomach and wing bones, but my

heart was bursting with excitement. Also, a little terror, but mostly excitement. I wasn't yet sure what secret they were all keeping but didn't really care. I mean, how bad could it be?

I stepped out of the channel before the sparkly smoke had even cleared, halting abruptly at the sight of the boy pacing the hallway. He looked up, body so tensed, I imagined he was holding his breath.

Before I could think of what it might look like to my parents, I ran and threw myself in his arms.

And he caught me.

Where I strangled his neck, he barely applied any pressure to my back, probably worried about hurting me. Unless he was scared of my father. That could be it.

"Aren't you happy to see me?" I whispered into the perfect mahogany crests of his hair.

I felt him swallow. Once. Twice. "Oh, Feather . . ." Two loaded words.

He finally tightened his grip, and it clipped the noose around my heart.

"I'm feeling a little left out," I heard Noah quip.

Adam grunted, but even his grunt was thick with emotion. After he set me down, I hugged the friend, who'd repeatedly had my back.

"You're not in too much pain?" he asked.

"Not anymore." I smiled to erase the smudge of worry creasing his brow, then circled back toward Adam, who curled his arm around my waist and tucked me so close into his side that I could feel his heart thumping through the layers of our clothes.

"Nice tee." He nodded to the purple pub shirt Galina had dropped off in my room before leaving to see her mother, swearing she wouldn't return to Chicago alone.

"Why, thank you. It's my favorite."

Although he swallowed a little hard, he also breathed a little easier.

Ama smiled at the sight of us. Apa grumbled. Tobias sounded sort of chirpy, even though he appeared bone-weary. Gabriel was quiet and attentive.

"Come. I've cleared the cafeteria." Tobias gestured toward the infamous Viennese cafeteria, whose ceiling had led Ama to paint the one in our guild. I'd seen pictures of the mural but never the real thing, and although this wasn't a museum tour, I was excited to finally lay my eyes on one of the many sources of contention between Mira and Tobias.

Noah chewed on his lip as we followed our parents. "I should probably—leave you guys. I'll just pace this nice, white hallway."

Adam nodded to the cafeteria. "Noah, you're family."

He rubbed the side of his freshly-buzzed fade. "Yeah. Okay." He glanced at Gabriel, who was waiting for us, and must've read something in his expression because he backed up. "Tell you what? As soon as whatever great reveal is revealed, just come and get me, okay? I'll be in our room."

He turned the corner at the same time as Gabriel entered the cafeteria, leaving Adam and me alone.

He spun me to face him. "Whatever happens in there, Naya, it won't change how I feel about you."

My heart skipped over a few beats as a smile took over my lips. "How *do* you feel about me?"

His eyes raked over every inch of my face. "Like I've been searching for you my entire life."

Be still, my heart.

I pressed up on my toes and kissed him. It didn't last half as long as I wished. Then again, I wanted to kiss him until my very last breath, and since I was immortal, that would've made our parents wait a *really* long time, and their patience, especially Apa's, was worn thin.

Even though it killed me to pare my lips off Adam's, I rocked back onto my heels. "I adore you, Adam no-last-name, grumpy-most-of-the-time, romantic-the-rest-of-the-time. My first. My last. My everything."

"Did you just rip off a Barry White song?"

"He did sing it so well."

"I bet you can sing it better." He speared his fingers through mine and winked. "At least as well as the sparrows."

Resting my head on his shoulder, I hummed the tune all the way to the cafeteria.

ADAM

ANGELIC FACT #500
A FEATHER IS A FEATHER IS A FEATHER

"Wow." Naya tipped her head back, large eyes drinking in the vast mural adorning the cafeteria's glass dome.

Although I'd often admired it as a child, I rarely looked up nowadays, taking it for granted. I realized I took a lot of things for granted. Like having doting fathers. So few parents took an interest in their children's upbringing. Another thing I'd taken for granted was the existence of feathers on my wing bones.

I traced the chaotic blonde waves flowing without obstruction down Naya's spine. If only I could've unhooked my wings and grafted them onto her back.

Asher cleared his throat, impatience carved across his face.

I squeezed Naya's hand, then nodded to the table at which our parents had taken residence.

"Nice ceiling, Tobias." Naya smiled at my father, wrapping the hand not looped through mine around my arm, as though to add an extra point of contact.

I caught Asher's narrowed glare.

"Make sure to tell Mira all about it." A smile danced on the edges of Apa's mouth like a flame atop a candle.

"Oh, I will. Although, admittedly, our ceiling's nicer." Naya winked at her mother.

"Naturally," Apa said, his smile firming up.

As we took our seats around the table, the atmosphere changed. Stiffened. Toughened. Even Asher, always so poised and collected, shifted in the seat he dwarfed. Celeste reached out and snagged one of his hands. When her fingers closed around his, all the air seemed to leave his lungs.

"Are we related?" Naya asked, barely no pause between each word. "Is that why we both have black wings and were born on the same day?"

I blinked at her, surprised she still thought this. When the adults exchanged wary looks, my palms grew damp and my heart still.

We couldn't be related. Angels, please no. If Naya was my sister—

"No." Asher's answer was low, yet smacked my dread away.

"Thank Elysium." Naya blew out such a long breath that it seemed she'd purged my lungs along with her own.

"No, Starlight, thank your father." Celeste looked up at Asher, her expression crammed with so many emotions, her face was inscrutable.

Naya frowned, while I kept holding still, waiting for everything to start making sense.

"Do you want me to tell them, Asher?" Tobias asked.

The seraphim's face was haunted, his eyes glassy. "No." He closed his lids, pulled in a deep breath, then opened his eyes and fastened them to his daughter. "I was hoping to tell you this story only once you'd ascended, but—" His voice broke. "But you've met, and—" Another pause. "Before I begin, I want you to understand that keeping this a secret wasn't intended to hurt you but to protect you. We wanted you both to live normal lives and never worry about . . . about how you—"

"How we?" I asked, when no one added to Asher's stop-and-go speech, which was mostly all stops.

Apa leaned forward, hands clasped on the table in front of him. "How you two came to be."

Naya's dark eyebrows bent. "We're not children of extra-marital affairs?"

"No. Or maybe." Apa heaved in a sigh. "We don't know who your parents are."

"Our *parents?*" I repeated. "Are you guys saying you're not . . . them?"

Naya's fingers grew so cold that it felt like clutching snow. "I don't understand," she murmured. "You aren't . . . my father?" Her voice splintered on those last two words.

"I am, just not biologically."

I stared into Apa's clear blue eyes, at the chiseled lines of the face I'd spent my whole life hunting for resemblances to my own. I'd come up with so many. "What happened? The angels who made us didn't want anything to do with us?"

"Your bodies' biological parents are both human. Your souls' biological parents are"—Asher's gaze slipped to me—"were angels."

"You aren't making any sense, Apa," Naya whispered. "You make us sound like car parts that were assembled."

"In a way, you were assembled, *levsheh*. I—" Asher scrubbed a hand down his face. Inhaled. Expelled that breath. "I made you. Both of you. I'm—I'm the one who placed your angelic souls into two new bodies."

Naya gasped. "You reincarnated us?"

"What was wrong with our old bodies? Were they outdated?" Great. Now, I was cracking jokes. Just great.

Celeste smiled but then bit the smile off her lips. "Your original bodies died."

"But angels are immortal." Naya's forehead was notched with confusion.

"Winged angels are immortal." The comment Dov had thrown at me before dropping me into the tree resounded against the throbbing walls of my skull, finally making sense. "We must've been nephilim."

Naya's lips parted a little, then some more.

Where I could see how I could've been a fallen angel, Naya's soul was so kind and light . . .

"Did we not make it?" she asked. "Is that why you're both so hard on me about ascending?"

"No, but there is a reason why your ascension . . . *both* your ascensions are of great magnitude." Asher looked between Naya and me. "I'll get to that in a minute."

"You did make it, Naya." Celeste's whiskey-colored eyes glistened with moisture. "But then you asked"—her gaze lifted to Asher—"you asked Asher to burn your wings because you wanted to return to Earth."

Her confession blew out Naya's pupils until her eyes were twin pools of starless sky. "I . . . ? Why?"

"For him." Asher nodded at me. "You made me burn your wings to return to Adam."

Her head jerked toward me. Coward that I was, I couldn't meet her eyes. "I was already a nephilim. That's why she gave up her immortality, isn't it?"

Asher nodded.

Earning feathers wasn't easy, but we had ten years. Unless I'd been the biggest tool born to Elysium, then I didn't see how I'd failed. "How did I lose my wings?"

"You never had any," Asher said.

This time, my eyebrows dipped. "I thought I was a fallen angel?"

Asher dragged his fingertip over a vein in the quartz tabletop. "You were born to a fallen angel."

"Fallen angels can have babies?" Naya's pitch was a full octave higher than normal.

"Not usually, but I suspect that Mikaela—Adam's soul's birth mother—was pregnant before she relinquished her wings to remain with her mortal husband, and somehow managed to keep the baby." A drumroll of silence agitated the air. "Anyway, he was never brought into a guild, so his wing bones never developed, but he had angel-blood, so he was labeled a nephilim."

I felt Naya's wide eyes sliding over my hard profile. I still couldn't look at her, the shame of having made her fall from celestial grace burning a hole in my gut. "Was his name . . . in his first life, was his name Jarod?"

I froze, on the outside and on the inside.

"Yes," Celeste said.

"Wow . . . well, at least one mystery's solved." Naya tugged on my hand, but I still wouldn't look at her.

"Do you also remember Naya's original name, Adam?" Celeste was staring at me.

They were all staring at me. I finally unfroze and shifted in my seat. And then I pulled my hand out of Naya's, crossed my arms, and leaned back, spine and shoulders as rigid as the chair under my nephilim ass. "No."

NAYA

*A*dam snatched his hand from mine. When I touched his thigh, he shifted so that my fingers fell away. For the life of me, I didn't understand why he was acting so aloof. Because he couldn't remember me while I'd never forgotten him?

"Her name was Leigh, even though she used to pronounce it Lay not Lee," Ama said. "She was my best friend. And Eve's, too."

My gaze snapped to my mother's in time with my heart. Wait, *what?*

Ama swallowed. "You were four years older than me and like a sister. When Asher accepted to burn your wings and sent you back to Earth, I was fifteen. I was so mad at you for having decided to give them up. So mad." A sad smile bowed her lips. "Anyway, the day after you got back . . . You ran off to find Jarod. To tell him you were back. For good." Ama looked at Adam. "You ran the Parisian mob, a job you inherited from your uncle. Your uncle was the one to raise you, as well as a woman called Muriel Moreau. You used to call her Mimi. She was like a mother to you."

That name or was it the nickname seemed to prick Adam's pupils, spreading the black over the green.

"I thought . . . I thought that was *your* adoptive mother's name, Ama?"

"It became mine, because, believe it or not, after Adam was killed and you decided to—" She shuddered. "Well, Mimi and I found each other, and she ended up raising me." Ama spread her fingers, studying all the rings gleaming there. "She's in Elysium, waiting for the two of you. You and her, Naya, are the reasons I completed my wings. Initially, that is. Then I had to go and fall in love with your father, and well, the rest is history."

"A complicated one," I murmured, trying to draw lines and connect dots. "So, you mentioned you put us inside new bodies. Did you"—I licked my lips, the name Valentine Tremblay echoing against the tender walls of my skull—"steal them and erase their souls?"

"No," Ama said. "The children were both stillborn."

Well, that explained my biological mother's shock at Pablo's phone call.

"Your father placed your souls inside these two infants and carried you . . . *home*."

My father, who wasn't my father but my creator, cleared his throat. "At first, I hesitated to smuggle your souls into Elysium but feared one of the Seven would uncover your existence and request your removal." His eyes took on a faraway sheen, as though he'd traveled back in time. "I could've slipped you into mortal wombs but didn't want either of you to be raised outside of guilds, nor did I want to have to steal you away from mortal parents." He nodded to Adam. "I gave you to Tobias, Adam, because he was the only person I trusted. And I kept you, Naya, because . . . because . . ." He rubbed his jaw, his fingers catching on his week-old stubble.

"Because you felt guilty for burning my wings?"

"There was a little of that. At first." His face softened with a smile. "But there was also a lot of selfishness. You had—*have*—such a beautiful soul, *motasheh*."

He hadn't called me sweet doll in ages and it made my heart throb a little harder than it already was.

Adam's hands curled around his biceps, his knuckles white against his olive skin. "How come Naya remembers my name, but I have no memory of hers?"

"For the same reason some humans remember people or experiences from past lives. Soul cleansing is a delicate process. You strip the soul too thoroughly, and you can end up causing more harm than good." It was Gabriel who explained this. He hadn't spoken until then, so hearing his voice was jarring.

"Why did you take away our memories, Apa?"

My father blinked at me. Was he surprised by my enquiry? "Apa?" he croaked.

I reached over the table, palm up. He took my hand without hesitation. "You made me. Maybe not with your blood, but with your heart. You and Ama will forever be my parents, even if I have another set out there. Or two..."

"You've actually met your soul's parents a few times," Ama said.

"Really?"

Ama drummed her fingertips against the table. "They asked to meet you when they learned about you."

"But I thought... but I thought no one knew about us?"

"Dov knew what we were." Adam's voice was so chilling it rained goosebumps over my skin.

"Every ascended knows." Tobias sighed. "When you two were four, Claire started snooping around, because she and Asher never saw eye-to-eye, and she was looking for a reason to kick him off the Council. When she uncovered that both he and I had children born on the same day, it pricked her curiosity."

"She managed to uncover our secret." Apa's jaw squared, turning so angular that he seemed more statue than human. "And she brought it to the attention of Elysians."

"She asked for your expulsions." The hollows of Gabriel's cheeks deepened as though he were sucking air faster than he was expelling it.

I frowned. "Our expulsions?"

"From guilds." Ama spun one of her numerous rings. "She didn't want you to be raised by angels."

"But then—" Claire's face materialized between us like a holographic image. She'd never shown me much affection, but she'd never shown her daughter or granddaughter any either, so I hadn't felt singled out. "Are you saying she wanted to prevent us from developing wing bones?"

"The Council put it up to a vote. Since you're both sitting here today, you can imagine what the majority decided." Apa smiled, but it didn't reach his eyes. Because the voting hadn't been unanimous? "However, no more nephilim souls are allowed to be collected until your ascension," he added. "*Both* of your ascensions. Which is one of the reasons I've been so hard on you, Naya. So impatient."

"Not that I ever considered quitting, Apa, but now I have even more of a reason to ascend. *We*"—I turned toward Adam, who still wouldn't look at me—"have even more of a reason to succeed. Right, Adam?"

After almost a full minute, he gave a sharp nod. What in the worlds was going on with him? He couldn't possibly be mad at my father for what he'd done?

"Adam?" Tobias tilted his head. "What is it, *vehnleh*?"

Adam stared at his father, eyes so flinty it made my heart ache for Tobias. Clearly, he wasn't taking this news as well as I was. "Why bring me back if I was such a horrible person?"

Ama shook her head. "You weren't horrible, Adam."

"I was the leader of the bloody mob. I made Naya—or Leigh, or whatever her name was—give up her plucking immortality. So what I want to understand is why the Abaddon you decided it was a good idea to give me a second chance. So I could drag her down again? Because, apparently, that's done."

"Adam," I hissed. "My lost feathers aren't your fault!"

He side-eyed me, and I took that as a little win.

"The fault is mine. Dov's. Claire's. But certainly not yours."

He huffed out a grunt. "That's not what your father thinks, Feather."

Ama's dimples cleaved her cheeks. "You call her Feather." It wasn't so much a question as a gasped insight.

"Yeah. Why?"

"Jarod used to call Leigh that."

"Aha! So you do remember me!" That won me another side-eye, a teeny bit softer this time.

Although his arms stayed crossed, he sat up in his chair. "So? Why did you bring me back, Seraph? You've never really liked me. You still don't like me much."

"That's not true," Tobias butted in.

"Oh, come on, Apa." Adam rolled his eyes while his father opened his wider.

And then he blinked hard. I imagined that, like my father, he'd been worried Adam may not consider him as such anymore, which struck me as ironic, considering these two men had risked their wings and hearts for us. These *three* men and *one* woman.

"Asher just likes to act like a big, old brute," Tobias said, knuckling his eye, "but he's a total softie."

"*Total* softie," Ama and I said at the very same time, which made us exchange a conspiratorial grin.

To think my best friend became my mother . . . Admittedly a little weird, but in the grand scheme of things, being a reincarnated nephilim definitely took the cake.

"I brought you back, because I stole your first chance at getting wings, and I wanted to right my wrong."

My father's answer made the smile trip off my face.

"I met you, Adam—well, Jarod. I met Jarod when he was eight. I was an ishim back then. I'm the one who found you carrying a bloodied knife in your hands. The knife that stopped your mother's heart. Matricide is a terrible crime, but killing an angel . . . Well, our world doesn't forgive that. I ranked you a permanent Triple that day, even though you shouldn't have been in the mortal sinner system since you had angel-blood."

"That's how Leigh found you. She decided to reform you." Ama glanced at my father, whose eyes didn't stray off Adam's.

"When she realized you'd been judged wrongfully . . ." Apa's eyes grew wet. "How you hated me, *levsheh*."

I was glad I didn't remember that.

He took in a shuddering breath. "You demanded I bring Jarod's case up with the Seven and have his permanent rank changed to a non-permanent one, so you could reform him. So his soul had a chance to redeem itself."

"And did you?"

"Eventually, yes. But it didn't change the fact that he was a nephilim, and nephilim souls aren't allowed to enter our world. Which is why, when you ascended and found out Jarod would never join you, you asked me to strip you of your silver wings."

Adam shifted again in his chair.

"I had silver wings?"

"Pure silver. And peach hair, which you absolutely abhorred," Ama said with a wistful smile. "We think that's why your wings sparkle. Because of your pure verity heritage."

Tobias wet his mouth. "We didn't know you'd have black wings, but when Naya sprouted her first feathers, we braced ourselves that

CISS, S
0880
Friday, May 10, 2024

31183212252008

you would too, Adam. We're sorry we lied to you, children, but we were only ever trying to protect you."

I shot Tobias a smile since Adam was wallowing in too much self-loathing to display his gratitude.

"You should've let me rot in peace, Seraph."

His fathers went paler than the abounding quartz.

"Don't say that!" I snapped.

"You lost your wings. Twice. You lost them twice!"

"I chose to have my wings burned the first time. Keyword, *I*, Adam. Not you. Me. As for that second time you're referring to, well, it hasn't happened. I lost my *feathers* not my wing bones. And you know what? Not only will I gain them all back, but I'll complete them before you." I lifted my chin, daring him to contradict me.

"Is that a challenge?"

Without lowering my chin, I said, "Maybe."

The dimple, which had been absent from Adam's cheek, returned. The sight of it made my heart pound so fast that I worried my skin was going to burst into glitter, which would be all sorts of embarrassing in front of our parents.

Please don't turn on. Please—

I lit up.

Crappy crap crap.

I sank low in my chair. "So, um . . . who are my soul's parents?"

Ama smiled. Tobias and Gabriel, too. The only one who wasn't amused by my public display of glitter was my father. Not amused at all.

Adam finally uncrossed his arms and reached for my hand under the table, and even though it didn't flick off my smolder, it did ease my sparking nerves.

"Sofia and Raphael."

I remembered them—the beautiful verity with golden hair and green eyes and her husband, a pure verity with solid silver wings and copper hair. They'd visited a few times over the course of my life. They were nice but aloof. Then again, most angels were both, but especially verities since they spent the least time with fletchings.

Except the two seated at our table.

For all my father's attempt to seem aloof, his heart was goo when it came to those he loved. And well, Tobias *was* goo. Not just his heart, but all of him.

As I tightened my grip on Adam's hand, it struck me that I'd died to be with him. No wonder I'd fallen for him so quickly this time around too. The boy had existed under my skin. Inside my soul.

Which made me wonder . . . "Are we soulmates?"

My father choked on his spit and started hacking. "Soulmates?" he wheezed, while Tobias reached over and thumped him on the back.

"Apa, don't pretend they're a human fabrication. Ama told me they existed."

"Celeste!" my father hissed.

"Oh, please." My mother rolled her eyes. "Out of all the secrets our kind keeps, that's really the silliest one. Especially since our children all spend so much time wondering about it. We honestly may as well tell them the truth." Apa and Gabriel stared at my mother as though she'd just unwrapped someone else's present. "Fletchings are completely capable of concentrating on their wings *and* hearts. Back me up, Tobias?"

Tobias threaded his fingers through his inky hair. "I *have* heard my fletchings discuss it at great lengths. Which isn't to say they should know . . . *everything*." He sent my mother a pointed look.

I stared between Ama, who was crushing her smile between her teeth, and Tobias, who was spearing his hand through his hair a few more times. "Well now, you guys *have* to tell us."

"Absolutely not," Apa said.

"Don't you want me to concentrate on my wings, Apa?" Thankfully, my sparkle had faded.

"Ha!" A grin burst over Ama's lips, which won her one heck of a glower from Apa, which won *him* another dramatic eye-roll.

"Are you blackmailing me, *levsheh*?" he asked slowly.

"I am. I mean, now's the time, right? It's not like I can lose any feathers for extorting information."

"And you claimed she was the sweet one?" Tobias fake-shuddered. "She's ruthless."

"Celeste's influence."

Ama smiled proudly then held out her hand behind Apa's back, and Tobias high-fived her.

Adam squeezed my fingers. "How old are you guys?" he asked, making sure to sound totally bored.

"How *young*," Gabriel corrected with a quiet smile and a wink.

Adam shook his head but smiled back at his father. I wanted to bottle that smile and spritz him with it whenever his temper got the upper hand.

Apa leaned back in his chair and crossed his arms, but instead of looking stiff, he finally looked at ease. "Tell you what, Nayaleh, when you get to five hundred feathers, I'll tell you myself."

"One-hundred."

"Four."

"One-hundred."

"Three."

"Two-hundred, and that's my final offer." I held out the hand not clutched in Adam's. "Deal?"

Apa narrowed his eyes on my hand, and although he drew the moment out, he leaned over and shook it.

"I'll hold you to it."

"I'm aware, *levsheh*."

Three sparrows swooped into the cafeteria and drew figure-eights over our heads, spilling their beautiful arias, enchanting this strange moment. As we admired their little show, Tobias got up and went to get us cake. The absolute *best* cake in the world made with chocolate and apricot preserves.

I may have stolen the slice he'd placed in front of his son.

"So, you roasted Dov's soul?" Adam slung that in rather abruptly, but I supposed it was necessary we discuss the traitorous ishim now that we were done discussing our origin. "What are you planning on doing about Seraph Claire?"

NAYA

My father glanced at the swooping sparrows still filling the cafeteria with their lovely song. "Claire's channel key is gone, and so is her title."

"Why did she want us to fail, Apa?" I asked.

"Because if you two manage—"

"*Once* you two ascend," Tobias corrected my father.

My father's throat rolled with a swallow. I supposed he'd stay worried until my feathers sealed to my wing bones. "Once you two ascend, the law about saving nephilim souls will be ratified, and she's staunchly opposed to it."

"Eve didn't know, right, Ama?" I felt like a traitor for asking, but better a traitor than a fool.

My mother shook her head. "No, Starlight, she didn't know."

I set my fork down. "Will you kick Claire out of Elysium?"

"Not until you ascend." At my frown, Apa added, "I want to keep my eye on her."

"Thought you were planning on keeping an eye on me?"

My father planted his elbows on either side of his untouched slice of cake and linked his fingers. And then he smiled. "I meant a metaphorical eye on Claire. I've entrusted her *care*"—from the sound of his voice, I fathomed he meant torture—"to my colleagues, so that you, baby girl, have my full and undivided attention."

A smile squeaked onto my lips. "Awesome."

Tobias dragged Apa's plate over to him and Gabriel. "You may as well get to know your future son-in-law."

"Tobias." My father enunciated each and every letter in his friend's name, while my mother tipped her head back and laughed, which made Tobias chuckle in turn.

Where I became an overheating mosh pit of nerves, Adam remained remarkably calm. He even smiled.

"You're happy about this?" I hissed at him.

"I'm happy someone's going to ensure you're earning your feathers, since I'm obviously not a good influence."

"Don't say that."

His smile softened. "But it's true." He squeezed my hand. "Before we all disperse, Seraph, I'd like to discuss what we did and why we did it."

He better be talking about shorhim, because I was so not discussing my private life with our parents.

"We were misguided, but guarding humans . . . we touched so many lives. Saved so many innocents."

My father seemed to grow taller in his chair. "All you did was alter timelines."

Adam's lips pressed together.

"That's not all we did. We stopped bad men, Apa! We uprooted evil. The same way you just did by burning Dov's soul and—" He hadn't killed Claire yet, but he'd put an end to her reign of terror.

To think I'd once believed angels superior to humans . . .

"*Levsheh*, I'm not depreciating what you children did. I think—well, I think it could've been better thought-out"—he glared at the space over my shoulders where my black feathers used to be, where they'd be again soon—"but your hearts were in the right place. And although I'll always encourage you to help someone in need, until you earn your wings, I don't want you getting sidetracked. When you ascend, when you *both* ascend, I'll put a shorhim faction up for a vote. Does that sound fair?"

It did.

"How about . . . ?" Ama's eyes filled with that fire she'd had long before she'd been bestowed actual angelic fire.

"I'm not going to like this, am I?"

"It's a fantastic idea." She grinned as excitedly as Lyla every time she saw Nitznootz, and my heart twanged with jealousy, because my sister was Celeste and Asher's flesh, blood, and soul, and I wasn't.

My flesh and blood belonged to two mortals I'd never met, and my soul to two ascended I *had* met but whom I didn't feel all that much for. Which, come to think of it, was strange. Shouldn't my soul have recognized them?

Maybe Leigh hadn't loved her parents like I . . . like I loved mine.

My jealousy sank back at the realization that Celeste and Asher were the ones who'd always been there for me. Who'd kissed my tears away and chased the monsters under my crib. Who'd held my hand and played with me and read me stories. They were the ones who loved me unconditionally. In every way that mattered, they were my parents.

I refocused on what Ama was saying, dimples grooving her cheeks. "It's about time we amend the scale system."

"Celeste—"

She pressed her finger to Apa's lips. "No talking until I'm done. The system is archaic. You said it yourself."

Apa's eyes rounded as though she were suffocating him with that single digit.

"And honestly, honey, this isn't a big ask," she continued. "I think the Seven of you—Six—need to amend the scoring so that, even when our children are signed up to sinners, they can earn feathers for little acts of kindness, and instead of just one feather, like they earn when they're not signed up to anyone, they should earn like, ten."

"Ten?" Apa seemed to rock back in his chair. "Why not fifty while you're at it?"

"Sure." Ama kept smiling, even though she was fully aware my father had tossed out the number ironically.

"You know, Asher, I agree with Celeste." Tobias nodded enthusiastically. "I think fifty might be a bit much but ten sounds reasonable."

"Of course you agree with Celeste. You two are always conspiring against me."

"Not against you, *aheevaleh*." Ama squeezed his cheek. "*For* you."

My father emitted a grunt that wasn't very angelic. "Most sinners that fletchings reform aren't worth ten feathers."

"Okay, fine. Five, then." Ama made a great show of conceding.

I looked at Adam, found his dimple pressed in deep.

When he caught me watching him, he drew his thumb over my knuckles and leaned over. "They're quite entertaining when they get together, aren't they?"

"They most certainly are." I rested my head on Adam's shoulder and stared adoringly at the adults who were bickering like school children. "Eternity with them will be so much fun."

Adam smiled and kissed my temple, imprinting the curve of his mouth on one more part of my body. "Eternity with you, Feather."

"What's next? Abolishing the rule about bad words costing feathers?" Apa tossed one big hand in the air.

I snuck my arm around Adam's waist and sighed in utter bliss.

"Any chance you could make that happen?" Ama asked my father, who turned a shade redder.

"It would be convenient for our son." Gabriel's gaze on Adam was as weightless as a caress.

That made my father's attention veer back to us. He didn't smile, merely sighed in resignation. He'd had eighteen years to prepare himself for my encounter with Adam, but apparently, eighteen years hadn't been long enough.

I mouthed, *Ni aheeva ta*, which made his temper deflate like a soufflé, whose sweet steam curled around us, inexplicably ferrying a name into my mind—*Mimi*.

Ama had mentioned Muriel Moreau had been a passionate baker. Had she made me soufflés in my past life?

"I'll see what I can do," my father finally said.

Adam scooted his chair back and pulled me up. "We'll be back."

"Where are you going?" Apa asked.

"I'm going to give Naya a tour of the guild," Adam called out.

"Better not be a tour of his bedroom." I heard Apa mutter, which brought my internal temperature to a sweltering six-hundred or so degrees. "You've got fifteen minutes, *Kalkohav*, or I'll—"

"Here. Have some cake." Just before I turned the corner, I caught Tobias stuffing my father's mouth with a piece of *sachertorte*. "Give our poor children a break."

Ama laughed as Apa tried to form words around his gooey mouthful of jam and chocolate. Tobias winked while Gabriel shook his head at his husband's antics.

"I love your fathers," I said, as we raced down the white halls of Adam's childhood home.

"Maybe they're your soulmates too." His tone was as bright as the sky above us.

I grinned as we turned a corner, and he twirled me, so that my back was flush with the quartz.

"As long as you love me more."

"I died for you, Adam."

He raised my hand to his mouth. "No, you died for Jarod." He pressed a kiss to my knuckles, then flipped my hand over and, against my palm, he whispered, "You'll live for me."

NAYA

After we left Vienna, after we dropped Ama off back in New York, my father directed me to the ranking room, but I stole his hand and asked him for one more trip before I got to work, and he begrudgingly indulged me.

Which is how I ended up in the guild that had forever changed my life.

"Where are we going, Starlight? To your hovel to collect your suitcase?"

My suitcase was unfortunately in the Dunmore manor, or at the bottom of their swamp, or in that closet they made available to guests. "I didn't come for my clothes."

"Then what did you come back here for?"

I extended my arms when we reached the rain-splattered pavement beyond the cornflower-blue door. "To visit a friend."

His eyebrows dipped. "Which one? You have so many now."

"Is that humor I detect, Apa?"

He smiled, and it ironed out some of the furrows that had creased his brow since he'd found me in Venezuela. "So, where to, Starlight?"

"The hospital."

His eyebrows jolted, clearly not expecting *that* to be my destination. "Which one? There are many."

I gave him the name of the hospital Emmy had been airlifted to yesterday after her parents had come to collect her from the one in Caracas. Pablo hadn't done many things right in his short life, but at least, he'd kept that one promise to me.

"How did you know where she'd be?" Apa asked, as we landed in front of the imposing modern structure.

"I checked the holo-ranker. It indicated this hospital. I imagine she'll be in here for a while if it's showing as her residence."

My father didn't remove his dust as we forded through the buzzing hallways, past clanking hospital beds and rushing nurses to Room 303. "Do you want me to stay out of sight?"

"Up to you, Apa. Am I visible?"

He nodded.

I knocked on the door before pressing it open.

Emmy turned her gauze-wrapped head. When her eyes alighted on mine, her lashes fluttered. "Naya?" Her voice was as dim as the sky beyond the lone window of her small, private room. "You're alive?"

"I am."

I looked over my shoulder to see if Apa would follow, but he shook his head.

I returned my attention to the girl who looked like she'd slipped into a ring between two heavyweight fighters. "How are you feeling?"

"Like I got shot in the head." Her voice caught, and her lips squeezed. "What happened, Naya? What happened to us?"

I walked closer to her bed. "We got caught between two men who valued their lives over ours."

"What I'm asking is—What I'm asking is why did this happen to us? To Grayson? How come no one saw what was happening? How come no one tried to stop them?"

We'd tried to stop them, and in a way, we had. Even though Emmy wouldn't see our mission as a success, even though I shouldn't either, considering all I'd lost, we'd accomplished what we'd come to Venezuela to do—we'd stopped an act of terrorism and saved the Circle Girls.

Except Natasha...

Emmy's hand shook, rustling the papery sheet shrouding her body. I stole it and gripped it. "I'm so sorry about Grayson." I wanted to tell her he was in a better place but didn't, because telling her he was in a better place wouldn't bring him back.

"If only I'd never received that email." A tear slid down her cheek.

That's right. That's how she'd gotten embroiled with the Circle Girls, by an anonymous invitation. Claire or Dov must've sent it to her to lure Adam. Or was it to lure me? Did it matter?

What was done was done, and even though they'd won the first round, they'd lost the ultimate one. My wing bones may have been bare, but I still had a soul and a body, unlike Dov, and love and support in spades, unlike Claire.

"I'm sorry. For telling them I didn't know you and for stealing your jacket." More tears chased the one that had fallen.

"You're forgiven, Emmy." I squeezed her hand. "But I'd like you to make me a promise."

"Anything."

"Live your life in a way that would've made Grayson proud, all right?"

She sniffed. "All this crying's hurting my brain."

"Then no more tears." I leaned over her and kissed her salted cheek. "Only smiles from now on."

"Those hurt my face."

I grinned. Always so dramatic. "How are your parents holding up?"

"They're so mad"—she released a honking sob—"and so fucking sad."

With time, their anger would wane and so would their grief. Humans were strong like that, stronger than I'd been in my previous lifetime.

I placed her hand back on her abdomen.

"Do you need a place to stay? Because I haven't rented out the apartment. In case . . ."

"I'm going to do some traveling."

"Can I call you?"

"I no longer have a phone." But even if I'd had one, I wouldn't have encouraged her to call. Not so much because I was jealous of her past relationship with Adam, but because I wasn't looking for a human friend. Lying was too exhausting. I strode over to the door.

"Make the world a better place. And a prettier one. You're so talented at interior decorating. Don't let it go to waste."

She rubbed the tears from her cheeks as I slipped out of her room and out of her life.

Apa must've just finished a call, because he slipped his phone into the back pocket of his suede pants. "How is she?"

"In pain but alive."

"Thanks to you, *Kalkohav*. Her guardian angel." His tone was light but not teasing.

"Angels. Plural. Not just me. And maybe. Or, maybe it was just luck." I looked over my shoulder at the girl who'd gone back to staring at the sky.

"Give me a second." He stepped toward her and laid his palm on her head.

Since she didn't yelp when flames licked the gauze, I imagined Apa had kept himself concealed.

When he was done, he returned to me. "They'll call her healing a miracle."

"Touched by an angel," I murmured as Emmy reached up and fingered her forehead, a dent appearing between her eyebrows. "Wish you could make more miracles happen."

My father's arm draped around my shoulders, but just as suddenly as it landed, it sprang off.

"What?"

He stared at my back. In shock and then in utter joy. "My wonderful, darling child."

My lashes reeled up as I crooked my arm to reach my spine. "They're back?"

Apa's eyes shone as though he were about to cry. "They're back."

"Are they still black?"

He released a soft snort. "Were you expecting them to grow out some other color? What was it you wanted when you were a child?"

"Rainbow wings. And no, I wouldn't want them to be any other color than the way they were. The way you made me."

I wasn't ashamed of my history. Perhaps I should've been. After all, I'd been a nephilim, the black sheep of our race. Was one still, I supposed. But I chose to see my wings, not as proof of having fallen, but as proof of having risen.

After stroking the new growths, I banished them into the ether and eased my father's arm around my shoulders. As we retraced our steps to the hospital exit, I asked, "Tell me something, when you decided to raise me as your daughter, did you foresee yourself actually loving me?"

His heavy breath fluttered a piece of my hair. "I foresaw myself protecting you and meeting all your needs, but I didn't foresee how you'd wrap my soul around your little finger."

"So we *became* soulmates . . ." I mused.

Although he didn't break his stride, I felt his head rock from side-to-side.

I tried again. "How come you were so certain I'd recognize Adam?"

"*Motasheh*, what was it we negotiated? Three hundred feathers?"

"Two hundred. Nice try, though."

"Nice try yourself."

I beamed up at him, and eventually, he returned my smile and wore it from one guild to the next. When we landed in New York, our first destination was the ranking room.

I took a seat in front of a holo-ranker and pressed my palm against the glass panel. "Who am I signing up to?"

He stared at my hand almost a full minute before he spoke a name that pinned my breath to my lungs.

"Calliope Underwood?" I repeated, all breathily, wondering if it was a coincidence.

"I hear she needs someone to succor her soul."

My heart stilled. Started. Stilled. "Where did you hear that from?"

"Another friend of yours."

"How cryptic." Before he could change his mind, I traced her name on the glass, and the girl Galina had told me all about materialized in 3-D before me. I pressed my palm against the glass, twining our fates together. "I'm guessing you know what she did?"

"I'm all caught up."

"And you're really okay with me helping a Triple?"

"Not all Triples deserve their scores. Now, go to your room. Your mother left you something."

I hiked up an eyebrow. "New clothes?"

"Go." He gave me a little shove. "I'll wait for you in the children's wing."

I turned, treading backward. "Should I pack a bag?"

"A change of clothes and your toiletries. You're not moving out of the guilds this time, so traveling to your closet will be a cinch."

When I pushed open the door of my room, a gasp tumbled from my lips. There, pacing my quartz floor, white hair wrapped in a high bun with a pink ribbon, was the girl I'd always considered like a sister. "Raven?"

"Oh my angels, Naya!" She leaped toward me and flung her arms around my rigid figure. "I missed you so much."

"Yeah?" My tone was as stiff as my posture. "So much that you didn't call me when you came down to meet Nitznootz?"

She pressed me away, her eyes, the color of frozen waves. "I couldn't call you."

"Why? Did you lose my number?"

"No." She wiped tears off her pale cheeks. "You know how I am about secrets."

"You hate them."

"I positively hate them."

"I still don't understand what that has got to do with you breaking your promise. You didn't even call."

"Honey, I was so scared that I'd spill your parents' secret."

"That's why you didn't reach out to me?"

"When I learned what you were, Naya—" She dented her lip.

"You were disgusted?"

"No. Never. I was shocked, that's for sure. But never disgusted." She tangled her fingers around mine, and it reminded me so acutely of the day her pale blue feathers had bound to her wing bones that my heart gave a sad thump.

I'd lost my best friend that day. My big sister. My sidekick. My confidant.

"The minute I got my key, I came down, ready to call you, but then I ran into Lyla, and it reminded me so much of the age you were when we became friends, and I . . . I choked. I was so certain I would do or say something that would ruin everything that I rushed back up." Her lips pressed together, attempting to shape a smile that didn't even last a heartbeat. "I'm sorry for being such a coward."

I closed my fingers around hers. "You're not a coward. I probably would've done the same."

She sniffed, her wet gaze darting to my shoulders.

"Heard about my downy demise, huh?" I imagined there wasn't an angel on Earth, in Elysium, or in Abaddon who hadn't heard of the archangel's daughter's epic fail.

"I always hated that woman, but now . . . Angels help me when I come into my angel-fire."

I didn't want to discuss Claire. I wanted to discuss Raven and Elysium and all our months apart. "I don't have long. Apa's waiting for me. He sent me to pack and pick up something Ama—"

"He meant me. Your mother came to get me."

My eyes veered off the room I'd been scanning for a pile of new clothes, or possibly, a cell phone. "He knows you're here?"

"He does. He told me I couldn't keep you too long but mentioned you'd be staying inside guilds. So, slumber party tomorrow night in Chicago?"

"Yes. Absolutely yes!" I smothered her with a hug, and she smothered me right back.

As I packed, she regaled me with stories about the land of angels, and I told her all about Adam and the guardian angel mission.

We'd only chipped the tip of the iceberg when we arrived in the children's wing, but we'd have tomorrow, and every day after that. After a long but tearless hug, Raven sat down with Lyla and Nitznootz, while Apa and I set sail for my next mission.

We arrived in Chicago as a coral dawn infused the clear blue sky. I extended my arms for a lift, but Apa tipped his head to the side.

"I've allowed someone else to taxi you to your destination, but I *will* be flying right above you, Starlight."

I whipped my head toward the road, finding Adam leaning against the frame of his parked motorcycle. Even though my skin didn't light up, my heart totally did.

"Adam's reforming Calliope's grandfather, so he's headed where you're headed."

"You're letting us—you're—" I squealed and hooked my arms around my father's neck to drag him down for a hug. "*Thank you, thank you, thank you.*" I stamped a kiss on both his cheeks, then released him and skipped toward Adam.

But then I thought skipping was a little childish, so I swaggered.

Adam's dimple grew and grew as I neared him. Just before reaching him, I made my feathers appear and twirled.

When I spun back, his dimple was gone, and his eyes glittered like the new growths on my back. "Already?"

"We do have a bet going." I winked at him, which made his lips part around a chuckle. "And by the way, I'm driving."

"Are you now?" He pressed away from the black frame of the bike, and although he glanced over my shoulder at our one-person audience, he slanted his head over mine and stole a kiss. Although, was it stealing when all my kisses belonged to him? "I'm so proud of you, Feather."

Even though I hadn't gone to see Emmy for personal gain, I was pretty damn proud of myself too. Nine feathers. Raven had counted them. "So how'd you swing getting us assigned to grandfather and granddaughter?"

"I raised a few convincing arguments, insisting on the easy hundred-feather gain."

"Easy, huh?"

"Calliope has a good soul."

"On second thought, why don't I fly you both? It'll save us time." Apa hovered one story-high, great copper-tipped wings shimmering like the fringe of hoops in Galina's ear.

"Didn't know you were on the clock, Apa."

"You have a thousand feathers to earn, baby girl."

"Nine-hundred and ninety-one. And five whole years ahead of me."

"I implore you, Starlight, for the sake of my heart, don't pull a Celeste."

I laughed. "I promise I won't wait till the very last minute."

Although Apa didn't laugh, his eyes glittered like his wings, because his plea had conveniently reminded him that five years was ample time to succeed.

If Claire had bided her time . . .

Nope. Not going there. "Ready to go save some souls, Adam?"

"When you are, Feather."

I tossed my leg over the warm frame and seized the grips as he climbed on behind me. When his arms laced around my torso and his palms settled against my ribs, eliciting little pulsations everywhere, I asked, "So, how does this work?"

"You have to roll the—"

I peeled away from the curb with a squeal of rubber.

Adam wrangled my hair to bring his mouth to my ear. "Gently."

I eased my grip, and the bike lurched to a stop.

"Not that gently." There was an edge of humor to his tone. "I'm starting to think you have only two speeds—fast and stop."

My throat and jaw heated, since, knowing him, he was referring to our first time.

"Since when do you drive motorcycles, *Kalkohav*?" Apa shrilled, voice crammed with nerves.

Even though we were stopped in the middle of the street, I craned my head to say, "Since right now."

"Elysium give me strength," I heard him mutter.

"How about we try this again?" Adam covered my hands with his and throttled the bike, which purred and darted smoothly down its lane.

Hands, breaths, and heartbeats entwined, bodies so close they were almost one, Adam and I set off on our road trip to redemption.

ADAM

4 YEARS LATER

ANGELIC FACT #100
HAVING WINGS DOESN'T MAKE ONE NOBLE;
IT SIMPLY MAKES ONE FLY.

She buttoned up a light jacket over navy scrubs that tugged around her abdomen. Fear, fatigue, and dread deepened the lines rimming her tired green eyes and puckered lips. Her boss wanted to put her on maternity leave, but from the watercooler gossip I'd overheard on the pediatric ward, Aicha Bennani had refused.

This was her first pregnancy since me, the baby whose umbilical cord had been wrapped too tight and too long around his neck.

It was the first time curiosity blew me Aicha's way, even though it wasn't my first trip to Paris. After Naya had earned her five-hundredth feather, she and I had decided to take a much-needed break. Although we'd discussed tropical destinations, we'd picked one that was anything but—Paris.

I'd booked a fancy hotel that had eaten away at a whole year's worth of my allowance, but damn if it hadn't been worth every penny. It had given us the privacy we so rarely had and a sanctuary to return to after treading across streets sheeted in snow, adding our footprints to the ones Jarod and Leigh had left behind twenty-two years earlier. To this day, the knowledge I'd been another man, a mob boss at that, was jarring. Obviously, it beat uncovering I was some yellow-vested social servant, but still . . . leader of the plucking mafia.

After our parents' big reveal, I'd researched Jarod Adler. Had even found a picture of him and Leigh at the opera. Seemingly, their only one together. I'd studied the two strangers, my gaze clinging to the emerald earrings shivering on the peach-haired angel's lobes. The awareness that they'd meant something to me was overwhelming, but more so, was the awareness that I couldn't remember what.

I wasn't angry with Asher for stripping my soul of my past life. I understood he'd had no choice, but at times, I wished I could locate a shred of the man I'd been and the woman I'd loved.

Naya had caught me looking at the opera picture, and her gaze, like mine, had stuck to the earrings. *"You gave those to me."* She remembered too much and I, too little. When she'd rubbed her chest, the memory apparently stirring heartache, I'd pulled her onto my lap and banded my arms around her waist to remind her that we existed.

During that same trip, we'd visited my old home on Place des Vosges, a dwelling that had been known as the Demon Court, but which had been converted by Mimi into a refuge for underprivileged kids.

Hand-in-hand, Naya and I had stood in front of the crimson carriage doors. When she'd suggested ringing, I'd gripped her hand and held her back, not ready to amble through the theater of my past and walk down the darkened wings where I'd spilled blood and had mine spilled in turn. But a teenaged girl had stepped out then, and I'd glimpsed a snow-dusted statue enthroned at the heart of a cobbled courtyard.

My breath had sawed through my lungs, and my skin had crawled. I'd pulled Naya away and beat a path far from that stone woman. Although Naya had tried to elicit words from me during our hour-long trek back to the hotel, I hadn't been able to speak. Barely been able to breathe.

We'd spent the rest of our trip bundled between silken sheets or sampling delicacies from Parisian bakeries. At the tail-end of our pilgrimage, Boone, Levi, Galina, and Noah had stopped by to see us. The six of us often met up, so their visit hadn't come as a surprise. What had, though, was the news of Galina's imminent ascension.

Teary-eyed, we'd hugged it out, making her swear to call as soon as she got her channel key.

A year later, Noah and Boone had joined Galina in the land of angels.

Although losing Galina had been hard, saying goodbye to Noah had rent my plucking heart.

And now, a year later, it was almost our turn.

"*Ton sac! Balances ton sac!*" *Your bag! Hand over your bag!* A red scooter had screeched to a halt beside Aicha, who'd taken her usual seat beneath the bus shelter that carried her to her two-bedroom walk-up in a neighboring arrondissement. "I said, give me your fucking bag!"

The jerk of Aicha's shoulders had me vaulting off the bike I'd parked in a pocket of darkness.

When the ski-masked kid on the back brandished a knife and hopped off, I charged across the road. The driver saw me through the eyeholes of his own mask and yelled at his friend to hurry, but I was already on him.

I kicked over the bike, sending the bunghole sprawling. Rage striking my temples, I pounded over to his friend, who swung around and came at me with his steak knife. I seized his wrist and twisted it so hard that his bones cracked in multiple places.

He yelped.

The knife plinked.

I kicked it away, just as fists pummeled my kidneys, knocking the breath from my lungs.

"*Kaskaseem tobahat,*" I growled, cinching the throat of the weeping turd, whirled, then grabbed a fistful of Muhammad Ali's fake Vuitton shirt, and banged their heads so hard against each other, they shrieked. Before the blood gushing from their noses could sprinkle my brand-new kicks, I shoved them both to the ground.

"I c-called the p-police." Aicha pressed one protective palm to her abdomen while the other shook so hard around her phone that her elbow bobbed up and down. "*Merci.*"

She was tall, taller than I'd imagined from the distance I'd kept. Nonetheless, I had a full head on her. Naya often joked I'd only stop growing once my wings were complete. Guessed we'd see once my soulhalf earned her missing thirty-two feathers . . . I was waiting on her before going for my absent three.

Aicha hadn't blinked once since I'd turned toward her. I hadn't either.

"Do we . . .? Do we know each other?" A furrow dented the space over a nose that had the same jagged topography as mine. Here I'd thought I'd gotten the bump from one too many fights.

"No." My crowd-cheer chime went off, but I didn't reach into my pocket, hypnotized by the stranger who'd occupied my thoughts often since I'd seen her face on our TV back in Chicago.

"Who are you?" Her eyes, the same leafy green as mine, sparkled in the yellow light trickling off the bus shelter.

"*Personne.*" *No one.* When police sirens sounded, my wings snapped out, and I took a step back.

Her dark eyebrows bent. Arched. Bent. "Can you stay until the police get here, *personne*?"

If I did, they'd question me. "See that motorcycle?" I hooked a thumb toward my bike. "I'll be right there and won't leave until they show up."

"The police are going to wonder how I took those boys down. What do I tell them?"

The sirens wailed louder.

"Tell them some passerby helped you but don't point me out." As I turned, one of the guys crawled onto his palms and knees. I drove my foot into his spine, flattening him against the asphalt. He grunted like the human swine he was and settled back beside his soundless and motionless buddy.

Her expression warped so suddenly I worried it had to do with the baby. But then she murmured, "Chicago." Her fingers spread wider across her abdomen. "That's why you look familiar. You're the boy—"

"Sorry, but I've got no clue what you're talking about." If the lie cost me a feather, I didn't feel it. The only thing I felt were the rapid thrusts of my heart and the October breeze combing through my feathers. "Take care, ma'am."

I sprinted back to my ride, then threw my leg over the seat and throttled the grips, just as my phone went off again. I didn't hear it over the ear-shredding sirens as much as feel it vibrate against my thigh.

Aicha was still observing me, the gyrating lights atop the cop cars painting the whites of her eyes and the silver streaks in her black hair blue.

Two officers got out, shearing off my sight of the woman who'd gifted me this body while all I'd gifted her was heartache and now confusion. Before the uniforms could spot me, I gunned the engine and shot into the dark.

When a few minutes later, my phone prickled my leg *again*, I swerved to the curb and cut the engine. My heart, which had been thudding punitively since I'd breached the distance between myself and Aicha, beat out of alignment when I noticed that all three calls had originated from Apa.

Swallowing, I hit dial. The night-soaked sidewalk vanished, and Naya appeared, kneeling on her glittering feathers. Her dress was black instead of blue, her tears red instead of transparent, but her wing bones were the same as they'd been then—bare.

I blinked the haunting sight away. There was no reason for me to worry. She had seven months left and only thirty-two feathers to earn. The sinner she'd signed up to was worth thirty-seven.

She'd complete her wings in no time.

She'd be fine.

The second Apa answered, my voice scraped up my throat. "What's wrong? Is it Naya?"

"Adam." My father sounded all choked up. "*Vehnleh.*"

Ribs aching, I sputtered, "What happened?"

Angels, please let it not be Naya. Please, please, plea—

"We're so proud."

"So proud," Papa Gabriel's voice echoed over Apa's.

Huh? "Of?"

"You!" my fathers said in unison.

Pinching the bridge of my nose, I released a mammoth exhale. "What have I done that's got the two of you so . . . enthused?"

"You're—" Apa started, but Papa cut him off with a loud, "Done!"

"With what?"

Papa chortled. "Your wings, Adamleh."

My neck cracked from how fast my gaze whizzed to the appendages adorning the back of my leather jacket. I tried to magick them away, but my tar-colored feathers didn't disappear.

Fuuuck.

Shiiit.
No hot jab of pain.
No downy drift.
How? I hadn't signed onto anyone. I was waiting for Naya to catch up, and—
Aicha!
The goons.
The edict Asher had passed after the debacle in Venezuela: five feathers for every life saved.

I gripped my temples and kneaded them as my fathers reminded me I had twenty-four hours to ascend, but they expected me home in twenty, twenty-two max.

I wasn't ready, but promised I'd be there, then hung up and called Naya.

She picked up after the first ringtone. "I'm on my way back to—"

"Are you done?" I barked.

"—the hotel. With what?"

"With your mission. Are you done?"

"Not yet. I'll probably need another week or . . ." Her voice faded, then erupted against my pulsating eardrum, "Why?"

"Can you finish tonight?"

"No, Adam. What's going on?"

I gripped the base of my neck, feeling my apple jump beneath my palm. "Fuck."

"Adam, you're scaring me. What happened?"

"I fucking completed my wings."

Silence.

A car horn bleeped from her end, so I knew she was still there.

"Fuck. Fuck. Fuck. I'm so fucking sorry, Feather."

"Are you trying to make up for all the years you weren't allowed to curse?" Her voice was light. Teasing.

"I don't want to leave you," I choked out.

Another long beat of silence palpitated between us. "How long do you have before—before you need to go?"

I swallowed. "It just happened."

More angelsdamn silence.

"Where are you?" I rasped.

"On the Champs-Elysées. Two blocks from the hotel."

"Okay. I'll be there in fifteen." I hung up and jetted off through the quiet streets of the French capital. Nine minutes later, after running every red light, and almost getting mowed down by a garbage truck, I reached the hotel, parked in front, tossed the keys to the valet, then dashed through the lobby and up to the suite.

Naya was standing in the living room, typing something on her phone. When the door clapped shut, she spun on a pair of thigh-high, heeled boots. My grief took a back seat to a bunch of other emotions as I took in the silken white shirt that she'd belted and worn as a dress.

I walked up to her and palmed the bare skin between the tops of her boots and the bottom of her dress, my thumbs settling on the crease beneath her perfect ass. "You wore *that* to go meet your sinner?"

She clasped my corded neck with one hand and the lapel of my jacket with the other. "You're done," she murmured, eyes glimmering. "I can't believe you're done."

"Don't change the subject."

"My dress is a non-subject, Adam."

"Your dress is very much a subject. Especially since I'm not going to be around to—" My throat and eyes stung so hard I thought I was going to start bawling.

She craned her neck, sending her waterfall of pale-blonde locks tumbling down her back and past her belt. "You beat me."

My throat worked around swallow after jagged swallow. Knowing that if I opened my mouth, I'd croak out my pain, I pressed my lips against hers, then gripped her ass and lifted her off the ground.

She didn't try to talk any more than I did as she kissed me back, her mouth as gentle and as soft as the fingers she twined through my hair to anchor my face to hers.

I walked over to the bed and laid her down, leaning in so our lips wouldn't separate.

I wasn't ready to go a day without seeing her.

Without tasting her.

Without hearing her.

I rued the assholes who'd attacked Aicha. Who'd forced me to break the promise I'd made to wait for her. I hoped that attacking me with their dirty knife and dirtier fists had shot their scores up to one hundred.

Naya's fingers slipped back down my neck, across the expanse of black feathers soldered to my back and stretching out so fast and far that my right wing grazed the heavy burgundy brocade framing the French doors of our private terrace.

She spiraled her fingers to my front, fraying a path between our bodies until she reached the waistband of my pants. After unbuttoning them, she gripped my cock and tugged until my anger and distress were replaced by such acute need that everything inside of me tapered to a single point—her.

Forever her.

The other half of my soul.

Noah had been wrong about Naya and me being soulmates; we were more than that—soulhalves—which was why Asher had kept us apart, even though he'd only speculated as much. It wasn't until Naya and I had met in our new bodies that he'd known. After all, there was no separating soulhalves, and the moment our paths had collided, living without each other became inconceivable.

As I devoured Naya's mouth, and she worked me to a blinding frenzy, I shoved aside the scrap of silk and lace between her legs and pushed my fingers knuckle-deep inside her warmth.

Paring my lips from hers, I rasped, "Don't make me wait, Feather. You know how much I hate waiting."

Her lashes sat low over her eyes, shielding them from me.

I slipped my thumb over her clit and drew small circles. "Look at me, baby."

Instead of lifting her lids, she lowered them completely.

"Naya, please."

Tears glided out the corners of her eyes, crystal rivulets that vanished into her pale locks.

"Feather..."

Her spine arched, and a sob-moan slipped from her parted lips. I kissed it away, kissed away the next sound too. I was storing them for all the days and nights I'd pace the Canyon of Reckoning, waiting for her to arrive.

If only they'd allow me back down immediately, but Asher had explained that newly-formed wings took a few months to settle, like drying clay.

On a breathy gasp, Naya came over my hand, and I came over that dress I didn't want her wearing again anyway.

I kissed the salt off her lids and then off her temples. "I'm going to sic your father on you."

Her eyes opened. "What?" she croaked.

"I want you up there with me, and I'm not waiting a whole angelsdamn week."

She wiped her hand over her dress before raising it to my face to push away the dark curls stuck to my brow. "Don't worry. Please don't worry. I'll be—"

"Your father will love it. It'll remind him of the good old days."

She smiled gently. "If it makes you feel better."

"It'll make me feel better."

Her smile sprinkled light into her dark eyes.

Angels, I was going to miss looking into them.

She splayed her fingers on the back of my head and towed my face down to hers. "Swear you won't worry."

I was about to snort, because until she joined me, I'd worry, but then I remembered I could lie to my soul's content, so I said, "Sure, Feather. I won't worry. Not. One. Fucking. Bit." Although I hated that I'd lost control over my ascension, there were definitive perks to having my feathers sealed to my bones.

She shook her head. "Liar."

"I could never lie to my soulhalf."

She pinched my arm.

I peered at the reddening skin and finally . . . *finally*, I smiled. "All the abuse I endure in the name of love."

She rolled her eyes. "I wonder if you were this droll in your previous life."

"Probably not. Mob bosses are reputed to be pitiless assholes."

"I wouldn't have loved a heartless man."

"No, Mademoiselle Moreau, you wouldn't have loved a *soulless* man, and I had a soul." Grazing her sensitive flesh with my scabbed knuckles, I drew her underwear low and settled myself between her thighs. "A soul that already belonged to you." I parted her slick heat with my swollen tip. "That will *always* belong to you." I thrusted in, and she moaned. "Can you imagine, Feather? Stuck together for all of eternity?" I drew out, then slammed back in.

Her lids slid shut. "How terrifying," she murmured, her raucous words warming my lips.

"You meant to say, *thrilling*, right?"

Even though her eyes remained closed, a smile curved her mouth. "I can't wait."

"I can't either." I drove so hard into her body that I cut off my own breath. "So don't fucking make me."

Her wings materialized beneath her body, and her skin lit up, and I dove, soul-first, into her starlit ocean of beauty.

ADAM

22 HOURS AND 54 MINUTES LATER

ANGELIC FACT #999
SOULS, LIKE HEARTS, CAN BREAK

"We have to go, Adamleh." Apa's lips were twisted into a grim expression that mirrored my other father's.

For all their thrill, they understood I was leaving a part of my soul behind. After all, they, too, were soulhalves.

I wanted to rip out handfuls of my feathers. I'd even asked Asher if he could burn one away when he'd come to collect his daughter minutes ago, tearing her from my arms. Woefully, not even archangels possessed that sort of magic.

Apa cupped both sides of my face, forcing my burning eyes to his. "Asher will take care of her. And she'll be with you again before you know it."

"Six minutes," Papa murmured over my shoulder.

I shut my eyes and jammed down the ball of grief that had gained so much breadth in my throat, I hadn't even been able to whisper goodbye to Naya. I'd just stared at her inflamed lids and shiny eyes, at her trembling body nestled in the crook of her father's big arm.

I stopped resisting my fathers' pull, finally letting them tug me into the channel. The beam of Elysian light singed my already tender lids.

Asher wouldn't let anything happen to her.

She'd be fine.

When the vision of her kneeling amid her feathers creeped back inside my mind, I shoved my eyes open and forewent blinking for so many minutes that when the channel smoke cleared, I was blinded.

Elysium was white and glowy.

So. Very. White.

Like the guilds, but tenfold. Even the wingless souls bobbing in the dark air were whitish and luminescent. Well, *soul*. Currently, just one was in attendance. A woman with burgundy lipstick and a sprinkling of fine lines that seemed to deepen at the sight of me.

She landed, hand lifting toward my cheek, as though to stroke it. "*Mon Ange, comme tu es beau.*" *My angel, how handsome you are.*

My ears began to buzz, and then I sucked in a breath that got stuck beside my giant lump of grief.

That raspy voice.

That lemony sweet scent.

"Mimi?"

Her palm settled, caressed, and emotion varnished her navy irises. "*Bienvenue, mon amour.*" *Welcome, my love.*

Although it felt traitorous to experience anything but grief, I couldn't help the deluge of heartbeats pelting my ribs as I leaned into her touch and soaked up her welcome.

NAYA

I peered up at my father, at the proud smile denting the corners of his mouth, at the sheen of emotion glossing his aquamarine eyes. "Ready, my darling daughter?"

My heart jounced, floated, as weightless as the thousand feathers garnishing my wing bones like black tinsel. "I'm ready."

I'd barely slept in the six days since Adam had ascended, working relentlessly on helping my sinner improve, not only swiftly but lastingly, and yet I felt buoyant and alert.

Although I had no doubt my diet composed exclusively of caffeine and cake was impacting my disposition, it was the excitement of being reunited with all my loved ones that made my blood feel effervescent.

Ama tightened the arm she'd speared through mine when she'd come to collect me from the playroom where I'd spent my last hour on Earth with Lyla. Although there'd been tears, there'd been so much laughter and smiles. And hugs. So many hugs. I could still feel the imprint of my sister's slight body against mine. I'd even gotten a hug from aloof Arden, who promised to keep my sister and Nitznootz entertained during my Elysian sabbatical.

"Your hand, *Kalkohav*." Apa held out his palm.

Keeping one arm laced through my mother's, I slipped my fingers over his and gripped his wrist. The sparkling smoke churned and thickened, and the Elysian light grew so bright that I was momentarily blinded. But I didn't want to close my eyes. I didn't want to miss a second of my first sight. Or, I supposed, second...

Although Adam had always insisted that our first kiss happened in that elevator in Venezuela, to this day, romantic-me considered the furtive brush of our lips back in the English inn our first. He insisted that had been an accident, but since he'd lost a feather claiming this, I was perfectly aware there had been nothing accidental about his mouth sweeping over mine.

"Welcome to the land of angels," Ama murmured as the twinkling vapors cleared.

Of course, the first thing I saw wasn't the vast trench of illuminated quartz, or the pearlescent arch glowing like a magical horseshoe. It was a pair of leathery-black wings, tucked in so tight they barely protruded from the leather jacket Adam had worn the night his fathers had carried him away from me.

"Just land already if your wings are cramping," Adam snarled at Noah, who hovered beside a woman I assumed was human—*had been* human—since no wings jutted from her back, and yet...

And yet, she was flying.

Neshamim. Soul. The word came to me as I regarded her, endeavoring to comprehend why this woman seemed familiar. Had our paths crossed on Earth?

She landed in front of me, a smile drawing up lips painted a deep crimson. "*Enfin...*" Finally...

She'd been waiting for me?

As I took in the gap between her teeth, the luminous navy of her irises, and the auburn hair pulled into an elaborate knot, I gasped, "Mimi?"

A sheen glossed her eyes. "You remember me?" she asked in French.

The air around us seemed to grow sweeter, as though Muriel Moreau had been spun from sugar. I remembered that I'd loved her, that I'd trusted her, and that she'd loved and trusted me. "*Oui.*"

I peered over her shoulder at Adam, who still hadn't turned. Had he remembered her? Before I could ask, Noah was landing beside me, expelling a sigh so deep it dispersed the remaining threads of channel smoke webbing the dusky air around me.

He scooped me into a giant hug. "Not that I didn't enjoy

camping out in the Canyon for the past week, but thank fork my favorite black-wing has arrived."

I laughed as we pulled away. "You don't have a favorite black-wing, Noah."

"At the moment, I do." He smiled down at me. "I may change my mind tomorrow."

I thought I heard Adam scoff, but Apa's voice carried over my soulhalf's.

"I'll be right back, Starlight. Don't move. Celeste, Mimi, shall we?" He tipped his head toward the quartz city silvered by stars and moonlight.

"If it's to retrieve who I think it is, then abso-feathering-lutely." Ama sprang upward, Mimi at her side.

After casting me one more tender look, the stranger, who already felt like a grandmother, trailed after my parents.

They swooped beneath the Pearly Arch, and then farther, past a smoking waterfall, one of several that crashed down the fire-lit walls of the capital. I wasn't sure if it was because of the mural in the Viennese cafeteria or because of memories from my previous life, but the sight wasn't bewildering. It was . . . familiar.

"They're going to get Claire," Noah explained. "Which reminds me. I promised the others I'd tell them the second you arrived. Be right back."

He sprang into the air, leaving me alone with the black-winged angel, who'd finally turned to face me.

"Six days, Naya," Adam finally said between clenched teeth. "I've been up here waiting. Six. Days."

I smiled. "Not my fault you had to go play hero and finish your wings first. Have you picked your prize? After all, you won the bet."

His jaw flexed like the tendons in his neck. "Yeah, I've picked it. I'm keeping you to myself for twice the time you made me wait."

I stepped lithely toward him and laced my arms around his taut waist. "You're going to sequester me for twelve whole days?"

"Thirteen."

I couldn't help the smile that cleaved my face. The same way I couldn't help the single tear that spilled over, because, angels how I'd missed this man.

He swept away the salty track before sliding his hand to the back of my head, his fingers catching in all the knots that had formed during my blustery flight over Paris. "I've missed you so fucking much, Feather."

"Still at it with the cursing, I see."

The line of his steel lips finally slackened, and the dimple I adored appeared. Even though I was wearing five-inch stilettos, I pressed up on tiptoe to reach his mouth, but before our lips could meet, the air churned with raised voices and powerful wing beats, which made both of our necks tip backward.

A cloud of angels as dense as a swarm of locusts was rolling in. On the frontline, were my parents and the woman who'd desperately tried to keep me out of Elysium.

Claire landed, ropy black hair settling like a noose around her ghostly pale throat. She gathered her dark locks and pushed them behind the starchy bodice of her shapeless black tunic.

My parents landed next, both retracting their wings. Six males followed suit. I recognized Eve's father from Arden's birthday parties, which he'd never failed to attend, unlike his wife... *ex*-wife. The others, I recognized because of the circlets atop their heads—the Council of Seven... now, Six.

Eve landed alongside Mimi a second later. And then Noah, Raven, Galina, and Boone plopped like raindrops around Adam and me. Where Raven launched herself at me, squeezing in a hug even though the atmosphere was rife with tension, Galina and Boone settled on wide smiles.

"Your moment of reckoning has finally arrived, Claire." My father's voice boomed. "The Council has found you guilty on all counts—conspiracy, malice, and deceit."

Although Claire's expression was smooth and devoid of emotion, her green eyes flared. "Won't you speed things up already?" She narrowed her eyes on me. "I've been waiting four years."

I crossed my arms in front of my chest, as though to shield my soul from this spiteful wretch.

Adam wound his hand around my waist, hooked my hip, and pulled me into his side. "We don't even get a *thank you for making it, kids?*"

Claire's lips thinned. "Why would I thank abominations?"

Intakes of air hissed over the silence that tailed her cruel words.

"Because we're your ticket back to a guild." I envied how calm Adam sounded.

She snorted. "I'm done with this world."

"You don't want to be"—I swallowed, because although I'd had years to get used to the idea, it hadn't become any less odd—"reincarnated?"

"And grow black feathers that showcase my nephilim status? No." She turned toward my father. "Asher, I suppose you're going to officiate?"

"Did you expect me to give someone else the privilege?" Apa's tone was so blistering I was surprised Claire's fuchsia feathers hadn't gone up in flames from just his words.

As though she, too, felt the heat, Claire vanquished her wings. "I request that my soul be incinerated."

Because she feared no one would reincarnate her nephilim soul or because she couldn't live without Dov? Had he been her soulhalf?

Adam's fingers quarried my hip as he forced me back a step . . . two, as though worried Claire's funeral pyre would be so violent, the flames would jump onto our wings.

The channel billowed then, and Tobias almost tripped over Mira as they both rushed out, followed by an even-keeled Gabriel.

"Did we miss it?" Tobias panted, his eyes circling the assembly before falling over Claire. "Guess not. The winged roach still breathes."

"Not for long, Tobias." Claire smiled, and it was so chilling that it made my arms dig harder into my torso.

"*Lehatsamehot!*" Apa roared.

Claire's eyes bulged as her wings popped back into existence. "Why did you—"

Before she could finish her sentence, Apa and the black-skinned seraphim streamed fire over her bright feathers, eliciting a soul-deep cry from the former archangel.

"You didn't actually expect us to make it quick and painless, did you, Claire?" Apa's voice blazed as hot as the infernal flames chewing through her metallic-tipped feathers.

Shrieking, Claire fell to her knees, before collapsing face-first into the quartz.

The stench of burning feathers stung my eyes and made both my shoulders and spine ache.

When I whimpered, Adam twirled me into his hard chest and pressed his mouth against my forehead. I gulped in his scent to clear away Claire's and buried my head in the scoop of his shoulder until the screams and crackling abated.

"I'm sorry for acting so barbarically in front of you, Starlight." My father's voice made me pull my face away from Adam and peek up. "I shouldn't have subjected you to this."

I licked my lips, not wanting to sling more guilt onto his shoulders by explaining it was the memory of my own wings' incineration that had upset me. "Is she gone?"

"She's gone."

"Forever?"

"Forever."

Beyond Apa's tense shoulder, I spotted Eve and her father, both dry-eyed, as though unaffected by Claire's passing. As though relieved by it.

As my gaze cycled back to the two most important men in my life, it snagged on a face I hadn't seen in four years—Grayson. He shot me a smile so wide it displayed all his teeth. All his *straight* teeth. I guessed he'd had them fixed when he entered Elysium. The same way he'd had his features chiseled and sprinkled with fine wrinkles, as though to make up for his missed opportunity to age back on Earth.

The black archangel, who'd assisted Apa, cut off my line of sight. "Welcome, Naya. I'm Seraph Daniel, but you may call me Daniel." He extended his hand, and I shook it.

"I've heard so much about you, Daniel." My parents' first and foremost ally in their cause. "I'm glad to finally be able to put a face to your name."

His grip was as honeyed as his smile.

The other archangels came to introduce themselves next, but none instructed me to drop their titles.

After they left, Adam murmured into my ear, "Our thirteen days together start now."

Goosebumps rippled over my skin.

"Shall we see how useful these things are?" He tipped his head to his wings.

"Wait." I pulled back so I could look him in the eye. "You haven't flown yet?"

"I was waiting for you."

"You hate waiting."

"I hate a lot of things, Feather." He stole my hands from where they rested laxly at my sides and threaded our fingers together, then brought them up to his lips and kissed them. "But none of them apply to you."

"Gag." Galina made a retching sound, which earned her Adam's flipped finger.

Noah and Boone jumped into the sky and extended their wings. And then Galina and Raven sprang up.

"Our turn." I dipped my head and spread my wings.

Adam's unfolded unhurriedly, sending every angel and soul in a ten-feet radius scattering, and then he leaned over. "Ready to conquer the sky, Feather?"

"Only you would see flying as a war to be won."

He pressed his still curving lips to mine as our souls, hearts, and bodies took flight, and our feathers coalesced with the brilliant night sky.

Epilogue

5 months later — Naya

"Everyone's ready and—"

I turned away from the window overlooking the glittery sea that puffed under a cobalt sky iced in stars.

Months had passed since my ascension, and yet the sight of the gauzy Elysian ocean and the glowing Nirvana mountains hadn't lost their enchanting splendor. The same way the man I turned toward now, the one standing by the bronze door of our home in the Hadashya, never ceased to enthrall me.

A forest-green leather tunic with a gilt mandarin collar and cuffs to match stretched over the broad cut of his shoulders, which seemed to have expanded since we'd ascended, probably from all those games of ultimate sky-Frisbee he and Noah had invented a month into our arrival and which had caught like angel-fire throughout Elysium.

Every city now boasted its own team, but the capital's—*ours*—was, wings down, the best. Although I didn't play, Boone, Raven, Galina, and Grayson had all signed up, and many others, angels and souls alike. I never missed a game, which I watched from atop the Canyon cliffs, seated between Ama and Mimi, consuming pastries from the picnic spread Mimi prepared for each game. Eve and her on-again-off-again erelim partner would join more often than not.

Sometimes, after long and taxing Council meetings, Apa would emerge from the Shevaya and meet us in the Canyon. Twice, he and

Tobias had played, which had drawn a crowd as thick and wide as the one that had gathered the night Claire had ceased to exist.

"Holy father of angels," Adam rasped, as he finally released the heavy door, cutting us off from the bustling street beyond.

As he advanced toward me, his wings snapped out. And out. He'd winged me thousands of times in the four years we'd been together, and yet the sight of his attraction still made my heart skip and my skin erupt, as though my blood was laced with liquid starshine.

He took the hand resting in the folds of my dark emerald gown and twirled me, his gaze consuming the panel of green leather stitched between my gold choker and matching belt, and the swaths of gossamer silk that spilled like vines over my knee-high gladiator sandals. Eve, who'd designed the dress, had even added a chain of handstitched flowers that trickled down the runnel between my black wings.

When our fronts realigned, Adam ran the tip of his index finger over the gold girdling my neck, then moved it down the bodice, tracking the seam of my ribs. His fingertip skipped across the cool surface of the belt before parting the fluid green swaths that joined at my navel.

Gaze caressing my bare, smoldering legs, he hooked his finger into the bottom of my bodysuit and snapped it open.

"I thought everyone was ready." My voice thickened and billowed like the *ayim* beyond our window as his finger glided against me.

"They are." He nosed the underside of my jaw, tipping my head back and sprinkling my skin with his heady kisses.

"Then we should get"—I gripped his biceps as he plunged, not one, but two fingers inside my heat—"going."

"If you'd wanted us to be on time, you shouldn't have worn a fuck-me dress." His mouth covered mine before I could protest that my dress was entirely decorous.

A waste of breath anyway. Adam deemed everything I wore an enticement to kiss, lick, or—My train of thought derailed, as his proficient fingers tormented and teased.

He penetrated my mouth deeper, first with his tongue, and then with his whisper. "*Naida neshahadzaleh.*" *My exquisite soulhalf.*

He was the exquisite one. His fingers were—

I gasped as the magic he stirred enveloped me whole, and my heart banged out beats that were so loud and close together, my pulse was surely vibrating the quartz walls of the Canyon. I hummed and thrummed, and although my feet were firmly planted on the ground, my body felt as though it had taken flight. His kisses and caresses turned languid as he carried me down from the high he'd given me.

Once my breathing smoothed, he pulled his mouth and fingers away. "*Now*, we can go."

"No." The word came out so jaggedly that his eyebrows slanted. "It's not as though the ceremony can take place without us." I reached around his leather tunic to comb my fingers through his feathered V.

He stayed perfectly still for two heartbeats, and then he was unzipping his pants and pushing them as far down as his black cavalier boots allowed. He scooped me up, folds of silk and flesh parting as my legs circled his waist.

I welcomed him into my slippery heat, my hands never breaking their stride. He pumped into me, emerald eyes alternately blazing and blanking with lust. My abdomen pulsed, and I couldn't tell if it was another orgasm building or my soul trying to nestle against his, but the pulsating grew violent like his thrusts.

He pinned me to the wall, rolling his hips while kneading my bare ass and waxing poetic. I shattered again, the sensation deliciously abrupt, and then he erupted, rasping the nickname he'd given me in another life before dubbing me with it again in this one.

I kissed his beautiful lips one more time before he set me back on my feet. "*Now*, we can go."

After cleaning ourselves up and straightening our clothes, we soared out of the Hadashya, toward the Pearly Arch where our families, closest friends, and the Seven—Noah's mother, Lyssa, had joined the crowned fray last month after a unanimous vote —awaited us.

"They're here!" Raven announced to the small cluster of winged and unwinged beings as Adam and I swooped past a colony of sparrows.

Apa stopped pacing the knoll that spilled from the Arch to the Lev and looked up, his lips reedy with frustration. "What is it we've been called upon to celebrate, Daughter?"

Nodding to Mira, whom I'd tasked to fetch Ama, I looped my arm through his and led him up the hill toward Daniel.

The grooves in my father's forehead deepened as he glanced between his fellow seraphim and me. And then his nostrils flared, and his gaze snapped to Adam. "I understand you kids live modern lives, but he hasn't even asked for my permission. The least he could've done was ask for my permission. I *may* have given it," he added in a surly tone. "And where the Abaddon is your mother?"

I laughed while Adam, who stood between his fathers, crossed his arms and smirked. "I'll make sure to remind him when he feels ready to make an honest woman out of me, but tonight isn't about us. Tonight is about you, Apa."

My father's gaze veered back to me. "Me?"

"Isn't it time you made an honest woman out of Ama? I mean, you two have *children* together. Not to mention your souls are bound for all of eternity. What more motivation do you need?"

My father opened his mouth to speak, probably to counter the issue wasn't motivation but permission. In the end, no words came out. He turned toward Daniel and parted his mouth again, but again, no sound escaped.

The five other archangels landed on either side of Daniel, who smiled at my father. "Your daughter is alarmingly smart, Asher."

Still, my father said nothing, but his gaze slowly returned to me.

"Remember how we'd allotted you one month to find a consort, and by failing to do so, you reneged on your chance to wed until your resignation?" Seraph Gideon asked.

"How could I forget?"

The blond archangel fingered the embellished collar of his cranberry jumpsuit, the shade of which matched his wings to perfection. "Well, Naya has found a loophole in our celestial marriage law."

I flipped Apa's hand to press the ring I'd had made for my mother into his palm, an exact replica of one of his feathers. I'd had an amethyst feather fashioned for his finger, which Mimi was currently keeping safe in the pocket of her navy trousers. "I know Ama doesn't care all that much about celestial customs, but I know they matter to you."

Apa stared at the miniaturized version of his feather that wrapped around itself, twinkling turquoise and copper. "What loophole?" he murmured.

"Your *neshahadza* wasn't of legal age during the courtship window we'd allotted you," Daniel explained.

My father's gaze bounced over the faces of his brethren.

"Your soulhalf had to be eighteen or an ascended to be eligible." Lyssa had been present during my appeal, which had coincided with her first day on the job. "Since Celeste was only fifteen at the time, it nulls the month you were given."

My father's eyes were as wide as Lyla's now. How I wished she could've come. We'd agreed with Ama that we'd hold a second ceremony in the guild as soon as I was allowed to return to Earth.

Apa closed his fingers around the ring. "I can't believe you did this, Starlight."

I couldn't tell if he was touched or peeved that I'd not only gone behind his back but also organized the ceremony, down to the wedding bands. Yes, Ama was sort of in on it . . . as of last week.

I swallowed. "Don't you want to marry her, Apa?"

Tobias raised his voice. "I'm certain Celeste will raise no objection to keep living in sin."

Pink streaks slashed my father's cheekbones as he sent a scathing look Tobias's way. His friend merely smirked, and although he and Adam didn't share DNA, they certainly shared the same crooked grin.

"You know me too well, Tobias." Ama's voice fell over the assembly as she landed beside me in a flowy white gown pricked over with glowing Nirvana blooms. The same flowers Mimi had braided into a crown to sit atop Ama's waist-long locks, lending her an ethereal light. She kissed my cheek and murmured, "The rings are genius, Starlight. We should make them a thing."

I blushed at the compliment.

"You want to marry me, Celeste?" Apa's complexion was still mottled.

She shrugged. "Why not?"

I grinned.

Apa did not. "*Why. Not?*" He drew out each word. Each letter from each word.

Mimi clasped my hand and towed me back, glowing with pride and joy as though it was her own child standing beneath the Pearly Arch, which, in a way, it was.

Ama held out the amethyst feather that could've fit two of her fingers. "We may as well tie our wings, *aheevaleh*. Everyone's already here, and—"

"You knew?" Apa sputtered. "You *all* knew?"

"Well, we are *all* here, Asher." Tobias swept a hand to encompass the small crowd. "So it goes without saying that yes, we knew."

Mira, who'd landed beside Tobias, released what sounded like a chortle. A chortle? Mira? Even Tobias frowned at her, which made her lips flatten immediately.

"Surprise?" Noah ventured, which earned him an asinine stare from my father. Cowed, he backed up, inadvertently crushing Galina's foot, who groused about putting him on a bird-seed diet.

"He's all bark and no bite," Raven whispered to Noah, effectively calming him. What calmed him further was when she linked her arm through his.

Those two had been dancing around each other for a while now, forever tag teaming in sky-Frisbee and hanging out after the rest of us retired to our beds. Boone was convinced they'd hooked up, but Raven and I told each other everything, so I knew they hadn't, yet.

After all, what was the rush when your days were infinite?

"Asher." Ama curled her hand around Apa's neck to tip his face down. "Will you marry me, you big, surly man?"

My father's lips were stone for so long I actually feared he'd refuse. But then one corner curled up. "Why not?"

Ama laughed, then forced his mouth down to hers.

Daniel *tsk*ed. "First, the vows. Then you may make a saint out of your sinner."

Apa snorted, but stole my mother's hand from his neck and clasped it in his, before pivoting toward Daniel.

I whistled, and two sparrows approached. I hummed a melody, which they amplified, and then more sparrows arrived and strengthened the tune.

After Daniel had blessed them, I added words to the harmony carried by my rainbow-winged choir. Lyrics I'd written for the man and woman with fierce souls and fiercer hearts, who'd moved Elysium and Earth, to give two fallen angels a second chance.

As my song came to an end, and my parents sealed the ceremony with a kiss, Adam strolled over to me.

"Think I should ask him for your hand in marriage tonight,

Feather?" His arm brushed across the silken flowers cloaking my spine. "He seems in a rather jovial mood."

"Perhaps, let's keep him that way, *mon amour*. For Celeste's sake. I'm sure she'd much prefer Asher focus on her tonight, than on you." Mimi gave Adam a wink and my fingers a light squeeze before gliding up toward the newlyweds to congratulate them.

A snort blustered through the flyaways framing my face. "Fine. I'll wait."

"Look at you. Becoming so patient."

He side-eyed me, and I grinned.

"I didn't say I'd wait *long*." Adam splayed his hand on my abdomen, stroking the soul pulsating beneath.

"That eager to wear my glittery black feather around your finger?"

"That eager to claim you as mine."

"I'm already yours." I turned in his arms to cup his bristly jaw and lure his emerald eyes to mine. "Always have been and forever will be. In every lifetime, Adam."

His wings unspooled from their bones to curl around mine. "How about we stop at this one, Feather?"

ACKNOWLEDGMENTS

What an adventure my angels have taken me on. When I wrote FEATHER two years ago, I never imagined my *Romeo & Juliet* retelling would evolve the way it did. That Jarod and Leigh would get a chance at a Happily Ever After.

But here we are.

Here *they* are.

Together and alive.

I won't hide that STARLIGHT was a very difficult book to write, because Adam and Naya aren't Jarod and Leigh, and yet, in many ways, they are. Although mired in their past, my heroes were essentially new characters. As much as I wanted Adam to resemble Jarod, and Naya to resemble Leigh, it would've been wrong to write them that way, because they didn't have the same education and upbringing, and weren't the same age.

I did try to preserve what you loved best about my star-crossed lovers and incorporate those traits into their reincarnations. I can only hope I've succeeded.

As usual with my books, there are many subplots and themes. Although I won't speak about all of them, my revenge killer, Calliope, was greatly inspired by the heroine in S.T. Abby's *Mindf*ck series*. (S.T. Abby was one of author C.M. Owens' pseudonyms.) Although I never got to meet Owens, and now never will because she left this world too soon, her stories live on inside my mind and heart, and I cannot urge you enough to look her up and pick up her books. I have no doubt she's reached Elysium and is regaling angels with her imagination.

Now, onto the reason this part is called acknowledgments.

I'm going to start by thanking you, my reader, for the enthusiasm and support you've shown my angels. If *Starlight* exists, it's entirely thanks to you and your outpouring of love for Leigh and Jarod.

To my editor, Becky, and proofreader, Kate, thank you for keeping an eye on my angels' behavior and their creator's grammar. Your suggestions and corrections helped make my prose smolder.

To my beta reader, Maria Silk, thank you for reading an early version. Your feedback was invaluable and helped me reshape so many important scenes.

To Rose Griot, thank you for giving Adam a voice. Without your early love for his chapters, he wouldn't have gotten to narrate this story, and what a shame that would've been. He was such a fun character to explore and write.

To my family, my real-life angels, thank you for enduring all the ups and downs that accompanied *Starlight*'s manufacture. I apologize for the thousands of times I proclaimed, "I'm almost done!" with such enthusiasm that I actually started to believe I was. Until I opened my word file the following morning and realized I still had so much farther to go.

I love you more than all my characters and stories, even though I do love my supernaturals to bits.

And now, onto the next adventure. Buckle up for some sexy fae and sexier crow shifters in *House of Beating Wings*. Make sure to follow me on Instagram (@olives21) for all the news on this upcoming series.

Eternally yours,

Olivia

ALSO BY OLIVIA WILDENSTEIN

PARANORMAL ROMANCE
The Lost Clan **series**
ROSE PETAL GRAVES
ROWAN WOOD LEGENDS
RISING SILVER MIST
RAGING RIVAL HEARTS
RECKLESS CRUEL HEIRS

The Boulder Wolves **series**
A PACK OF BLOOD AND LIES
A PACK OF VOWS AND TEARS
A PACK OF LOVE AND HATE
A PACK OF STORMS AND STARS

Angels of Elysium **series**
FEATHER
CELESTIAL
STARLIGHT

The Quatrefoil Chronicles **series**
OF WICKED BLOOD
OF TAINTED HEART

CONTEMPORARY ROMANCE
GHOSTBOY, CHAMELEON & THE DUKE OF GRAFFITI
NOT ANOTHER LOVE SONG

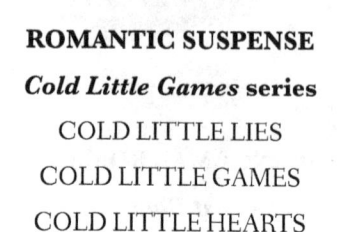

ROMANTIC SUSPENSE
Cold Little Games series
COLD LITTLE LIES
COLD LITTLE GAMES
COLD LITTLE HEARTS

ABOUT THE AUTHOR

USA TODAY bestselling author Olivia Wildenstein grew up in New York City and earned her bachelor's in comparative literature from Brown University. After designing jewelry for a few years, Wildenstein traded in her tools for the writing life, which made more sense considering her college degree.

When she's not sitting at her computer, she's psychoanalyzing everyone she meets (Yes. Everyone), eavesdropping on conversations to gather material for her next book, and attempting not to forget one of her kids in school.

She has a slight obsession with romance, which might be the reason why she writes it. She's a hybrid author of over a dozen Young Adult love stories.

oliviawildenstein.com
press@oliviawildenstein.com